BILLY SUMMERS

By Stephen King and published by Hodder & Stoughton

NOVELS:

Carrie
'Salem's Lot
The Shining
The Stand
The Dead Zone
Firestarter
Cujo
Cycle of the Werewolf
Christine
Pet Sematary
IT
The Eyes of the Dragon
Misery
The Tommyknockers
The Dark Half
Needful Things
Gerald's Game
Dolores Claiborne
Insomnia
Rose Madder
Desperation
Bag of Bones
The Girl Who Loved Tom Gordon
Dreamcatcher
From a Buick 8
Cell
Lisey's Story
Duma Key
Under the Dome
11.22.63
Doctor Sleep
Mr Mercedes
Revival
Finders Keepers
End of Watch
Sleeping Beauties (with Owen King)
The Outsider

Elevation
The Institute
The Dark Tower I: The Gunslinger
The Dark Tower II:
The Drawing of the Three
The Dark Tower III: The Waste Lands
The Dark Tower IV: Wizard and Glass
The Dark Tower V: Wolves of the Calla
The Dark Tower VI: Song of Susannah
The Dark Tower VII: The Dark Tower
The Wind through the Keyhole:
A Dark Tower Novel

As Richard Bachman

Thinner
The Running Man
The Bachman Books
The Regulators
Blaze

STORY COLLECTIONS:

Night Shift
Different Seasons
Skeleton Crew
Four Past Midnight
Nightmares and Dreamscapes
Hearts in Atlantis
Everything's Eventual
Just After Sunset
Stephen King Goes to the Movies
Full Dark, No Stars
The Bazaar of Bad Dreams
If It Bleeds

NON-FICTION:

Danse Macabre
On Writing (A Memoir of the Craft)

STEPHEN KING

BILLY SUMMERS

A NOVEL

HODDER &
STOUGHTON

First published in Great Britain in 2021 by Hodder & Stoughton
An Hachette UK company

4

Grateful acknowledgement is made for permission to reprint
excerpts from the following copyrighted material:
THE TEDDY BEARS' PICNIC
Words by JIMMY KENNEDY, Music by JOHN W. BRATTON
©1932 by WC MUSIC CORP (ASCAP) and EMI MUSIC PUBLISHING LTD (PRS)
Reproduced by permission of ALFRED MUSIC and B FELDMAN & CO LTD/EMI MUSIC
PUBLISHING LTD, London W1T 3LP

A CIP catalogue record for this title is available from the British Library

Hardback ISBN 978 1 529 36572 6
Trade Paperback ISBN 978 1 529 36571 9
eBook ISBN 978 1 529 36569 6

Typeset in Bembo by Palimpsest Book Production Ltd, Falkirk, Stirlingshire

Printed and bound in Great Britain by Clays Ltd, Elcograf S.p.A.

Hodder & Stoughton policy is to use papers that are natural, renewable
and recyclable products and made from wood grown in sustainable forests.
The logging and manufacturing processes are expected to conform to
the environmental regulations of the country of origin.

Hodder & Stoughton Ltd
Carmelite House
50 Victoria Embankment
London EC4Y 0DZ

www.hodder.co.uk

Thinking of Raymond and Sarah Jane Spruce

'I once was lost, but now am found.'

Amazing Grace

BILLY SUMMERS

CHAPTER 1

1

Billy Summers sits in the hotel lobby, waiting for his ride. It's Friday noon. Although he's reading a digest-sized comic book called *Archie's Pals 'n' Gals*, he's thinking about Émile Zola, and Zola's third novel, his breakthrough, *Thérèse Raquin*. He's thinking it's very much a young man's book. He's thinking that Zola was just beginning to mine what would turn out to be a deep and fabulous vein of ore. He's thinking that Zola was – is – the nightmare version of Charles Dickens. He's thinking that would make a good thesis for an essay. Not that he's ever written one.

At two minutes past twelve the door opens and two men come into the lobby. One is tall with black hair combed in a 50s pompadour. The other is short and bespectacled. Both are wearing suits. All of Nick's men wear suits. Billy knows the tall one from out west. He's been with Nick a long time. His name is Frank Macintosh. Because of the pomp, some of Nick's men call him Frankie Elvis, or – now that he has a tiny bald spot in back – Solar Elvis. But not to his face. Billy doesn't know the other one. He must be local.

Macintosh holds out his hand. Billy rises and shakes it.

'Hey, Billy, been awhile. Good to see you.'

'Good to see you too, Frank.'

'This is Paulie Logan.'

'Hi, Paulie.' Billy shakes with the short one.

'Pleased to meet you, Billy.'

Macintosh takes the *Archie* digest from Billy's hand. 'Still reading the comics, I see.'

'Yeah,' Billy says. 'Yeah. I like them quite a bit. The funny ones. Sometimes the superheroes but I don't like them as much.'

Macintosh breezes through the pages and shows something to Paulie Logan. 'Look at these chicks. Man, I could jack off to these.'

'Betty and Veronica,' Billy says, taking the comic back. 'Veronica is Archie's girlfriend and Betty wants to be.'

'You read books, too?' Logan asks.

'Some, if I'm going on a long trip. And magazines. But mostly comic books.'

'Good, good,' Logan says, and drops Macintosh a wink. Not very subtle, and Macintosh frowns, but Billy's okay with it.

'You ready to take a ride?' Macintosh asks.

'Sure.' Billy tucks his digest into his back pocket. Archie and his bosomy gal pals. There's an essay waiting to be written there, too. About the comfort of haircuts and attitudes that don't change. About Riverdale, and how time stands still there.

'Then let's go,' Macintosh says. 'Nick's waiting.'

2

Macintosh drives. Logan says he'll sit in back because he's short. Billy expects them to go west, because that's where the fancy part of this town is, and Nick Majarian likes to live large whether home or away. And he doesn't do hotels. But they go northeast instead.

Two miles from downtown they enter a neighborhood that looks lower middle-class to Billy. Three or four steps better than the trailer park he grew up in, but far from fancy. No big gated houses, not here. This is a neighborhood of ranch houses with lawn sprinklers twirling on small patches of grass. Most are one-story. Most are well maintained, but a few need paint and there's crabgrass taking over some of the lawns. He sees one house with a piece of cardboard blocking a broken window. In front of another, a fat man in Bermuda shorts and a wifebeater sits in a lawn chair from Costco or Sam's Club, drinking a beer and watching them go by. Times have been good in America for awhile now, but maybe that is going to change. Billy knows neighborhoods like this. They are a barometer, and this one has started to go down. The people who live here are working the kind of jobs where you punch a clock.

Macintosh pulls into the driveway of a two-story with a patchy lawn. It's painted a subdued yellow. It's okay, but doesn't look like a place where Nick Majarian would choose to live, even for a few days. It looks like the kind of place a machinist or lower-echelon airport employee would live with his coupon-clipping wife and two kids, making mortgage payments every month and bowling in a beer league on Thursday nights.

Logan opens Billy's door. Billy puts his *Archie* digest on the dashboard and gets out.

Macintosh leads the way up the porch steps. It's hot outside but inside it's air conditioned. Nick Majarian stands in the short hallway leading down to the kitchen. He's wearing a suit that probably cost almost as much as a monthly mortgage payment on this house. His thinning hair is combed flat, no pompadour for him. His face is round and Vegas tanned. He's heavyset, but when he pulls Billy into a hug, that protruding belly feels as hard as stone.

'Billy!' Nick exclaims, and kisses him on both cheeks. Big hearty smacks. He's wearing a million-dollar grin. 'Billy, Billy, man, it's good to see you!'

'Good to see you, too, Nick.' He looks around. 'You usually stay somewhere fancier than this.' He pauses. 'If you don't mind me saying.'

Nick laughs. He has a beautiful infectious laugh to go with the grin. Macintosh joins in and Logan smiles. 'I got a place over on the West Side. Short-term. House-sitting, you could call it. There's a fountain in the front yard. Got a naked little kid in the middle of it, there's a word for that . . .'

Cherub, Billy thinks but doesn't say. He just keeps smiling.

'Anyway, a little kid peeing water. You'll see it, you'll see it. No, this one isn't mine, Billy. It's yours. If you decide to take the job, that is.'

3

Nick shows him around. 'Fully furnished,' he says, like he's selling it. Maybe he sort of is.

This one has a second floor where there are three bedrooms and two bathrooms, the second small, probably for the kids. On the first floor there's a kitchen, a living room, and a dining room that's so small it's actually a dining nook. Most of the cellar has been converted into a long carpeted room with a big TV at one end and a Ping-Pong table at the other. Track lighting. Nick calls it the rumpus room, and this is where they sit.

Macintosh asks them if they'd like something to drink. He says there's soda, beer, lemonade, and iced tea.

'I want an Arnold Palmer,' Nick says. 'Half and half. Lots of ice.'

Billy says that sounds good. They make small talk until the drinks come. The weather, how hot it is down here in the border south. Nick wants to know how Billy's trip in was. Billy says it was fine but doesn't say where he flew in from and Nick doesn't ask. Nick says how about that fuckin Trump and Billy says how about him. That's about all they've got, but it's okay because by then Macintosh is back with two tall glasses on a tray, and once he leaves, Nick gets down to business.

'When I called your man Bucky, he tells me you're hoping to retire.'

'I'm thinking about it. Been at it a long time. Too long.'

'Truth. How old are you, anyway?'

'Forty-four.'

'Been doing this ever since you took off the uniform?'

'Pretty much.' He's pretty sure Nick knows all this.

'How many in all?'

Billy shrugs. 'I don't exactly remember.' It's seventeen. Eighteen, counting the first one, the man with the cast on his arm.

'Bucky says you might do one more if the price was right.'

He waits for Billy to ask. Billy doesn't, so Nick resumes.

'The price on this one is very right. You could do it and spend the rest of your life someplace warm. Drinking piña coladas in a hammock.' He busts out the big grin again. 'Two million. Five hundred thousand up front, the rest after.'

Billy's whistle isn't part of the act, which he doesn't think of as an act but his *dumb self*, the one he shows to guys like Nick and Frank and Paulie. It's like a seatbelt. You don't use it because you expect to be in a crash, but you never know who you might meet coming over a hill on your side of the road. This is also true on the road of life, where people veer all over the place and drive the wrong way on the turnpike.

'Why so much?' The most he's ever gotten on a contract was seventy K. 'It's not a politician, is it? Because I don't do that.'

'Not even close.'

'Is it a bad person?'

Nick laughs, shakes his head, and looks at Billy with real affection. 'Always the same question with you.'

Billy nods.

The dumb self might be a shuck, but this is true: he only does bad people. It's how he sleeps at night. It goes without saying that he has made a living *working* for bad people, yes, but Billy doesn't see this as a moral conundrum. He has no problem with bad people paying to have other bad people killed. He basically sees himself as a garbageman with a gun.

'This is a very bad person.'

'Okay . . .'

'And it's not my two mill. I'm just the middleman here, getting what you could call an agenting fee. Not a piece of yours, mine's on the side.' Nick leans forward, hands clasped between his thighs. His expression is earnest. His eyes are fixed on Billy's. 'The target is a pro shooter, like you. Only this guy, he never asks if it's a bad person or a good person. He doesn't make those distinctions. If the money's right, he does the job. For now we'll call him Joe. Six years ago, or maybe it was seven, it don't matter, this guy Joe took out a fifteen-year-old kid on his way to school. Was the kid a bad person? No. In fact he was an honor student. But someone wanted to send the kid's dad a message. The kid was the message. Joe was the messenger.'

Billy wonders if the story is true. It might not be, it has a fairy tale fabulism to it, but it somehow feels true. 'You want me to hit a hitter.' Like he's getting it straight in his mind.

'Nailed it. Joe's in a Los Angeles lockup now. Men's Central. Charged with assault and attempted rape. The attempted rape thing, tell you what, if you're not a Me Too chick, it's sorta funny. He mistook this lady writer who was in LA for a conference, *feminist* lady writer, for a hooker. He propositioned her – a bit on the hard side, I'd guess – and she pepper-sprayed him. He popped her one in the teeth and dislocated her jaw. She probably sold another hundred thousand books out of that. Should have thanked him instead of charging him, don't you think?'

Billy doesn't reply.

'Come on, Billy, think about it. The man's offed God knows how many guys, some of them very hard guys, and he gets pepper-sprayed by a dyke women's libber? You gotta see the humor in that.'

Billy gives a token smile. 'LA's on the other side of the country.'

'That's right, but he was *here* before he went *there*. I don't know why he was here and don't care, but I know he was looking for a poker game and someone told him where he could find one. Because see, our pal Joe fancies himself a high roller. Long story short, he lost a lot of money. When the big winner came out around five in the morning, Joe shot him in the gut and took back not just his money but *all* the money. Someone tried to stop him, probably another moke who was in the game, and Joe shot him, too.'

'He kill both of them?'

'Big winner died in the hospital, but not before he ID'd Joe. Guy who tried to intervene pulled through. He also ID'd Joe. You know what else?'

Billy shakes his head.

'Security footage. You see where this is going?'

Billy does, absolutely. 'Not really.'

'California's got him for assault. Which'll stick. The attempted rape would probably get thrown out, it's not like he dragged her into an alley or anything, in fact he fucking offered to *pay* her, so it's just solicitation, DA won't even bother about that. With time served, he might get ninety days in county. Debt paid. But *here* it's murder, and they take that very serious on this side of the Mississippi.'

Billy knows it. In the red states they put stone killers out of their misery. He has no problem with that.

'And after looking at the security footage, the jury would almost certainly decide to give old Joey the needle. You see that, right?'

'Sure.'

'He's using his lawyer to fight extradition, no big surprise there. You know what extradition is, right?'

'Sure.'

'Okay. Joe's lawyer is fighting it for all he's worth, and the guy ain't no ambulance chaser. He's already got a thirty-day delay on a hearing, and he'll use it to figure out other ways to stall, but in the end he's gonna lose. And Joe's in an isolation cell, because somebody tried to stick a shiv into him. Old Joey took it away and broke his wrist for him, but where there's one guy with a shiv, there could be a dozen.'

'Gang thing?' Billy asks. 'Crips, maybe? They got a beef with him?'

Nick shrugs. 'Who knows? For now, Joe's got his own private quarters, doesn't have to get slopped with the rest of the hogs, gets thirty minutes in the yard all by his lonesome. *Also* meantime, the lawyer-man is reaching out to people. The message he's sending is that this guy will talk about something very big unless he can get a pass on the murder charge.'

'Could that happen?' Billy doesn't like to think so, even if the man this Joe killed after the poker game was a bad person. 'The prosecutors might take the death penalty off the table, or maybe even step it down to second-degree, or something?'

'Not bad, Billy. You're on the right track, at least. But what I'm hearing is that Joe wants all the charges dismissed. He must be holding some high cards.'

'He thinks he can trade something to get away with murder.'

'Says the guy who got away with it God knows how many times,' Nick says, and laughs.

Billy doesn't. 'I never shot anyone because I lost money in a poker game. I don't play poker. And I don't *rob*.'

Nick nods vigorously. 'I know that, Billy. Just bad people. I was only busting your chops a bit. Drink your drink.'

Billy drinks his drink. He's thinking, Two million. For one job. And he's thinking, What's the catch?

'Someone must really want to stop this guy from giving up whatever he's got.'

Nick points a finger gun at him like Billy has made an amazing leap of deduction. 'You know it. Anyway, I get a message from this local guy, you'll meet him if you take the job, and the message is we're looking for a pro shooter who's the best of the best. I think that's Billy Summers, case fuckin closed.'

'You want me to do this guy, but not in LA. Here.'

'Not me. I'm just the middleman, remember. It's someone else. Someone with very deep pockets.'

'What's the catch?'

Nick turns on the grin. He points another finger gun at Billy. 'Straight to the point, right? Straight to the fuckin point. Except it's not really a catch. Or maybe it is, depending on how you feel. It's time, you see. You're going to be here . . .'

He waves his hand to indicate the little yellow house. Maybe the neighborhood it sits in, as well – the one Billy will discover is called Midwood. Maybe the whole city, which sits east of the Mississippi and just below the Mason–Dixon Line.

'. . . for quite awhile.'

4

They talk some more. Nick tells Billy that the location is set, by which he means the place Billy will shoot from. He says Billy doesn't have to decide until he sees it and hears more. Billy will get that from Ken Hoff. He's the local guy. Nick says Ken is out of town today.

'Does he know what I use?' This isn't the same as saying he's in, but it's a big step in that direction. Two million for mostly sitting around on his ass, then taking one shot. Hard to turn down a deal like that.

Nick nods.

'Okay, when do I meet this Hoff guy?'

'Tomorrow. He'll give you a call at your hotel tonight, time and place.'

'If I do it, I'll need some kind of a cover story for why I'm here.'

'All worked out, and it's a beaut. Giorgio's idea. We'll tell you tomorrow night, after you meet with Hoff.' Nick rises. He sticks out his hand. Billy shakes it. He has shaken with Nick before and never likes it because Nick is a bad guy. Hard not to like him a little, though. Nick is also a pro, and that grin works.

5

Paulie Logan drives him back to the hotel. Paulie doesn't talk much. He asks Billy if he minds the radio, and when Billy says no, Paulie puts on a soft rock station. At one point he says, 'Loggins and Messina, they're the best.' Except for cursing at a guy who cuts him off on Cedar Street, that's the extent of his conversation.

Billy doesn't mind. He's thinking of all the movies he's seen about robbers who are planning one last job. If noir is a genre, then 'one last job' is a sub-genre. In those movies, the last job always goes bad. Billy isn't a robber and he doesn't work with a gang and he's not superstitious, but this last job thing nags at him just the same. Maybe because the price is so high. Maybe because he doesn't know who's paying the tab, or why. Maybe it's even the story Nick told about how the target once took out a fifteen-year-old honor student.

'You stickin around?' Paulie asks when he pulls the car into the hotel's forecourt. 'Because this guy Hoff will get you the tool you need. I could have done it myself, but Nick said no.'

Is he sticking around? 'Don't know. Maybe.' He pauses getting out. 'Probably.'

6

In his room, Billy powers up his laptop. He changes the time stamp and checks his VPN, because hackers love hotels. He could try googling Los Angeles County courts, extradition hearings have got to be matters of public record, but there are simpler ways to get what he wants. And he wants. Ronald Reagan had a point when he said trust but verify.

Billy goes to the *LA Times* website and pays for a six-month subscription. He uses a credit card that belongs to a fictitious person named Thomas Hardy, Hardy being Billy's favorite writer. Of the naturalist school, anyway. Once in, he searches for *feminist writer* and adds *attempted rape*. He finds half a dozen stories, each smaller than the last. There's a picture of the feminist writer, who looks hot and has a lot to say. The alleged attack took place in the forecourt of the Beverly Hills Hotel. The alleged perpetrator was discovered to be in possession of multiple IDs and credit cards. According to the *Times*, his real name is Joel Randolph Allen. He beat a rape charge in Massachusetts in 2012.

So Joe was pretty close, Billy thinks.

Next he goes to the website of this city's newspaper, once again uses Thomas Hardy to get through the paywall, and searches for *murder victim poker game*.

The story is there, and the security photo that runs with it is pretty damning. An hour earlier the light wouldn't have been good enough to show the doer's face, but the time stamp on the bottom of the photo is 5:18 A.M. The sun isn't up but it's getting there, and the face of the guy standing in the alley is as clear as you'd want, if you were a prosecutor. He's got his hand in his pocket, he's waiting outside a door that says LOADING ZONE DO NOT BLOCK, and if Billy was on the jury, he'd probably vote for the needle just on the basis of that. Because Billy Summers is an expert when it comes to premeditation, and that's what he's looking at right here.

The most recent story in the Red Bluff paper says that Joel Allen has been arrested on unrelated charges in Los Angeles.

Billy is sure that Nick believes he takes everything at face value. Like everyone else Billy has worked for over the years he's been doing this, Nick believes that outside of his awesome sniper skills, Billy is a little slow, maybe even on the spectrum. Nick believes the *dumb self*, because Billy is at great pains not to overdo it. No gaping mouth, no glazed eyes, no outright stupidity. An *Archie* comic book does wonders. The Zola novel he's been reading is buried deep in his suitcase. And if someone searched his case and discovered it? Billy would say he found it left in the pocket of an airline seat and picked it up because he liked the girl on the cover.

He thinks about looking for the fifteen-year-old honor student, but there isn't enough info. He could google that all afternoon and not find it. Even if he did, he couldn't be sure he was looking at the right fifteen-year-old. It's enough to know the rest of the story Nick told checks out.

He orders a sandwich and a pot of tea. When it comes, he sits by the window, eating and reading *Thérèse Raquin*. He thinks it's like James M. Cain crossed with an EC horror comic from the 1950s. After his late lunch, he lies down with his hands behind his head and beneath the pillow, feeling the cool that hides there. Which, like youth and beauty, doesn't last long. He'll see what this Ken Hoff has to say, and if that also checks out, he thinks he will take the job. The waiting will be difficult, he's never been good at that (tried Zen once, didn't take), but for a two-million-dollar payday he can wait.

Billy closes his eyes and goes to sleep.

At seven that evening, he's eating a room service dinner and watching *The Asphalt Jungle* on his laptop. It's a jinxed one last job picture, for sure. The phone rings. It's Ken Hoff. He tells Billy where they'll meet tomorrow afternoon. Billy doesn't have to write it down. Writing things down can be dangerous, and he's got a good memory.

CHAPTER 2

1

Like most male movie stars – not to mention men Billy passes on the street who are emulating those movie stars – Ken Hoff has a scruff of beard, as if he forgot to shave for three or four days. This is an unfortunate look for Hoff, who is a redhead. He doesn't look rough and tough; he looks like he has a bad sunburn.

They are sitting at an umbrella-shaded table outside an eatery called the Sunspot Café. It's on the corner of Main and Court. Billy guesses the place is plenty busy during the week, but on this Saturday afternoon it's almost deserted inside, and they have the outside scatter of tables to themselves.

Hoff is maybe fifty or a hard-living forty-five. He's drinking a glass of wine. Billy has a diet soda. He doesn't think Hoff works for Nick, because Nick is based in Vegas. But Nick has his fingers in many pies, not all of them out west. Nick Majarian and Ken Hoff may be connected in some way, or maybe Hoff is hooked up with the guy who is paying for the job. Always assuming the job happens, that is.

'That building across the street is mine,' Hoff says. 'Only twenty-two stories, but good enough to make it the second highest in Red Bluff. It'll be the third highest when the Higgins Center goes up. That's gonna be thirty stories high. With a mall. I've got a piece of that one, too, but this one? Strictly my baby. They laughed at Trump when he said he was gonna fix the economy, but it's working. It's working.'

Billy has no interest in Trump or Trump's economy, but he studies the building with professional interest. He's pretty sure it's where he's supposed to take the shot. It's called the Gerard Tower. Billy thinks that calling a building that has only twenty-two stories a tower is a little overblown, but he supposes in this city of small brick buildings, most of them shabby, it probably seems like a tower. On the well-tended and -watered greensward in front of it is a sign reading OFFICE SPACE AND LUXURY APARTMENTS NOW AVAILABLE. There's a number to call. The sign looks like it's been there awhile.

'Hasn't filled the way I expected,' Hoff says. 'The economy's booming, yeah, people with money falling out of their asses and 2020 is going to be even better, but you'd be surprised how much of that is Internet-driven, Billy. Okay to call you Billy?'

'Sure.'

'Bottom line, I'm a little bit tight this year. Cash flow problems since I bought into WWE, but three affils, how could I say no?'

Billy has no idea what he's talking about. Something about pro wrestling, maybe? Or the Monster Truck Jam they keep advertising on TV? Since Hoff clearly thinks he should know, Billy nods his head as if he does.

'The local old money assholes think I'm overextended, but you have to bet on the economy, am I right? Roll the dice while the dice are hot. Takes money to make money, yeah?'

'Sure.'

'So I do what I have to do. And hey, I know a good thing when I see it and this is a good deal for me. A little risky, but I need a bridge. And Nick assures me that if you were to get caught, I know you won't but if you did, you'd keep your mouth shut.'

'Yes. I would.' Billy has never been caught and doesn't intend to get caught this time.

'Code of the road, am I right?'

'Sure.' Billy has an idea that Ken Hoff has seen too many movies. Some of them probably in the 'one last job' sub-genre. He wishes the man would get to the point. It's hot out here, even under the umbrella. And muggy. This climate is for the birds, Billy thinks, and probably even they don't like it.

'I got you a nice corner suite on the fifth floor,' Hoff says. 'Three rooms. Office, reception, kitchenette. A kitchenette, how about that, huh? You'll be okay no matter how long it takes. Snug as a bug in a rug. I'm not gonna point, but I'm sure you can count to five, right?'

Sure, Billy thinks, I can even walk and chew gum at the same time.

The building is square, your basic Saltine box with windows, so there are actually two corner suites on the fifth floor, but Billy knows which one Hoff means: the one on the left. From the window he traces a diagonal down Court Street, which is only two blocks long. The diagonal, the path of the shot he'll take if he takes the job, ends at the steps of the county courthouse. It's a gray granite sprawl of a building. The steps, at least twenty, lead up to a plaza with blindfolded Lady Justice in the middle, holding out her scales. Among the many things he will never tell Ken Hoff: Lady Justice is based on Iustice, a Roman goddess more or less invented by the emperor Augustus.

Billy returns his gaze to the fifth-floor corner suite and once more eyes the diagonal. It looks to him like five hundred yards from the window to the steps. That's a shot he is capable of making even in a strong wind. With the right tool, of course.

'What have you got for me, Mr Hoff?'

'Huh?' For a moment Hoff's *dumb self* is on full view. Billy makes a curling gesture with the index finger of his right hand. It could be taken to mean *come on*, but not in this case.

'Oh! Sure! What you asked for, right?' He looks around, sees no one, but lowers his voice anyway. 'Remington 700.'

'The M24.' That's the Army classification.

'M . . .?' Hoff reaches into his back pocket, takes out his wallet, and thumbs through it. He removes a scrap of paper and looks at it. 'M24, right.'

He starts to put the piece of paper back in his wallet, but Billy holds out his hand.

Hoff hands it over. Billy puts it in his own pocket. Later, before he goes to see Nick, he'll flush it down the toilet in his hotel room. You don't write stuff down. He hopes this guy Hoff isn't going to be a problem.

'Optics?'

'Huh?'

'Scope. The sight.'

Hoff looks flustered. 'It's the one you asked for.'

'Did you write that down, too?'

'On the paper I just gave you.'

'Okay.'

'I've got the, uh, tool in a—'

'I don't need to know where. I haven't even decided if I want this job.' He has, though. 'Does the building over there have security?' Another *dumb self* question.

'Yeah. Sure.'

'If I do take the job, getting the tool up to the fifth floor will be on me. Are we good on that, Mr Hoff?'

'Yeah, sure.' Hoff looks relieved.

'Then I think we're done here.' Billy stands and holds out his hand. 'It was very nice meeting you.' It wasn't. Billy isn't sure he trusts the man, and he hates that stupid scruffy beard. What woman would want to kiss a mouth surrounded by red bristles?

Hoff shakes. 'Same here, Billy. This is just a squeeze I'm going through. You ever read a book called *The Hero's Journey*?'

Billy has, but shakes his head.

'You should, you should. I just skimmed the literary stuff to get to the main part. Straight to the meat of a thing, that's me. Cut through the bullshit. Can't remember the name of the guy who wrote it, but he says every man has to go through a time of testing before he becomes a hero. This is my time.'

By supplying a sniper rifle and an overwatch site to an assassin, Billy thinks. Not sure Joseph Campbell would put that in the hero category.

'Well, I hope you pass.'

2

Billy supposes he'll get a car eventually if he stays here, but right now he doesn't know his way around and he's happy to let Paul Logan drive him from the hotel to where Nick is 'house-sitting.' It's the McMansion Billy was expecting yesterday, a cobbled-together horror-show on what looks like two acres of lawn. The gate to the long curving driveway swings open at a touch of Paulie's thumb to the gadget on his visor. There is indeed a cherub peeing endlessly into a pool of water, and a couple of other statues (Roman soldier, bare-breasted maiden) that are lit by hidden spots now that dusk is here. The house is also lit, the better to show off its wretched excess. To Billy it looks like the bastard child of a supermarket and a mega-church. This isn't a house, it's the architectural equivalent of red golf pants.

Frank Macintosh, aka Frankie Elvis, is waiting on the endless porch to receive him. Dark suit, sober blue tie. Looking at him you'd never guess that he began his career breaking legs for a loan shark. Of course that was long ago, before he moved up to the bigs. He comes halfway down the porch steps, hand outstretched, like the lord of the manor. Or the lord of the manor's butler.

Nick is once more waiting in the hall, one much grander than that of the humble yellow house in Midwood. Nick is built big, but the man with him is enormous, way north of three hundred. This is Giorgio Piglielli, of course known to Nick's Las Vegas cadre as Georgie Pigs (and also never to his face). If Nick is a CEO, then Giorgio is his chief operating officer. For them both to be here, so far from their home base, suggests that what Nick called the agenting fee must be very high. Billy has been promised two million. How much have these guys been promised, or already pocketed? Someone is very worried about Joel Allen. Someone who probably owns a house like this, or one even uglier. Hard to believe such a thing is possible, but it probably is.

Nick claps Billy on the shoulder and says, 'You probably think this fat-ass is Giorgio Piglielli.'

'Sure looks like him,' Billy says cautiously, and Giorgio gives a chuckle as fat as he is.

Nick nods. He's got that million-dollar grin on his face. 'I know it does, but this is actually George Russo. Your agent.'

'Agent? Like in real estate?'

'Nope, not that kind.' Nick laughs. 'Come on in the living room. We'll have drinks and Giorgio will lay this out for you. Like I said yesterday, it's a beaut.'

3

The living room is as long as a Pullman car. There are three chandeliers, two small and one big. The furniture is low and swoopy. Two more cherubs are supporting a full-length mirror. There's a grandfather clock that looks embarrassed to be here.

Frank Macintosh, the leg-breaker turned manservant, brings them drinks on a tray: beer for Billy and Nick and what looks like a chocolate malted for Giorgio, who seems determined to ingest every calorie possible before dying at the age of fifty. He chooses the only chair that will fit him. Billy wonders if he'll be able to get out of it without help.

Nick raises his glass of beer. 'Here's to us. May we do business that makes us happy and leaves us satisfied.'

They drink to that, then Giorgio says, 'Nick tells me that you're interested, but you haven't actually signed on for this yet. Still in what could be called the exploratory phase.'

'That's right,' Billy says.

'Well, for the purposes of this discussion, let's pretend that you're on the team.' Giorgio sucks on the straw in his malted. 'Man, that's good. Just the ticket on a warm evening.' He reaches into the pocket of his suitcoat – enough fabric there to clothe an orphanage, Billy thinks – and produces a wallet. He holds it out.

Billy takes it. A Lord Buxton. Nice, but not fancy. And it's been slightly aged, with a couple of scuffs and nicks in the leather.

'Look through it. It's who you'll be in this godforsaken burg.'

Billy does. Seventy dollars or so in the billfold. A few pictures, mostly of men who could be friends and women who could be gal pals. Nothing to indicate he has a wife and kids.

'I wanted to Photoshop you into one,' Giorgio says, 'standing at the Grand Canyon or something, but nobody seems to have a photo of you, Billy.'

'Photos can lead to trouble.'

Nick says, 'Most people don't carry pictures of themselves in their wallets, anyway. I told Giorgio that.'

Billy continues to go through the wallet, reading it like a book. Like *Thérèse Raquin*, which he finished while eating supper in his room. If he stays here, his name will be David Lockridge. He has a Visa card and a Mastercard, both issued by Seacoast Bank of Portsmouth.

'What are the limits on the plastic?' he asks Giorgio.

'Five hundred on the Master, a thousand on the Visa. You're on a budget. Of course, if your book works out like we hope it will, that could change.'

Billy stares at Giorgio, then at Nick, wondering if this is some kind of set-up. Wondering if they've seen through the *dumb self.*

'He's your *literary* agent!' Nick nearly shouts. 'Is that a hoot, or what?'

'A writer is my cover? Come on, I never even finished high school. Got my GED in the sand, for God's sake, and that was a gift from Uncle Sam for dodging IEDs and mujies in Fallujah and Ramadi. It won't work. It's crazy.'

'It's not, it's genius,' Nick says. 'Listen to the man, Billy. Or should I start calling you Dave now?'

'You're never calling me Dave if this is my cover.'

Too close to home, far too close. He's a reader, that's for sure. And he sometimes dreams of writing, although he's never actually tried his hand except for scraps of prose here and there, which he always destroyed.

'It'll never fly, Nick. I know you guys have already started this going . . .' He raises the wallet. '. . . and I'm sorry, but it just won't work. What would I say if someone asked what my book was about?'

'Give me five minutes,' Giorgio says. 'Ten, tops. And if you still don't like it, we all part friends.'

Billy doubts if that's true but tells him to go ahead.

Giorgio puts his empty malted glass on the table (probably a Chippendale) beside his chair and belches. But when he turns his full attention on Billy, he can see what Georgie Pigs really is: a lean and athletic mind buried inside the ocean of blubber that will kill him before many more years. 'I know how it sounds at first blush, you being the kind of guy you are, but it *will* fly.'

Billy relaxes a little. They still believe what they see. He's safe on that score, at least.

'You're going to be here for at least six weeks and maybe as long as six months,' Giorgio says. 'Depends on how long it takes for the moke's lawyer to run out the string fighting extradition. Or until he thinks he has a deal on the murder charge. You're getting paid for the job, but you're also getting paid for your time. You get that, right?'

Billy nods.

'Which means you need a reason to be here in Red Bluff, and it's not exactly a vacation spot.'

'Truth,' Nick says, and makes a face like a little kid looking at a plate of broccoli.

'You also need a reason to be in that building down the street from the courthouse. You're writing a book, that's the reason.'

'But—'

Giorgio holds up a fat hand. 'You don't think it'll work, but I'm telling you it will. I'm going to show you how.'

Billy looks doubtful, but now that he's over his fear that they've seen through the camouflage of the *dumb self*, he thinks he can see where Giorgio is going. This might have possibilities.

'I did my research. Read a bunch of writers' magazines, plus a ton of stuff online. Here's your cover story. David Lockridge grew up in Portsmouth, New Hampshire. Always wanted to be a writer but barely finished high school. Worked construction. You kept writing, but you were a hard partier. Lots of drinking. I thought about giving you a divorce but decided it would be a lot to keep straight.'

For a guy who's smart about guns but not about much else, Billy thinks.

'Finally you get going on something good, okay? There's a lot of talk in the blogs I read about writers suddenly catching fire, and that's what happens to you. You write a bunch, maybe seventy pages, maybe a hundred—'

'About what?' Billy's actually starting to enjoy himself now, but he's careful not to show it.

Giorgio exchanges a glance with Nick, who shrugs. 'Haven't decided that yet, but I'll come up with someth—'

'Maybe my own story? Dave's story, I mean. There's a word for that—'

'Autobiography,' Nick snaps, like he's on *Jeopardy!*

'That might work,' Giorgio says. His face says *nice try, Nick, but leave this to the experts*. 'Or maybe it's a novel. The important thing is you never talk about it on orders from your agent. Top secret. You're writing, you don't keep that a secret, everybody you meet in the building will know the guy on the fifth floor is writing a book, but nobody knows what it's about. That way you never get your stories mixed up.'

As if I would, Billy thinks. 'How did David Lockridge get from Portsmouth to here? And how did he wind up in the Gerard Tower?'

'This is my favorite part,' Nick says. He sounds like a kid listening to a well-loved story at bedtime, and Billy doesn't think he's faking or exaggerating. Nick is totally on board with this.

'You looked for agents online,' Giorgio says, but then hesitates. 'You go online, don't you?'

'Sure,' Billy says. He's pretty sure he knows more about computers than either of these two fat men, but that is also information he doesn't share. 'I do email. Sometimes play games on my phone. Also, there's ComiXology. That's an app. You download stuff. I use my laptop for that.'

'Okay, good. You look for agents. You send out letters saying you're working on this book. Most of the agents say no, because they stick with the proven earners like James Patterson and the Harry Potter babe. I read a blog that said it's a catch-22: you need an agent to get published, but until you're published you can't get an agent.'

'It's the same in the movies,' Nick puts in. 'You got your famous stars, but it's really all about the agents. They have the real power. They tell the stars what to do, and boy, they do it.'

Giorgio waits patiently for him to finish, then goes on. 'Finally one agent says yeah, okay, what the fuck, I'll take a look, send me the first couple of chapters.'

'You,' Billy says.

'Me. George Russo. I read the pages. I flip for them. I show them to a few publishers I know—'

The fuck you do, Billy thinks, you show them to a few *editors* you know. But that part can be fixed if it ever needs to be.

'—and they also flip, but they won't pay big money, maybe even seven-figure money, until the book is finished. Because you're an unknown commodity. Do you know what that means?'

Billy comes perilously close to saying of course he does, because he's getting jazzed by the possibilities here. It could actually be an excellent cover, especially the part about being sworn to secrecy concerning his project. And it could be fun pretending to be what he's always sort of wished he could be.

'It means a flash in the pan.'

Nick flashes the money grin. Giorgio nods.

'Close enough. Some time passes. I wait for more pages, but Dave doesn't come through. I wait some more. Still no pages. I go to see him up there in lobsterland, and what do I find? The guy is partying his ass off like he's Ernest fuckin Hemingway. When he's not working, he's either out with his homeboys or hungover. Substance abuse goes with talent, you know.'

'Really?'

'Proven fact. But George Russo is determined to save this guy, at least long enough to finish his book. He talks a publisher into contracting for it and paying an advance of let's say thirty or maybe fifty thou. Not big money, but not small money either, plus the publisher can demand it back if the book doesn't show up by a certain deadline, which they call a delivery date. But see, here's the thing, Billy: the check is made out to *me* instead of to *you*.'

Now it's all clear in Billy's mind, but he'll let Giorgio spin it out.

'I have certain conditions. For your own good. You have to leave lobsterland and all your hard-drinking, coke-snorting friends. You have to go somewhere far away from them, to some little shitpot of a town or city where there's nothing to do and no one to do it with even if there was. I tell you I'm gonna rent you a house.'

'The one I saw, right?'

'Right. More important, I'm going to rent you office space and you're going to go there every weekday and sit in a little room and pound away until your top secret book is done. You agree to those terms or your golden ticket goes bye-bye.'

Giorgio sits back. The chair is sturdy, but still gives out a little groan.

'Now if you tell me that's a bad idea, or even if you tell me it's a good idea but you can't sell it, we'll call the whole thing off.'

Nick holds up a hand. 'Before you say anything, Billy, I want to lay out something else that makes this good. Everybody on your floor will get acquainted with you, and a lot of other people in the building, too. I know you, and you've got another talent besides hitting a quarter at a quarter of a mile.'

Like I could do that, Billy thinks. Like even Chris Kyle could.

'You get along with people without buddying up to them. They smile when they see you coming.' And then, as if Billy had denied it: 'I've seen it! Hoff tells me that a couple of food wagons stop at that building every day, and in nice weather people line up and sit outside on the benches to eat their lunches. You could be one of those people. The time waiting doesn't have to be for nothing. You can use it to get accepted. Once the novelty of how you're writing a book wears off, you'll be just another nine-to-fiver who goes home to his little house in Midwood.'

Billy sees how that could happen.

'So when it finally goes down, are you a stranger no one knows? The outsider who must have done it? Uh-uh, you've been there for months, you make chit-chat in the elevator, you play dollar poker with some of the collection agency guys from the second floor to see who buys the tacos.'

'They are going to know where the shot came from,' Billy says.

'Sure, but not right away. Because at first everyone will be looking for that outsider. And because there's going to be a diversion. Also because you've always been fucking Houdini when it comes to disappearing after the hit. By the time things start to settle, you'll be long gone.'

'What's the diversion?'

'We can talk about that later,' Nick says, which makes Billy think Nick might not have made up his mind about that yet. Although with Nick, it's hard to tell. 'Plenty of time. For now . . .' He turns to Giorgio, aka Georgie Pigs, aka George Russo. *Over to you*, the look says.

Giorgio reaches into the pocket of his gigantic suit jacket again and pulls out his phone. 'Say the word, Billy – the word being the passcode of your favorite offshore bank – and I'll send five hundred grand to it. It'll take about forty seconds. Minute and a half if the connection's slow. Also plenty of walking-around money in a local bank to get you started.'

Billy understands they're trying to rush him into a decision and has a brief image of a cow being driven down a chute to the slaughterhouse, but maybe that's just paranoia because of the enormous payday. Maybe a person's last job shouldn't just be the most lucrative; maybe it should also be the most interesting. But he would like to know one more thing.

'Why is Hoff involved?'

'His building,' Nick says promptly.

'Yeah, but . . .' Billy frowns, putting an expression of great concentration on his face. 'He said there's lots of vacancies in that building.'

'The corner spot on the fifth floor is prime, though,' Nick says. 'Your agent, Georgie here, had him lease it, which keeps us out of it.'

'He also gets the gun,' Giorgio says. 'May have it already. In any case, it won't be traced back to us.'

Billy knows that already, from the way Nick has been careful not to be seen with him – no, not even on the porch of this gated estate – but he's not entirely satisfied. Because Hoff struck him as a chatterbox, and a chatterbox isn't a good person to have around when you're planning an assassination.

4

Later that night. Closing in on midnight. Billy lies on his hotel room bed, hands beneath the pillow, relishing the cool that's so ephemeral. He said yes, of course, and when you say yes to Nick Majarian, there's no going back. He is now starring in his own last job story.

He had Giorgio send the $500,000 to a bank in the Caribbean. There's a good amount of money in that account right now, and after Joel Allen dies on those courthouse steps, there will be a good deal more. Enough to live on for a long, long time if he's prudent. And he will be. He doesn't have expensive tastes. Champagne and escort services have never been his thing. In two other banks – local ones – David Lockridge will have an additional $18,000 to draw on. It's plenty of walking-around money, but not enough to twang any federal tripwires.

He did have a couple of other questions. The most important was how much lead time he could expect when the deal was about to go down.

'Not a lot,' Nick said, 'but it won't be "He's gonna be there in fifteen minutes," either. We'll know right after the extradition is ordered, and you'll get a call or a text. It'll be twenty-four hours at the very least, maybe three days or even a week. Okay?'

'Yeah,' Billy said. 'Just as long as you understand I can't guarantee anything if it is fifteen minutes. Or even an hour.'

'It won't be.'

'What if they don't bring him up the courthouse steps? What if they use another door?'

'There is another door,' Giorgio said. 'It's the one some of the court-house employees use. But you'll still have a sightline from the fifth floor and the distance is only sixty yards or so longer. You can do that, can't you?'

He could, and said so. Nick lifted a hand as if to wave away a troublesome fly. 'It'll be the steps, count on it. Anything else?'

Billy said there wasn't and now he lies here, thinking it over, waiting for sleep. On Monday he'll be moving into the little yellow house, leased for him by his agent. His *literary* agent. On Tuesday, he'll see the office suite Georgie Pigs has also leased for him. When Giorgio asked him what he'd do there, Billy told him he'd start by downloading ComiXology to his laptop. And maybe a few games.

'Be sure to write something between funnybooks,' Giorgio said, half-joking and half not. 'You know, get into character. Live the part.'

Maybe he will. Maybe he will do that. Even if what he writes isn't very good, it will pass the time. Autobiography was his suggestion. Giorgio suggested a novel, not because he thinks Billy's bright enough to write one but because Billy could say that when someone asked, as someone will. Probably lots of someones, once he gets to know people in the Gerard Tower.

He's slipping toward sleep when a cool idea wakes him up: why not a combination of the two? Why not a novel that's actually an autobiography, one written not by the Billy Summers who reads Zola and Hardy and even plowed his way through *Infinite Jest*, but one written by the other Billy Summers? The alter ego he calls his *dumb self*? Could that work? He thinks yes, because he knows that Billy as well as he knows himself.

I might give it a try, he thinks. With nothing but time on my hands, why not? He's thinking about how he might begin when he finally drifts off.

CHAPTER 3

1

Billy Summers once more sits in the hotel lobby, waiting for his ride.

It's Monday noon. His suitcase and laptop case are beside his chair and he's reading another comic book, this one called *Archie Comics Spectacular: Friends Forever*. He's not thinking about *Thérèse Raquin* today but what he might write in the fifth-floor office he's never seen. It isn't clear in his mind, but he has a first sentence and holds onto it. That sentence might connect to others. Or not. He's prepared for success but he's also prepared for disappointment. It's the way he rolls and it's worked out pretty well so far. In the sense, at least, that he's not in jail.

At four minutes past twelve, Frank Macintosh and Paulie Logan enter the lobby dressed in their suits. There are handshakes all around. Frank's pompadour appears to have had an oil change.

'Need to check out?'

'Taken care of.'

'Then let's go.'

Billy tucks his *Archie* book into the side pocket of his bag and picks it up.

'Nah, nah,' Frankie says. 'Let Paulie. He needs the exercise.'

Paulie holds his middle finger against his tie like a clip, but he takes the bag. They go out to the car. Frank drives, Paulie sits in back. They drive to Midwood and the little yellow house. Billy looks at the balding lawn and thinks he'll water it. If there's no hose, he'll buy one. There's a car in the driveway, a subcompact Toyota that looks a few years old, but with Toyotas, who can really tell?

'Mine?'

'Yours,' Frank says. 'Not much, but your agent keeps you on a tight budget, I guess.'

Paulie puts Billy's suitcase down on the porch, takes an envelope from his jacket pocket, removes a keyring, unlocks the door. He puts the keys back in the envelope and hands it to Billy. Written on the front is *24 Evergreen Street*. Billy, who didn't check the street sign yesterday or today, thinks, Now I know where I live.

'Car keys are on the kitchen table,' Frank says. He holds out his hand again, so this is goodbye. That's okay with Billy.

'Shake her easy,' Paulie says.

Less than sixty seconds later they're gone, presumably back to the McMansion with the endlessly peeing cherub in the gigantic front yard.

2

Billy goes upstairs to the master bedroom and opens his suitcase on a double bed that looks freshly made. When he opens the closet to put things away, he sees it's already loaded with shirts, a couple of sweaters, a hoodie, and two pairs of dress pants. There's a new pair of running shoes on the floor. All the sizes look right. In the dresser he finds socks, underwear, T-shirts, Wrangler jeans. He fills up the one empty drawer with his own stuff. There's not much. He thought he'd be buying more clothes at the Walmart he saw down the way, but it seems like that won't be necessary.

He goes down to the kitchen. The Toyota keys are on the table beside an engraved card that says KENNETH HOFF and ENTREPRENEUR. Entrepreneur, Billy thinks. There's a word for you. He turns the card over and sees a brief note in the same hand as on the envelope containing the housekeys: *If you need anything, just call.* There are two numbers, one for business and one for cell.

He opens the refrigerator and sees it's stocked with staples: juice, milk, eggs, bacon, a few bags of deli meats and cheeses, a plastic carton of potato salad. There's a rack of Poland Spring water, a rack of Coke, and a sixpack of Bud Light. He pulls out the freezer drawer and has to smile because what's in there says so much about Ken Hoff. He's single and until his divorce (Billy's sure there was at least one), he has been fed and watered by women, starting with a mother who probably called him Kenny and made sure he got his hair cut every two weeks. The freezer is stuffed with Stouffer's entrees and frozen pizza and two boxes of ice cream novelties, the kind that come on a stick. There are no vegetables, fresh or frozen.

'Don't like him,' Billy says aloud. He's not smiling anymore.

No. And he doesn't like what Hoff is doing in this. Aside from Hoff being too out front after the deal goes down, there's something Nick's not telling him. Maybe that doesn't matter. Maybe it does. As Trump says at least once a day, Who knows?

3

There's a hose in the basement, coiled up and dusty. That evening, as the heat of the day is starting to fade a little, Billy lugs it outside and hooks it up to the faucet bib on the side of the house. He's standing on the front lawn, dressed in jeans and a T-shirt, spraying the grass, when a man comes over from next door. He's tall, his own tee blinding white against very black skin. He's carrying two cans of beer.

'Hi, neighbor,' he says. 'Brought you a cold one to welcome you to the neighborhood. Jamal Ackerman.' He's got both beers in one big hand and holds out the other.

Billy shakes. 'David Lockridge. Dave. And thanks.' He twists the hose shut. 'Come on inside. Or we can sit out on the steps. I haven't really got the place sorted out yet.' No need of the *dumb self* here; in Midwood he can be a more regular self.

'Porch steps'll do fine,' Jamal says.

They sit. They open the cans: *fsst*. Billy tips his to Jamal's and says, 'Thanks.'

They drink. They survey the lawn.

'It'll take more than water to bring that mess back,' Jamal says. 'I've got some Miracle-Gro, if you want to use some. They had a BOGO deal at the Wally World Garden Center last month and I have plenty.'

'I might take you up on that. I'm planning a trip to Wally World myself. I might get a couple of chairs for the porch. But probably not until next week. You know how it is, new place and all.'

Jamal laughs. 'Do I ever. This is the third house we've lived in since I got married in '09. First one was her mom's.' He pretends to shiver.

Billy smiles. 'Got two kids, ten and eight. Boy and a girl. When they bug you, cause they will, holler them back home.'

'If they don't break the windows or light the place on fire, they won't bug me.'

'You buying or renting?'

'Leasing. I'll be here awhile, don't know just how long. I'm . . . it's a little embarrassing to come right out and say it, but I'm writing a book. Trying, anyway. Looks like there's a chance I can get it published, might even be some real money in it, but I'll have to buckle down. I've got an office in town. The Gerard Tower? At least I think I do. I'm going to look at it tomorrow.'

Jamal's eyes have gotten very wide. 'An author! Living right here on Evergreen Street! I'll be goddamned!'

Billy laughs and shakes his head. 'Easy, big fella. I'm just a wannabe for now.'

'Still, man! Wow. Wait 'til I tell Corinne. We gotta have you over to dinner some night. We'll be able to tell people we knew you when.'

He holds up a hand. Billy slaps him five. *You get along with people without buddying up to them*, Nick said. It's true and it's not a shuck. Billy likes people, and he likes to keep them at arm's length. It sounds like a contradiction, but it's not.

'What's it about, your book?'

'Can't tell you.' This is where the editing begins. Giorgio may think he knows it all from reading a few writers' magazines and online posts, but he doesn't. 'Not because it's a big secret or something, but because I've got to keep it bottled up. If I start talking about it . . .' He shrugs.

'Yeah, man, got it.' Jamal smiles.

And so, yeah. Just like that.

4

That night Billy browses Netflix on the big TV in the rumpus room. He knew it was a thing these days but has never bothered to investigate it when there are so many books to read. There's so much to watch as well, it seems. The sheer volume of choices is intimidating and he decides to go to bed early instead of watching anything. Before undressing, he checks his phone and finds a text from his new agent.

GRusso: 9 AM at Gerard Tower. Don't drive. Uber.

Billy doesn't have a David Lockridge phone – neither Giorgio nor Frank Macintosh gave him one – and he doesn't have a burner. He decides to use his personal since Giorgio already did. With the encrypted messaging app it should be all right. And Billy has something he really needs to say.

Billy S: OK. Don't bring Hoff.

Dots roll as Giorgio composes his reply. It doesn't take long.

GRusso: Have to. Sorry.

The dots disappear. Discussion over.

Billy empties his pockets and puts his pants in the washing machine along with everything else. He does this slowly, brow furrowed. He doesn't like Ken Hoff. Did not like him, in fact, even before he opened his mouth. Gut reaction. What Giorgio's parents and grandparents would have called *reazione istintiva.* But Hoff is in it. Giorgio's text made that clear: *Have to.* It's not like Nick and Giorgio to bring a local into their business, especially not life-and-death business like this. Is Hoff in it because of the building? Location, location, location, as the real estate guys like to say? Or because Nick isn't local himself?

Neither of those things quite excuse Ken Hoff in Billy's mind. *I'm a little bit tight this year* he'd said, but Billy guesses you had to be more than a little bit short in the shekels department to get involved in an assassination plot. And from the very first – the macho beard scruff, the Izod shirt, the Dockers with the slightly frayed pockets, the Gucci loafers worn at the heel – Hoff smelled to Billy like the guy who would be first to flip in an interrogation room if offered a deal. Deals, after all, were what the Ken Hoffs of the world made.

He turns in and lies in the dark, hands under the pillow, looking up at nothing. Some traffic on the street, but not much. He's wondering when two million dollars starts to look like not enough, when it starts to look like dumb money. The answer seems obvious: after it's too late to back out.

5

Billy Ubers to the Gerard Tower, as instructed. Hoff and Giorgio are waiting in front. The face-bristles still make Hoff look (to Billy, at least) like a hobo instead of a cool dude, but otherwise he's squared away in a summerweight suit and subdued gray tie. 'George Russo,' on the other hand, looks larger than ever in an unfortunate green shirt, untucked, and blue jeans with enough ass in them to make a puptent. Billy supposes it's that fat man's idea of how a big-time literary agent dresses for a visit to sticksville. Propped between his feet is a laptop case.

Hoff seems to have pulled back on the salesman *bonhomie*, at least a little. Possibly at Giorgio's request, but he still can't resist a jaunty little salute: *mon capitaine.* 'Good to see you. The security guy on duty this morning – and most weekdays – is Irv Dean. He'll want your driver's license and a quick snap. That okay?'

Because it has to be if they're going to proceed, Billy nods.

A few workbound people are still crossing the lobby to the elevators. Some wear suits, some of the women are in those high heels Billy thinks of as click-clack shoes, but a surprising number are dressed informally, some even in branded tees. He doesn't know where they work, but it's probably not meeting the public.

The guy sitting at the concierge-type stand at the lobby's center is portly and elderly. The lines around his mouth are so deep they make him look like a life-sized ventriloquist's dummy. Billy guesses retired cop, now only two or three years from total retirement. His uniform consists of a blue vest with POLK SECURITY on it in gold thread. A cheap hire. More evidence that Hoff is in trouble. Big trouble, if he's solely on the hook for this building.

Hoff turns on his charm turbocharger, approaching the old guy with a smile and outstretched hand. 'How's it going, Irv? All okay?'

'Fine, Mr Hoff.'

'Wife tip-top?'

'The arthritis bothers her some, but otherwise she's fine.'

'This is George Russo, you met him last week, and this is David Lockridge. He's going to be our resident author.'

'Pleased to meet you, Mr Lockridge,' Dean says. A smile lights up his face and makes him look younger. Not much, but a little. 'Hope you'll find some good words here.'

Billy thinks that's a nice thing to say, maybe even the best thing. 'I hope so, too.'

'Mind me asking what your book is about?'

Billy puts a finger to his lips. 'Top secret.'

'Okay, I hear you. That's a nice little suite on five. I think you'll like it. I have to take your picture for your building ID, if that's okay?'

'Sure.'

'Got a DL?'

Billy hands over the David Lockridge driver's license. Dean uses a cell phone with GERARD TOWER Dymo'd on the back to photograph first his license and then Billy himself. Now there's a picture of him on this building's computer servers, retrievable by anyone with authorization or hacking skills. He tells himself it doesn't matter, this is his last job, but he still doesn't like it. It feels all wrong.

'I'll have the card for you when you leave. You need to use it if there's nobody here at the stand. Just put it on this reader gadget. We like to know who's in the building. I'll be here most of the time, or Logan when I'm off, and when we are, we'll sign you in.'

'Got it.'

'You can also use your card for the parking garage on Main. It's good for four months. Your, uh, agent paid for that. It'll open the barrier as soon as I put you in the computer. Parking on the street when court's in session, forget it.' Which explains the Uber. 'There's no assigned space in the garage, but most days you'll find a spot on the first or second level. We're not overcrowded just now.' He gives Ken Hoff an apologetic look, then returns his attention to the new tenant. 'Anything I can do for you, just tap one-one on your office phone. Landline's installed. Your agent there took care of that, too.'

'Mr Dean has been very helpful,' Giorgio says.

'It's his job!' Hoff exclaims cheerfully. 'Isn't it, Irv?'

'Absolutely right.'

'You say hi to your wife, tell her I hope she feels better. Those copper bracelets are supposed to help. The ones they advertise on TV?'

'Might give them a try,' Dean says, but he looks dubious, and good for him.

When they pass the security stand, Billy sees that Mr Polk Security has a copy of the *Sports Illustrated* swimsuit issue in his lap. There's a bodacious babe on the cover, and Billy makes a mental note to pick one up. The *dumb self* likes sports, and he likes babes.

They take the elevator up to five and step out in a deserted corridor.

'There's an accounting office down there,' Hoff says, pointing. 'Two connecting suites. Also some lawyers. There's a dentist on this side. I think. Unless he moved out. I guess he did, because the plaque on the door is gone. I'll have to ask the rental agent. Rest of the floor is unoccupied.'

Oh, this guy is in real trouble, Billy thinks again. He risks a glance at Giorgio, but Giorgio – *George* – is gazing at the door behind which there is now no dentist. As if there was something there to see.

Near the end of the hall, Hoff reaches into his suitcoat pocket and produces a little cloth keycard wallet with GT stamped on the front in gold. 'This is yours. Also two spares.'

Billy touches one of the keycards to the reader and steps into what would be a small reception area if this were a going business. It's stuffy. Stale.

'Jesus, someone forgot to turn on the air conditioning! Just a second, wait one.' Hoff punches a couple of buttons on the wall controller and has an anxious moment when nothing happens. Then cool air begins to whoosh from an overhead vent. Billy reads Hoff's relief in the slump of his shoulders.

The next room is a big office that could double as a small conference room. There's no desk, just a table long enough for maybe six people, if they crammed in shoulder to shoulder. On it is a stack of Staples notebooks, a box of pens, a landline telephone. This room – his writing studio, Billy supposes – is even hotter than the antechamber because of the morning sun flooding in. No one has bothered to lower the blinds, either. Giorgio flaps the collar of his shirt against his neck. 'Whew!'

'It'll cool quick, real quick,' Hoff says. He sounds a bit frantic. 'This is a great HVAC system, state of the art. It's starting already, feel it?'

Billy doesn't care about room temperature, at least for the time being. He steps to the right side of the big window facing the street and looks down that diagonal to the courthouse steps. Then he traces another diagonal to the small door further on. The one courthouse employees use. He imagines the scene: a police car pulling up, or maybe a van with SHERIFF'S DEPARTMENT or CITY POLICE on the side. Law enforcement gets out. Two at least, maybe three. Four? Probably not. They will open the door on the curb side if it's a car. The back doors if it's a van. He'll watch Joel Allen clear the vehicle. There will be no problem picking him out, he'll be the one bracketed by cops and wearing handcuffs.

When the time comes – if it comes – there will be nothing to this shot.

'Billy!' Hoff's voice makes him jerk, as if waking him from a dream.

The developer is standing in the doorway of a much smaller room. It's the kitchenette. When Hoff sees he has Billy's attention, he gestures around palm up, pointing out the mod cons like a model on *The Price Is Right*.

'Dave,' Billy says. 'I'm Dave.'

'Right. Sorry. My bad. You got your little two-burner stove, no oven but you got your microwave for popcorn, Hot Pockets, TV dinners, whatever. Plates and cookware in the cupboards. You got your little sink to wash up your dishes. Mini-fridge. No private bathroom, unfortunately, the men's and women's are at the end of the hall, but at least they're at your end. Short walk. And then there's this.'

He takes a key from his pocket and reaches up to the rectangular wooden panel above the door between the office/conference room and the kitchenette. He turns the key, pushes the panel, and it swings up. The space inside looks to be eighteen inches high, four feet long, two feet deep. It's empty.

'Storage,' Hoff says, and actually mimes shooting an invisible rifle. 'The key's so you can lock it on Fridays, when the cleaning staff—'

Billy almost says it, but Giorgio beats him to it, and that's good because he's supposed to be the thinker, not Billy Summers. 'No cleaning in here. Not on Fridays, not on any other day. Top secret writing project, remember? Dave can keep the place neatened up himself. He's a neat guy, right, Dave?'

Billy nods. He's a neat guy.

'Tell Dean, tell the other security guy – Logan, yeah? – and tell Broder.' To Billy he says, 'Steven Broder. The building super.'

Billy nods and files the name away.

Giorgio hoists the laptop bag onto the table, pushing aside the tools for writing by hand (a gesture Billy finds both sad and somehow symbolic), and unzips it. 'MacBook Pro. Best money can buy, state of the art. My present to you. You can use your own if you want to, but this baby . . . all the bells and whistles. Can you get it going okay? There's probably an instruction book, or something . . .'

'I'll figure it out.'

No problem there, but something else might be. If Nick Majarian hasn't rigged this beautiful black torpedo so he can use it as a kind of magic mirror into what Billy writes in this room, he has missed a trick. And Nick doesn't miss many.

'Oh sugarpie, that reminds me,' Hoff says, and hands Billy another of his engraved cards along with the key to the cubby over the door to the kitchenette. 'WiFi password. Totally safe. Secure as a bank vault.'

Bullshit, Billy thinks as he puts the card in his pocket.

'Well,' Giorgio says, 'I guess that's about it. We'll leave you to your creative endeavors. Come on, Ken.'

Hoff seems reluctant to leave, as if he feels there should be more to show. 'You call me if you need anything, Bi . . . Dave. Anything at all. Entertainment, maybe? A TV? Maybe a radio?'

Billy shakes his head. He has a considerable musical library on his phone, mostly country and western. He has many things to do in the days ahead, but at some point he'll find time to rip his tunes to this fine new laptop. If Nick decides to listen in, he can catch up on Reba and Willie and all Hank Junior's rowdy friends. And maybe he'll write that book after all. On his own laptop, which he trusts. He will also take security measures on both lappies – the new one and his personal, which is an old pal.

Giorgio finally gets Hoff out and Billy is on his own. He goes back to the window and stands there tracing both diagonals: the one leading to the wide stone steps and the one leading to the employees' door. Again he imagines what will happen, seeing it vividly. Real-world events are never quite the same as the ones you see in your head, but this work always begins with the seeing. It's like poetry that way. The things that change, the unexpected variables, the revisions: that stuff has to be dealt with when it comes up, but it starts with the seeing.

His phone dings with a text.

GRusso: Sorry about H. I know he's a bit of an asshole.
Billy S: Do I need to see him again?
GRusso: Don't know.

Billy would prefer something more definitive, but this will do for now. It will have to.

6

When he gets back to what he supposes is now home, his new David Lockridge building ID is in his pocket. Tomorrow he'll be driving his new used car to work. On the porch, leaning against the door, is a bag of Miracle-Gro lawn food with a note taped to it: *Thought you could use this! Jamal A.*

Billy gives the house next door a wave, although he's not sure there's anyone there to see; it's still half an hour shy of noon. Probably both Ackermans work. He takes the lawn food inside, props it in the hall, then drives to Walmart, where he buys two burner phones (an heir and a spare) and a couple of flash drives, although he'll probably need just the one; he could put the complete works of Émile Zola on a single thumbie and barely fill a corner of the space available.

He also impulse buys a cheap AllTech laptop, which he puts in his bedroom closet, still in the carton. He pays cash for the phones and the flash drives. He uses his David Lockridge Visa for the laptop. He has no immediate plans for the burners, may never even use them. It all depends on his exit strategy, which at this point is only a shadow.

He stops at Burger King on the way back, and when he gets to the yellow house, a couple of kids on bikes are in front of it. A boy and a girl, one white and one black. He guesses the girl must belong to Jamal and Corinne Ackerman.

'Are you our new neighbor?' the boy asks.

'I am,' Billy says, and thinks he'll have to get used to being one. It might even be fun. 'I'm Dave Lockridge. Who are you?'

'Danny Fazio. This is my bud Shanice. I'm nine. She's eight.'

Billy shakes hands with Danny, then with the girl, who looks at him shyly as her brown hand disappears into his white one. 'Nice to meet you both. Enjoying your summer vacation?'

'Summer reading program's okay,' Danny says. 'They give out stickers for each book you read. I've got four. Shanice got five, but I'll catch up. We're going over my house. After lunch, a bunch of us gonna play Monopoly down the park.' He points. 'Shan brings the board. I'm always the racecar.'

Kids on their own in the twenty-first century, Billy marvels, how about that. Only then he notices the fat guy two houses down – wife-beater, Bermudas, grass-stained sneakers – keeping an eye on him. And on how he behaves with these kids.

'Well, seeya later, alligator,' Danny says, mounting his bike.

'After awhile, crocodile,' Billy responds, and both kids laugh.

That afternoon, after taking a nap – he supposes that he's allowed an afternoon nap, now that he's a writer – he takes the sixpack of Bud from the fridge. He leaves it on the Ackermans' porch with a note that says *Thanks for the lawn fertilizer – Dave.*

Off to a good start here. And downtown? He thinks so. He hopes so.

Except maybe for Hoff. Hoff bugs him.

7

That evening, while Billy's putting down lawn food, Jamal Ackerman comes over with two of the beers that were in Billy's fridge. Jamal is wearing a green coverall with his name in gold thread on one breast and EXCELLENT TIRE on the other. With him, holding a can of Pepsi, is a young boy.

'Hey there, Mr Lockridge,' Jamal says. 'This little man is my son, Derek. Shanice says you met her already.'

'Yes, with a little man named Danny.'

'Thanks for the beers. Hey, what is that you're using? Looks like my wife's flour sifter.'

'Exactly what it is. I thought about buying a lawn spreader at Walmart, but for this so-called lawn . . .' He looks at the small bald patch and shrugs. 'Too much expense for too little return.'

'Looks like it works fine. Might even give it a try myself. But what about in back? That's a lot bigger.'

'It needs to be mown short first, and I don't have a mower. Yet.'

'You can borrow ours, can't he, Dad?' Derek says.

Jamal ruffles the kid's hair. 'Any time.'

'No, that's too much,' Billy says. 'I'll buy one. Always supposing I get traction on the book I'm trying to write and stick around.'

They go over to the porch and sit on the steps. Billy opens the beer and drinks. It hits the spot and he says so.

'What's your book about?' Derek asks. He's sitting between them.

'Top secret.' Smiling as he says it.

'Yeah, but is it make-believe or true?'

'A little of both.'

'That's enough,' Jamal says. 'It's not polite to pry.'

A woman is approaching from one of the houses at the far end of the street. Mid-fifties, graying hair, bright lipstick. She's holding a high-ball glass and walking not quite straight.

'That's Mrs Kellogg,' Jamal says, keeping his voice low. 'Widow lady. Lost her husband last year. Had a stroke.' He gazes thoughtfully at Billy's excuse for a lawn. 'While mowing the grass, actually.'

'Is this a party, and can I crash it?' Mrs Kellogg asks. Even though she's still on the walk and there's no breeze, Billy can smell the gin on her breath.

'As long as you don't mind sitting on the steps.' Billy gets up and offers his hand. 'Dave Lockridge.'

And now here comes the guy who was keeping an eye on Billy's interaction with Shanice and Danny. He's swapped his wifebeater and Bermudas for a pair of jeans and a Masters of the Universe T-shirt. With him is a tall, scrawny blonde in a housedress and sneakers. From next door – bearing what looks like a plate of brownies – comes Jamal's wife and daughter. Billy invites them all inside, where they can sit in actual chairs.

Welcome to the neighborhood, he thinks.

8

The Masters of the Universe guy and his skinny blonde wife are the Raglands. The Fazios also show up – although without their son – and the Petersons from the far end of the block, with a bottle of red wine. The living room fills up. It's a nice little impromptu party. Billy enjoys himself, partly because he doesn't have to work at projecting the *dumb self*, partly because he likes these people, even Jane Kellogg, who is pretty tight and has to keep visiting the bathroom. Which she calls the biffy. And by the time they all drift away – early, because tomorrow is a working day – Billy knows he will fit in here. He will be of interest because he's writing a book and that makes him something of an exotic, but that will pass. By midsummer, always supposing Joel Allen doesn't show up early for his date with a bullet, he'll be just another guy on the street. Another neighbor.

Billy learns that Jamal is the foreman at Excellent Tire, and Corrie is – small world – a steno at the courthouse. He learns that Diane Fazio keeps an eye on Shanice during summer vacation while Jamal and Corrie are at work. Shanice's brother Derek goes to day camp and will go to basketball camp in August. He learns that the Dugans, who moved out of the yellow house very suddenly last October (skedaddled is how Paul Ragland puts it), were 'snooty,' and Dave Lockridge is, consequently, a good change. After the shot, they'll tell reporters that he seemed like such a nice man. That's okay with Billy. He thinks of himself as a nice man, one with a dirty job. At least, he thinks, I never shot a fifteen-year-old on his way to school. Supposing Joel Allen, aka 'Joe,' actually did that.

Before bed, he unboxes his AllTech laptop, powers it up, and googles Ken Hoff. He's quite the mover and shaker in Red Bluff. He's an Elk. He's in Rotary. He was president of the local Jaycees chapter. Chairman of the local Republican Party during the 2016 election cycle, and there's a picture of pre-beard scruff Ken wearing a red MAGA hat. He was on the city planning board but stepped down in 2018 after accusations of conflict of interest. He owns half a dozen downtown buildings, including the Gerard Tower, which Billy supposes makes him a kind of Donald Trump Mini-Me. He owns three TV stations, one here in Red Bluff and two in Alabama. All three are affiliated with World Wide Entertainment, which probably explains Hoff's reference to WWE. He's divorced not once but twice. That means hellimony. Plans to build a golf course were scrapped late last year. Plans for another downtown building are on hold. So is Hoff's application for a casino license. All in all, it's a picture of a man whose small-time business empire is teetering. One push and off the cliff it will go.

Billy hits the rack and lies staring up into the dark with his hands under the pillow. He's starting to understand why Nick was attracted to Ken Hoff and why Ken Hoff was attracted to Nick. Nick can be charming (that million-dollar grin), and he's smarter than the average bear, but when you get right down to it, he's a hyena and what hyenas are good at is sizing up the passing herd and picking out the one that's limping. The one that will soon fall behind. Ken Hoff is the patsy. Not for the killing, he'll have a cast-iron alibi for that, but when the cops start looking for the guy who ordered the killing, they won't find Nick. They'll find Ken. Billy decides that's okay with him.

He's used up the reservoir of cool under the pillow, so he rolls over on his right side and goes to sleep almost at once.

Being a good neighbor is tiring.

CHAPTER 4

1

The next day Billy hooks up his new MacBook in the office on the fifth floor and downloads a solitaire app. There are a dozen different versions. He opts for Canfield and rigs the computer to leave a five-second pause before each move. If Nick or Giorgio should choose to look in and monitor his activities (or maybe Frankie Elvis would be given that task), they will have no idea the computer is playing solo.

Billy goes to the window and looks out. Both sides of Court Street are lined with parked cars, many of them police cruisers. The umbrella-shaded tables outside the Sunspot Café are filled with people eating doughnuts and Danish. A few people are descending the wide court-house steps, but a lot more are on their way up. Some trot, showing off their aerobic fitness. Others plod. Most of the plodders are lawyers, identifiable by their huge, boxy briefcases. Court will soon be in session.

As if to underline this, a small bus − once red, now wash pink − trundles slowly down the choked street, passes the steps, and stops outside the smaller door at the righthand end of the big stone building. The door of the bus folds open. A cop gets out, then a conga-line of prisoners in orange jumpsuits, then another cop. The jumpsuits perp-walk around the bus's snub nose. The door of the employees' entrance opens and the men in the jumpsuits go inside, where they'll wait to be arraigned. Interesting, and worth filing away, but Billy believes Nick is right: when Allen comes, he'll be escorted up the steps to the main entrance. Not that it matters. The shot will be almost the same either way. What's important is that Court Street is a busy place during the working week. There may be fewer people out and about in the afternoons, but most arraignments take place in the morning.

You've always been fucking Houdini when it comes to disappearing after the hit, Nick said. *By the time things start to settle, you'll be long gone.*

He'd better be, because disappearing is part of what they're paying him for. A large part. Nick surely knows that using Billy has certain advantages if he botches the disappearance. He has no friends or relatives that can pressure him – or be *used* to pressure him – into giving up the name of his employer. And while Nick might consider Billy far from the brightest bulb in the chandelier, he knows his hired gun is smart enough to realize he can't trade a name for a reduction to homicide in the second or manslaughter. When you shoot a man with a sniper rifle from the fifth floor of a building where you've been set up for weeks or months, there could be no argument about the charge. That's premeditation in big red letters and only murder in the first would do.

Yet if Billy were caught there's one offer the prosecution *could* make, and Nick would know that, too. This is a death penalty state. A smart DA might well offer Billy a shot at life in Rincon Correctional instead of the needle. If he talked. Billy supposes that if it came to that, he actually could still keep Nick out of it. He could name Ken Hoff, because Hoff wouldn't live long if the cops grabbed Billy Summers coming out of Gerard Tower. Hoff might not live long in any case. When dealing with Nick Majarian's ilk, patsies rarely did.

Billy might not live long even so, because safe is always better than sorry. He might fall down a flight of prison stairs with his hands cuffed behind his back. He might be stabbed in the shower with a sharpened toothbrush or have a bar of soap stuffed down his throat. He could hold his own against one guy, maybe even two, but faced with a posse of 88s or three or four widebodies from People Nation? No. And does he want to spend life in prison in any case? Also no. Better dead than caged. He guesses Nick knows that, too.

None of it will be an issue if he isn't caught. He never has been, seventeen times he's gotten away clean, but he's never been faced with a situation like this one. It's not like shooting from an alley with a car nearby to carry you away, the best route out of town carefully marked.

How did you disappear after you'd gunned a man down from the fifth floor of a downtown office building, with a shit-ton of city and county cops right across the way? Billy knows how it would work in a movie: the bad-guy shooter would use a sound-and-flash suppressor. That's not an option in this case. The range is just a little too long, and he won't get a second chance if he misses the first time. Also, there's going to be the unmistakable *crack* of the bullet breaking the sound barrier. A suppressor can do nothing about that. Billy has a personal issue, as well: he has simply never trusted potato-busters. Put a gadget on the end of a good rifle and you're taking a risk of fucking up your shot. So it's going to be loud, and while the source may not be immediately identifiable, when people stop cringing and look up, they're going to see a window on the fifth floor from which a small circle of glass is missing. Because these windows don't open.

The problems don't daunt Billy. On the contrary, they engage him. The way the prospect of certain dangerous escapes – being chained up inside a safe and thrown into the East River, or dangling from a skyscraper in a straitjacket – no doubt engaged Houdini. Billy doesn't have a whole plan yet, but he's got a start. The parking garage was a little more loaded on the first two levels than Irv Dean had indicated, maybe today's court docket is especially heavy, but by the time Billy got to Level 4, he had his pick of spots. Privacy, in other words, and privacy is good. Billy is sure Houdini would have agreed with that.

He goes back to the table, where the expensive Mac Pro is still playing Canfield. He powers up his own laptop and goes to Amazon. You can buy anything at Amazon.

2

A stretch of curb in front of Gerard Tower has been stenciled AUTHORIZED PARKING ONLY. At quarter past eleven a truck with a big sombrero on the side pulls up there. Below the sombrero, JOSE'S EATS. And below that, TODOS COMEN! People start leaving the building, trundling toward the truck like ants drawn to sugar. Five minutes later another truck pulls up behind the first. On the side of this one is a grinning cartoon boy woofing down a double cheeseburger. At eleven-thirty, while people are lined up for burgers and fries and tacos and enchiladas, a hotdog wagon appears.

Time to eat, Billy thinks. Also time to meet some more neighbors.

There are four people waiting for the elevator, three men and a woman. All are dressed for business and all look to be in their mid-thirties, the woman maybe even younger. Billy joins them. One asks if he's the new writer in residence . . . as if Billy has supplanted an old one. Billy says he is and introduces himself. They do likewise: John, Jim, Harry, Phyllis. Billy asks what's good down below. John and Harry suggest the Mexican wagon. 'Excellent fish tacos,' John says. Jim says the burgers aren't bad and the onion rings are A-plus. Phyllis says she has her face fixed for one of Petie's chili dogs.

'None of it's haute cuisine,' Harry says, 'but it beats brown-bagging it.'

Billy asks about the café across the street and all four shake their heads. Such instant unanimity strikes Billy funny and he has to grin.

'Stay away from it,' Harry says. 'Crowded at lunch.'

'And the prices are high,' John adds. 'I don't know about writers, but when you work for a start-up law firm, you have to watch your nickels and dimes.'

'Lots of lawyers in the building?' Billy asks Phyllis as the elevator doors open.

'Don't ask me, ask them,' she says. 'I'm with Crescent Accounting. Answer the phone and check tax returns.'

'Quite a few of us legal beagles,' Harry says. 'Some on three and four, a few more on six. I think there's a start-up architectural firm on seven. And I know there's a photography studio on eight. Commercial stuff for catalogs.'

John says, 'If this place was a TV show, they'd call it *The Young Lawyers*. The big firms are mostly two or three blocks over, other side of the courthouse on Holland Street and Emery Plaza. We stay close and get crumbs from the big boys' table.'

'And wait for the big boys to die,' Jim adds. 'Most of the lawyers in the old-line firms are dinosaurs who wear three-piece suits and sound like Boss Hogg.'

Billy thinks of the sign in front: OFFICE SPACE AND LUXURY APARTMENTS NOW AVAILABLE. It looked like it had been there awhile, and like Hoff, it had a certain whiff of desperation. 'I'd guess your firm got a break on the lease.'

Harry gives Billy a thumbs-up. 'Bang. Four years at a price just north of incredible. And the lease will hold even if the guy who owns the building, Hoff's his name, goes into Chapter 11. Ironclad. It gives us little fellas some time to get traction.'

'Besides,' Jim says, 'a lawyer who gets screwed on his own lease agreement deserves to go broke.'

The young lawyers laugh. Phyllis smiles. The doors open on the lobby. The three men forge ahead, intent on chow. Billy crosses the lobby with Phyllis at a more leisurely pace. She's a good-looking woman in an understated way, more daisy than peony.

'Curious about something,' he says.

She smiles. 'It's a writer's stock in trade, isn't it? Curiosity?'

'I suppose so. I'm seeing a lot of people dressed casual. Like them.' He points to a couple just approaching the door. The guy is wearing black jeans and a Sun Ra tee. The woman with him is in a smock top that declares her pregnant belly rather than hiding it. Her hair is pulled back in a careless ponytail secured with a red rubber band. 'Don't tell me those two are lawyers or architectural assistants. I guess they could be from the photography studio, but there's a whole herd of them.'

'They work for Business Solutions on the second floor. The *whole* second floor. It's a collection agency. We call them BS for a reason.' She wrinkles her nose as if at a bad smell, but Billy doesn't miss the touch of envy in her voice. Dressing for success may be exciting at first, but as time passes it must become a drag, especially for women – the good hair, the good makeup, the click-clack shoes. Surely this nice-looking woman from the accounting firm on the fifth floor must from time to time think about how much of a relief it would be to just slop on a pair of jeans and a shell top, add a dash of lipstick, and call it good.

'You don't need to dress up when you spend the day working the phones in a great big open-plan office,' Phyllis says. 'Your targets don't see you when you're telling them to cough up the cash or the bank will slap a lien on your house.' She stops just shy of the doors, looking thoughtful. 'I wonder what they make.'

'I guess you don't crunch their numbers.'

'You guess right. But keep us in mind if you hit big with your book, Mr Lockridge. We're also a new firm. I think I've got a card in my purse . . .'

'Don't bother,' Billy says, touching her wrist before she can do any serious digging. 'If I hit it big, I'll just come down the hall and knock on your door.'

She gives him a smile and an appraising look. There's no engagement or wedding ring on her third finger left, and Billy thinks that in another life, this is when he'd ask her to come for a drink after work. She might say no, but that look, up from under her lashes, along with the smile, makes him think she'd say yes. But he won't ask. Meet people, yes. Get liked and like in return, yes. But don't get close. Getting close is a bad idea. Getting close is dangerous. Maybe after he retires that will change.

3

Billy gets a burger dragged through the garden and sits on one of the plaza benches with Lawyer Jim, whose actual name is Jim Albright. 'Try one of these,' he says, holding out a fat onion ring. 'Fucking delicious.'

It is. Billy says he's got to get some of those and Jim Albright says goddam right you do. Billy gets his rings in a little paper boat along with some packets of ketchup and goes back to sit with Jim.

'So what's your book about, Dave?'

Billy puts a finger to his lips. 'Top secret.'

'Even if I signed an NDA? Johnny Colton specializes in em.' He points to one of his colleagues, over by the Mexican wagon.

'Not even then.'

'I admire your discretion. I thought writers loved to talk about what they're working on.'

'I think writers who talk a lot probably don't write a lot,' Billy says, 'but since I'm the only writer I actually know, I'm really just guessing.' Then, and not entirely to change the subject, either: 'Look at the guy over there at the hotdog wagon. That's an outfit you don't see every day.'

The man he's pointing to has joined some of his colleagues at the Mexican food wagon. Even among the other Business Solutions employees, this one stands out. He's wearing gold parachute pants that take Billy back to his Tennessee childhood, when some of the would-be town sharpies wore such gear to the Friday night dances at the Rollerdome. Above it is a paisley shirt with a high collar, like the ones worn by British Invasion rock groups in old YouTube videos. The ensemble is finished off with a porkpie hat. From beneath it, lush black hair spills to his shoulders.

Jim laughs. 'That's Colin White. Quite the fashion plate, ain't he? Gay as hell and cheerful as a Sunday afternoon in Paris. Most of the BSers stick to their own. Earning their beer and skittles by dunning people at the end of their financial rope doesn't exactly make them popular and they know it, but Colin's a regular social butterfly.' Jim shakes his head. 'At least at lunch he is. I have to wonder what he's like when he's on the clock, hectoring widows and busted-up vets out of their last quarters and dimes. He must be good at the job, because there's a lot of turnover at that company and he's been here longer than I have.'

'How long is that?'

'Eighteen months. Sometimes Col comes to work wearing a kilt. Serious! Sometimes a cape. He's also got a Michael Jackson outfit – you know, the cavalry officer deal with the epaulets and the brass buttons?'

Billy nods. Colin White is currently holding a cardboard box with a couple of tacos in it. He stops to talk with Phyllis, and something he says causes her to throw back her head and laugh.

'He's a doll,' Jim says, with what sounds like genuine affection.

Phyllis strolls off and sits with a few other women. A couple of Colin White's cohorts make room for him. Before sitting down, he puts one foot behind the other and executes a quick turn that would have done the Gloved One proud. Billy puts him at five-nine, five-ten at most. Another piece of the plan. Maybe. Level 4 in the parking garage, maybe more laptops, and now Colin White. A bird of rare plumage.

4

That afternoon he sets the Mac Pro to playing itself at cribbage, with a five-second delay before each Player 1 move. He also sets it so that Player 2 will beat Player 1 every time. That should hold any lookie-loos for an hour or so. Then he powers up his own Mac, returns to Amazon, and buys two wigs: a blond one with short hair and a black one with long hair. In other circumstances he would have these sent to a store-front mail drop, but on this job there's no point, not when David Lockridge will be ID'd as the shooter before the sun goes down on the day it happens.

With the wigs taken care of, he puts one of the blank Staples note-books beside his personal lappie and begins a virtual tour of houses and apartments for rent. He finds a number of possibles, but any boots-on-the-ground investigation will have to wait until he gets his goods from Amazon.

It's only two o'clock when he finishes his virtual house-hunting, too early to call it a day. It's time to actually start writing. He's thought about this quite a lot. At first he assumed he would use his own machine for that. Using the Pro might mean his employer – and possibly his 'literary agent' – could be reading over his shoulder, which makes him think of the telescreens in *1984*. Would Nick and Giorgio be suspicious if they looked in and didn't see any copy? Billy thinks they would be. They wouldn't say anything, but it might give them the idea that Billy knows more about snooping and hacking than he wants them to know.

And there's another reason to write on the Pro, even though it may be bugged. It's a challenge. Can he really write a fictionalized *dumb self* version of his own life story? Risky, but he thinks maybe he can. Faulkner wrote dumb in *The Sound and the Fury*. *Flowers for Algernon*, by Daniel Keyes, is another example. There are probably more.

Billy quits the automated cribbage game and opens a blank Word document. He titles it **The Story of Benjy Compson** – a nod to Faulkner he's sure neither Nick nor Giorgio will tip to. He sits for several seconds, drumming his fingers on his chest and looking at the blank screen.

This is a crazy risk, he thinks.

This is the last job, he thinks, and types the sentence he's been holding in his mind for just this occasion.

The man my ma lived with came home with a broke arm.

He looks at this for almost a minute, then types again.

I don't even remember his name. But he was plenty mad. I guess he must have went to the hospital first because it was in a cast. My sister

Billy shakes his head and fixes it so it's better. He thinks so, anyway.

The man my ma lived with came home with a broke arm. I guess he must have went to the hospital first because it was in a cast. My sister was trying to bake cookies and she burnt them. I guess she forgot to keep track of the time. When that man came home he was plenty mad. He killed my sister and I don't even remember his name.

He looks at what he's written and thinks he can do this. More, he wants to do this. Before starting to write, he would have said *Yes I remember what happened, but only a little.* Only now there's more. Even that short paragraph has unlocked a door and opened a window. He remembers the smell of burned sugar, and seeing smoke seep out of the oven, and the chip on the side of the stove, and flowers in a teacup on the table, and some kid outside chanting 'One p'tater two p'tater three p'tater *four.*' He remembers the heavy clod-clod-clod of that man's boots coming up the steps. That man, that boyfriend. And now he even remembers the name. It was Bob Raines. He remembers thinking when he heard that man use his fists on Ma, *Bob is raining. Bob is raining on Ma.* He remembers her smiling after and saying *He didn't mean it.* And *It was my fault.*

Billy writes for an hour and a half, wanting to bolt ahead but holding himself back. If Nick or Giorgio or even Elvis is looking in, they must see the *dumb self* going slowly. Struggling for every sentence. At least he doesn't have to deliberately misspell words; the ones the computer doesn't correct automatically it underlines in red.

At four o'clock he saves what he's written and shuts down. He finds he's looking forward to picking up the thread tomorrow.

Maybe he's a writer after all.

5

When he gets back to Midwood, Billy finds a note thumbtacked to his door. It's an invitation to have ribs and slaw and cherry cobbler at the Raglands' down the street. He goes because he doesn't want to be seen as standoffish, but with no enthusiasm, expecting an after-dinner conversation over cans of suds having to do with commie college kids this and dirty immigrants that. He is stunned to discover that Paul and Denise Ragland voted for Hillary Clinton and can't stand Trump, who they call 'President Crybaby.' Proving once more, Billy supposes as he walks home, that you can't judge a man by his wifebeater.

He's already been sucked in by a Netflix show called *Ozark* and is ready to start the third episode when his cell phone – his David Lockridge cell – dings with a text. George Russo, ever the concerned agent, wants to know how his first day went.

DLock: Pretty well. I did some writing.

GRusso: Good to hear. We'll make you a bestseller yet. Can you drop by Thurs night? 7 PM, dinner. N wants to talk to you.

Nick is still in town, then, and probably in Vegas withdrawal.

DLock: Sure. But no H.

GRusso: Absolutely not.

That's good. Billy thinks he could live long and die happy if he never saw Ken Hoff again. He turns off the TV and goes to bed. He slips easily into sleep, and at some point just before dawn's prologue, he slips just as easily into a nightmare. Which he will write down tomorrow, as Benjy Compson. Changing the names to protect the guilty.

6

The man my ma lived with came home with a broke arm. I guess he must have went to the hospital first because it was in a cast. My sister was trying to bake cookies and she burnt them. I guess she forgot to keep track of the time. When that man came home he was plenty mad. He killed my sister and I don't even remember his name. He started yelling as soon as he came in. I was on the floor of the trailer, putting together a 500 piece jigsaw puzzle that when it was done would be 2 kittens playing with a ball of yarn. I could smell the booze he was drinking even with the smoke from the cookies and found out later he got into a fight at Wally's Tavern. He must have lost because he had a black eye too. My sister

Catherine was her name, although that's not the one he'll use – almost but not quite. Catherine Ann Summers, just nine on the day she died. Blonde. Small.

My sister Cassie was at the table we ate off, coloring in her book. She would have turned 10 in 2 or 3 months and she was looking forward to being in 2 figures instead of just 1. I was 11 and suppose to be looking out for her.

The boyfriend was yelling and waving at the smoke which only just started before he came in, asking what did you do what did you do and Cathy

Billy deletes that fast, hoping nobody is looking right then.

Cassie said I was baking cookies I guess they burnt I am sorry. And he said you are a stupid little bitch I don't believe how stupid you are.

He open the oven door and more smoke come out. If we had a smoke detector it would have gone off but we didn't have one in our trailer. He picked up a dish towel and started flapping it at the smoke. I would have got up to open the outside door but it was open already. The boyfriend reached in to get that cookie sheet. He grab it with his good hand but the dish towel slipped and he burnt his hand and spilled those cookies that were in shapes I helped Cassie cut out and they went all over the floor. Cassie got down to pick them up and that's when he started killing her. Or maybe it happened right away when he swatted her with that cast upside her head and she flew into the wall. Out like a light anyway but maybe still alive only then he started kicking her with these boots he always wore that my ma called motorhuckle boots.

Stop it your killing her I said but he didn't stop until I said stop it you son of a bitch bully chickenshit fucker STOP HURTING MY SISTER. So then I went to tackle him and he push me down

Billy gets up and goes to the window of the office that is now – he supposes – his writing room. People are coming and going on the courthouse steps, but he doesn't see them. He goes into the little kitchenette for a drink of water. He spills a bit of it because his hands are trembling. They don't tremble when he's going to take a shot, they are always stone-steady then, but they are now. Not a lot, but enough to spill some water. His mouth and throat are dry and he drinks down the whole glass.

It has all come back to him and it all makes him ashamed. He will leave what he has written about trying to tackle Bob Raines, because it puts a layer of heroic fiction over the truth, which is close to unbearable. He didn't tackle Bob Raines while Bob Raines was kicking his sister and stepping on her and crushing her fragile chest on which no breasts would ever appear. Billy was supposed to take care of her. *Take care of your sister* was the last thing Ma always said when she left for her job at the laundry. But he didn't take care of her. He ran. He ran for his life.

But it was in my mind even then, he thinks as he goes back to the table and the laptop. It must have been, because it wasn't our room I ran for.

'I ran for theirs,' Billy says, and picks up where he left off.

So then I went to tackle him and he push me down and I got up and ran down the trailer to their room at the end and slam the door behind me. He started pounding on it right away, calling me every name in the book and said if you don't open this door right now Benjy you are going to be one sorry-ass motherfucker. Only I knew it didn't matter if I opened the door or not because he'd do me like he did Cassie. Because she was dead, even a kid of 11 could see that.

Ma's boyfriend use to be in the army and he kept his footlocker at the end of the bed with a blanket over it. I pushed the blanket off and open the footlocker. He had a padlock for it but hardly ever used it, maybe never. If he had've I wouldn't be writing this because I would be dead. And if that gun of his hadn't been loaded I would be dead but I knew it was because he kept it loaded in case of what he called burg-gurg-gurglers.

Burg-gurg-gurglers, Billy thinks. Christ, how it all comes back.

He bust in the door like I was pretty sure he would

Not pretty sure, Billy thinks, I knew. Because it was nothing but fiberboard. Cathy and I used to hear them going at it just about every night. In the afternoon, if Ma came home early. But that was another fiction he would leave.

and when he come in I was sitting with my back against the foot of the bed with his gun pointing at him. It was an M9X19 that took 15 Parabellum rounds. I didn't know that then of course but I knew it was heavy and I held it in both hands against my chest. He said give that to me you useless piece of shit don't you know kids ain't supposed to play with guns.

Then I shot him, dead center mass. He just stood there in the doorway like nothing happen but I knew it did because I saw the blood fly out of his back. The M9 recoiled against my chest

Billy remembers making an *uh* sound. And burping. And later on he had a bruise there above his sternum.

and he fell down. I went over to him and said to myself that I might have to shoot him again. If I had to I would. He was my mother's boyfriend but he was wrong. He was a bad guy!

'Except he was dead,' Billy says. 'Bob Raines was dead.'

He thinks briefly of deleting everything he's written, it's awful, but saves it instead. He doesn't know what anyone else might think, but Billy thinks it's good. And good that it's awful, because awful is sometimes the truth. He guesses he really is a writer now, because that's a writer's thought. Émile Zola might have thought the same when he was writing *Thérèse Raquin*, or when Nana gets sick and all of her beauty rots away.

His face feels hot. He goes back to the kitchenette and splashes water on it, then stands bent over the little sink with his eyes shut. The memory of shooting Bob Raines doesn't bother him, but it hurts to remember Cathy.

Take care of your sister.

Writing is good. He's always wanted to do it, and now he is. That's good. Only who knew it hurt so much?

The landline phone rings, making him jump. It's Irv Dean, telling him he has a package from Amazon. Billy says he'll come right down and pick it up.

'Man, that company sells everything,' Irv says.

Billy agrees, thinking You don't know the half of it.

7

It's not the wigs; even with Amazon's speedy delivery, those won't come until tomorrow. What he's got today would fit in the cubby over the doorway between the office and the kitchen, but Billy has no intention of stowing it there; all his Amazon swag is going back to the yellow house in Midwood.

He opens the box and takes out the things he ordered one by one. From Fun Time Ltd in Hong Kong is a box containing a mustache made of real human hair. Blond, like one of the wigs he's ordered. It's a little bushy; when the time comes he'll trim it. He wants to disguise, not to stand out. Next is a pair of horn-rimmed glasses with clear lenses. These are surprisingly hard to find. You can buy reading glasses at any drugstore, but Billy's vision is 20/10 and even slight magnification gives him headaches. He tries them on and finds the fit is a little loose. He could tighten the bows, but won't. If they slide down his nose a bit, they'll give him a scholarly air.

Last, the most expensive item, the *pièce de résistance*. It's a silicone pregnancy belly, sold by Amazon but made by a company called MomTime. It was expensive because it's adjustable, allowing the wearer to look anywhere from six to nine months pregnant. It attaches with Velcro straps. Billy knows that these fake bellies are notorious shoplifting tools, big-box security personnel are told to be on the lookout for them, but Billy has not come to this small city to shoplift, and it won't be a woman wearing it when the time comes.

That will be his job.

CHAPTER 5

1

Billy shows up at Nick's borrowed McMansion a bit before seven on Thursday evening. He has read somewhere that the polite guest arrives five minutes early, no more and no less. Paulie is the official greeter this time. Nick is once more waiting in the hall, thus out of sight of any passing law enforcement drones – unlikely but not impossible. His smile is turned up to maximum, arms outstretched to enfold Billy in a hug.

'Chateaubriand on the menu. I got a cook, I don't know what he's doing in this rinky-dink town, but he's great. You're going to love it. And save some room.' He holds Billy back at arm's length and drops his voice to a hoarse whisper. 'I heard a rumor about Baked Alaska. You have to be tired of microwave dinners, right? Right?'

'That's right,' Billy says.

Frank appears. In an ascot and a pink shirt, with his hair combed in gleaming swoops and swirls piled high above an Eddie Munster widow's peak, he looks like the hoodlum in a gangster movie who gets killed first. He's got some glasses and a big green bottle on a tray. 'Champers. Mote and Shandon.'

He sets down the tray and eases the cork from the bottle's neck. No pop and no splurt. Frankie Elvis may not know French, but his opening technique is superb. So is his pour.

Nick lifts a glass. The others do likewise. 'To success!'

Billy, Paulie, and Frank clink and drink. The Champagne goes pleasantly to Billy's head at once, but he refuses another glass. 'I'm driving. Don't want to get stopped.'

'That's Billy,' Nick says to his amigos. 'Always thinking two steps ahead.'

'Three,' Billy says, and Nick laughs like this is the funniest thing he's heard since Henny Youngman died. The amigos dutifully follow suit.

'Okay,' Nick says. 'Enough with the bubble-water. *Mangiamo, mangiamo.*'

It's a good meal, starting with French onion soup, progressing to beef marinated in red wine, and ending with the promised Baked Alaska. It's served by an unsmiling woman in a white uniform, except for the dessert course. Nick's hired chef wheels that in himself to the expected applause and compliments, nods his thanks and leaves.

Nick, Frank, and Paulie carry the conversation, which is mostly about Vegas: who is playing there, who is building there, who is looking for a casino license. As if they don't understand that Vegas is obsolete, Billy thinks. Probably they don't. There is no sign of Giorgio. When the serving woman comes in with after-dinner liqueur, Billy shakes his head. So does Nick.

'Marge, you and Alan can leave now,' Nick says. 'It was a great meal.'

'Thanks, but we've just started to clean up the—'

'We'll worry about that tomorrow. Here. Give this to Alan. Car-fare, my old man would have said.' He pushes some bills into her hand. She mutters that she will and turns to go. 'And Marge?'

She turns back.

'You haven't been smoking in the house, have you?'

'No.'

Nick nods. 'Don't linger, okay? Billy, let's you and me go in the living room for a little chin-chin. You guys, find something to do.'

Paul tells Billy it was good seeing him and heads for the front door. Frank follows Marge into the kitchen. Nick drops his napkin into the smeared remains of his dessert and leads Billy into the living room. The fireplace at one end is big enough to roast the Minotaur. There are statues in niches and a ceiling mural that looks like a porno version of the Sistine Chapel.

'Great, isn't it?' Nick says, looking around.

'It sure is,' Billy says, thinking that if he had to spend too much time in this room, he might lose his mind.

'Sit down, Billy, take a load off.'

Billy sits. 'Where's Giorgio? Did he go back to Vegas?'

'Well, he might be there,' Nick says, 'or he might be in New York or Hollywood talking to movie people about this great book he's agenting.'

None of your business, in other words, Billy thinks. Which is, in a way, fair enough. He's just an employee, after all. What they'd call a hired gun in the old Western movies Mr Stepenek used to like.

Thinking of Mr Stepenek makes him think of a thousand junked cars – it seemed like a thousand to a kid, anyway, and maybe there really were that many – with their cracked windshields winking in the sun. How many years since he last thought of that automobile grave-yard? The door to the past is open. He could push it shut, latch and lock it, but he doesn't want to. Let the wind blow in. It's cold but it's fresh, and the room he's been living in is stuffy.

'Hey, Billy.' Nick is snapping his fingers. 'Earth to Billy.'

'I'm here.'

'Yeah? Thought for a minute I lost you. Listen, are you actually writing something?'

'I am,' Billy says.

'Real life or made up?'

'Made up.'

'Not about Archie Andrews and his friends, is it?' Smiling.

Billy shakes his head, also smiling.

'They say that a lot of people writing fiction for the first time use their own experiences. "Write what you know," I remember that from senior English. Paramus High, go Spartans. That the case with you?'

Billy makes a seesaw gesture with one hand. Then, as if the idea has just occurred to him: 'Hey, you aren't getting up on what I'm writing, are you?' A dangerous question, but he can't help himself. 'Because I wouldn't want—'

'God, no!' Nick says, sounding way past surprised, sounding actually shocked, and Billy knows he's lying. 'Why would we do that even if we could?'

'I don't know, I just . . .' A shrug. '. . . wouldn't want anyone peeking. Because I'm no writer, just trying to stay in character. And passing the time. I'd be embarrassed for anyone to see it.'

'You put a password on the laptop, right?'

Billy nods.

'Then nobody will.' Nick leans forward, his brown eyes on Billy's. He lowers his voice like he did when telling Billy about the Baked Alaska. 'Is it hot? Threesomes, and all that?'

'No, huh-uh.' A pause. 'Not really.'

'Get some sex in there, that's my advice. Because sex sells.' He chuckles and goes to a cabinet across the room. 'I'm going to have a splash of brandy. Want some?'

'No thanks.' He waits for Nick to come back. 'Any word on Joe?'

'Same old same old. His lawyer's appealing the extradition like I told you and the whole thing is on hold, maybe, who knows, because Johnny Judge is off on vacation.'

'But he's not talking about what he knows?'

'If he was, *I'd* know.'

'Maybe he might have an accident in jail. Never get extradited at all.'

'They're taking very good care of him. Out of gen-pop, remember?'

'Oh yeah. Right.' *That seems a little convenient* is an observation Billy can't make. It would be a bit too smart.

'Be patient, Billy. Settle in. Frankie says you're meeting the neighbors out there in Midwood.'

So. He hasn't seen Frank in the neighborhood, but Frank has seen him. Nick is checking his sexy new lappie at will and also keeping an eye on him at his temporary home. Billy thinks again of *1984*.

'I am.'

'And in the building?'

'There too, sure. Mostly at lunch. The food wagons.'

'That's great. Blend in with the scenery. Become *part* of the scenery. You're good at that. I bet you were good at it in Iraq.'

I was good at it everywhere, Billy thinks. At least after I killed Bob Raines I was.

Time to change the subject. 'You said there was going to be a diversion. Said we'd talk about it later. Is this later enough?'

'It is.' Nick takes a mouthful of brandy, swirls it around like it's mouthwash, swallows. 'Happens to feed into an idea I wanted to try out on you. The diversion is going to be a couple of flashpots. Do you know what those are?'

Billy does, but shakes his head.

'Rock bands use em. There's a bang and a big flash of light. Like a geyser. When I know for sure that Joe is coming east, I'll have a couple planted near the courthouse. One for sure in the alley that runs behind that café on the corner. Paulie suggested putting one in the parking garage, but it's too far away. And besides, what terrorist blows up a fucking parking garage?'

Billy makes no attempt to hide his alarm. 'Planting those things isn't going to be Hoff's job, is it?'

Nick doesn't bother to swirl the second mouthful of brandy, just gulps it down. He coughs, and the cough turns into a laugh. 'What, you think I'm stupid enough to give a job like that to a *grande figlio di puttana* like him? I'd be sad if that was your opinion of me. No, I've got a couple of my guys coming in. Good boys. Trustworthy.'

Billy thinks, You don't want Hoff placing the flashpots, because that could come back to you, but you don't mind him procuring the gun and placing it in the shooter's nest, because that will come back to me. How stupid do you think *I* am?

'I'll probably be in Vegas when this thing goes down, but Frankie Elvis and Paul Logan will be here with the two other guys I'm bringing in. If you need anything, they'll take care of you.' He leans forward again, earnest and smiling. 'It's going to be a beautiful thing. The gunshot goes, scaring everybody. Then the flashpots go – *BOOM, BOOM!* – and anybody who's not running already starts running then and screaming their heads off. Active shooter! Suicide bombers! Al-Qaeda! ISIS! Whatever! But the *real* beauty of it? Unless somebody breaks a leg running away, nobody gets hurt except for Joel Allen. That's his real name. Court Street is in a panic, and that brings me to what I wanted to talk to you about.'

'Okay.'

'Now I know you're used to planning your own getaways, and you've always been good at it – fucking Houdini, like I said – but Giorgio and I had a little idea. Because . . .' Nick shakes his head. 'Man, this could be a tough one, even for you and even if we panic the street with the flash-bangs. Which we will. If you've already got something worked out, go with God. But if you don't . . .'

'I don't.' Although he's getting there. Billy gives a big *dumb self* smile. 'Always happy to listen, Nick.'

2

He's home – he guesses the yellow house *is* home, at least for a while – by eleven P.M. All of his Amazon swag is in the closet. It would have stayed there until he got the call that Allen is headed east from Los Angeles, but things have changed. Billy is uneasy.

He takes the stuff out to the car and stows it in the trunk. He won't be spending all of tomorrow in the fifth-floor office, and that's okay. The nice thing about being the Gerard Tower's writer in residence is that he's not a working stiff who has to keep regular hours. He can come in late and leave early. He can take a stroll if the urge strikes him. If anyone asks he can say he's working over a new idea. Or doing research. Or just taking an hour or two off. Tomorrow he will stroll nine blocks to 658 Pearson Street. It's a three-story house on the border of municipal downtown. Billy has already looked at the house on Zillow, but that's not good enough. He wants eyes on.

He locks the car and goes back inside. He brought the shiny new MacBook Pro back from his office and parked it on the kitchen table. Now he opens it and reads what he's written as Benjy Compson. It's only a couple of pages, ending with Benjy shooting Bob Raines. He reads it over three times, trying to see it as Nick must have. Because Nick *has* read it, after that crack about writers using their own experiences Billy has no doubt of it.

He doesn't care if Nick finds out about his childhood, for all Billy knows Nick has checked that out already. What Billy does care about is protecting the *dumb self*, at least for now. He won't be able to sleep until he makes sure that there's nothing in those two or three pages that makes him seem too smart. So he goes over it a fourth time.

At last he shuts the laptop down. He doesn't think there's anything in the prose that a C student in English couldn't have written, assuming most of it really happened. The spelling is mostly good, and the punctuation, but Nick would chalk that up to autocorrect. Although the Word program isn't able to detect the difference between can't and cant, the computer always turns dont into don't, it underlines misspellings in red, it even notes the most egregious grammatical lapses. The verb tenses in what he's written come and go, which is fine because that's above the computer's pay grade . . . although the day will probably come when it flags those, too.

But he's uneasy.

He's never had reason to distrust Nick, who is undoubtedly a bad person but who has always played straight with Billy. He is not playing straight now, or he wouldn't have denied cloning the Pro. Would not have cloned it in the first place. Billy feels he can still assume the job is straight, the first quarter of the payout is in his bank account, five hundred thousand dollars, tall tickets, but this whole thing still feels wrong. Not big wrong, just a little wonky. It's like one of those shots you sometimes see in a movie where the camera has been slightly tilted to give you a sense of disorientation. Dutching is what movie people call that kind of tilt, and that's how this job feels: dutched. Not enough to call it off, which he might not be able to do anyway now that he's said yes, but enough to be concerning.

And there's the getaway plan Nick sprang on him. *If you've already got something worked out, go with God,* he'd said. *But if you don't, me and Giorgio had an idea that might work fine.*

Nick's idea isn't a problem because it's bad; it's not. It's good. But disappearing after the job is done has always been Billy's responsibility, and for Nick to get in his business like that is . . . well . . .

'Dutched,' Billy murmurs to his empty kitchen.

Nick said that six weeks ago, when this job looked like becoming a reality, he sent Paul Logan up to Macon and told him to buy a Ford Transit van, not new but not more than three years old. Transits were the workhorses of Red Bluff's Department of Public Works fleet. Billy has already seen several, painted yellow and blue with the motto WE ARE HERE TO SERVE painted on the sides. The brown Transit Frank bought in Georgia was now in a garage on the outskirts of town, painted in DPW colors and with the DPW motto.

'I'll have a good idea of when Allen's extradition is getting close,' Nick said. He was sipping a little more brandy. 'Those guys I told you about – the ones coming in – will start being out and about in that van, always looking busy but not really *doing* anything. Never staying too long in one place but always near the courthouse and the Gerard Tower. An hour here, two hours there. Becoming part of the scenery, in other words. Like you, Billy.'

On the day of Allen's arrival, Nick said this bogus DPW van would be parked around the corner from the Gerard Tower. The bogus city workers would maybe open a manhole cover and pretend to be doing something inside. When the shot came, and the flashpot explosions, people would run everywhere. Including from the Gerard Tower and including Billy Summers, who would race around the corner and into the back of the van. There he would jump into a pair of DPW coveralls.

'The van pulls around to the courthouse,' Nick said. 'Cops are already on the scene. My guys – and you – pile out and ask if there's anything they can do to help. Put up sawhorses to block the street, or something. In all the confusion, it will look a hundred per cent natural. You see that?'

Billy saw. It was bold and it was good.

'The cops—'

'They probably tell us to get lost,' Billy said. 'We're city workers but we're civilians. Is that right?'

Nick laughed and clapped his hands. 'See? Anyone who thinks you're stupid is full of shit. My guys say yes sir, officers, and off you drive. And you keep driving. After switching vehicles, of course.'

'Driving to where?'

'De Pere, Wisconsin, a thousand miles from here. There's a safe house. You stay there a couple of days, relax, check your bank account for the rest of your payday, think about how you're going to spend your money. After that you're on your own. How does it sound?'

It sounded good. Too good? A possible set-up? Unlikely. If anyone in this deal is being set up, it's Ken Hoff. Billy's problem with Nick's unexpected offer is that he's never had to depend on other people to disappear before. He doesn't like it but that wasn't the time to say so.

'Let me think about it, okay?'

'You bet,' Nick said. 'Plenty of time.'

3

Billy hauls his suitcase out of the master bedroom closet. He puts it on the bed and unzips it. It looks empty, but it's not. The lining has a Velcro strip running along the underside. He pulls the lining up and takes out a small flat case. It's the kind smart people – those who read more challenging stuff than *Archie* digests and supermarket checkout lane scandal papers – might call an etui. There's a wallet inside with credit cards and a driver's license issued to Dalton Curtis Smith, of Stowe, Vermont.

There have been many other wallets and IDs during Billy's career, not one for each of his assassinations (he calls them what they are) but at least a dozen, leading up to the current one belonging to a make-believe individual named David Lockridge. Some of his previous selves had good ID, some not so good. The credit cards and DL in the David Lockridge wallet are very good indeed, but the stuff in the flat gray case is better. The stuff in there is gold. Putting it together has been the work of five years, a labor of love going back to when he decided he must eventually get out of a business that makes him – admit it – just another bad person.

Dalton Smith isn't just a Lord Buxton wallet with a legit-looking driver's license inside; Dalton Smith is practically a real person. The Mastercard, the Amex card, and the Visa all get used regularly. Ditto the Bank of America debit card. Not every day, but often enough so the accounts don't gather dust. His credit rating isn't excellent, which might draw attention, but it's very good.

There's a Red Cross blood donor card, his Social Security card, and Dalton's membership in an Apple User Group. No *dumb self* here; Dalton Curtis Smith is a freelance computer tech with a fairly lucrative sideline that allows him to go wherever the wind blows him. Also in the wallet are pictures of Dalton with his wife (they were divorced six years ago), Dalton with his parents (killed in the ever-popular car crash when Dalton was a teenager), Dalton with his estranged brother (they don't talk since Dalton found out his brother voted for Nader in the 2000 election).

Dalton's birth certificate is in the etui, and references. Some are from individuals and small businesses whose computers Dalton has fixed, others from people who have rented to him in Portsmouth, Chicago, and Irvine. His go-to guy in New York, Bucky Hanson, has created some of these references; Bucky is the only person Billy trusts completely. Others Billy created himself. Dalton Smith never stays long in one place, a tumbling tumbleweed is he, but when he's *in situ*, he's a very good tenant: neat and quiet, always pays the rent on time.

To Billy, Dalton Smith with his low-key but impeccable bona fides is as beautiful as a snowfield without a single track on it. He hates the idea of defacing that beauty by putting Dalton to work, but isn't this exactly what Dalton Curtis Smith was created for? It is. One last job, the *ever-popular* last job, and Billy can disappear into a new identity. Probably not live the rest of his life in it, but even that's possible, assuming he can get out of this town without being burned; the five hundred thousand down payment has already made the rounds and finished up at Dalton's bank account in Nevis, and half a mil's the biggest sign that Nick isn't playing this funny. When the work is done, the rest will follow.

Dalton's DL headshot shows a man of about Billy's age, maybe a year or two younger, but he's blond instead of dark. And he has a mustache.

4

The next morning, Billy parks on the fourth level of the garage near the Gerard Tower. After making certain adjustments to his appearance, he walks in the opposite direction. This is Dalton Smith's maiden voyage.

When the city is small, small distances can make a big difference. Pearson Street is only nine blocks from the Main Street parking garage, a brisk fifteen-minute walk (Gerard Tower still looms close enough to be clearly seen), but this is a different world from the one where guys in ties and gals in click-clack shoes man and woman their posts and lunch in the kind of restaurants where the waiter hands you a wine list along with the menu.

There's a corner grocery, but it's closed up. Like many declining neighborhoods, this one is a food desert. There are two barrooms, one closed and the other looking like it's just hanging on. A pawn-shop that doubles as a check-cashing and small-loans business. A sad little strip mall a bit further on. And a line of homes that are trying to look middle class and not getting there.

Billy guesses the reason for the area's decline is the vacant lot right across the street from his target house. It's a big expanse of rubbly, trash-strewn ground. Cutting through it are rusting railroad tracks barely visible in high weeds and summer goldenrod. Signs posted at fifty-foot intervals read CITY PROPERTY and NO TRESPASSING and DANGER KEEP OUT. He notes the jagged remains of a brick building that once must have been a train station. Maybe it served bus lines as well – Greyhound, Trailways, Southern. Now the city's land-based transportation has moved elsewhere, and this neighborhood, which might have been busy in the closing decades of the last century, is suffering from a kind of municipal COPD. A rusty shopping cart lies overturned on the sidewalk across the way. A tattered pair of men's undershorts flap from one of its wheels in a hot wind that tousles the hair of Billy's blond Dalton Smith wig and flutters his shirt collar against his neck.

Most of the houses need paint. Some have FOR SALE signs in front of them. 658 also needs paint, but the sign in front reads FURNISHED APARTMENTS FOR RENT. There's a real estate agent's number to call. Billy notes it down, then goes up the cracked cement walk and looks at the line of doorbells. Although it's just a three-story, there are four bells. Only one of them, second from the top, has a name: JENSEN. He rings it. At this time of day there's probably nobody home, but his luck is in.

Footsteps descend the stairs. A youngish woman peers through the dirty glass of the door. What she sees is a white man in a nice open-collared shirt and dress pants. His blond hair is short. His mustache is neatly trimmed. He wears glasses. He's quite fat, not to the point of obesity but getting there. He doesn't look like a bad person, he looks like a good person who could stand to drop twenty or thirty pounds, so she opens the door, but not all the way.

As if I couldn't push my way in and strangle you right there in the foyer, Billy thinks. There's no car in the driveway or parked at the curb, which means your husband's at work, and those three unmarked bells strongly suggest that you are the only person in this old faux Victorian.

'I don't buy from door-to-door salesmen,' Mrs Jensen says.

'No, ma'am, I'm not a salesman. I'm new in the city and looking for an apartment. This looks like it might be in my price range. I just wanted to know if this is a nice place. My name's Dalton Smith.'

He holds out his hand. She gives it a token touch, then draws her own hand back. But she's willing to talk. 'Well, it's not the greatest area, as you can see, and the nearest supermarket's a mile away, but me and my husband haven't had any real problems. Kids get into that old trainyard across the way sometimes, probably drinking and smoking dope, and there's a dog around the corner that barks half the night, but that's about the worst of it.' She pauses and he sees her look down, checking for a wedding ring that's not there. '*You* don't bark at night, do you, Mr Smith? By which I mean parties and loud music.'

'No, ma'am.' He smiles and touches his stomach. The fake pregnancy belly has been inflated to about six months. 'I like to eat, though.'

'Because there's a clause about excessive noise in the rental agreement.'

'May I ask how much you pay per month?'

'That's between me and my husband. If you want to live here, you'd have to take it up with Mr Richter. He's the man that handles this place. Couple of others down the block, too . . . although this one's nicer. *I* think.'

'Completely understood. I apologize for asking.'

Mrs Jensen thaws a little. 'I will tell you that you don't want the third floor. That place is a hotbox, even when the wind blows from across the old trainyard, which it does most of the time.'

'No air conditioning, I take it.'

'You take it right. But when it comes on cold weather, the heat's okay. Course you have to pay for it. Electricity, too. It's all in the agreement. If you've rented before, I guess you know the drill.'

'Boy, do I ever.' He rolls his eyes and finally gets a smile out of her. Now he can ask what he really wants to ask. 'What about the downstairs? Is that a basement apartment? Because it looks like there's a bell—'

Her smile widens. 'Oh yes, and it's quite nice. Furnished, like the sign says. Although, you know, just the basics. I wanted that one, but my husband thought it would be too small if our application gets approved. We're trying to adopt.'

Billy marvels at this. She has just revealed a crucial piece of her heart – of her *marriage's* heart – after she balked at revealing how much rent she and her husband pay. Which he asked not because he really wanted to know but because it would make him seem plausible.

'Well, good luck to you. And thanks. If this Mr Richter and I see eye to eye, maybe you'll see more of me. You have a good day, now.'

'You too. Nice to meet you.' This time she holds out her hand for a real shake, and Billy thinks again about what Nick said – *You get along with people without buddying up to them.* Nice to know that works even if you look fat.

As he walks down the sidewalk, she calls after him, 'I bet that basement apartment stays nice and cool even in the hottest weather! I wish we'd taken it!'

He gives her a thumbs–up and heads back toward downtown. He has seen all he needs to see and has come to a decision. This is the place he wants, and Nick Majarian doesn't need to know a thing about it.

Halfway back he comes to a hole–in–the–wall store that sells candy, cigarettes, magazines, cold drinks, and burner phones in blister packs. He buys one, paying cash, and sits on a bus bench to get it up and running. He will use it as long as he has to, then dispose of it. The others as well. Always supposing the deal goes down, the cops are going to know right away that it was David Lockridge who assassinated Joel Allen. They will then discover that David Lockridge is an alias of one William Summers, a Marine vet with sniper skills and sniper kills. They will also discover Summers's association with Kenneth Hoff, the designated fall guy. What they must not discover is that Billy Summers, aka David Lockridge, has disappeared into the identity of Dalton Smith. Nick can never know that, either.

He calls Bucky Hanson in New York and tells Bucky to send the box marked *Safeties* to his Evergreen Street address.

'So this is it, huh? You're really pulling the pin?'

'Looks like it,' Billy says, 'but we'll talk some more.'

'Sure we will. Just make sure it isn't collect from some tooliebop city jail. You're my man, hoss.'

Billy ends the call and makes another. To Richter, the real estate guy who is serving as rental agent for 658 Pearson.

'I understand it's furnished. Would that include WiFi?'

'Just a second,' Mr Richter says, but it's more like a minute. Billy hears paper rustling. At last Richter says, 'Yes. Put in two years ago. But no television, you'd have to supply that.'

'All right,' Billy says. 'I want it. How about I drop by your office?'

'I could meet you there, show you the place.'

'That won't be necessary. I just want it as a base of operations while I'm in this part of the country. Could be a year, could be two. I travel quite a bit. The important thing is the neighborhood looks quiet.'

Richter laughs. 'Since they demolished the train station, you bet it is. But the people out there might trade a little more noise for a little more commerce.'

They set a time to meet the following Monday and Billy returns to Level 4 of the parking garage, where his Toyota is parked in a dead spot neither of the security cameras can see. If they can see at all; they look mighty tired to Billy. He removes the wig, the mustache, the glasses, and the fake pregnancy belly. After stowing them in the trunk, he takes the short walk back to Gerard Tower.

He's there in time to get a burrito from the Mexican wagon. He eats it with Jim Albright and John Colton, the lawyers from five. He sees Colin White, the dandy who works for Business Solutions. Today he's looking mighty cute in a sailor suit.

'That guy,' Jim says, laughing. 'He's quite the bandbox, isn't he?'

'Yes,' Billy agrees, and thinks, A bandbox who's just about my height.

5

It rains all weekend. On Saturday morning Billy goes to Walmart where he buys a couple of cheap suitcases and a lot of cheap clothes that will fit his overweight Dalton Smith persona. He pays cash. Cash has amnesia.

That afternoon he sits out on the porch of the yellow house, watching the grass in his front yard. Watching it rather than merely looking at it, because he can almost see it perking up. This is not his house, not his town or state, he'll leave without a look back or single regret, but he still feels a certain proprietorial pride in his handiwork. It won't be worth mowing for a couple of weeks, maybe not even until August, but he can wait. And when he's out there, zinc ointment on his nose, mowing in gym shorts and a sleeveless tee (maybe even a wifebeater), he'll be one step closer to belonging. To blending in with the scenery.

'Mr Lockridge?'

He looks next door. The two kids, Derek and Shanice Ackerman, are standing on *their* porch, looking at him through the rain. It's the boy who's spoken. 'My ma just made sugar cookies. She ast me to ast you if you want half a dozen.'

'That sounds good,' Billy says. He gets up and runs through the rain. Shanice, the eight-year-old, takes his hand with a complete lack of self-consciousness and leads him inside, where the smell of fresh-baked cookies makes Billy's stomach rumble.

It's a neat little house, tight and shipshape. There are about a hundred framed photos in the living room, including a dozen on the piano that holds pride of place. In the kitchen, Corinne Ackerman is just removing a baking sheet from the oven. 'Hi, neighbor. Do you want a towel for your hair?'

'I'm fine, thanks. Ran between the raindrops.'

She laughs. 'Then have a cookie. The kids are having milk with theirs. Would you like a glass? There's also coffee, if you'd prefer that.'

'Milk would be fine. Just a little.'

'Double shot?' She's smiling.

'Sounds about right.' Smiling back.

'Then sit down.'

He sits with the kids. Corinne puts a plate of cookies on the table. 'Be careful, they're still hot. Your take-homes will be in the next batch, David.'

The kids grab. Billy takes one. It's sweet and delicious. 'Terrific, Corinne. Thank you. Just the thing on a rainy day.'

She gives her kids big glasses of milk, Billy a small one. She pours her own small glass and joins them. The rain drums on the roof. A car goes hissing by.

'I know your book is top secret,' Derek says, 'but—'

'Don't talk with your mouth full,' Corinne admonishes. 'You're spraying crumbs everywhere.'

'*I'm* not,' Shanice says.

'No, you're doing good,' Corinne says. Then, with a sideways glance at Billy: 'Doing well.'

Derek has no interest in grammar. 'But tell me one thing. Is there blood in it?'

Billy thinks of Bob Raines, flying backward. He thinks of his sister with all her ribs broken — yes, every fucking one — and her chest stomped in. 'Nope, no blood.' He takes a bite of his cookie.

Shanice reaches for another. 'You can have that one,' her mother says, 'and one more. You too, D. The rest are for Mr Lockridge and for later. You know your dad likes these.' To Billy she says, 'Jamal works six days a week and overtime when he can get it. The Fazios are good about keeping track of these two while we're both at work. This is not a bad neighborhood, but we've got our eye on something better.'

'Movin on up,' Billy says.

Corinne laughs and nods.

'I don't ever want to move,' Shanice says, then adds with a child's charming dignity: 'I have *friends*.'

'So do I,' Derek says. 'Hey, Mr Lockridge, do you know how to play Monopoly? Me'n Shan are going to play, but it's stupid with just two and Mom won't.'

'Mom won't is right,' Corinne says. 'Most boring game in the world. Get your father to play with you tonight. He will, if he's not too tired.'

'That's *hours* away,' Derek says. 'I'm bored right now.'

'Me too,' Shanice says. 'If I had a phone, I could play Crossy Road.'

'Next year,' Corinne says, and rolls her eyes in a way that makes Billy think the girl has been phone-campaigning for quite a while. Maybe since the age of five.

'*Do* you play?' Derek asks, although without much hope.

'I do,' Billy says, then leans across the table, pinning Derek Ackerman with his eyes. 'But I have to warn you that I'm good. And I play to win.'

'So do I!' Derek is smiling below a milk mustache.

'So do *I*!' Shanice says.

'I wouldn't hold back just because you're kids and I'm a grownup,' Billy says. 'I'd wound you with my rental properties, then kill you with my hotels. If we're going to play, you have to know that up front.'

'Okay!' Derek says, jumping up and almost spilling the rest of his milk.

'Okay!' Shanice cries, also jumping up.

'Are you kids going to cry when I win?'

'No!'

'No!'

'Okay. As long as we have that straight.'

'Are you sure?' Corinne asks him. 'That game, I swear it can go on all day.'

'Not with me rolling the dice,' Billy says.

'We play downstairs,' Shanice says, and once more takes his hand.

The room down there is the same size as the one in Billy's house, but it's only half a man-cave. In that part, Jamal has set up a work space with tools pegged to the wall. There's also a bandsaw, and Billy notes with approval that there's a padlocked cover over the on/off switch. The kids' half of the room is littered with toys and coloring books. There's a small TV hooked up to a cheap game console that uses cassettes. To Billy it looks like a yardsale purchase. Board games are stacked against one wall. Derek takes the Monopoly box and puts the board on a child-sized table.

'Mr Lockridge is too big for our chairs,' Shanice says, sounding dismayed.

'I'll sit on the floor.' Billy removes one of the chairs and does so. There's just room for his crossed legs under the table.

'Which piece you want?' Derek asks. 'I usually take the racing car when it's just me 'n Shan, but you can have it if you want.'

'That's okay. Which one do you like, Shan?'

'The thimble,' she says. Then adds, rather grudgingly, 'Unless you want it.'

Billy takes the top hat. The game begins. Forty minutes later, when Derek's turn comes around again, he calls for his mother. '*Ma!* I need advice!'

Corinne comes down the stairs and stands with her hands on her hips, surveying the board and the distribution of Monopoly money. 'I don't want to say you kids are in trouble, but you kids are in trouble.'

'I warned them,' Billy says.

'What do you want to ask me, D? Keep in mind your mother barely passed Home Economics back in the day.'

'Well, here's my problem,' Derek says. 'He's got two of the green ones, Pacific and Pennsylvania, but I got North Carolina. Mr Lockridge says he'll give me nine hundred dollars for it. That's three times what I paid, but . . .'

'But?' Corinne says.

'But?' Billy says.

'But then he can put houses on the green ones. And he already has *hotels* on Park Place and Boardwalk!'

'So?' Corinne says.

'So?' Billy says. He's grinning.

'I gotta go to the bathroom and I'm almost broke anyway,' Shanice says, and gets up.

'Honey, you don't need to announce your bathroom calls. You just need to say excuse me.'

Shanice says, with that same winning dignity, 'I'm going to *powder my nose*, okay?'

Billy bursts out laughing. Corinne joins him. Derek pays no attention. He studies the board, then looks up at his mother. 'Sell or not? I'm almost out of money!'

'It's a Hobson's choice,' Billy says. 'That means you have to decide between taking a chance or standing pat. Between you and me, D, I think you're kinda sunk either way.'

'Think he's right, hon,' Corinne says.

'He's really lucky,' Derek says to his mother. 'He landed on Free Parking and got all the money in there and it was a *bundle*.'

'Also I'm really good,' Billy says. 'Admit it.'

Derek tries to scowl, but can't manage it for a long time. He holds up the deed with the green stripe. 'Twelve hundred.'

'Done!' Billy cries, and hands over the cash.

Twenty minutes later the children are bankrupt and the game is over. When Billy stands up, his knees crack and the kids laugh. 'You guys lost, so you have to put the game away, right?'

'That's the way Daddy plays, too,' Shanice says. 'But sometimes *he* lets us win.'

Billy leans down, smiling. 'I don't do that.'

'Big bully,' she says, and giggles with her hands over her mouth.

Danny Fazio comes jingling down the stairs in a yellow rain slicker and unbuckled galoshes that gape like funnels. 'Can I play?'

'Next time,' Billy says. 'I make it a policy to only beat up on kids once a weekend.'

It's just more joking around, what these kids might call throwing shade, but suddenly he sees burned cookies littering the floor in front of the stove in their trailer and the cast on Bob Raines's arm thudding against the side of Cathy's face and it isn't funny anymore. The three kids laugh because to them it is. None of them have watched their sister being stepped on by a drunken ogre with a fading mermaid on his arm.

Upstairs, Corinne gives him a bag of cookies and says, 'Thank you for making a rainy day so much fun for them.'

'I had fun, too.'

He did. Right up until the end. When he gets home he throws the cookies into the trash. Corinne Ackerman is a good little baker, but he can't think of eating cookies now. He can't even bear to look at them.

6

On Monday he goes to see the rental agent, who does business in the sad little strip mall three blocks from 658. Merton Richter's office is a hole-in-the-wall two-roomer between a tanning salon and the Jolly Roger Tattoo Parlor. Parked in front is a blue SUV, pretty old, with a stick-on sign on one side (RICHTER REAL ESTATE) and a long scratch on the other. The guy gives Dalton Smith's painstakingly crafted references a cursory glance, then hands them back along with a rental agreement. The places where Billy is supposed to sign have been highlighted in yellow.

'You could tell me it's a little over-market,' Richter says, as if Billy had protested, 'and you might be right, but only a little, considering the furnishings and the WiFi. And with no street parking until six P.M., the driveway is a real convenience. You'll be sharing it with the Jensens, of course—'

'I'm planning to keep my car in a municipal garage for the most part. I can use the exercise.' He pats his fake belly. 'The rent does seem a little high, but I want the place.'

'Sight unseen,' Richter marvels.

'Mrs Jensen spoke well of it.'

'Ah, I see. In any case, if we're in agreement . . .?'

Billy signs the form and writes his debut check as Dalton Smith: first month, last month, and a damage deposit that's fucking outrageous unless the cookware is All-Clad, the china Limoges, and the lamps come with Tiffany shades.

'IT guy, huh?' Richter says, stashing the check away in his desk drawer. He pushes an envelope marked KEYS across the desk, then whacks his old PC like you'd whack a dog you don't have much use for but keeps hanging around. 'I could sure use some help with this balky bitch.'

'I'm off the clock,' Billy says, 'but I can give you some advice.'

'Which is?'

'Replace it before you lose everything. Do you hook me up with heat, electric, water, and cable?'

Richter smiles as if giving Billy a prize. 'Nope, that's all you, brother.' And offers his hand.

Billy could ask Richter what he actually does for his commission, the agreement is pretty obviously a form printed off the Internet with the local details dropped in, but does he care? Not at all.

7

Billy would like to get back to his story (it seems premature to call it a book, and maybe unlucky as well), but there's more to do. When the banks open on Tuesday, he goes to SouthernTrust and withdraws some of the walking-around money that has been deposited in a David Lockridge account. He goes to three different chain stores and buys three more laptop computers, all for cash, all cheap off-brands like the AllTech. He also buys a cheap table model TV. That he pays for with a Dalton Smith credit card.

Next on his list is leasing a car. He stashes his Toyota in a garage on the other side of town from the one he uses as David Lockridge, not wanting to chance anyone from his building seeing him in his Dalton Smith rig. That would be a small chance, at this time of day all the worker bees should be in the hive, but taking even small chances is stupid. It's how people get nailed.

When he's put on the wig, glasses, mustache, and big belly, he calls an Uber and asks to be driven to McCoy Ford, on the western edge of the city. There he leases a Ford Fusion for thirty-six months. The dealer reminds him that if Billy drives it over 10,500 miles per year, he'll pay a pretty hefty overcharge. Billy doubts if he'll even put three hundred miles on the Fusion. The important thing is that Billy has wheels Nick knows about, and Dalton Smith now has wheels Nick *doesn't* know about. It's a precaution in case Nick should be planning something hinky, but it's more. It's keeping Dalton Curtis Smith separate from what's going to happen on those courthouse steps. Keeping him clean.

Billy parks his new ride next to his old ride (different garage, same upper-level blind spot) long enough to transfer the TV and new laptops to the Fusion. Also the cheap suitcases he stashed in the Toyota's trunk late last night. They are filled with the cheap Walmart clothes. He drives the Fusion to 658 Pearson Street and parks in the driveway, which is your basic asphalt stub with grass growing up the middle. He hopes Mrs Jensen will see him moving in, and he's not disappointed.

Does Dalton Smith see her looking down from her second-story window? Billy decides he doesn't. Dalton is a computer nerd, lost in his own world. He struggles and puffs two of the suitcases up to the door and uses his new key to unlock it. Nine steps down take him to the door of Dalton Smith's new apartment, where he uses another key. The door opens directly onto the living room. He drops the bags on the industrial carpet and walks around, checking out the four rooms – five, if you count the bathroom.

The furnishings are quite nice, Richter said. That's not true, but they're not terrible, either. The word *generic* comes to mind. The bed's a double, and when Billy lies down on it there are creaks but no springs poking at him, so that's a win. There's an easy chair in front of a table obviously meant to hold a small TV like the one he bought at Discount Electronics. The chair is comfortable enough, but the zebra-striping is almost the stuff of nightmares. He'll want to cover it with something.

On the whole, he likes the place. He goes to the one narrow window, which is set at lawn-level. It's almost like looking out through a periscope, Billy thinks. He digs the perspective. It feels cozy, somehow. He likes his Midwood neighbors, especially the Ackermans next door, but he thinks he likes this place better. It has a sense of safety. There's an old couch that also looks comfortable, and he decides he'll move it to where the zebra-striped chair is now, so he can sit on it and look out at the street. People passing on the sidewalk might look at the house, but most won't glance down at these basement windows and see him looking back. It's a den, he thinks. If I have to go to ground, this is where I should do it, not some safe house in Wisconsin. Because this place is actually *in* the gr—

There's a light knock from behind him, actually more of a rattle. He turns and sees Mrs Jensen standing in the door he left open, twiddling her fingernails on the jamb.

'Hello, Mr Smith.'

'Oh, hi.' His Dalton Smith voice is slightly higher than the one he uses as Billy Summers and David Lockridge. A little breathy, maybe a touch of asthma. 'You caught me moving in, Mrs Jensen.' He gestures to the suitcases.

'Since we're going to be neighbors, why don't you call me Beverly?'

'Okay, thanks. And I'm Dalton. Sorry I can't offer you coffee or anything, no supplies yet—'

'I totally understand. Moving in's crazy, isn't it?'

'It sure is. The good part is that I travel a lot, so I don't have a lot. Seen more motels than I ever wanted to. Spending the rest of this week in Lincoln, Nebraska, then Omaha.' Billy has found that if you lie about business travel to cities of secondary size and importance in the economic scheme of things, people believe you. 'I've got a few more things to bring in, so if you'll excuse me . . .'

'Do you need help?'

'No, I'm fine.' Then, as if reconsidering: 'Well . . .'

They go out to the Fusion. Billy gives her the three off-brand computers. With the boxes in her arms, she looks like a woman who delivers for Domino's. 'Gosh, I better not drop these, they're brand new. And probably worth a fortune.'

They're only worth about nine hundred dollars, but Billy doesn't contradict her. He asks if they're too heavy.

'Pooh. Less than a laundry basket of wetwash. Are you going to set all of these up?'

'As soon as I get the power on, yes,' Billy says. 'It's how I do my business. Some of it, anyway. Most I outsource.' *Outsource* is one of those impressive-sounding words that might mean anything. He hefts out the carton containing the TV. They go up the walk, through the open front door, down the stairs.

'Come on up once you're a little bit settled,' Beverly Jensen says. 'I'll put on the coffee pot. And I can give you a doughnut, if you don't mind day-old.'

'I never say no to a doughnut. Thank you, Mrs Jensen.'

'Beverly.'

He smiles. 'Beverly, right. One more suitcase to bring in and then I'll be with you.'

Bucky has sent Billy's box, the one marked *Safeties*. Dalton Smith's iPhone is in it, and once he's unloaded the Fusion, Billy uses it to make some Dalton Smith calls. By the time he's drunk a cup of coffee and eaten a doughnut in the Jensens' second-floor apartment, listening with apparent fascination as Beverly tells him all about her husband's problems with the boss at the company where he works, the power is on in his new place.

His below-ground den.

8

He's at 658 until mid-afternoon, unpacking the cheap clothes, booting up the cheap computers, and shopping at the Brookshire's a mile away. Except for a dozen eggs and some butter, he steers clear of perishables. Most of what he buys is stuff that will keep when he's not here: canned goods and frozen dinners. At three o'clock he drives the leased Fusion back to the fourth level of Parking Garage , and after making sure he's unobserved, removes the glasses and fake facial hair. Getting rid of the fake belly is an incredible relief, and he sees he'll need to get some baby powder if he wants to avoid a rash.

He drives the Toyota back to Parking Garage #1, then returns to the fifth floor of the Gerard Tower. He doesn't work on his story, and he doesn't play games on the computer, either. He just sits and thinks. No rifle in the office, nothing more lethal than a paring knife in one of the kitchenette's drawers, and that's okay. It may be weeks or even months before Billy needs a gun. The assassination might not even happen at all, and would that be so bad? In monetary terms, yes. He'd lose one-point-five mill. As for the five hundred thousand he's already been paid, would the person who ordered the assassination – the one Nick is go-betweening for – want the money back?

'Good luck with that,' Billy says. And laughs.

9

As he walks, *plods*, back to the parking garage, Billy is thinking about bigamy.

He's never been married once, let alone to two different women at the same time, but now he knows how that must feel. In a word, exhausting. He's getting his feet set in not just two different lives but three. To Nick and Giorgio (also to Ken Hoff, which he hates), he's a gun for hire named Billy Summers. To the inhabitants of the Gerard Tower, he's a wannabe writer named David Lockridge. Ditto the residents of Evergreen Street in Midwood. And now, on Pearson Street – nine blocks from Gerard Tower and four safe miles from Midwood – he is an overweight computer geek named Dalton Smith.

Come to think of it, there's even a fourth life: that of Benjy Compson, who is just enough not-Billy so Billy can look at painful memories he usually avoids.

He started writing Benjy's story on a laptop he's pretty sure (no, positive) has been cloned because it was a challenge, and because it's that fabled *last job*, but he now understands there was a deeper, truer reason: he wants to be read. By anyone, even a couple of Vegas hardballs like Nick Majarian and Giorgio Piglielli. Now he understands – he never did before, never even considered it – that any writer who goes public with his work is courting danger. It's part of the allure. *Look at me. I'm showing you what I am. My clothes are off. I'm exposing myself.*

As he approaches the entrance to the parking garage, deep in these thoughts, there's a tap on his shoulder that makes him jump. He turns and sees Phyllis Stanhope, the woman from the accounting firm.

'I'm sorry,' she says, taking a step back. 'I didn't mean to startle you.'

Has she seen something in that unguarded moment? A flash of who he really is? Is that what the backward step was about? Maybe. If so, he tries to dismiss it with an easy smile and the absolute truth. 'It's fine. I was just a million miles away.'

'Thinking about your story?'

About bigamy. 'That's right.'

Phyllis falls in step beside him. Her handbag is slung over one shoulder. She's also wearing a child's backpack with SpongeBob on it and has exchanged her click-clack shoes for white socks and sneakers. 'I didn't see you at lunch today. Did you eat at your desk?'

'I was out and about. Still trying to get settled in. Plus I had a long talk with my agent.'

He did in fact speak with Giorgio, although it wasn't a long talk. Nick has returned to Vegas, but Giorgio is in residence at the McMansion, and he brought the two new guys – Reggie and Dana are their names – with him. Billy doesn't think Nick and Georgie Pigs are tag-teaming him, exactly, but this is a very big deal for them and Billy would be surprised if they were careless. Shocked, really. The one they may actually be keeping an eye on is Ken Hoff. The patsy in waiting.

'Besides, even when a writer's not at his desk, he's working.' He taps his temple.

She returns his smile. It's a good one. 'I bet that's what they all say.'

'In truth, I seem to have hit a little bit of a roadblock.'

'Maybe it's the change of scene.'

'Maybe.'

He doesn't think there actually is a roadblock. He hasn't written anything beyond that first episode, but the rest is right there. Waiting. He wants to get to it. It means something to him. It's not like journaling, it's not an effort to make peace with a life that has in many ways been unhappy and traumatic, it's not confessional even though it may amount to a confession. It's about power. He's finally tapped into power that doesn't come from the barrel of a gun. Like the view from his new apartment's ground-level windows, he likes it.

'In any case,' he says as they reach the entrance to the parking garage, 'I plan to buckle down. Starting tomorrow.'

She raises her eyebrows. 'Jam yesterday, jam tomorrow—'

He chimes in and they finish together. 'But never jam today!'

'In any case, I can't wait to read it.' They start up the ramp. It's deliciously cool after the hammerstroke sun on the street. She stops halfway to the first turn. 'This is me.' She beeps her keyfob. The taillights of a little blue Prius respond. Two bumper stickers flank her license plate: OUR BODIES, OUR CHOICES and BELIEVE THE WOMEN.

'You're apt to get keyed with those,' Billy says. 'This is a deep red state.'

She lifts her purse in front of her and gives a smile unlike the one she greeted him with. This is more of a Dirty Harry smile. 'It's also a concealed carry state, so if anyone tries to key off my bumper stickers, they better do it while I'm not around.'

Is that more show than go? The little accountant lady putting on a badass front for a man she might be interested in? Maybe, maybe not.

Either way, he admires her for being out front about what she believes. For being brave. This is how a good person acts. At least it is when they're being their best selves.

'Well, I'll see you around the campus,' Billy says. 'I'm up a few levels.'

'Couldn't find anything closer? Really?'

He could say it's because he came in late today, but that might come back to bite him, because he always parks on Four. He hoists a thumb. 'Less chance of a bump-and-run up there.'

'Or getting your bumper stickers keyed off?'

'I don't have any,' Billy says, and adds the absolute truth: 'I like to fly under the radar.' Then, on impulse (and he is rarely an impulsive man), he says what he's promised himself he would not. 'Come for a drink with me sometime. Want to?'

'Yes.' With no hesitation, as if she's just been waiting for him to pop the question. 'What about Friday? There's a nice place two blocks over. We can go dutch. I always go dutch when I have a drink with a man.' She pauses. 'At least the first time.'

'Probably a good policy. Drive safe, Phyllis.'

'Phil. Call me Phil.'

He gives her taillights a wave before walking the rest of the way up to the fourth level. There's an elevator, but he wants the walk. He wants to ask himself why the fuck he did what he just did. Or what about playing Monopoly with Derek and Shanice Ackerman, especially when he knows they'll want a return engagement the coming weekend, and he'll probably oblige? What happened to getting friendly, but not too close? Can you be part of the scenery when you're in the foreground?

The short answer is no.

CHAPTER 6

1

Summer rolls along. Hot and humid days of blaring sunshine are punctuated by sudden thunderstorms, some of them vicious with throats full of hail. A couple of tornados strike, but on the outskirts, none downtown or in Midwood. When the storms blow out, they leave streets that steam and dry quickly. Most of the apartments on the upper floors of the Gerard Tower are empty, either unoccupied or deserted by their residents for cooler climes. Most of the businesses remain fully staffed, because most of them are young firms still struggling to find their footing. Some, like the law firm down the hall from Billy's office, are start-ups that didn't even exist two years ago.

Billy and Phil Stanhope go for that drink, in a pleasant wood-paneled bar adjacent to what Billy guesses is one of the Bluff's better restaurants, where steaks are the specialty of the house. She has a whiskey and soda ('My dad's tipple,' she says). Billy has an Arnold Palmer, explaining he's off alcohol, even beer, while working on his book.

'I don't know if I'm actually an alcoholic, the jury's out on that,' he says, 'but I've had trouble with the booze.' He gives her the backstory he's been given by Nick and Giorgio: too much drinking back home in New Hampshire with too many party animal friends.

They spend a pleasant enough half-hour, but he senses her interest in him – as anything more than a friend, that is – is not as strong as he maybe had hoped it would be. He thinks it's the gulf between what's in their glasses. Drinking whiskey with a man who's drinking an iced tea–lemonade mix is like drinking alone, and maybe (the quick color that dashes into her cheeks as she takes down what's in hers suggests it might be so) Phil has a booze problem herself. Or will, in the coming years. It's too bad things are as they are because he wouldn't mind taking her to bed, but keeping it friendly does lessen the chance of complications. He won't fade entirely into the background with her – there is that liking, on both their parts – but no forensic unit will ever find his fingerprints in her bedroom. That's good. For both of them. Yet even getting this close, exchanging life summaries (hers real, his bogus) is too close, and he knows it.

Dalton Smith has a backstory that doesn't include problems with booze, so he can have a beer on the back stoop of 658 Pearson with Beverly's husband. Don Jensen works for a landscaping company called Growing Concern. He's totally down with that other Don, the one who sits in much grander digs at 1600 Pennsylvania Avenue. He especially agrees with the other Don when it comes to the issue of immigration ('Don't want to see America painted brown,' he says), even though a large part of Growing Concern's workforce consists of undocumented aliens who don't speak English ('Although they *do* speak food stamps,' he says). When Billy points out the contradiction, Don Jensen waves it away ('Movie stars come and go, but wetbacks are forever,' he says). He asks Billy where he's off to next and Billy says a couple of weeks in Iowa City. Then on to Des Moines and Ames.

'You sure don't spend much time here,' Don says. 'Seems like a waste of rent money.'

'Summer's always my busy time. And I need a place to hang my hat. You may see more of me this fall.'

'I'll drink to that. Want another beer?'

'No thanks,' Billy says, getting up, 'I've got some work to do.'

'Nerd,' Don says, and gives him an affectionate clap on the back.

'Guilty as charged,' Billy says.

On Evergreen Street, the Raglands – Paul and Denise – invite him over for barbecued chicken from Big Clucks. For dessert, Denise serves strawberry shortcake made in her own kitchen. It's delicious. Billy has seconds. The Fazios – Pete and Diane – invite him over for Friday pizza, which they eat in the downstairs rumpus room, watching *Raiders of the Lost Ark* along with Danny Fazio and the Ackerman kids from across the street. The movie works as well for them as it did for Billy and Cathy when they went to see it at a third-run showing at the old Bijou. Jamal and Corinne Ackerman have him over for tacos and chocolate silk pie. It's delicious. Billy has seconds. He's put on five pounds. Not wanting to look like the neighborhood freeloader, he buys a grill at Walmart, using one of his David Lockridge credit cards, and invites all three families, plus Jane Kellogg, the widow who lives at the far end of the block, over for burgers and hotdogs in his backyard. Which, like the front one, is enjoying a nice revival under his supervision.

The weekend Monopoly games continue. Now they draw kids from all over the neighborhood, not just Evergreen Street, everyone vying to dethrone the champ. Billy takes them all to the cleaners. One Saturday, Jamal Ackerman takes a seat at the board, claiming the racecar as his token ('Come on, White America,' he says to Billy with a grin). He's a little tougher than the kids, but not much. After seventy minutes he's broke and Billy is gloating. It's Corinne who finally takes him down, on the last Saturday before school reconvenes. All the kids who've been kibitzing applaud when Billy declares bankruptcy. So does Billy. Corinne bows, then takes a picture of the board that Billy is careful not to be in. Not that it matters much. This is the age of the cell phone camera, and he's sure he's on Derek's. Probably on Danny Fazio's, too. The Ackerman kids are looking at Billy with shining eyes as they applaud. These games have become important to Derek and Shanice. To all the kids, but especially to them, because they were there when the Saturday games started. *He* has become important to them, and he's going to let them down. He doesn't believe (or can't, or refuses to) that he is actually going to break their hearts when he kills Joel Allen, but he knows they will be shocked and shaken. Disillusioned. Dutched. He can tell himself, if not by me then by someone else (and does), but it won't wash. This is not how a good person behaves. But the situation is inflexible. He more and more hopes Allen will avoid extradition, or be killed in lockup, or even escape, rendering the whole thing moot.

Weekdays he eats on the plaza of the Gerard Tower, if it's not too hot. He makes it his business to strike up an acquaintance with Colin White, the flashy dresser. White comes across not as a stereotypical gay man but as an actual caricature, a figure of fun out of a 1980s sitcom. He's all breathy voice and exaggerated gestures and great big ohmygod eyerolls. He calls Billy *darling* and *honeypie*. Once Billy gets past that, he discovers a man of great wit. *Cutting* wit. And when the eyeballs aren't rolling, they are sharply observant. Later, after the deed is done, there will be many descriptions of David Lockridge. Some, including Phyllis Stanhope's, will be good, but Billy thinks that this man's will be the most accurate. He intends to use Colin White, but in the meantime he needs to be careful of him. Billy has the *dumb self*; he thinks Colin White has a *silly fucker self*. It takes one to know one.

One day while they're sitting on a bench in the plaza's scant noontime shade, Billy asks Colin how he can do his job of cozening people out of a few bucks when he's basically, face it, a pretty nice guy, not to mention as gay as Aunt Maudie's Easter hat. Colin puts a hand to the side of his face, gives Billy a wide-eyed ingenue's stare, and says, 'Well . . . I sort of . . . *change*.' The hand drops. The pleasant smile (enhanced by just the barest touch of lip gloss) disappears. So does the lilting delivery. The voice that comes out of wispy Colin White, today dressed in his gold parachute pants and high-collared paisley shirt, is that of a pissed-off lawyer.

'Ma'am, I don't know who you've been soft-soaping, but I am immune. You're all out of time. You want to keep your car? Because if I hang up on you without getting something, *and I mean more than a promise*, my next call is going to be to the repo company we use. Cry all you want, I'm immune to that, too.' He sounds it. 'I need sixty bucks on my screen in the next ten minutes. Fifty at the very least, and only because I got up on the right side of the bed this morning.'

He stops, looking at Billy with wide eyes (enhanced by just a trace of liner). 'Does that help you understand?'

It does. What it doesn't help Billy to understand is whether Colin White is a good person or a bad one. Perhaps he's both. Billy has always found this a troubling concept.

2

He gets texts from his 'agent' on his David Lockridge phone that summer, sometimes once a week, sometimes twice.

GRusso: Your editor hasn't had a chance to read your latest pages yet.

GRusso: I called your editor but he was out of the office.
GRusso: Your editor is still in California.

And so on. The one he's waiting for, the one meaning that a California judge has approved Allen's extradition, will be **Your editor wants to publish.** When Billy gets that, he'll begin his final preparations.

Giorgio's final text will read **The check is on the way.**

3

Nick returns from Vegas in mid-August. He calls Billy and tells him to arrive at the McMansion after dark, an instruction Billy hardly needs. They sit down to a late dinner at nine-thirty. There's no help – Nick cooks himself, veal parmigiana, not great but the Pinot Noir is good. Billy takes only a single glass, mindful of the drive back.

Frankie, Paulie, and the new guys, Reggie and Dana, are in attendance. They praise the meal extravagantly, including the dessert, which is a supermarket poundcake garnished with either Cool Whip or Dream Whip. Billy knows the taste. He ate his share as a kid on Friday nights at the Stepenek house, which he and Robin and Gad – plus other assorted inmates – called the House of Everlasting Paint.

That place is on his mind a lot these days. Robin, too. He was crazy for that girl. Soon he will be writing about her, although he'll change her name to something similar. Rikki, or maybe Ronnie. He'll change all the names, except maybe for the one-eyed girl.

Most of Nick's crew, the guys Billy thinks of as the Vegas hardballs, have names ending in -ie, like characters in a Coppola or Scorsese movie. Dana Edison is different. He's a redhead with a tight little manbun in back to make up for what he's lost in front – his forehead looks more like a runway. Frankie Elvis, Paulie, and Reggie are muscular boys. Dana is slight, and looks out at the world through rimless spectacles. At first glance you might take him to be inoffensive, a Mr Milquetoast, but the eyes behind the specs are blue and cold. Shooter's eyes.

'No word on Allen yet?' Billy asks when the meal is finished.

'As a matter of fact, there is.' Then, to Paulie: 'Don't you light that fuckin stinkbomb in here, there's a no-smoking clause in the lease. Violation is cause for immediate termination plus a thousand-dollar fine.'

Paulie Logan looks at the cheroot he's taken from the pocket of his pink Paul Stuart shirt like he doesn't know where it came from and puts it back with a muttered apology. Nick turns back to Billy.

'Allen is gonna be in court the Tuesday after Labor Day. His lawyer will try for another continuance. Will he get it?' Nick lifts his hands, palms up. 'Maybe, but what I'm hearing from my friends in LA is this judge is a grumpy old cunt.'

Frank Macintosh laughs, then stops and crosses his arms over his chest when Nick frowns at him. Nick has been in a shitty mood most of the night. Billy thinks he wants to be back in Vegas, listening to some oldtimer – Frankie Avalon, maybe Bobby Rydell – sing 'Volare.'

'They tell me this has been a rainy summer here, Billy. That true?'

'It comes and goes,' Billy says, thinking of his lawn in Midwood. It's as green as the felt on a new pool table. Even the grass in front of 658 Pearson looks better, and the brick jaw of the train station across the street is hidden by high-sprouting weeds.

'When it comes, it comes hard,' Reggie says. 'Not much like Vegas, boss.'

'Can you make the shot in the rain?' Nick asks. 'That's what I want to know. And I want the truth, not some optimistic bullshit.'

'Unless it's pouring cats and dogs, sure.'

'Good. Good. We'll hope the cats and dogs stay home. Come in the library with me, Billy. Want to talk to you a little more. Then you can go home and get your beauty rest. You guys find something to do. Paulie, if you smoke that thing outside, don't let me find the butt on the lawn tomorrow.'

'Okay, Nick.'

'Because I'll look.'

Paul Logan and the three Vegas imports troop out. Nick takes Billy into a room lined floor to ceiling with books. Cunning little spotlights shine down sprays of light on leatherbound sets. Billy would love to browse those shelves – he's pretty sure he sees the complete works of both Kipling and Dickens – but that's not the sort of thing the Billy Nick knows would do. The Billy Nick knows sits in a wingback chair and gives Nick his best wide-eyed receptive look.

'Have you seen Reggie and Dana around?'

'Yes. Once in awhile.' They drive a DPW panel truck. Once they were parked at the curb in front of the Gerard Tower, where the food trucks roost at lunchtime. They were fiddling with a manhole cover. Another time he saw them on Holland Street, kneeling down and shining their lights into a sewer grate. They were wearing gray coveralls, city gimme caps, work boots.

'You'll see them more. They look okay?'

Billy shrugs.

Nick returns it with an impatient look. 'What does that mean?'

'They looked okay.'

'Not attracting any special attention?'

'Not that I saw.'

'Good. Good. The truck's in the carriage house here. They don't take it out every day, at least not yet, but I want people to get used to seeing them cruising around.'

'Blending into the scenery,' Billy says with his best *dumb self* smile.

Nick points a finger gun at him. It's his trademark, Billy knows, probably picked it up from some Vegas lounge act, but Billy doesn't care for having even a make-believe gun pointed at him. 'Exactly right. Hoff deliver your weapon yet?'

'No.'

'You seen him?'

'No, and don't much want to.'

'Okay.' Nick sighs and runs a hand through his hair. 'Probably you'd like to sight the gun in, right? Take a few shots out in the country?'

'Maybe,' Billy says, but he won't risk shooting, even out in the toolies where every stop sign has been riddled with bullet holes. He can zero the rifle with an iPhone app and a laser gadget they sell on Amazon.

Nick leans forward, hands clasped in front of his considerable basket. He wears an expression of friendly concern. To Billy it makes him look like an imposter. 'How are you doing out there in . . . what's it called? Midwood?'

'Midwood, yeah. Pretty good.'

'Kind of a shithole, I know, but the payoff will be worth it.'

'Yeah.' Thinking it's actually a pretty nice neighborhood.

'Keeping a low profile?'

Billy nods. No need for Nick to know about the Monopoly games, or the get-together in his backyard, or the drink he had with Phil Stanhope. Now or ever.

'Have you thought any more about the getaway plan I mentioned to you? Because, as you see, the boys will be ready when it's time. Reggie's no rocket scientist, but Dana is a thinking cat. And both of them can drive.'

'I just run around the corner, right? And get in the back of the van.'

'Right, and change into one of the coveralls like the ones the city employees wear. You guys ask the cops if you can help with crowd control or something.' Like Billy has forgotten all this. 'If they say yes – they probably won't, but if they do – you pitch right in. Either way, you'll be out of state and on your way to Wisconsin by nightfall. Maybe sooner. So what do you think?'

Billy pictures himself not on his way to Wisconsin but lying dead beside a county road in a ditch along with the beer cans and discarded Big Mac boxes. That picture is very clear.

He smiles – *big* smile – and says, 'It sounds good. Better than anything I could have thought up.'

Which is bullshit, what he's thought up seems strong to him no matter how much he turns it this way and that. There are risks, but they are minimal. Nick doesn't need to know his actual getaway plan. He may be pissed off later, but really, how pissed can he be if the job gets done?

Nick rises to his feet. 'Good. Glad to help you out, Billy. You're a good man.'

No I'm not, and neither are you. 'Thanks, Nick.'

'Last job, huh? You really mean that?'

'I do.'

'Well come here, bambino, and give me a hug.'

Billy does.

It isn't that he doesn't trust Nick, he thinks on his way back to the yellow house. It's just that he trusts himself more. Always has, always will.

4

A couple of days later there's a knock on the door of his little office suite. Billy has been writing, lost in a past that's partly Benjy Compson's but mostly his. He saves his work, shuts down, and opens the door. It's Ken Hoff. He looks like he's lost ten pounds since Billy saw him in June. The scruff on his face is scruffier than ever. Maybe he still thinks it makes him look like the leading man in an action movie, but to Billy he looks like a guy one day off a five-day drunk. His breath doesn't help. The mint he's chewing can't disguise the shot or two he had on his way here, at ten-forty in the morning. His tie is natty, but his shirt is wrinkled and a bit untucked on one side. This is trouble on two legs, Billy thinks.

'Hello, Billy.'

'It's Dave, remember?'

'Sure, Dave, right.' Hoff looks over his shoulder, making sure there's no one in the hall that might have overheard his mistake. 'Can I come in?'

'Sure, Mr Hoff.' He's not going to call the man who's essentially his landlord Ken. He stands aside.

Hoff takes another look over his shoulder and comes in. They're standing in what would be the reception area if this was an actual business office. Billy closes the door. 'What can I do for you?'

'Nothing, I'm fine.' Hoff wets his lips and Billy realizes the man is afraid of him. 'Just came by to see if everything was, you know, all right. If you needed anything.'

Nick sent him, Billy thinks. The message? You got off on the wrong foot with Billy and he's our man on the spot, so get right with him.

'Just one thing,' Billy says. 'You'll make sure the merch is there when I need it, right?' Meaning the M24. What Hoff called a Remington 700.

'That's all in hand. All in hand, my friend. Do you want it now, or—'

'No. One of our friends will tell you when it's time. Until then, keep it someplace safe.'

'No problem. It's in my—'

'I don't want to know. Not yet.' Sufficient unto the day is the evil thereof, he thinks. Book of Matthew. What he wants on this day is to get back to what he was doing. He had no idea how good writing could make you feel.

'Okay, sure. Listen, you want to go for a drink sometime?'

'That wouldn't be a good idea.'

Hoff smiles. Probably it's charming when he's on his game but he's not on it now. He's in a room with a paid killer. That's part of it but not all of it. This is a man who feels the walls closing in, and Billy doesn't think it's because Hoff suspects he might be played for a patsy. He should know but he doesn't. Maybe he can't conceive of it, the way Billy can't conceive of black holes far out in space as actual real things.

'It'd be okay. You're a *writer*, after all. Socially, you're in my zone.'

Whatever that means, Billy thinks. 'Wouldn't be good later. For you. You could answer any questions, say you had no idea what I was really doing here, but it'd be better if the questions never got asked.'

'But *we're* good, Billy, right?'

'It's Dave. You need to get used to that so you don't slip up. And sure, we're good, why wouldn't we be?' Billy gives him the wide-eyed *dumb self* look.

It works. This time Hoff's grin is marginally more charming, because his tongue doesn't come out to slurp his lips in the middle of it. 'Dave now and forever. I won't forget again. You're sure you don't need anything? Because, hey, I own the Carmike Cinema at the Southgate Mall, nine screens, got IMAX coming in next year. I could get you a pass, if you—'

'That would be great.'

'Terrific. I'll bring it around this aftern—'

'Why don't you mail it? Here, or to the address on Evergreen Street. You've got it, right?'

'Sure, yeah. Your agent gave it to me. All the big pictures play in the summer, you know.'

Billy nods as if he can't wait to go see a bunch of actors in super-suits.

'And listen, Dave, I've got an in at an escort service. Very nice girls, very discreet. I'd be happy to—'

'Better not. Low profile, remember?' He opens the door. Hoff isn't just trouble, Hoff is an accident waiting to happen.

'Irv Dean treating you all right?'

The security guard who works days in the lobby. 'Yeah. He and I match for buck scratch-off tickets sometimes.'

Hoff laughs too loudly, then looks over his shoulder again for people who might overhear. Billy wonders if Colin White and the other staff members of Business Solutions have Ken Hoff on their call list. Probably not. The people Ken is in debt to – and he *is* in debt, Billy is sure of it – don't call you on the phone. At a certain point they just come to your house, drown your dog in the swimming pool, and break your fingers on the hand that doesn't write the checks.

'Good, that's good. And Steve Broder?' Off Billy's blank look: 'Building manager.'

'Haven't even seen him,' Billy says. 'Listen, Ken, thanks for stopping by.' Billy puts an arm around the shoulders of the man's wrinkled shirt, escorts him into the hall, and turns him toward the elevators.

'You bet. And I'll be johnny on the spot with that item.'

'I know you will be.'

Hoff starts down the hall, but just when Billy thinks he's rid of him, Hoff comes back. No hiding the desperation in those eyes now. He speaks low. 'We're really good, right? I mean, if I did anything to offend you, or piss you off, I apologize.'

'Really good,' Billy says. Thinking, This guy could blow. And if he does, it won't be Nick Majarian on ground zero. It'll be me.

'Because I need this,' Hoff says. Still speaking low. Smelling of Certs and booze and Creed cologne. 'It's like I'm a quarterback and my receivers are covered but then a slot opens up, opens like magic, and I – you know, I—'

In the middle of this strangled metaphor the door to the lawyers' office down the hall opens. Jim Albright steps out, headed for the bathroom. He sees Billy and lifts a hand. Billy lifts his in return.

'I get it,' Billy says. 'Everything's going to be fine.' And because he can think of nothing else, 'Touchdown ahead.'

Hoff brightens. 'Third and goal!' he says. He grabs Billy's hand, gives it a brisk shake, then heads down the hall, trying to look jaunty.

Billy watches him until he steps into the elevator car and disappears from view. Maybe I should just run, he thinks. Buy a beater as Dalton Smith and run.

But he knows he won't, and the pending million-five is only half of the reason. What's waiting for him in the office/conference room is the other half. Maybe more than half. What Billy most wants to do isn't play Monopoly or drink beer with Don Jensen or go to bed with Phil Stanhope or shoot Joel Allen. What he most wants to do is write. He sits down and powers up the laptop. Opens the document he's been working on and falls into the past.

CHAPTER 7

1

I went over to him and said to myself I might have to shoot him again. If I had to I would. He was my mother's boyfriend but he was wrong. He looked dead but I had to make sure so I lick my hand good and wet and kneeled down beside him. I put my wet hand in front of his mouth and nose so I could feel if there was still any breath in him. There wasn't so then I knew for sure he was dead.

I knew what to do next, but first I went over to Cassie. I was hoping but I knew she was dead too. Had to be, with her chest all crush like it was. But I lick my hand good and wet again and put it in front of her mouth but there was no breath in her either. I held her in my arms and cried, thinking of what my mom always said when she left for the laundry, take care of your sister. But I didn't take care of her. I should have shot that son of a bitch before, that would have been taking care of her. And it would have been taking care of my mother too because I knew he hit her sometimes and she would laugh at her black eye or split lip and say we were just rassling around Benjy and I hit my face. Like I would believe that. Even Cassie didn't believe that and she was only 9.

After I finished crying I went to the phone. It worked. It didn't always but that day it did because the bill was paid. I call 911 and a lady answered.

I said hello, my name is Benjy Compson and I just killed my mothers boyfriend after he killed my sister. The lady asked me if I was sure the man was dead. I said I was. She said what is your address son. I said it is 19 Skyline Drive in the Hillview Trailer Park. She said is your mother there. I said no, she is at the 24 Hour Laundry in Edendale where she works.

She said are you sure your sister is dead. I said I was because he stomped on her and crush her chest all in. I said I lick my hand and felt for breath and there wasn't any. She said okay son you stay where you are and officers will be with you shortly. I said thank you ma'am.

You might think police would be coming already what with the gunshot and all, except the trailer park was on the edge of town and people were always popping off at deers and coons and woodchucks in their gardens. Besides, this was Tennessee. People shoot guns there all the time, in Tennessee it's like a hobby.

I thought I heard something, like maybe mom's boyfriend was getting up to make a run at me even though he was dead. I knew he couldn't do that except I was thinking of a movie I sneaked into. I sneaked Cassie in with me and she hid her eyes at the gorie parts and later she had night-mares and I knew it was mean of me to take her. I don't know why I took her. I think there's something mean in people and sometimes it comes out like blood or puss. I would take that movie back if I could but not shooting the boyfriend. He was a bad, bad person to kill a harmless little girl. I would have done it even if it meant going to the reform school.

Anyway there are only zombies in horror movies. He was dead as dogshit. I wondered if I should put a blanket or something over Cassie but thought no, that would be sad and awful, so I call the 24 Hour Laundry from the paper taped to the wall where the phone was. A lady answered 24 Hour Laundry and I said my name is Benjy Compson and I have to talk to my mother Arlene Compson, she works on the mangle. She said is this an emergency. I said yes ma'am it is. She said we're awfully busy this morning, what is this big emergency. Which I thought was nosey and snotty, maybe just because I was so upset but I don't think so. I said my sister is dead. That is the big emergency. She said oh my God are you sure and I said please let me speak to my mom. Because I had enough of that nosey bitch.

I waited and then mom came on the phone all out of breath and said Benjy what happened? This better not be a joke. And I thought it would be better for all of us if it was a joke but it's not. I said her boyfriend came in all drunk with his arm in a cast and killed Cassie and tried to kill me but I shot him dead. I said the police are coming, I can hear the sirens, so you come home and don't let them take me to jail because it was him or me.

I went out on the top step of the trailer, which weren't really steps at all but cement blocks my mom's last boyfriend, the one before the bad boyfriend, made into steps. That one's name was Milton and he was okay. I wish he stayed but he left. He didn't want the responsibility of two kids, mom said. Like it was our fault. Like we ask to be born. Anyway I went out on those steps because I didn't want to be in the trailer with dead people. I kept asking myself if Cassie could really be dead and telling myself yes she really is.

The first cops came and I was telling them what happen when my mom came. The cops tried to keep her from going in but she went in anyway and when she saw Cassie she scream and moaned and carry on so much I put my hands over my ears. And I was mad at her. I thought what did you think was going to happen. He hit us before just like he hit you so what did you think would happen. Sooner or later bad people do bad things, even a kid knows that.

By then all our neighbors were out and looking. One of the cops was nice. He sat me in the cop car where the neighbors couldn't look so easy and give me a hug. He said he had some candy in the glove compartment and did I want a piece and I said no thank you. He said okay Benjy just tell me what happened. So I did. I don't know how many times I told that story but it was quite a few. Anyway I started to cry and the cop give me another hug and called me a brave kid and I wished my mother would have a boyfriend like that guy.

While I was sitting in the cop car and telling what happened, more cops came and a van that said MAYVILLE POLICE FORENSICS UNIT. One cop from the van took pictures and I later saw some at the hearing but not the bodies. I don't know why the people at the hearing felt like I couldn't look at pictures of bodies I already saw in person. But what I want to say is that one of the pictures that man took got in the newspaper. It showed the cookies my sister made, how they were scattered all over the floor. Underneath it said SHE WAS KILLED FOR COOKIES. I never forgot that, how it was mean and true at the same time.

I had to go to the hearing. It wasn't with a judge but with 3 people. They were 2 men and 1 woman who looked like teachers and talked like teachers. There was nobody in the room except for them and me and my mother and the cops who were first to get to the trailer, which they called 'the scene.' We didn't have a lawyer like in Law & Order on TV and we didn't need one. The woman said I was a brave boy and told my mother I should get counseling. My mother said that was a good idea, then later said to me some people think money grows on trees.

We go to leave and I thought it was over but then I of the men said just a minute, Mrs Compson. I need to say something. I need to say that you have to shoulder some of the blame for this tragedy. Then he told a story about how a scorpion beg a ride across a raging river from a kind-hearted frog but halfway across the scorpion stung the frog and the frog said why did you do that, now we will both drown and the scorpion said it is my nature to sting and you knew I was a scorpion when you let me ride on your back.

Then the man said you picked up a scorpion Mrs Compson and he stung your little girl to death. You could have lost your son as well. You didn't but this trommer will be with him for the rest of his life. I suggest the next time you come across a scorpion you crush it under your foot instead of giving it a ride.

My mom got all red in the face and said how dare you. I never would have put my children at risk if I knew something like this could happen. The man said you are keeping custody of young Benjamin because we can't prove otherwise. But if you did not have warnings of Mr Russell's violent nature, maybe only a few, maybe many, I would be very surprised.

My mother started to cry and that made me want to cry. She said you are so unfair, sitting there on your high horse. When was the last time you had to do 40 hours of sweat-labor to bring home groceries? He said this isn't about me, Mrs Compson. You have lost one child because of poor choices, don't lose the other. This hearing is closed.

2

At some point during that summer – his season of many identities – Billy re-reads the story of Bob Raines's death and the hearing that followed. Then he goes to the window and looks out at the courthouse, where a sheriff's car has pulled up to the curb. Two cops in county brown get out of the front seat. One opens the back door and they wait for the man in there to climb out. The prisoner is rangy and skinny, wearing carpenter's jeans that bag in the seat and a bright purple sweatshirt – too hot for this day – that has the Arkansas Razorback on it. Even at five hundred yards he looks to Billy like one sad fucking sack. Each cop takes an arm and they lead him up the wide steps toward whatever justice awaits him. It's exactly the shot Billy will have to make when (and if) the time comes, but he barely sees it. He's thinking about his story.

He set out to tell it as the *dumb self*, but it turned into something else and he only realized it after reading it cold. The *dumb self* is there, all right, any reader (Nick and Giorgio, for instance) would say the man who wrote it sticks mostly to *Star* magazine, *Inside View*, and *Archie* funnybooks, but there's something more. It's the voice of the *child self*. Billy never set out to write in that voice – consciously, at least – but that's what he did. It's as if he has been regressed under hypnosis. Maybe that's what writing is, when it really matters.

Does it matter? When the only people who'll ever see it are him and a couple of Vegas hardballs who may already have lost interest?

'It does,' Billy says to the window. 'Because it's mine.'

Yes, and because it's true. He's changed the names a little – Cassie instead of Cathy, and his mother's name was Darlene, not Arlene – but mostly it's true. The child's voice is true. That voice never had a chance to speak, not even at the hearing. He answered the questions he was asked but no one asked how it felt to hold Cathy with her crushed chest. No one asked how it felt to be told *take care of your sister* and fail at the most important job in the whole round world. No one asked how it felt when you held your wet hand in front of your sister's mouth and nose, hoping even though you knew hope was gone. No one ever knew that the gun's recoil had made him burp as if he had done no more than drink a soda fast. Not even the cop who hugged him asked those questions, and what a relief it is to let that voice speak.

He goes back to the open MacBook and sits down. Looks at the screen. He thinks, When I get to the Stepenek House part – only I'll call it Speck House – I can let that voice be a little more grownup. Because I was a little more grownup.

Billy begins to tap the keys, slowly at first, then picking up speed. The summer rolls on around him.

3

After the hearing me and my mom went back home. We buried Cassie. I don't know who buried the boyfriend and don't care. In the fall I went back to school where some of the kids started calling me Bang Bang Benjy and I got held back that year. I didn't get in trouble for fighting but I skipped school a lot and my mother said I had to smarten up if I didn't want to get taken away and put into a foster home. I didn't want that so next year I tried harder and passed my courses. When I got sent to Speck House it wasn't my fault, it was my mom's.

She started drinking heavy after Cassie died, mostly at home but sometimes she would go out to bars and sometimes bring a man home with her. To me those men all looked like the bad boyfriend, assholes in other words. I don't know why my mother would go back to the same types of men after what happened but she did. She was like a dog that pukes and then laps it up. I know how that sounds, but I will not take it back.

Her and those men, there were three at least and maybe five, would go in the bedroom and she said they were just rassling around but of course by then I was older and knew they were fucking. Then one night when she was drinking in the trailer she went out to the 7-11 for a box of Cheezits and on her way back she got pulled over. She was charged with drunk driving and put in the jail for 24 hours. She got to keep me that time too, but she lost her license for six months and had to take the bus to the laundry.

A week after she got her license back she got stopped for drunk driving again. There was another hearing, this time just about me, but what do you know, that same man who told the story about the scorpion and the frog was sitting at the table along with 2 new ones! He said you again. My mother said that's right, me again and you know I lost my daughter. You know what I've been through. The man said I do know, and you don't seem to have learned your lesson, Mrs Compson. My mom said you have never walked in my shoes. She had a lawyer that time but he didn't say much. After, she gave him hell and asked what he was good for. The lawyer said you haven't given me much to work with, Mrs Compson. She said you're fired. He said you can't fire me because I quit.

When we came back to the hearing room a day later they said I would have to go into foster care at a place called Speck House because she was an unfit mother. She said you are bullshit artists and I will fight this all the way to the supreme court. The man who told the story about the frog and the scorpion said have you been drinking. My mother said kiss my ass you fat bastard. He didn't come back on her for that but said you have 24 hours to put Benjy's things together, Mrs Compson, and to say goodbye. It will mean more to him if you're sober when you do it. Then him and the other 2 walked out.

We took the bus home. My mother said we're going to run away, Benjy. We will go to another town and change our names. We will start over. But we were still there the next day, and that was my last day in Hillview Trailer Park, the last day I lived with my mother. A county cop came to take me to the Speck House. I wished the cop had been the one who hug me, but it was another one. Deputy Malkin wasn't so bad though.

Anyway, mom didn't make trouble because she was sober. She said to the cop I put off packing his things because I didn't want to think this would really happen. Give me 15 minutes. The cop said that was quite all right and waited while she pack me a duffle full of clothes. He waited outside. Then she made me 2 PB&J sandwiches and put them in a lunch sack and told me to be a good boy. Then she started to cry and I did too. It was her fault I had to go away, everything was her fault, she was the one who gave the scorpion a ride and she was the one who kept getting drunk and blaming it on Cassie being dead, but I cried because I loved her.

When we went outside, the cop said I could probably call when I got to Speck House in Evansville. My mother told me to call Mrs Tillitson next door and said to the cop it's because right now our phone isn't working. Which meant the bill wasn't paid again. Deputy Malkin said that sounds like a plan and told me to hug my mom. I did. I smelled her hair because it always smell good. It took about 2 hours to get to Evansville. I sat up front. Behind the front seats there was a wire thing that made the back into a cage. The cop said if I stayed out of trouble I would never have to ride back there. He asked me if I would stay out of trouble and I said yes but I was thinking that when you were riding to a foster home in a cop car you are in trouble already.

I ate 1 of the PB&Js and saw she put a devil-egg in the lunch sack too and that made me cry again, thinking of her hands doing that. The cop patted my shoulder and said it gets better, son. His little nametag said F.W.S. MALKIN. I asked him what F.W.S. stood for because I thought it was some kind of special job. He said it stood for his name, which was Franklin Winfield Scott Malkin but he said you can call me Frank, Benjy.

I wasn't crying then but he must have seen I was sad and maybe scared too, because he reach over and pat me on the shoulder and said you'll be okay, Benjy. There are lots of nice kids there. They all get along and if you mind your p's and q's, you will get along, too. I know all the foster situations in the tri-counties and the Specks aren't the worst. They are not the best either but we haven't ever had any trouble with them. Some of the things I've seen, you don't want to know. If you behave and go along to get along you will be fine.

I said I miss my mother. He said of course you do and when she gets her feet back planted on the ground, there'll be another hearing and you can go home. In the meantime, she can come on Wednesday evenings and any time Saturday or Sunday up to 7 oclock. Be sure to tell her that when you speak to her.

Only my mom never did get her feet back planted on the ground. She kept drinking and got a boyfriend who gave her crystal meth and when you get on that stuff you're feet hardly ever get to the ground because you are high most of the time. At first she come to see me quite a lot, then once in a while, then hardly ever, and then she stopped coming at all. The last time she come some of her teeth were gone and her hair was dirty. She said I hate for you to see me like this Benjy and I said I hate it, too. I said you are a mess. By then I was a teenager, and teenagers say anything to hurt when *they* are hurting.

Speck House was out in the country. It was rickety but big like a mansion with rooms everywhere, 3 stories. Maybe even 4. It look good outside but inside it was old and drafty and leaky and cold in wintertime. Cold as a whore's fuck in a freezer, Ronnie used to say. But I didn't know it was old when I got there, I thought it was new because rickety or not it had bright red paint and blue trim. I found out pretty soon that the Speck foster kids painted it every year and got $2 dollars an hour. One year it was green with white trim and then yellow with green trim. You can see why me and Ronnie called it the House of Everlasting Paint! The year I left to join the Marines it was back to red and blue. Ronnie said it's only paint holding this rambling wreck together, Benjy. That was a joke, she was always joking around, but it was also true. I guess most jokes have some truth in them, and that is what makes them funny.

Deputy F.W.S. Malkin said the Specks weren't the worst or the best, and that turned out to be true. I was there 5 years by the time I was old enough to sign for the Marines and sometimes Mrs Speck would slat me side of the head with a towel or dishrag, but she never hit me with her hand and she never hit one of the little kids like Peggy Pye who was six and had her eye put out by a cigarette. When she slat me side of the head I deserved it. I only saw Mr Speck slat kids a couple of times. Once it was when Jimmy Dykeman broke a storm window throwing stones and once when he caught Sara Peabody dancing around Peggy and singing Peggy Pye, Peggy Pye, cross my heart and hope to die, Peggy Pye with just one eye. Mr Speck slap her face for that. Sara was a mean girl, a bad person. Once when I asked her what she wanted to be when she grew up she said I'm going to be a call girl and fuck famous men to get their money. Then she laughed like it was a joke so maybe it was.

The Specks weren't good people or bad people, just people living on money they got from the state of Tennessee. They passed all their inspections. We went to school on the bus and always in clean clothes, and when I decided to join the Marines, Mr Speck went with me to one hearing so I could get emancipated from my mother and another one so he could become my legal guardian. That way he could sign the paper and I could join at 17 and a half instead of waiting to 18. I thought my mother might show up at the emancipation hearing but she never did, and how could she when she didn't know there was going to be one? I would have told her but she was gone from the trailer park and also the apartment where she lived for a while with the boyfriend that turned her into a meth-head. After those 2 hearings Mr Speck said to me God help you now you can do what you want, Benjy. I said I don't believe in God and he said you will, give it time.

What I learned in the House of Everlasting Paint: There aren't just 2 kinds of people, good and bad, like I thought when I was a kid who got most of his ideas on how people act from TV. There are 3. The third type of people go along to get along, like Deputy F.W.S. Malkin told me to do. Those are the most people in the world and I think they are gray people. They will not hurt you (at least on purpose) but they won't help you much, either. They will say do what you want and God help you.

I think in this world you have to help yourself.

When I came to the House of Everlasting Paint, there were 14 kids counting me. Ronnie said that was good because 13 was an unlucky number.

The youngest was Peggy Pye, who still wet her britches sometimes. There were twins, Timmy and Tommy, who were 6 or 7. The oldest kid was Glen Dutton, he was 17 and went in the army not too long after I came. He didn't need Mr Speck to become his legal guardian and sign for him, though, his mother did it because Glen said he would send her the lottment. Glen said to me and Ronnie, that bitch would sign me into slavery with the ragheads if there was money in it for her. Glen was big and curse all the time, even more than Ronnie who could swear like a sailor, but he never bullied the smaller kids. He was a whiz of a painter too, always up on the highest scaffold.

When Deputy Malkin pulled his cop car into the driveway, I was almost blinded by what was next door. It was junk cars far as I could see, not just a few but hundreds. They went up this one hill and I soon found out they also went down the other side, getting older and rustier as they went. The sun was reflecting off all the windshields of the cars that still had windshields. Maybe half a klick down from the Speck House there was a green auto body shop made of corrugated metal. I could hear people inside running noomatic drills and wrenches. Out in front was a sign that said SPECK'S AUTO PARTS and SMALL REPAIRS and BEST BUYS LOWEST PRICES.

Deputy Malkin said that's Speck's brother's place, quite the eyesore isn't it. It's just outside the county zoning, which is how he gets away with it. Your Speck is just *inside* the county zoning, which is why he had to put up a chainlink fence around the sides and back. I'm telling you so you won't look at all that fence and think you're going to a prison. That auto graveyard is a dangerous place, Benjy. Off limits for a reason. Don't take it into your head to go there, all right? I said yes but of course I did. Me and Glen and Ronnie and Donnie. Just me and Ronnie and sometimes Donnie after Glen left for the army, then mostly just me when Ronnie ran away. Sometimes I wonder where she got off to. I hope she's all right. It was sad without her. Maybe that's why I went into the Marines, but if I am going to tell the truth, I might have gone anyway.

The 5 years I was a Speck Boy was long enough to see the House of Everlasting Paint change color 3 times. There are some things that stand out from when I was there, like the time I got suspended from school for fighting when 2 boys called me Bang Bang Benjy, which had happened many times before but that time I got sick of it. They were bigger but I kept fighting even after one of them black my eye and the other one almost bust my nose. That one, his name was Jared Klein, I got hold of his pants and yank them down so everyone saw his pee-stained underwear. He got teased about that plenty which served him right.

Another thing that stands out is when Peggy Pye had to go to the hospital with pneumonia. Then a week later, or maybe it was 10 days, Mrs Speck got us all together in the living room to pray because she said Peggy passed on and went up to heaven to be with Jesus and now she could see out of both her eyes. Donnie Wigmore said I hope the food is better up there and Mr Speck told him keep your smart remarks to yourself if you don't want me to slat you one. Anyway we prayed for Peggy's soul and Ronnie had to put her hand over her mouth to keep from laughing at what Donnie said only she was crying too. Other kids were also crying because Peggy was everyone's 'pet.' I didn't cry but I felt bad. Later on when me and Ronnie and Glen and Donnie were out in Demo Derby, Ronnie cried some more. Glen hug her and Ronnie said Peg was a sweetie wasn't she and Glen said yes she sure was.

Then she hug on me and I hug on her and that was one happy thing that come out of Peggy dying because I was in love with Ronnie Givens. I knew nothing could come of that because she was 2 years older and crushing big on Glen, but you can't help how you feel. Feelings are like breathing, they come in and go out.

Demo Derby was what we called the car junkyard behind the House of Everlasting Paint and next to Speck's Auto Parts. It was our special place. Being told to stay away from there made us want to go even more. Ronnie said it was like the Forbidden Fruit Tree Eve wasn't supposed to eat from in the Garden of Eden. Glen wave his hand at the rows and rows of junk cars with all those windshields reflecting and turning one sun into hundreds of suns and he said this is a whole motherfucking orchard, which made me and Ronnie laugh.

When we went there we would look for the best cars, like Cadillacs and Lincolns and Beemers, or once there was this old Mercedes limo with it's whole rear end gone. Glen always carry a broom and whoomp the seats a couple of times before we got in to scare away the mice if there were any. Once he scared out a big rat. Donnie was with us and he said there goes Mr Speck and we laughed fit to split. Anyway we would sit in those cars and pretend they were whole and we were going someplace.

We could get into the Demo Derby easy because there was a hole in the chainlink fence at the back corner of the playground and once Glen said who knows how many fucked-up foster kids have gone through this hole and where they are now. That made us all laugh but then Ronnie said probably noplace good. Donnie laughed at that too, but me and Glen didn't. I looked at him and he looked at me and we were both thinking 'noplace good'!

Sometimes Glen would sit behind the wheel and pretend to drive and Ronnie would sit in the shotgun seat. Sometimes it would be the other way around, and when Glen was in the shotgun seat he might yell stuff like WHOA RONNIE DON'T HIT THAT FUCKIN DOG and Ronnie would turn the wheel and pretend to swerve. Glen would flop over with his head in her lap and Ronnie would push him away and say buckle your seatbelt dumbass.

I would always sit in back, with Donnie if he came with us but mostly on my own. Which I preferred. A couple of times Glen brought a can of beer which we would pass around until it was gone. Then Ronnie would give us Certs to take the smell off our breath. Once Glen brought 3 cans and we got a little bit high and Ronnie swooped the wheel back and forth and Glen said don't get pulled over by 5–0, girlfriend. They laughed at that but I didn't because my mother really did get pulled over by 5–0 and it was no joke.

Donnie smoked. I don't know if the same person who got Glen his beers got Donnie his cigs, but he kept a pack of Marlboros behind a loose board under his bed. He mostly did it out back by the kitchen, but one day he pulled out his smokes when we were sitting in a big old Buick Estate wagon and pretending to drive to Vegas where we would play roulette and shoot craps. Ronnie said don't you dare light up out here where there's all these dry weeds and spilled oil. Donnie said what are you on the rag or something. Glen turned around and made a fist and said take that back unless you want to eat your front teeth. Later on, when I was in Fallujah, this one time I saw Sargent West shoot an RPG into an insurgent safe house in the part of town we called the Pizza Slice, and it blew sky-high because of all the ammo inside. Lucky we didn't all get killed because we weren't expecting it. That made me think of how Donnie also used to smoke sometimes in the supply shed, where the Specks stored all their paint. That was probably a lot more dangerous than out in the Demo Derby.

Donnie took it back but Ronnie punched Glen a good hard one on the shoulder. I don't need you to stand up for me Dutton, she said.

When Ronnie called you by your last name, you knew she was mad. She turned around to the back seat and said I don't need to be on the rag to worry about fire Wigmore because I got this. She held out her arm and showed the shiny burn scar there. We all seen that before. It went from halfway up her forearm just about all the way to her shoulder. Her parents got burnt up in a housefire, you see. Ronnie, she jump out of a 2nd story window just about in time with her arm burned and part of her leg on that side and her hair on fire. That's how she wound up in the Speck House of Everlasting Paint when her one relative, an aunt, said I am not taking her. The one time she visited Ronnie in the hospital she said I raised two of my own, both hellions, and that's enough. Ronnie said she couldn't blame her for that.

I know what fire can do, she said. If I ever forget I only need to look at this arm to remember. Donnie said he was sorry, and I did too. I didn't have anything to apologize for, I just felt bad because she got burned but also happy because it wasn't her face, which was pretty. Anyway we was all friends again after that, although Donnie Wigmore was never a friend to me like Ronnie and Glen were.

4

'We had some good times in the Demo Derby,' Billy says.

He's looking out the window at the courthouse again. August has given way to September, but still the heat shimmers. He can see waves of it coming off the street. It reminds him of the way the air used to shimmer above the big incinerator behind the House of Everlasting Paint's kitchen.

The Specks were the Stepeneks, Ronnie Givens was Robin Maguire, Glen Dutton was Gadsden Drake. Gadsden after the Gadsden Purchase, Billy figured. He had read a book while still in the Marines, *Slavery, Scandal, and Steel Rails*, which had covered the purchase of that arid chunk of land from Mexico. He'd read it in Fallujah, between Operation Vigilant Resolve in April of '04 and Phantom Fury in November. Gad said that before his mother died of lung cancer, she'd told him that his long-gone daddy had been a history teacher, so it made a degree of sense. *I might not be the only Gadsden in the world*, he said once while they were out in Demo Derby, pretending to go somewhere, *but I bet there's not more than a dozen. With it as a first name, that is.*

Billy has changed the names of his friends, but Demo Derby was always Demo Derby, and they really did have some good times there before Gad joined the army and Robin ran off to . . . what did she tell him?

'To seek my fortune in seven-league boots,' he says. That was it. Only her boots hadn't been of the seven-league variety, just scuffed suede with tired elastic sides.

I loved her among the wrecks, Billy thinks, and goes back to write another paragraph or two before calling it a day.

CHAPTER 8

1

Two bad things happen on Labor Day weekend. One is stupid and alarming, the other casts a light on the rather unpleasant person Billy never meant to become. Taken together, they make him realize that the sooner he gets out of Red Bluff, the better. I never should have taken a job with such a long lead time, he thinks when the weekend is over, but there was no way to know.

To know what? That the Ackermans and the others on Evergreen Street would take such a liking to him, for one thing. That he would take a liking to them, for another.

There's a parade downtown on the Saturday of the holiday weekend. Billy and the Ackermans go in a van Jamal borrowed from Excellent Tire. Shanice holds her mother's hand on one side and Billy's on the other as they work through the crowd and find a place on the corner of Holland and Main. When the parade actually comes, Jamal perches his daughter on his shoulders and Billy hoists Derek onto his. The kid feels good up there.

The parade is okay, even letting a kid who is later going to find out he was sitting on the shoulders of an assassin is okay . . . sort of. The stupid and alarming thing, the *lapse*, comes on Sunday. Next to the Midwood suburb of Red Bluff is the semi-rural town of Cody, and there a ratty little carnival set up shop during the last two weeks of summer, wanting a final shot of income before the kids go back to school.

Because Jamal still has the van and Sunday is nice, nothing will do but a trip to the carnival with the kids. Paul and Denise Ragland from down the street come along. The seven of them stroll the midway, eating sweet sausages and drinking sodas. Derek and Shanice ride the carousel, the Tooterville Trolley, and the Wild Cups. Mr and Mrs Ragland go off to play Bingo. Corrie Ackerman throws darts at water balloons and wins a spangly headband that says WORLD'S GREATEST MOM. Shanice tells her she looks cute, like a princess.

Jamal tries his hand at knocking over wooden milk bottles and wins nothing, but he bangs the Test Your Strength weight all the way to the top, ringing the bell. Corrie applauds and says, 'My hero.' For this feat of strength he gets a cardboard top hat with a paper flower stuck in the band. When he puts it on, Derek laughs so hard he has to cross his legs and then run for the nearest Porta-John so he won't wet his pants.

The kids ride a few more of the rides, but Derek won't go on the Wonky Caterpillar because he says it's for babies. Billy goes with Shan, and the fit is so tight that Jamal has to yank him out like a cork from a bottle when the ride is over. That makes them all laugh.

They are walking back to find the Raglands when they come to Dead-Eye Dick's Shooting Gallery. Half a dozen men are having a go with BB guns, shooting at five rows of targets moving in opposite directions, plus tin rabbits that pop up and down. Shanice points to a giant pink flamingo atop the wall of prizes and says, 'I'd love to have that for my bedroom. Could I buy it out of my allowance?'

Her father explains that it's not for sale, you have to win it.

'Then you win it, Dad!' she says.

The man running the shooting shy is wearing a striped shirt, a rakishly tilted straw boater, and a fake curly mustache. He looks like he belongs in a barber shop quartet. He hears Shanice and waves Jamal over. 'Make your little girl happy, mister, knock over three rabbits or four of the birds in the top row and she's going home with Freddy Flamingo.'

Jamal laughs and hands over five bucks for twenty shots. 'Prepare for disappointment, sweetie,' he says, 'but I might win you one of the smaller prizes.'

'You can do it, Dad,' Derek says stoutly.

Billy watches Jamal shoulder the rifle and knows he'll be lucky to wind up with one of the stuffed turtles that are the consolation prizes for two hits.

'Go for the birds,' Billy says. 'I know the rabbits are bigger, but you can only take snap shots when they pop up.'

'If you say so, Dave.'

Jamal pops off ten shots at the birds in the top row and hits exactly none. He lowers his sights, pops a couple of the lumbering tin moose in the bottom row, and accepts one of the turtles. Shanice eyes it without much enthusiasm but says thank you.

'What about you, hoss?' the barber shop quartet guy asks Billy. Most of his other customers have drifted away. 'Want to give it a try? Five bucks buys you twenty shots and you only need to hit four of the birdies to make your pretty little pal the happy owner of Frankie Flamingo.'

'I thought it was Freddy,' Billy says.

The concession guy smiles and tips his straw boater the other way. 'Frankie, Freddy, or Felicia, make a little girl happy.'

Shanice looks at him hopefully but says nothing. It's Derek who convinces him to do the stupid thing when he says, 'Mr Ragland says all these games are a cheat and nobody wins the big prizes.'

'Well, let's test that out,' Billy says, and lays down a five-spot. Mr Barber Shop Quartet loads a paper spill of BBs and hands Billy a rifle. A few other men and two women are currently at the shy's counter. Billy moves down partly to give them room, but also because he's noticed that the tin birds – plus the targets on the other four levels – slow down a bit before they turn out of sight. Probably the chain drives need to be oiled. Which is lazy. The shy's proprietor should pay for that.

'Are you going for the birds, Dave?' Derek asks. It's been quite awhile since they stopped calling him Mr Lockridge. 'Like you told Dad?'

'Absolutely,' Billy says. He takes a breath, lets it out, takes another and lets it out, takes a third and holds it. He makes no effort to use the little rifle's sight, which will be wildly out of true. He just snugs his head against the rifle's stock and fires quickly – *pop-pop-pop-pop-pop*. The first one misses; his next four knock over four tin birds. He knows he's doing a stupid thing and should quit, but he can't resist knocking over one of the rabbits when it rises from its hole.

The Ackermans applaud. So do the other shooters. And, to his credit, so does Mr Barber Shop Quartet before grabbing the pink flamingo and handing it over to Shanice, who hugs it and laughs.

'Wow, Dave!' Derek says. His eyes are shining. 'You rock!'

Now Jamal will ask me where I learned to shoot like that, Billy thinks. And then he thinks, How do you know you're an idiot? Because if everyone is looking at you, like they are now, you're an idiot.

It's actually Corrie who asks him, as they resume their stroll to the Bingo tent. Billy tells her it was in ROTC. That he was just naturally good at it. Telling her he killed at least twenty-five mujin in Fallujah, shooting from rooftops during the nine days of Operation Phantom Fury, would be a bad idea.

Oh, you think? he asks himself with a sarcasm that's very unlike him – in his thoughts or aloud.

The other thing – the character-check – happens on Monday, the actual holiday. Because he's a freelance writer working his own hours, he can take off when he wants and also work when others are enjoying a federally mandated day of rest. Gerard Tower is all but deserted. The lobby door is unlocked (such trusting souls in the border south), and no one is at the security stand. When the elevator passes the second floor, he hears no shouts as the denizens of Business Solutions psych each other up and no ringing phones. Apparently debtors are also getting the day off, and good for them.

Billy writes for two hours. He's almost up to Fallujah now, and wondering what he should say about it – a little, a lot, or maybe nothing at all. He shuts down and decides to put in an appearance at Pearson Street, re-establishing his existence with Beverly Jensen and her husband, who will no doubt be taking the day off. He drives over in his leased car, wig, mustache, and fake pregnancy belly in place. Don is mowing the lawn. Beverly is sitting on the stoop in unfortunate lime green shorts. The three of them bat the breeze a little, talking about how hot the summer has been, how glad they are it's over, and Dalton Smith's impending trip to Huntsville, Alabama, where he'll install a state-of-the-art computer system at the new Equity Insurance HQ. Shouldn't take too long. After that, he says, he hopes to be back for awhile.

'They sure do keep you on the hop,' Don says.

Billy agrees and then asks Beverly about her mother, who lives in

Missouri and has been poorly. Beverly sighs and says she's about the same. Billy says he hopes she'll be better soon and Beverly says she sure hopes so. As she's telling him this, Billy looks over her shoulder and sees Don slowly shaking his head. That he doesn't want his wife to know what he thinks about his mother-in-law's chances makes Billy like him. He thinks that Don Jensen would never tell his wife that her lime green shorts make her look fat.

He goes down to his pleasingly cool basement apartment. David Lockridge has his book and Dalton Smith has his laptops. Smith's work might not matter, but because it might matter a great deal somewhere down the line, he does it carefully (even though after working on Benjy Compson's story, it seems boring and mechanical). He finishes up with a quick review of the three screens. 10 FAMOUS CELEBS WHO ALMOST DIED; THESE 7 FOODS CAN SAVE YOUR LIFE; THE 10 MOST INTELLIGENT DOGS. Good clickbait. He posts them on facebook.com/ads. He really could do this for a living, but who would want to?

He shuts down, reads a little (he's currently on an Ian McEwan binge), then checks the fridge. The half-and-half is holding out, but the milk has gone spunky. He decides on a trip to the Zoney's Go-Mart to replace it. When he finds Don and Beverly still on the porch, now sharing a can of beer, he asks if they want anything.

Beverly asks if he'll see if they have any Pop Secret. 'We're going to watch something on Netflix tonight. You're welcome to join, if you want.'

He almost says yes, which is close to appalling. He tells them instead that he's going to make it an early night because he's driving to Alabama first thing in the morning.

He walks down to the sad little strip mall. Merton Richter's blue SUV with the scratched side is nowhere to be seen and the office is closed. So is the Nu You Tanning Salon, Hot Nails, and the Jolly Roger Tattoo Parlor. Beyond Hot Nails is an abandoned launderette and a Dollar Store with a sign in the window reading VISIT OUR NEW LOCATION IN PINE PLAZA. The Zoney's is at the very end. Billy gets his milk out of the cooler. There's no Pop Secret, but there's Act II, so he grabs a box of that. The clerk is a middle-aged woman with hennaed hair who looks like she's been down on her luck for awhile, maybe twenty years or so. She offers him a carry sack and Billy says no thank you. Zoney's uses plastic bags, which are bad for the environment.

On the way back, he passes two young men standing outside the abandoned launderette. One is white. The other is black. They are both wearing hoodies, the kind with kangaroo pockets in front. The pockets sag with the weight of what's inside them. Their heads are together as they murmur to each other. They give Billy identical glances of narrow assessment as he passes. He doesn't look at them directly but sees them perfectly well from the corner of his eye. When he doesn't slow, they go back to whispering together. They might as well be wearing placards around their necks that say WE PLAN TO CELEBRATE LABOR DAY BY ROBBING THE LOCAL ZONEY'S.

Billy walks out of the sad little strip mall and back to the street. He can feel them looking at him. There's no telepathy involved in that, unless it's the ordinary telepathy of someone who has survived a war zone with only a half-gone great toe and two Purple Hearts (long since discarded) to show for it.

He thinks of the woman who sold him his goods, a hard-luck mama from the look of her. Her luck isn't going to change on this holiday, either. Billy never considers going back to brace them, judging from their cranked-up expressions that would be a fine way to get killed, but he does consider calling 911. Only there are no pay phones in the vicinity, not anymore, and the phone he's carrying is Dalton Smith's. If he calls the cops, he'll burn it. Then the rest of his identity will catch fire, because what is it made of? Just paper.

He goes back to the apartment building instead and tells Beverly they didn't have any Pop Secret. She says Act II is fine. There's scant traffic on Pearson Street at the best of times, and it's even scanter on this holiday. He keeps his ear cocked for gunshots. He doesn't hear any. Which means nothing.

2

Billy downloaded an app for the local newspaper shortly after arriving in this city he can't wait to put behind him, and the following day he looks for a Zoney's robbery. He finds the story on the Close to Home page, just a snippet in a roundup of minor news items. It says two thieves armed with handguns made off with just under a hundred dollars (which would include my dollars and Beverly's, Billy thinks). The clerk, Wanda Stubbs, was alone in the store at the time. She was taken to Rockland Memorial, where she was treated for a head wound and released. So one of those scumbuckets hit her, probably with the butt of his gun, and probably because she wasn't emptying the register fast enough to suit him.

Billy can tell himself it could have been a lot worse (and does). He can tell himself the robbery would have gone down much as it did even if he had called 911 (and does). It doesn't change the fact that he feels like the priest and Levite who passed by on the other side of the road before a good Samaritan came along and saved the day.

Billy read the Bible from cover to cover while he was in the suck, every Marine got one on request. He has often regretted it and this is one of those times. The Bible has a story to puncture every equivocation and denial. The Bible – New Testament as well as Old – does not forgive.

3

Me and Mr Speck went to Chattanooga, which was where I joined the Marines. I thought I would have to go to a Marine base to sign up, but it was just an office in a shopping mall with a vacuum cleaner store on one side and a place to get your taxes written up on the other. There was a flag over the door with NOOGA STRONG printed on one of the stripes. In the window was a photo of a Marine that said THE FEW THE PROUD and DO YOU HAVE WHAT IT TAKES.

Mr Speck said are you sure you want to do this Benjy? and I said yes, but I wasn't. I don't think your sure of anything when you are seventeen and a half although you might pretend so as not to look like a total dub.

Anyway we went in and I talked to Staff Sergeant Walton Fleck. He asked me why I wanted to be a Marine and I said to serve my country, although the real reason was to get out of Speck House and out of Tennessee and start a life that didn't seem so sad. Glen and Ronnie were gone and Donnie was right when he said only the paint remains.

Next Staff Sergeant Fleck asked me if I thought I was tough enough to be a Marine and I said yes even though I wasn't sure of that either. Then he asked me if I thought I could kill a man in a combat situation and I said yes.

Mr Speck said can I talk to you for a minute, Sergeant, and Sergeant Fleck said he could. They sent me outside and Mr Speck sat down across the desk and started talking. I could have told the sergeant what happened with my mother's bad boyfriend, but I guess it was better to hear it from a 'responsible adult.' With all I have been through, back then and since, I have to wonder if there is such a thing.

After awhile they called me back inside and I wrote out what happened in the space marked Personal Information. Then I signed in four places, bearing down hard like the sarge told me to. When I was done he told me to be all present and accounted for on Monday. He said sometimes young men had to wait months for processing but I came at the right time. He said on Monday I would take my ASVAB test and my physical with the other 'new fish.' ASVAB is an aptitude test that helps them (the Marines) figure out how much you can do and how smart you are.

He asked if I had any tattoos and I said no. He asked if I wore eye-glasses some of the time and I said no. There were other things he said, like bring your Social Security card and if you wear an earring take it out. Then he said (I thought this was funny but kept a straight face) to be sure and wear undershorts. I said okay. He said if there's anything wrong with you that you didn't write down, you better tell me now and save yourself a trip. I said there wasn't.

Sergeant Fleck shook my hand and said if you've got a mind to hooraw you better hooraw this weekend because come Monday when you take that test you are going to be Mr Taking Care of Business. I said okay. He said never mind that, let me hear you say yes Staff Sergeant Fleck. So I said that and he shook my hand and said it was good to meet me. 'And you too sir,' he said to Mr Speck.

Going back, Mr Speck said he talked tough but I don't believe he ever killed anyone like you did, Benjy. He just didn't have that look about him.

By then Ronnie had been gone (in her 7-league boots) for 4 or 5 months, but before she went she let me make out with her in the Demo Derby. That was great, but when I wanted to go farther she laughed and push me away and said your too young but I wanted to give you something to remember me by. I said I would remember, and I do. I don't think you ever forget the first girl who gives you real kisses. She told me

4

Billy stops there, looking over the laptop and out the window. Robin told him that when she finally lit somewhere, she would write the Stepeneks so her friends from the House of Everlasting Paint could write back to her. She told Billy to do the same thing when he left.

'I'm guessing it won't be long before you're on your way,' she said that day as they sat in the smashed Mercedes. She had let him unbutton her shirt – that much she had allowed – and she was buttoning it up again as she spoke, hiding all that glory inside. 'But your idea about feeding yourself to the war machine . . . you need to re-think that, Billy. You're too young to die.' She kissed the tip of his nose. 'And too pretty.'

Billy starts to write this, only omitting that he had had the hardest, most painful, and most wonderful erection of his life during that all-too-short necking session, when his David Lockridge phone bings with a text. It's from Ken Hoff.

I have something for you. Probably it's time for you to take it.

And because he's probably right about that, Billy texts back **Okay.**

Hoff returns, **I'll come by your house.**

No, no, and no. Hoff at his house? Next door to the Ackermans, with whose kids Billy plays Monopoly on the weekends? Hoff will bring the rifle wrapped in a blanket, of course he will, as if anyone with half a brain and a single eye wouldn't know what was inside.

No, he texts. **Walmart. The Garden Center parking lot. 7:30 2nite.**

He waits, watching the dots as Hoff composes his reply. If he thinks the meeting place is negotiable, he's in for a surprise. But when the response comes back, it's brief: **OK.**

Billy shuts down his laptop without even finishing the last sentence. He's done for the day. Hoff poisoned the well, he thinks. Only he knows better. Hoff is just Hoff and can't help himself. The real poison is the gun. This thing is getting close.

5

At 7:25 Billy parks his David Lockridge Toyota in the Garden Center section of Walmart's giant parking lot. Five minutes later, at 7:30 on the dot, he gets a text.

Can't see you, too many cars, get out and give me a wave.

Billy gets out and waves, as if spotting a friend. A vintage cherry-red Mustang convertible – a Ken Hoff car if ever there was one – drives down one of the lanes and pulls in next to Billy's humbler vehicle. Hoff gets out. He looks better than the last time Billy saw him, and there's no alcohol on his breath. Which is a good thing, considering his cargo. He's wearing a polo shirt (with a logo on it, naturally), pressed chinos, and loafers. He's got a fresh haircut. Yet the essential Ken Hoff is still there, Billy thinks. The man's expensive cologne doesn't mask the smell of anxiety. He's not cut out for the heavy stuff, and bringing a gun to a hired killer is pretty damn heavy.

The rifle isn't wrapped in a blanket after all and Billy is willing to give him points for that. What Hoff hauls out of the Mustang's trunk is a tartan golf bag with four club heads sticking out. They gleam in the day's fading light.

Billy takes the bag and puts it in his own trunk. 'Anything else?'

Hoff shuffles his tasseled loafers. Then he says, 'Maybe, yeah. Can we talk for a minute?'

Because it might be prudent to know what's on Hoff's mind, Billy opens the passenger door of the Toyota and gestures for Hoff to get in. Hoff does. Billy goes around and sits behind the wheel.

'I just want to ask you to tell Nick that I'm okay. Can you do that?'

'Okay about what?'

'About everything. That.' He hoists a thumb behind him, meaning the golf bag in the trunk. 'Just make sure he knows I'm a stand-up guy.'

You've seen too many movies, Billy thinks.

'Tell him it's all good. Some of the people I owe money to are happy. Once you do your job, they'll all be happy. Tell him we all part friends and everybody goes their way. If I'm ever asked, I know nothing about nothing. You're just some writer I rented space to in one of my buildings.'

No, Billy thinks, you didn't rent space to me, you rented it to my agent, and George Russo is actually Giorgio Piglielli, aka Georgie Pigs, a known associate of Nikolai Majarian. You're the link and you know it, which is why we're having this conversation. You still think you can probably skate after the deal goes down. You have a right to think that, I guess, because skating is what you do. Trouble is, I don't think you could skate far after ten hours in an interrogation room with cops tag-teaming you. Maybe not even five, if they dangled a deal in front of you. I think you'd crack like an egg.

'Listen a minute.' Billy tries to sound kind, but hopefully in a straight-from-the-shoulder way: just two guys in a Toyota having a no-bullshit talk. Is it really the job of Billy Summers to keep this man-shaped annoyance in line? Wasn't he just supposed to be the mechanic, the one who can disappear like Houdini after the deal is done? That was always the deal before, but for two million . . .

Meanwhile, Hoff is looking at him eagerly. Needing that reassurance, that soothing syrup. It should have been George giving it, George is good at this stuff, but Georgie Pigs isn't here.

'I know this isn't your usual thing—'

'No! It's not!'

'—and I know you're nervous, but this isn't a movie star or a politician or the Pope of Rome we're talking about. This is a bad guy.'

Like you, Hoff's face says, and why not? That Billy won a pink flamingo for a cute little girl with ribbons in her hair doesn't matter. It's not what they call an extenuating circumstance.

Billy turns to face the other man squarely. 'Ken, I need to ask you something. Don't take it personally.'

'Okay, sure.'

'You're not wearing a wire or anything, are you?'

Hoff's shocked expression is all the answer Billy needs, and he cuts the man's confused gabble of protests short.

'Okay, fine, I believe you. I just had to ask. Now listen up. Nobody is going to set up a task force on this one. There's not going to be a big investigation. They'll ask you a few questions, they'll look for my agent and find out he's a ghost who fooled you with some good papers, and that will be it.' Balls it will. 'Do you know what they'll say? Not for the newspapers or TV, but among themselves?'

Ken Hoff shakes his head. His eyes never leave Billy's.

'They'll say it was a gang killing or a revenge thing and whoever did it saved the city the cost of a trial. They'll look for me, they won't find me, and the case will go in the open-unsolved file. They'll say good riddance to bad rubbish. Got it?'

'Well, when you put it that way . . .'

'I do. I do put it that way. Now go home. Let me take care of the rest.'

Ken Hoff suddenly moves toward him, and for a moment Billy thinks the man is going to slug him. Instead, Hoff gives him a hug. He looks better tonight, but his breath tells a different story. It doesn't stink of booze, but it stinks.

Billy suffers the hug, bad breath and all. He even hugs back a little. Then he tells Hoff to go on, for God's sake. Hoff gets out of the car, which is a relief (a *huge* relief), but then leans back in. He's smiling, and this smile looks real, as if it comes from the man inside. Apparently there is one.

'I know something about you.'

'What's that, Ken?'

'That text you sent me. You didn't write *garden center*, small *g* and small *c*. You wrote capital *G*, capital *C*. And just now you didn't say *between* themselves, you said *among*. You're not as dumb as you like to make out, are you?'

'I'm smart enough to know that you'll be fine if you keep it simple. You have no idea where I got the rifle and no clue what I was planning to do with it. End of story.'

'Okay. One other thing. A heads-up, like. You know Cody?'

Sure he does. The town where they went to the little shitpot of a carnival. At first Billy thinks Hoff's going to tell him that he was noticed there, because of his shooting. It's a paranoid thought, but before a job paranoia is just the way to be.

'Yes. It's not far from where I'm living.'

'Right. On the day this thing goes down, there's going to be a diversion in Cody.'

The only diversion Billy knows about are the flashpots, one in the alley behind the Sunspot Café, the other someplace close to the courthouse. Cody is *miles* from the courthouse, and Nick never would have told this moke about the flashpots, anyway.

'What kind of diversion?'

'A fire. Maybe a warehouse, there are a lot of them out that way. It'll happen before your guy . . . your target . . . gets to the courthouse. I don't know how long before. I just thought you'd like to know, in case you get a bulletin on your phone or computer or whatever.'

'Okay, thanks. And now it's time for you to beat it.'

Hoff gives him a thumbs-up and returns to his rich-boy car. Billy waits until he's gone and then heads back to Evergreen Street, driving carefully, aware that he's carrying a high-powered rifle in the trunk.

A warehouse fire in Cody? Really? Does Nick know? Billy doesn't think so, Nick would have told him about anything that might knock him off his rhythm. But *Hoff* knows. The question is whether or not he, Billy, tells Nick or Giorgio about this unexpected wrinkle. He thinks he'll keep it to himself. Ponder it in his heart, like Mary pondering the birth of baby Jesus.

He told Hoff to keep it simple. Except how simple can you keep it when, after three or four hours in that little interrogation room, the cops start asking you how you paid off all the creditors who were baying at your heels? By then they'd be calling him Ken instead of Mr Hoff, because that's what they do when they smell blood. Where did the money come from, Ken? Did a rich uncle die, Ken? There's still time to get out from under this. Is there something you'd like to tell us, Ken? *Ken?*

Billy finds himself wondering about the golf bag and the clubs that are inside it along with the gun. Is it Hoff's bag? If it is, has he thought to wipe the club heads, in case his fingerprints are on them? Better not to think about it. Hoff has made his bed.

But isn't that also true of Billy? He keeps thinking about Nick's escape plan. It's too good to be true, which is why Billy decided not to use it, and without letting Nick know. Because, hey – if you're going to get rid of the guy who brokered the deal and supplied the gun, why not get rid of the man who used the gun? Billy doesn't want to believe that Nick would do that, but he recognizes one incontrovertible fact: not wanting to believe stuff is how Ken Hoff got into a situation he's almost certainly never going to get out of.

And whose idea was a warehouse fire in Cody on the day of the assassination? Not Nick's, not Hoff's. So who?

It's all worrisome, but as he pulls into his driveway, he sees one thing that's good: his lawn looks terrific.

6

Through most of August Billy slept well. He drifted off to sleep thinking of nothing except what he would write the following day. There were only a few dreams of Fallujah and the houses with the green garbage bags fluttering from the palm trees in their courtyards. (How had they gotten up there? *Why* were they up there?) It was no longer his story, it was Benjy's story now. Those two things had begun to drift apart, and that was all right. He had once watched an interview with Tim O'Brien on YouTube, O'Brien talking about *The Things They Carried*. He said fiction wasn't the truth, it was the way to the truth, and Billy can now understand that. Especially when it came to writing about war, and wasn't that what his story was mostly about? Kissing in that ruined Mercedes with Robin Maguire, aka Ronnie Givens, had only been a truce. Most of the rest was fighting.

Tonight, with summer past and autumn on the come, he lies awake, troubled. Not by the gun in the golf bag. He's thinking about the job he's agreed to do with the gun. As a rule he never goes further than the two basics: taking the shot and getting out of Dodge. This time it's different, and not just because it's the last time he plans to take a life for pay. It's different because it has a smell, the way Hoff's breath had a smell when he snared Billy in that clumsy and unexpected embrace.

Somebody got in touch with Hoff, he thinks, then realizes that's not so. *Nobody* got in touch with Hoff, because Hoff is a nobody. He may *think* he's a somebody, with his real estate developments and his movie theaters and his red Mustang convertible, but he's just a big fish in a small pond, and not really that big, either. And this is a big deal. Lots of people are getting paid. Hoff himself, for one. Some of his debts are paid already, and he seems to think all of them will be cleared after Joel Allen goes down. Then there's Nick, and the troops Nick has fielded for this op. They are not squad strength, but almost. And maybe it is a squad. There could be more Nick hasn't told him about.

Nobody got in touch with Hoff. Somebody got in touch with *Nick*, and told him to bring Hoff on board. Billy remembers thinking, the first time he met with Hoff at the Sunspot Café, that Nick and Hoff must be affiliated. Now he's one step from being positive that's not true. Hoff wanted a casino license but didn't get one. Would that have happened if he were tight with Nick, who knows how to finagle such things? A casino was a license to print money, after all, and Hoff needs money.

Is the somebody behind this the same somebody who gave Hoff a heads-up about that putative warehouse fire in Cody? Maybe. Probably.

And consider Joel Allen, now incarcerated in Los Angeles. He's in protective custody, presumably as snug as a bug in a rug. He has a lawyer fighting extradition. Why, when Allen must know he'll be shipped back here eventually? It's not because the food is better in LA County. Is he buying time? Trying to make a deal with the somebody who set all this mishegas in motion, maybe using his lawyer as the go-between?

The somebody must know Allen will be sent back here eventually, and when he gets here, Billy Summers will put him down before he can trade what he knows. The somebody must know there's a risk Allen has an insurance policy – pictures, recordings, maybe a written confession to something (Billy can't imagine what). Only the somebody must feel the risk has to be taken, and that it's an acceptable one. The somebody could be right. Probably is. Guys like Allen don't take out insurance policies; guys like Allen feel invulnerable. He may be good at the paid hits, but the crimes that have gotten him in his current barrel of shit were crimes of impulse.

Besides, Mr Somebody may feel he has no choice. Whatever the secret is, it's bad. Allen can't be allowed to find himself standing trial in a death penalty state. Not with something hot he can trade.

Billy starts to drift into sleep. Before he goes under his last thought is of Monopoly, about how you try to stop the slide into bankruptcy by selling your properties one by one. It rarely works.

7

As he's getting into his car the next morning, Corrie Ackerman cuts across her lawn and his. She's got a brown bag, and something inside it smells delicious.

'I made cranberry muffins. Shan and Derek both get hot lunch at school, but they like a little something extra. I had these two left over. They're for you.'

'That's really nice,' he says, taking the bag. 'Are you sure you don't want to save at least one of them for Jamal when he comes home?'

'I did put one by for him, but I want you to eat both of these, you hear?'

'I think I can carry out that mission,' Billy says, smiling.

'You've lost weight.' She pauses. 'You're okay, right?'

Billy looks down at himself, surprised. Has he lost weight? It seems he has. A hole in his belt that used to go unused is now in service. Then he looks back at her. 'I'm fine, Corrie.'

'You look healthy enough, but that isn't what I meant. Or not all I meant. Is your book going okay?'

'Gangbusters.'

'Then maybe you just need to eat more. Healthy stuff. Greens and yellow vegetables, not just take-out pizza and Taco Bell. In the long run, bachelor food is worse than booze. You come to dinner tonight. Six o'clock. I'm making shepherd's pie. I load in the carrots and peas.'

'That sounds good,' Billy says. 'As long as I'm not putting you out.'

'You're not, and I need to say thank you. You have been very good to my kids. Shanice's crush on you got even bigger when you won her that flamingo.' She lowers her voice, as if imparting a secret. 'She changed its name from Frankie to Dave.'

As he drives toward downtown, Billy thinks of Shan changing her flamingo's name and feels happy because she did that and shame because the name is, after all, a lie.

8

That afternoon he leaves Gerard Tower and strolls a couple of blocks toward Pearson Street. He stops briefly to look into a narrow alley where there are a couple of dumpsters. He thinks it will do. He U-turns to the parking garage.

Later, on his way back to Midwood, he stops at the Walmart. Since coming to Midwood, he's always stopping here, it seems. As he stands in line at the checkout with his shopping basket, he thinks again about packing this job in. Just disappearing. Only Nick would come after him, and not just looking for a refund of the considerable sum that's already been paid on account. Billy is good at disappearing, but Nick wouldn't stop hunting. He'd start by sending a hardball to question Bucky Hanson, and that questioning would be rough, because Nick would figure if anyone had a line on Billy Summers's whereabouts, it would be his broker in New York. Bucky might end up without fingernails. He might end up dead. He deserves neither.

Nick would also send guys, probably Frankie Elvis and Paul Logan, to the neighborhood. The Fazios and the Raglands would be questioned. So would Jamal and Corrie. Maybe the kids? That was unlikely, grown men talking to kids attracted unwanted attention, but just the thought of those two questioning Shan and Derek makes him queasy.

There are two other things. He has never run out on a job, that's number one. Joel Allen has it coming, that's number two. He's a bad person.

'Sir? You're next.'

Billy comes back to the Walmart checkout lane. 'Sorry, I was woolgathering.'

'No worries, I do it all the time,' the checkout girl says.

He empties his carry-basket. There are bright green golf head covers with things like POW! and WHAM! printed on them, a gun cleaning kit, a set of wooden kitchen spoons, a big red bow with HAPPY BIRTHDAY on it in glitter, a light jacket with the Rolling Stones logo on the back, and a child's lunchbox. The checkout girl beeps the lunchbox last, then holds it up for a better look.

'Sailor Moon! Some little girl is going to love this!'

Shan Ackerman would love it, Billy thinks, but it's not for her. In a better world it would be.

9

That night, after dinner with the Ackermans (Corrie's shepherd's pie is delicious), he goes down to his basement rumpus room and slides the gun out of the golf bag. It's an M24, as specified, and it looks okay. He breaks it down, laying the pieces out on the Ping-Pong table, and cleans each one, over five dozen in all. He finds the telescopic sight in one of the golf bag's two zipper pockets. In the other pocket is a magazine, which holds five rounds of ammunition: Sierra MatchKing Hollow Point Boat Tails.

He will only need one.

10

When he enters the Gerard Tower lobby the next morning at quarter to ten, the strap of the golf bag is over his left shoulder. He has come in purposely late so that most of the business-gerbils will be running on their wheels. Irv Dean, the elderly security guy, looks up from his magazine – today it's *Motor Trend* – and gives him a grin. 'Goin on a golf adventure, Dave? Oh for the life of a writer!'

'Not me,' Billy says. 'I think it's the most boring game in the universe. These are for my agent.' He shifts the bag so Irv can see the big bow on the side, with its glittery letters. It's over the side pocket that now holds a loaded magazine instead of a couple of dozen tees.

'Well that's pretty damn nice of you. Expensive present!'

'He's done a lot for me.'

'Uh-huh, I hear that. Only Mr Russo doesn't exactly look cut out for the golf course.' Irv holds his hands out in front of him, indicating Giorgio's enormous front porch.

Billy is ready for this. 'Yeah, he'd probably drop dead of a heart attack by the third hole if he was walking, but he's got a custom golf cart. He told me he learned the game in college, when he was a lot slimmer. And you know what, the one time he talked me into going out on the course with him, he put a drive on that ball you wouldn't believe.'

Irv gets up and for a cold moment Billy thinks the old guy's cop reflexes have fired one last time and he means to inspect the clubs, which would save Joel Allen's life and maybe end Billy's. Instead he turns sideways and claps both hands to his own not inconsiderable hindquarters. 'This is where the power comes from.' Irv smacks himself again for emphasis. 'Right here. You ask any NFL lineman or home run hitter. Ask José Altuve. Five-six, but he's got an ass like a brick.'

'That must be it. George sure does have one hell of a boot.' Billy straightens one of the green club covers. 'Irv, you have a good day.'

'You do the same. Hey, when's his birthday? I'll get him a card or something.'

'Next week, but he may not be here. He's out on the west coast.'

'Palm trees and pretty girls by the swimming pool,' Irv says, sitting down. 'Nice. You staying late tonight?'

'Don't know. Have to see how it goes.'

'Oh for the life of a writer,' Irv says again, and opens his magazine.

11

In his office, Billy pulls off one of the green club covers – it's the one that says SLAM! Sticking out of the Remington's barrel is a curtain rod he hacksawed to the right length. Taped to the end of the rod is the bowl of a wooden serving spoon. With the green club cover snugged down over it, it looks enough like the head of a golf club to be one. He takes out the stock, barrel, and bolt of the 700. Then he pushes two of the clubs aside so he can remove the lunchbox, which is wrapped in a sweater to muffle any clinks and clunks. Inside are the smaller components – bolt plug, firing pin, ejector pin, floor-plate latch, all the rest. He puts the disassembled gun, plus the five-shot magazine, the Leupold scope, and a glass cutter, in the overhead cabinet between the office and the little kitchenette. He locks it and puts the key in his pocket.

He doesn't even try to write. Writing is done until this shit-show has been put to bed. He pushes aside the MacBook on which he's writing his story and opens his own. He types in the password, just a jumble of numbers and letters he's memorized (there's no giveaway sticky note hidden somewhere with the password written on it), and opens a file titled THE GAY BLADE. Said gay blade being Colin White of Business Solutions, of course. Listed there are ten flamboyant outfits Billy has observed Colin wearing to work.

There's no way of predicting which one Colin will be wearing on the day Joel Allen is delivered to the courthouse, and Billy has decided it doesn't matter. Not just because people believe their eyes even when their eyes are telling lies, but because it has to be the parachute pants. Sometimes Colin tops them with a wide-shouldered flower power shirt, sometimes with a tee that says QUEERS FOR TRUMP, sometimes with one of his many band shirts. It doesn't matter because the Colin people see will be wearing a jacket on top with the Rolling Stones lips logo on the back. He's never seen Colin in a jacket of any kind, not during the hot summer just past, but such a garment is certainly in his wheelhouse. And if the day of the shooting is hot, as fall weather tends to be here, the jacket will still be all right. It's a fashion statement.

When Nick's men in the fake DPW truck see Billy running past without stopping to get in, they won't think *Billy Summers is taking off*; they'll get a glimpse of the parachute pants and the shoulder-length black hair and think *There goes that fag in one of his flashy outfits, running for the hills*.

He hopes.

Still using his own laptop, Billy goes shopping on Amazon, specifying next-day delivery.

CHAPTER 9

1

A week passes. He keeps expecting to hear from Giorgio, but there's nothing. On Friday evening he invites his neighbors over for a backyard barbecue, and for awhile afterward he, Jamal, and Paul Ragland play three-way pass in Billy's backyard while the kids play tag, ducking under Paul and Jamal's throws, which are sizzling. Even though the glove Jamal found for Billy is a well-padded catcher's mitt, his hand is still stinging as he does up the few dishes. That's when his phone rings.

He goes to the David Lockridge one first, but it's not that one. Then to the Billy Summers phone, but it's not that one, either. Which leaves the one he didn't expect to ring at all. It has to be Bucky in New York, because he's the only one who has the Dalton Smith number. But as he picks it up off the Welsh dresser in the living room, he realizes that's not true. It was on the form he filled out for Merton Richter, the real estate agent, and he also gave it to Beverly Jensen, his upstairs neighbor.

'Hello?'

'Hi, neighbor.' It's not Beverly; it's her husband. 'How's Alabama?'

For a moment Billy has no idea what Jensen is talking about. He's frozen.

'Dalton? Did I lose you?'

It clicks into place. He's supposed to be in Huntsville, installing a computer system for Equity Insurance. 'No, I'm here. How is it? Hot, that's how it is.'

'Weather okay otherwise?'

Billy has no clue how the weather is in Huntsville, probably pretty much like here but who knows. If he'd had the slightest fucking idea Don Jensen might call, he'd have checked. 'Nothing special,' he says. 'What can I do for you?'

Well, we were wondering just who the hell you really are, he imagines Don saying. That fake belly might fool most people, but my wife spotted it from the get-go.

'I tell you what,' Don says, 'Bev's mother took a turn for the worse yesterday and died this afternoon.'

'Oh. I'm very sorry to hear that.' Billy actually is sorry. Maybe not 'very,' but at least 'sort of.' Beverly is no Corrie Ackerman, but she's okay.

'Yeah, Bev's pretty broken up about it. She's in the bedroom, packin and bawlin, bawlin and packin. We're flyin to St Louis tomorrow, then gotta rent a car at the airport and drive to this little shitsplat town called Diggins. It's not just the buryin, there's a bunch of affairs that need windin up. Gonna be there awhile.' Don sighs. 'I hate the expense, but some lawyer of hers gonna read the will on Tuesday, and I think there might be some money in it for us. That's how he sounds, but you know lawyers.'

'Cagey,' Billy says.

'That's right, cagey. Still, Annette was what you call a savin soul, and Bev's her only kid.'

'Ah.'

'We're apt to be there awhile is why I'm callin. Bev wanted to know if it'd be okay for me to put a key to our place under your door. When you get back from Bama, it'd be a favor if you'd check our fridge and water Bev's spider plant and her Busy Lizzie. Crazy about those things, even gives em names, do you believe it? If you're gonna be gone longer than a week, that's a head-scratcher. We don't know many people around here.'

Because there *aren't* many people around there, Billy thinks. He also thinks this is good. Better than good, a fantastic stroke of luck. He'll have the Pearson Street house entirely to himself, unless the Jensens come back before Joel Allen leaves California.

'If you can't do it . . .'

'I can and I'll be happy to. How long do you think you'll be gone?'

'No way of telling. At least a week, maybe two. I got a leave of absence from work. Without pay, accourse, but if there's money in it . . .'

'Right. I get it.' Better and better. 'And no problem on the plants. I expect to be back soon, and for quite awhile this time.'

'That's great. Bev told me to tell you that you can have anything out of the fridge you want. Better it gets used up than have it spoil, she says. Course, the milk may be gone, anyway.'

'Yes,' Billy says. 'I ran into that problem myself. You have a safe trip.'

'Thanks, Dalton.'

'You bet,' Billy says.

2

That night Billy lies in bed with his hands under the pillow, looking up at the misty oblong of yellowish light on the ceiling, thrown by the streetlight in front of the Fazios'. He keeps forgetting to get curtains. He thinks about doing it and then it slips his mind. Maybe now, with nothing to do but wait, he'll remember.

He hopes the waiting period will be short, not just because Don and Beverly being gone is so convenient but because the hours spent in Gerard Tower are going to hang heavy without Benjy's story to work on. Fallujah comes next, and Billy knows some of what he wants to say, some of the brilliant details he wants to capture. Those shredded garbage bags caught in the palm trees, blowing in the hot wind like flags. How the muj showed up in taxis to battle the Marines, piling out of them like clowns out of the little car at the circus. Only the circus clowns don't pile out guns up. How boys in 50 Cent and Snoop Dogg T-shirts served as ammo runners, darting through the rubble in their battered Nikes or Chuck Taylors. How a three-legged dog with half a human hand in its mouth went trotting through Jolan Park. Billy can see the white dust on that dog's paws so clearly.

The pieces are there, but no way he can put them together until this job is done. According to William Wordsworth, the best writing is about strong emotion recalled in tranquility. Billy has lost his tranquility.

Finally he slips into sleep, but the soft ding-dong of an arriving text awakens him at some dark hour. Ordinarily he might have slept through it, but now all his sleep is thin, with dreams that are mere wisps. It was always that way in the suck.

Three phones are lined up and charging on his nightstand: Billy's, Dave's, and Dalton's. It's the screen of his own that's lit up.

Db1Dom: Call me. There follows a number with a Las Vegas area code. **Db1Dom** is the Double Domino, Nick's casino hotel. In Billy's time-zone it's three o'clock. In Vegas, Nick is probably just preparing to turn in.

Billy calls. Nick answers and asks how Billy's doing. Billy says he's doing fine except for it being three o'clock in the morning.

Nick laughs cheerfully. 'Best time to call, folks are always home. I just got word that our friend will probably be coming your way next Wednesday. It would have been Monday, but he's got a little case of food poisoning, probably self-administered. His ride will take him to his hotel, where he'll spend the night. You follow?'

Billy follows. Allen's hotel will be the county jail.

'The next morning he'll be over your way for the A. You know what I mean?'

'Yes.' The arraignment.

'Did our redhaired friend get you what you wanted?'

'Yes.'

'It's okay?'

'Yes.'

'Good. Your agent will send you one more text, then you're on standby. After, you leave on your vacation. Got all that?'

'Yes,' Billy says.

'You'll want to pay the bill on this phone and any other you've been using. Follow me?'

'Yes,' Billy says. The way Nick keeps asking him if he's getting it is tiresome, but also good. Nick still thinks he's talking to a fellow whose brains are permanently on the dimmer switch. Destroy the Billy Summers phone, destroy the David Lockridge phone, destroy any burner phones he may have picked up along the way, roger that. The phone he'll keep is the one Nick doesn't know about.

'We'll talk down the line,' Nick says. 'Keep your phone for awhile if you want, but trash the text I sent you.' And he's gone.

Billy deletes the text, lies down, and is asleep in less than a minute.

3

It's a cool weekend. Fall, it seems, is finally arriving. Billy can see the first few dashes of color in the trees on Evergreen Street. There's Monopoly on Sunday afternoon, Billy playing against three kids with half a dozen more kibitzing around the board. The dice are usually his friend but not today. He rolls three doubles and winds up in jail on three consecutive turns, a statistical freak almost up there with picking all six Mega Millions numbers. He hangs in long enough for two of his opponents to go broke and then loses to Derek Ackerman. When the bank has taken his last mortgaged property, the kids all crow and pig-pile him, chanting *loser-loser-vodka-boozer*. Corrie comes downstairs to see what all the ruckus is about and yells through her laughter to get off him, let the man breathe.

'You got smoked!' Danny Fazio shouts gleefully. 'You got smoked by a *kid*!'

'I did,' Billy says, laughing himself. 'If I'd gotten all of the railroads instead of going to jail—'

Shan's friend Becky blows a raspberry at him and they all laugh some more. Then they go upstairs and eat pie in the living room, where Jamal is watching a baseball playoff game. Shan sits next to Billy on the couch, holding her flamingo in her lap. In the seventh inning, she goes to sleep with her head resting on Billy's arm. Corrie asks him to stay for supper, but Billy declines, saying he might catch an early movie. He's been hankering to see *Deadly Express*.

'I saw the previews for that one,' Derek says. 'It looks scary.'

'I eat lots of popcorn,' Billy says. 'It keeps me from being scared.'

Billy doesn't go to the movie but listens to a podcast review of it as he drives across town to the parking garage where his Ford Fusion awaits. Always safe, never sorry. He drives the Fusion to 658 Pearson Street and stows his Dalton Smith gear in the closet. Then he goes upstairs and waters Bev Jensen's spider plant and Busy Lizzie. The spider plant is going great guns, but the Busy Lizzie looks pretty wilted.

'There you go, Daphne,' Billy says. The little sign in front of the Busy Lizzie so identifies her. The spider plant is named – who knows why – Walter.

Billy locks up and leaves the house, wearing a gimme cap to cover his non-blond hair. Also sunglasses, although it's now almost dark. He returns the Fusion, drives his Toyota back to Midwood, watches some TV, goes to bed. He falls asleep almost immediately.

4

On Monday afternoon there's a knock on his door. Billy opens it with a sinking heart, expecting Ken Hoff, but it's not Hoff. It's Phyllis Stanhope. She's smiling, but her eyes are red and puffy.

'Take a girl to dinner?' Just like that. 'My boyfriend dumped me, and I need some cheering up.' She pauses, then adds: 'My treat.'

'No need of that,' Billy says. He has an idea where this might lead, and it's maybe not such a good idea, but he doesn't care. 'Happy to pick up the tab, and if you really don't like that, we can go dutch again.'

But they don't go dutch. Billy pays. He thinks she may have decided to celebrate the end of her affair by sleeping with him, and the three screwdrivers she downs – two before dinner and one during – only cement the idea. Billy offers her the wine list but she waves it away.

'Never mix, never worry,' she says. 'That's from—'

'*Who's Afraid of Virginia Woolf?*' Billy finishes, and she laughs.

She doesn't eat much of her dinner, says it was kind of a nasty breakup scene, part one in person and part two on the phone, and she's just not that hungry. What she really wants are those drinks. They may not be going dutch, but she needs some dutch courage for what comes next, which now seems not just possible but inevitable. And he wants it. It's been a long time since he's been with a woman. As Billy pays the check with one of his David Lockridge credit cards, he thinks of the kids piling on him and chanting *loser-loser-vodka-boozer*. And here, only a day later, is that very vodka boozer, a loser in love.

'Let's go to your place. I don't want to go to mine and look at his aftershave on the bathroom shelf.'

Well, Billy thinks, you can look at the aftershave on mine. You can even use my toothbrush.

When they get to the yellow house on Evergreen Street, she takes an appraising look around, compliments him on the *Doctor Zhivago* poster he bought in a downtown junkshop, and asks him if he has anything to drink. Billy has a six in the fridge. He asks her if she wants a glass, and Phil says she'll drink it right out of the can. He brings two into the living room.

'I thought you were off alcohol for the duration.'

He shrugs. 'Promises were made to be broken. Besides, I'm off the clock.'

They have barely opened them when she says 'It's hot in here' and starts unbuttoning her blouse. The beers will be open on the coffee table in the morning, flat and barely tasted.

The sex is good, at least for Billy. He thinks for her, too, but with women it's hard to tell. Sometimes they'd just like you to stop trying so hard and get off so they can go to sleep, but if she's faking it's a good fake. There comes a point, just before he can hold back no longer, when she makes an *mmmm* sound against his shoulder and digs in with her nails almost hard enough to bring blood.

When he rolls over to his side of the bed, she gives him a pat on the shoulder as if to say *good boy*. 'Please don't tell me that was a mercy fuck.'

'It wasn't, believe me,' he says. 'I won't ask you if it was a revenge fuck.'

She laughs. 'You better not.' Then she rolls over on her side, away from him. Five minutes later she's snoring.

Billy lies awake for awhile, not because she's snoring – they're ladylike snores, almost like purring – but because his mind won't turn off. He thinks her turning up the way she did and then coming home with him is like something out of a Zola novel, where every character has to be fully used and make one final appearance, like a curtain call. He hopes his own story isn't over, but guesses this part of it almost is. If he finishes his job and collects his pay, some new life (maybe as Dalton Smith, maybe as someone else) will begin. Maybe a better life.

He has realized for some time, probably since he started writing Benjy's story, that he can no longer live this one without choking. The idea – no, the *conceit* – that he only kills bad people will stretch just so far. There are good people sleeping in the houses on this very street. He's not going to kill any of them, but he supposes he'll kill something inside them when they find out why he was really here.

Is that too poetic? Too romantic? Billy thinks not. A stranger came, and he turned into a neighbor, but here's the punchline, he turned out to be a stranger all along.

Around three o'clock Billy awakes to hear Phil puking in the bathroom. The toilet flushes. Water runs. She comes back to bed. She cries a little. Billy pretends to be asleep. The crying stops. The snores recommence. Billy sleeps and dreams of garbage bags fluttering in palm trees.

5

He awakes shortly after six to the smell of coffee. Phil is in the kitchen, barefoot and wearing one of his button-up shirts.

'How did you sleep?' Billy asks.

'Fine. You?'

'Terrific. And that coffee smells really good.'

'I stole some of your aspirin. I guess I had one drink too many last night.' She gives him a look that's amusement and embarrassment, half and half.

'As long as you didn't steal any of my aftershave.' That makes her laugh. One-night hookups can lead to some grisly mornings after, he's suffered through a couple of those, but Billy thinks this one may be okay, and that's good. Phil is a nice woman.

When he offers to scramble some eggs she makes a face and shakes her head. He does get her to eat some unbuttered toast. After, he gives the bedroom and bathroom over to her so she can shower and dress in privacy. When she emerges, she looks fine. Her blouse is a little wrinkled, but otherwise she's good to go. She'll have a tale to tell later on, Billy thinks. My Night with a Killer. If she chooses to tell it, that is. She may not.

'Will you drive me home, Dave? I want to change my clothes.'

'Happy to.'

She pauses at the door and puts a hand on his arm. 'It wasn't revenge sex.'

'No?'

'Sometimes a girl just wants to be wanted. And you wanted me . . . didn't you?'

'Yes.'

She gives a brisk nod that says that's settled. 'And I wanted you. But

I think it's going to be the only time. Never say never, but that's my feeling.'

Billy, who knows it's going to be the only time, nods.

'Friends?' Phil asks.

He gives her a hug and a kiss on the cheek. 'To the end.'

It's still early, but Evergreen Street gets up early. Across the street, Diane Fazio is sitting in a rocker on her front porch. She's bundled up in a wooly pink housecoat, with a cup of coffee in one hand. Billy opens the passenger door of his Toyota for Phil. As he walks around the back to the driver's side, Diane gives him a neighborly thumbs-up.

Billy has to smile.

6

When the lunch trucks arrive, Billy goes down for a taco and a Coke. Jim Albright, John Colton, and Harry Stone – The Young Lawyers, like characters in a TV show or a Grisham novel – wave him over and ask him to sit with them, but Billy says he wants to eat at his desk and do a little more work.

Jim raises a finger and recites, 'No man on his deathbed ever said "I wish I had spent more time in the office." Oscar Wilde, just before he passed into the great beyond.'

He could tell Jim that Oscar Wilde's last words are actually reputed to have been *Either that wallpaper goes or I do*, but he just smiles.

The truth is he doesn't want to spend time with these guys now that the job is almost here, not because he doesn't like them but because he does. And Phil seems to have taken the day off. He hopes she'll take Wednesday and Thursday off too, but that's probably too much to hope for.

His Dalton phone starts to ring just as he re-enters his office. It's Don Jensen.

'Dollen my man! You back?'

'I am.'

'How you doon? How's Daffy and Woller?'

'All three of us are fine. How are you?' In the bag is how Don is from the sound of his voice, even though it's just a little past noon.

'Man, I've never been better.' Better comes out *bear*. 'Bevvie, too. Say hi, Bevvie!'

Distant but perfectly audible because she's yelling, Beverly says, 'Hi there, honey-bunny!' And shrieks with laughter. So she's been drinking, too. Not exactly in mourning, either of them.

'Bevvie says hi,' Don says.

'Yes, I heard her.'

'Dollen . . . buddy . . .' He drops his voice. 'We're rich.'

'Seriously?'

'Lawyer read the will this morning and Bevvie's mom left her everything. Stocks and bank accounts. Almost *two hunnert thousand dollars!*'

In the background Bevvie cheers, and Billy can't help but smile. She may be in mourning again when she sobers up, but right now these two apartment dwellers in one of the city's not-very-desirable neighborhoods are celebrating, and Billy can't blame them.

'That's great, Don. Really great.'

'How long you gonna be home this time? That's why I'm callin, Dollen.'

'Probably quite awhile. I've got a new contract for—'

Don doesn't wait for him to finish. 'Good, that's good. You keep waterin Daffy an Woller, because . . . you know what?'

'What?'

'Guess!'

'Can't guess.'

'Gotta, my computer compadre, gotta!'

'You're going to Disneyland.'

Don laughs so loudly that Billy pulls the phone away from his ear with a little wince, but he's also still smiling. A good thing has happened to decent people, and no matter what his own situation happens to be, he has to like it. He wonders if Zola ever wrote a development similar to this. Probably not, but Dickens, now—

'Close, Dollen, close. *We're goin on a cruise!*'

In the background, Beverly whoops.

'You gonna be around for a month? Maybe even six weeks? Because—'

At this point, Beverly snatches the phone, and Billy once more has to hold it a couple of inches away to spare his overtaxed eardrum. 'If you're not, just let em die! I can afford new ones! A whole greenhouse!'

Billy has time to offer her both condolences and congratulations, then it's Don again.

'And when we get back, we're movin. No more scenic view of that fuckin vacant lot across the street. Not that I'm dissin your apartment, Doll. Iss the one Bevvie always wanted.'

Bev cries, 'Not anymore!'

Billy says, 'I'll water Daphne and Walter, don't worry about that.'

'We'll pay you for it, Mr Computer Geek Plant Sitter! We can afford to!'

'No need. You're good neighbors.'

'You too, Dollen, you too. Know what we're drinkin?'

'Maybe Champagne?'

Billy once more has to hold the phone away from his ear. 'You hit the goddam nail on the goddam head!'

'Don't overdo it,' Billy says. 'And give Beverly my best, you hear? Sorry for her loss but glad for your gain.'

'I will, for sure. Thanks a million, buddy.' He pauses, and when he speaks again he sounds almost sober. Awed. '*Two hundred thousand dollars.* Do you believe it?'

'Yes,' Billy says. He ends the call and sits back in his office chair. He's getting a lot more than two hundred K, but he thinks Don and Beverly Jensen are really the rich ones. Yes sir, really the rich ones. Sentimental but true.

7

The next morning, as he's turning into the parking garage around the corner from Gerard Tower, his David Lockridge phone chimes with a text. He waits until he's parked on the fourth level, then reads it.

GRusso: The check is on the way.

Billy doubts it, it's only six-thirty on the west coast, but he understands that the check *will* be on the way soon enough. Allen is coming, probably on a commercial flight handcuffed to one of this city's detectives or a state cop, and that's good. Time to get the show on the road. Overtime.

He opens the back door of his car and takes a paper grocery bag from the seat. Crammed inside are the parachute pants and the silk jacket with the Rolling Stones lips on the back. This pair isn't gold, although the gold ones are Colin White's favorites. After some interior debate, Billy has decided that would be a little *too* flashy. The ones he ordered from Amazon are black with gold sparkles. He's sure Colin would adore them.

Billy has a story ready in case – unlikely but always possible – Irv asks him why he's coming to work with a grocery bag, but Irv is talking to several fine-looking ladies from Business Solutions and just gives him a distracted wave as Billy signs in and heads for the elevators.

In his office he opens the bag, rummages beneath the clothes, and takes out a sign he bought at Staples from a rack of them. It says SORRY CLOSED. A pair of sad cartoon faces flank the message. There's white space for a brief explanation beneath. Billy uses a Sharpie to print NO WATER USE 4 OR 6. He waves the sign in the air a few times, not wanting his message to smudge, then places it back in the bag. He adds the long-haired black wig, then puts the bag in the closet.

At his desk, he transfers the Benjy story to a thumb drive. Once that's done, he uses a suicide program to destroy everything on the MacBook Pro. It stays here. His fingerprints are all over it and everything else in this place, after all this time he'd miss some no matter how much he wiped, but that's okay. Once he takes the shot and sees Joel Allen lying dead on the courthouse steps, Billy Summers will cease to exist. As for his personal lappie . . . he could kill that one as well, leave it, and use one of the cheap new AllTechs at Pearson Street, but he doesn't want to. This one is coming along for the ride.

8

An hour later there's a knock on the outer door. He answers it, once more expecting Ken Hoff, maybe with a case of cold feet, and once again he's wrong. This time it's Dana Edison, one of the imported hard boys from Nick's Vegas team. He's not dressed in his DPW coverall today. Today he's Mr Nondescript in dark slacks and a gray sportcoat. He's a little man, bespectacled, and at first glance you might think he belongs in Phil Stanhope's accounting office at the other end of the hall. Take a closer look and you might – especially if you were a Marine – see something different.

'Hey there, fella.' Edison's voice is low and polite. 'Nick wanted me to have a word with you. Okay if I step in?'

Billy stands aside. Dana Edison breezes through the outer office in his neat brown loafers and into the small conference room that serves as Billy's writing studio. Not to mention his shooter's overlook. Edison moves with lithe confidence. He glances briefly at the table, where Billy's personal lappie is open with a half-played cribbage game in progress, then looks out the window. Tracing the line of fire Billy has traced himself many times over the summer. Only now summer is over and there's a snap in the air.

It's good that Edison gives him a little time, because here Billy has gotten used to being a pretty smart guy named David Lockridge and might have slipped. But when Edison turns back to him, Billy has his *dumb self* face on: eyes wide, mouth slightly ajar. Not enough to make him look like the village idiot, just enough so he looks like a man who might believe Zola is one of Superman's archenemies.

'You're Dana, right? I met you at Nick's.'

He nods. 'Also seen me and Reggie tooling around in that little city truck, yeah?'

'Yeah.'

'Nick wants to know if you're all ready for tomorrow.'

'Sure.'

'Where's the gun?'

'Well . . .'

Dana grins, showing teeth as small and neat as the rest of him. 'Never mind. But it's close, right?'

'You bet.'

'Got a glass cutter for that window?'

A stupid question, but that's okay. He's supposed to be a stupid man. 'Sure.'

'You don't want to use it today. The sun shines on this side of the building all afternoon and someone might see the hole.'

'I know that.'

'Yeah, I suppose you would. Nick says you were a sniper. Got some kills in Fallujah, yeah? How was that?'

'Good.' It wasn't. Neither is this conversation. Having Edison in this room is like having let in a small and very compact storm cloud.

'Nick wanted me to make sure you're straight on the plan.'

'I'm straight.'

Edison stays on message. 'You take the shot. Five seconds later, no more than ten, there's going to be a hell of a big bang from behind that café over there.'

'A flashpot.'

'A flashpot, right. That's Frankie's responsibility. Five seconds after that, no more than ten, one's going to go off behind the news and stationery shop on the corner. That's Paulie Logan. People are going to start beating feet. You'll join them, just one more office guy wanting a quick look at what happened and then wanting to get the hell out. You hook around the corner. The DPW truck will be there. Reggie will have the back doors open. I'll be behind the wheel. In you go and change into a coverall as fast as you can. Clear?'

It always was. Billy doesn't need a last-minute tutorial. 'Yes. Just one thing, Dana.'

'What might that be?'

'I've got stuff to do to get ready, and once I start doing it, there's no going back. Are you sure it's gonna be tomorrow?'

Dana starts to speak, to say of course, but Billy shakes his head.

'Think before you say anything. Think hard, because if something changes, this deal goes south, I'm gone and Joel Allen is still using his lungs. So . . . are you *sure?*'

Dana Edison looks closely at Billy, perhaps re-evaluating. Then he smiles. 'As sure as I am that the sun rises in the east. Anything else?'

'No.'

'Okay.' Edison heads back to the outer office, walking that springy walk. His manbun looks like a dark red doorknob. At the door, he turns and regards Billy with eyes that are bright and blue and expressionless. He says, 'Don't miss.' Then he's gone.

Billy goes back into his writing room and stares at the frozen cribbage game. He's thinking that Dana Edison said nothing about a possible warehouse fire in Cody, and he certainly would have if he knew about it. He's also thinking about the possibility that if he went with Nick's plan, he really might end up in a ditch on a country road with a hole in his forehead. If that were to happen, he guesses Edison would be the one to put it there. And who would end up with the owing million-five? Nick, of course. Billy would like to believe that's paranoid, but after Edison's visit it seems a little more likely. Surely the thought has at least crossed Nick's mind, despite their long association. Pinch off Ken Hoff, pinch off Billy Summers, and everyone walks away clean.

Billy closes down his computer. Writing his story has never felt so far away. Hell, today he can't even play cribbage.

9

On his way home he stops at Ace Hardware and buys the last thing he needs: a Yale padlock. When he arrives at his house – his last night here – there's a piece of paper on the top step of the porch, held down with a rock. He slides his laptop case off his shoulder, picks up the paper, sits, studies it, and thinks this is a curtain call he could have done without. It's a crayon drawing, obviously made by a child, but one who shows at least some talent. How much is impossible to tell, because the artist is currently only eight years old. At the bottom she has signed her name: Shanice Anya Ackerman. At the top, in capital letters: FOR DAVE!

The picture is of a smiling little girl with dark brown skin and bright red ribbons decorating her cornrows. In her arms is a pink flamingo, from whose head floats a series of hearts. Billy looks at it for a long time, then folds it and puts it in his back pocket. He has gotten himself into a box he never dreamed of. He would give anything, two-million-dollar payout included, to be able to turn the calendar back three months, to that hotel lobby where he sat reading *Archie's Pals 'n' Gals* and waiting for his ride. And when Frankie Elvis and Paul Logan came in, he would tell them to make his apologies to Nick, he's changed his mind. But there's no going back now, only forward, and when he thinks of Dana Edison perhaps stopping by this neighborhood to ask questions, maybe even putting those small neat hands of his on Shanice's shoulders, Billy presses his lips together so tightly that they disappear. He is in a box and all he can do is shoot his way out.

CHAPTER 10

1

Thursday morning. The day of. Billy gets up at five. He eats toast with a glass of water to wash it down. No coffee. No caffeine of any kind until the job is done. When he shoulders the 700 and looks through the Leupold scope, he wants his hands perfectly steady.

He puts his toast plate and the empty water glass in the sink. Lined up on the table are his four cell phones. He takes the SIM cards from three of them – the Billy-phone, the Dave-phone, the burner – and microwaves the cards for two minutes. He dons an oven glove, picks out the charred remains, and grinds them up in the garbage disposal. The three SIMless phones go in a paper bag. He adds the Dalton Smith phone, the Yale lock, and the plain gray gimme cap he wore to Pearson Street when he dropped off the Dalton Smith gear and watered Beverly's plants.

He stands in the doorway for a few moments, laptop slung over one shoulder, looking around. This isn't home, he hasn't really had a place he could call home since Officer F.W.S. Malkin drove him away from 19 Skyline Drive in the Hillview Trailer Park (and that wasn't much of one, especially after Bob Raines killed his sister), but he guesses this place has been close.

'Well okay then,' Billy says, and goes out. He doesn't bother to lock the door. No need for the cops to break it down. Bad enough that they'll assuredly trample all over the lawn he worked so hard to bring back.

2

Billy doesn't drive to the parking garage. The parking garage is done. At five to six he parks on Main Street a few blocks from the Gerard Tower. Plenty of curbside spaces at this hour and the sidewalk is deserted. His laptop is over his shoulder. The paper bag is in his hand. He leaves the keys in the Toyota's cup holder. Maybe somebody will steal it, although that's not actually necessary. Neither is dropping the three dead cell phones through three different sewer grates, always checking his surroundings to be sure he's not observed. It's what they called 'policing up the area' in the Marines. After he drops the third one, he checks to see if he brought Shan's drawing of her and the flamingo. The one whose name has been changed to Dave. It's there. Good. It's a keeper.

He cuts down Geary Street, walks a block away from Gerard Tower, and comes to the alley he scoped out. After again checking to make sure he's unobserved (also that there's no inconvenient wino sleeping it off in there), Billy enters the alley and crouches behind the second of two dumpsters. Trash pickup day in this city is Friday, so both are full and reeking. He stows his laptop and the gray gimme cap behind the dumpster, then scavenges a bunch of packing paper and covers them.

This part worries him more than taking the shot. Do you call that irony? He doesn't know. What he knows is that he doesn't want to lose the lappie any more than he wants to lose the copy of *Thérèse Raquin* he was reading when he came to this city (the book is safely stowed at 658 Pearson). Lucky charms are what they are. Like the baby shoe he carried during Operation Vigilant Resolve and most of Phantom Fury.

The chances of someone coming down this alley, looking behind the dumpster, lifting the garbage-bespattered packing paper, and stealing his laptop are small, and they'd never be able to crack the password, but the *object* matters. He can't bring it, though, because he can't leave Gerard Tower with it slung over his shoulder. He has seen Colin White with his phone, and a couple of times he's shown up for lunch still wearing the headset that must just about be a part of him, but Billy has never seen him with a laptop.

He gets to Gerard Tower at twenty past six. This street dead-ending at the courthouse will be a hive full of worker bees later on, but now it's a graveyard. The only person he sees is a sleepy-eyed woman putting out the breakfast specials signboard in front of the Sunspot Café. Billy wonders if the flashpot is already in place behind it, then dismisses the thought. The flashpots are not his problem, nor is the fire Ken Hoff promised out in Cody. Billy will take the shot no matter what. It's his job, and with his bridges burning one by one behind him, he means to do it. There's no other choice.

Irv Dean isn't at the security stand, and won't be until seven, maybe seven-thirty, but one of the building's two janitors is buffing the lobby floor. He looks up as Billy goes to the card reader to record his entry, just like a good boy should.

'Hey, Tommy,' Billy says, heading for the elevators.

'What're you doing here so early, Dave? God isn't even up.'

'I've got a deadline,' Billy tells him, thinking what an apt word that is for today's business. 'I'll probably be here until God goes back to bed.'

That makes Tommy laugh. 'Go get em, tiger.'

'That's the plan,' Billy says.

3

He takes the two paper bags down to the fifth-floor men's room. He stows his Colin White disguise, not neglecting the wig of long black hair (maybe the most important part), in the trash basket by the wash-basins, then covers it with paper towels. The sign and the padlock go on the door. The key goes in his pocket, along with Dalton's phone and the Benjy Compson flash drive.

Halfway back to his office, he has a nasty thought. There were a few moments on his way here when he lost focus, his mind on Shan's drawing instead of staying where it belonged, on this morning's prep-arations. Has he dropped the Dalton Smith phone into a sewer instead of one of the others? The idea is so terrible that in that moment he's positive that's just what he did, that when he reaches in his pocket he'll find the Billy-phone, or the Dave-phone, or that useless burner. If so, he can replace it, his Dalton Smith credit cards are all good, but what if Don or Beverly Jensen should call on the day or two before FedEx can deliver a new one to 658 Pearson? They'll wonder why he's out of touch. It might not matter, but it might. Good neighbors, *grateful* neighbors, might even call the police and ask them to check his basement apartment to make sure he's okay.

He grasps the phone, and for a moment just holds it, feeling like a roulette player afraid to look at the wheel and see which color the little ball has landed on. The worst thing – worse than the inconvenience, even worse than the potential danger – is knowing he was careless. He let his thoughts slip to the life that's now behind him.

He brings the phone out of his pocket and breathes a sigh of relief. It's the one that belongs to Dalton. He's gotten away with one potential mistake. He can't make another. The fates are unforgiving.

4

Quarter of seven. Billy goes to the local paper on his Dalton Smith phone and uses a Dalton Smith credit card to get behind the paywall. The front page headline has to do with the upcoming state elections, but near the bottom of the page, what would have been below the fold in the old days of actual newspapers, there's a headline reading ALLEN TO BE ARRAIGNED, CHARGED WITH HOUGHTON MURDER. The story begins, 'After a protracted extradition fight, Joel Allen will finally have the first of many days in court. Prosecutors plan to charge him with first-degree murder in the slaying of James Houghton, 43, and assault with intent to kill in the near-fatal shooting of . . .'

Billy doesn't bother with the rest, but he sets his phone to receive news alerts from the paper. He sits at the desk in the outer office and prints a note on a page torn from one of the Staples pads that have otherwise never been used. WORKING UNDER DEADLINE, PLEASE DO NOT DISTURB, it reads. He tapes it to the door and locks the door from the inside.

He takes the pieces of the Remington 700 from the overhead cabinet and lays them out on the table where he's done his writing. Seeing them there, like an exploded schematic in a firearms manual, brings back Fallujah. He pushes the memories away. That's another life that's behind him.

'No more mistakes,' he says, and puts the rifle together. Barrel, bolt, the extractor and ejector spring, the butt plate and butt plate spacer, all the rest. His hands move swiftly and almost of their own accord. He thinks briefly of that poem by Henry Reed, the one that begins *Today we have naming of parts. Yesterday, we had daily cleaning.* He pushes that away, too. No more thinking of little girls' pictures this morning and no poetry. Later, maybe. And maybe later he will write. Now he has to keep his mind on his business and his eyes on the prize. That he no longer cares much about the prize doesn't matter.

The scope comes last, and once again he uses the sighting app to make sure it remains accurate. *True-down*, they used to say. He runs the bolt three times, adds a drop or two of oil, and runs it again. There's no need of this when he only intends to fire once, but it's how he was taught. Last, he loads the magazine and cycles the bolt to move the killing round into the chamber. He lays the weapon with care (but no reverence, not anymore) on the table.

He uses a thumbtack, a length of string, and a Sharpie to trace a circle two inches in diameter on the window. He crisscrosses it with masking tape, then starts in with the glass cutter. His phone chimes softly while he's going round and round, but Billy doesn't even pause. It takes him awhile because the glass is thick, but in the end the circlet of glass comes out as neatly as the cork from a wine bottle. A breath of cool morning breeze slips in through the hole.

He checks his phone and sees he's gotten a text alert from the newspaper. Warehouse fire in Cody, a four-alarm job. Looking out the window, Billy can see a pillar of black smoke. He doesn't know where Ken Hoff got his information, but it was bang on the money.

It's now seven-thirty, and he is as ready as he can be. As ready as he needs to be, he hopes. He sits down in the chair where he has done his writing, hands clasped loosely in his lap, and waits. As he waited in Fallujah, high up and across the river from the Internet café run by the Arab who tattled on the Blackwater contractors and set off a fire-storm. As he did on a dozen rooftops, listening to gunfire and garbage bags rattling in palm trees. His heartbeat is slow and regular. There are no nerves. He watches the traffic pick up on Court Street. Soon all the parking spaces will be full. He watches customers enter the Sunspot Café. A few sit outside, where Billy sat months ago with Ken Hoff. A

Channel 6 news truck comes lumbering up the street, but it's the only one. Either the warehouse fire has drawn away the others, or Joel Allen isn't a big priority. Probably both, Billy thinks. He waits. The time passes. It always does.

5

The Business Solutions crew starts arriving at ten to eight, some carrying go-cups. They'll be hard at it by eight-fifteen, dunning folks who are over their heads in debt, translucent shades dropped over the big windows to discourage them from looking away from their work for even a few seconds. Some stop on their way to the lobby doors to stare at the pillar of black smoke rising over the courthouse from out Cody way. Colin White is among them. No coffee in a go-cup for him; he's got a can of Red Bull. Today he's wearing tie-dyed bellbottoms and a blaze orange T-shirt. Nothing like the outfit Billy's hidden away, but in the confusion it shouldn't matter.

More people arrive, but in this under-occupied building, not that many. Most are headed for the courthouse. At eight-thirty, Jim Albright and John Colton come down Court Street and cut across the plaza. They are carrying big boxy briefcases. And behind them, Phyllis Stanhope. Her fall coat has come out of its closet hibernation for the first time. It's scarlet, making Billy think of Little Red Riding Hood. He has a brief and vivid memory of her looking down at him, urging him deeper as he brushes her nipples with his thumbs. He pushes it away.

There are twelve people on the fifth floor, not counting Billy himself – five in the lawyers' office and seven in the accounting office. The people in the lawyers' office may or may not hear the shot, but Billy is counting on them hearing the bang when the first flashpot goes off. There will be a short pause as they look at each other, asking *what was that*, and then they'll hurry across the hall to the Crescent Accounting Service, because those are the windows facing Court Street. By then the second flashpot will have gone off. They'll crowd together and look out, trying to decide what has happened and what they should do. Go down or stay put? There will be differing opinions. He thinks it may be as long as five minutes before they decide to go down, because they have a high vantage point and all the hoohaw is either across the street, at the courthouse, or up on the corner at the news and stationery store. Billy won't need five minutes. Three should do it, maybe only two.

His phone chimes with another news push. The warehouse fire has spread to a nearby storage facility, and fire crews from other districts are on their way. Route 64 will be closed until at least noon. Motorists are advised to use State Road 47A. At five to nine, another push announces that the fire is being brought under control. So far there are no reported injuries or fatalities.

Billy is now sitting in front of the window with the Remington across his knees. The day is clear as a bell, the rain Nick fretted about hasn't happened, the breeze is no more than a refreshing breath, the Channel 6 film crew is all set and ready to record for News at Noon, so where is the star of the show? Billy expected Allen to be delivered in a county sheriff's vehicle rather than in the perp bus, and on the dot of nine, at which time he'd be escorted to a holding room until the judge was ready for him, but it's now five past and there's no sign of any official vehicle arriving from the county jail on Holland Street.

Ten past and still nothing. The breakfast crowd at the Sunspot is clearing out. Soon the woman in charge, no longer sleepy-eyed, will take in the signboard with the breakfast specials and replace it with the one for the lunch specials.

Quarter past nine and the smoke billowing above the courthouse seems to be thinning. Billy is starting to wonder if there's been a glitch. By twenty past he's sure of it. Maybe Allen's sick, or has made himself sick. Maybe somebody has attacked him in county. Maybe he's in the infirmary, or even dead. Maybe he's pretended to go mental in order to delay the arraignment. Maybe he actually *has* gone mental.

At nine-thirty, as Billy is considering his exit options – disassembling the gun will be step one, no matter what – a black SUV with COUNTY SHERIFF on the side glides onto Court Street. Blue lights are flashing on the roof and inside the grill. The small Channel 6 film crew, which has been lounging around, snaps to attention. A woman in a short dress the exact same red as Phil's fall coat steps out of the TV truck. She's holding a microphone in one hand and a small mirror in the other, to check her appearance. The mirror heliographs bright morning sun Billy's way and he turns his head to avoid the dazzle.

Two cops, walkies in hand, emerge from the courthouse and trot down the stone stairs as the SUV stops at the curb. The front passenger door opens and a portly man in a brown suit and a ridiculously large white Stetson gets out. A uniformed cop gets out on the driver's side. The TV crew is filming. The reporter starts to approach the portly man, who is surely the county sheriff. No one else would dare to wear a Stetson like that. The courthouse cops move to block the reporter, but the portly man beckons her forward. She asks a question and holds the mic to him for his reply. Billy can guess the gist of it: we know how to handle dangerous men like this, justice will be done, vote for me next November.

The reporter has her sound bite and takes a step back. The portly man turns to the SUV. The back door opens and another uniformed cop gets out. This one's an XL widebody. Billy raises the Remington to port arms, watching and waiting. The driver joins the widebody. They turn to the open door and now Joel Allen emerges. Because it's just the arraignment and there's no jury to impress, he's wearing an orange DOCC coverall instead of civvies. His hands are cuffed in front of him.

The reporter wants to ask Allen a question, probably something insightful like did you do it, but this time the portly man pushes out his hands at her. Allen is grinning at her and saying something. Billy doesn't need the scope to see that.

The humungous cop takes Allen by the elbow and turns him to the courthouse steps. They start their climb. Billy slides the barrel of the Remington through the hole in the glass. He snugs the butt plate into the hollow of his shoulder and puts his elbows on his slightly spread knees, for a shot like this all the support he needs. He looks into the scope and the scene down there jumps close. He can see the creases in the portly man's sunburned neck. He can see the keyring jingling and bouncing on the humungous cop's belt. He can see a tuft of Allen's light brown hair sticking up in the back. Billy will put the slug right through that cowlick and into the brain beneath. Into the secret Allen's been keeping, the one he's been hoping is his Get Out of Jail Free card.

This time the flash of memory is the kids pig-piling on him when Derek beat him in that last Monopoly game. He banishes it. Now it's just him and Allen. They are the only ones in the world. It comes down to this. Billy pulls in an easy breath, holds it, and takes the shot.

6

The force of the slug frees Allen from the grip of his cop minder. He flies forward with his arms out and hits the steps. The front of his skull gets there before the rest of him. The portly sheriff runs for cover, losing his ridiculous cowboy hat. The woman reporter also beats feet. The camera guy crouches reflexively but holds his ground. So does the widebody cop. The Dixie-fried Marine sergeant who signed Billy up would have loved both those guys. Especially the widebody, who takes one glance at Allen and then whirls, pulling his gun and looking for the source of the shot. This guy's got his shit together, and he's quick, but Billy has already withdrawn the 700. He drops it on the floor and goes into the outer office.

He peeks into the hall and sees no one. The first flashpot goes off. It's a good loud bang. Billy takes off, sprinting all-out for the men's, pulling the key from his pocket as he goes. He turns it in the base of the Yale lock and just as he slips inside the bathroom, he hears raised, excited voices from the far end of the hall. The Young Lawyers, plus their paralegal and their secretary, are headed across to Crescent Accounting, right on schedule.

Billy bends over the trash basket, tosses aside the paper towels, and grabs the components of his disguise. He yanks the parachute pants on over his jeans, pulls the drawstring, granny-knots it. There's no fly to zip. He puts on the Rolling Stones jacket. Then, looking in the wash-basin mirror, he dons the wig. The black hair only falls halfway down the nape of his neck, but it obscures his forehead to his eyebrows and the sides of his face.

He opens the men's room door. The hall is empty. The lawyers and accountants (Phil among them) are still gawking at the confusion below. Soon they will decide to exit the building, and at least some of them will take the stairs because they are too many for the elevator, but not yet.

Billy leaves the bathroom and starts down the stairs. He can hear commotion below him, plenty of it, but the flight between four and three is empty. The people on those floors are still gawking out the windows. Not on the second floor, though, that's all Business Solutions, and even without the translucent shades they wouldn't have the pano-ramic view offered by the street-facing windows higher up. He can hear them clumping down the stairs, babbling as they go. Colin White will be among them, but no one should notice he now has a doppelgänger, because Billy will be behind them and nobody is going to be looking back. Not this morning.

Billy pauses just above the second-floor landing. He stands there until the thundering herd has dried up, then continues down to the first floor, behind a man in khaki cargo shorts and a woman in unfortunate plaid slacks. For a moment he's forced to stop, probably because there's a jam-up in the door giving on the first-floor lobby. This makes him nervous, because folks from the upper floors will soon be coming down these stairs. Some of them will be people from five.

Then the crowd gets moving again, and five seconds later – while Jim, John, Harry, and Phil are still looking out from high above, Billy hopes – he's in the lobby. Irv Dean has abandoned his post. Billy can see him on the plaza, easy to pick out in his blue security vest. Colin White in his bright orange shirt is also easy to pick out. He's got his phone raised, taking video of the confusion: cops running up the street toward the smoke billowing from between the Sunspot Café and the travel agency next door, cops and bailiffs shouting for people to go back into the courthouse and shelter in place, people running down from more smoke on the corner, yelling their heads off.

Colin isn't the only one taking video. Others, apparently feeling that a raised iPhone makes them invulnerable, are doing the same. But they are the minority, Billy sees as he steps outside. Most people just want to get away. He hears someone yell *Active shooter!* Someone else is shouting *They bombed the courthouse!* Another bawls *Armed men!*

Billy cuts across the plaza to the right, onto Court Street Place. This short tree-lined diagonal will take him to Second Street, which runs behind the parking garage. He's not alone, over three dozen people are ahead of him and at least that many behind him, all using this route away from the chaos, but he's the only one who pays attention to the DPW Transit van parked at the curb. Dana is behind the wheel. Reggie, dressed in the regulation city coverall, is standing by the back door and scanning the crowd. Most of those fleeing Court Street are talking on their phones. Billy wishes he could pretend to do the same, but the Dalton Smith phone is in his jeans, under the parachute pants. A missed opportunity, but you can't think of everything.

He knows better than to drop his head because Dana or Reggie might notice that (more likely Dana), but he moves up beside a plump woman who is panting and holding her pocketbook to her breasts like a shield. As they approach the van, Billy turns his head to her and raises his voice in an approximation of Colin White's when Colin's doing his I'm-the-gayest-of-them-all shtick. 'What *happened*? Oh my *God*, what *happened*?'

'Some kind of terrorism thing, I think,' the woman replies. 'Jesus, there were *explosions*!'

'I *know*!' Billy cries. 'Oh my God, I *heard*!'

Then they're past. Billy risks one quick look over his shoulder. He has to make sure they aren't looking at *him*. Or coming after him. They're not. More people than ever are now using Court Street Place to get away; they crowd the sidewalk. Reggie is scoping them hard, standing on his tiptoes, trying to catch sight of Billy. Presumably Dana is, too. Billy speeds up, leaving the plump woman behind, weaving around others. Not quite race-walking, but almost. He turns left on Second Street, left again on Laurel, then right on Yancey. The exodus is behind him now. A young guy on the street grabs Billy by the shoulder, wanting to know what the hell is going on.

'I don't know,' Billy says. He shakes free and walks on.

Behind him, sirens rise in the air.

7

His laptop is gone.

Billy yanks out the packing paper, now splattered with globs of Chinese food from the overflowing dumpster, and uncovers nothing but old cobblestones. His mind sideslips back to Fallujah and the baby shoe. To Taco saying *You keep that thing safe, brah.* He kept it tied to his belt loop by the laces, bouncing against his hip with the rest of the things he carried. That they all carried.

He doesn't need the fucking laptop, he has the flash drive with Benjy's story on it, Rudy 'Taco' Bell and the others still unwritten but waiting in the wings. He can go on once he gets to the basement apartment. There's nothing on the lappie to connect him to his Dalton Smith life, even if someone, some supergeek out of a movie, could crack the password. The only connection to his Dalton Smith life besides the Jensens is Bucky Hanson, and he has only communicated with Bucky on a phone that no longer exists.

So let it go. No choice and no loss.

But it feels like such bad luck. Such a bad omen. Almost like a final summation of a shit job he should have known better than to take.

He pounds his fist against the side of the dumpster hard enough to hurt and listens to the sirens. Right now he's not worried about police, they are all headed to the courthouse, where some major clusterfuck is going down, but he has to worry about Reggie and Dana. Once they get tired of waiting, they'll either conclude Billy's gotten trapped in Gerard Tower or that he's crossed them up. They can't do anything if he's still in the building, but if he's decided to abandon the plan and strike out on his own, they can start cruising the streets and looking for him.

It's not like the baby shoe, Billy thinks. And hell, the baby shoe wasn't magic either, just magical thinking. The shit that happened after I lost it means nothing. Fortunes of war, baby, and so is this. Someone found the lappie and stole it, it's gone, and you have to get under cover before that Transit van shows up, rolling slow.

He thinks of Dana Edison's sharp little eyes behind those rimless spectacles. Billy got past those eyes once and doesn't want to risk giving the man a second chance. He has to get to the basement apartment on Pearson Street, and fast.

Billy gets to his feet and hurries to the mouth of the alley. He sees a few cars but no Transit van. He starts to turn right, then freezes, amazed and disgusted at his own stupidity. It's as if the *dumb self* has become his real self. He was just about to head for Pearson Street still wearing the wig, the Rolling Stones jacket, and the fucking parachute pants. Like wearing a neon sign saying CHECK ME OUT.

He runs back down the alley, stripping off the wig and jacket as he goes. Behind the dumpster again, he frees the waistband granny knot holding up the idiotic parachute pants, pushes them down, and steps out of them. He squats and bundles everything together. He shoves the bundle as deep as he can under the crumpled heaps of bespattered packing paper . . . and touches something. It's hard and thin. Can it be the brim of a gimme cap?

It is. Did he really push it that far behind the dumpster? He tosses it aside and reaches in deeper, leaning his shoulder against the dumpster's rusty side, the smell of Chinese food a miasma. His outstretched fingers brush something else. He knows what it is and can't believe it. He stretches further, his cheek now against the dumpster's rusty side, and grasps the handle of his laptop case. He pulls it out and looks at it unbelievingly. He could swear he didn't push it in that far, but it seems he did. He tells himself it's nothing like thinking he threw away the wrong phone, nothing at all like that, but it is.

Agreeing to be in this city so long was a mistake. Monopoly was a mistake. Having a backyard barbecue was a mistake. Knocking over those tin birds in the shooting gallery? Mistake. Having time to think and act like a normal person was the biggest mistake of all. He's not a normal person. He's a hired assassin, and if he doesn't think like who and what he is, he'll never get clear.

He uses a relatively clean swatch of the packing paper to wipe off the hat and the laptop case. He slings the strap over his shoulder and pulls on the gimme cap, which was once clean and is now grimy. He goes to the head of the alley and peers out again. A cop car comes squalling around the next corner, lights and siren. Billy pulls back until it passes. Then he heads out, walking briskly toward Pearson Street and the apartment building across from the demolished railway station. He thinks of Fallujah again, the endless sweeps through the narrow streets with the baby shoe bouncing against his hip. Waiting for the patrol to be over. Wanting to go back to the relative safety of the base a mile outside of town, where there would be hot food, touch football, maybe a movie under the desert stars.

Nine blocks, he tells himself. Nine blocks and you're home and dry. Nine blocks and this particular patrol is over. No movie under the stars, that was Billy Summers, but Dalton Smith has both YouTube and iTunes on one of his AllTech computers. No violence, no explosions, just people doing zany things. Plus kissing at the end.

Nine blocks.

8

He has done seven of those blocks, and the more modern part of the city is behind him, when he sees a city Transit van roll across an intersection ahead. Billy supposes it could be another DPW Transit, they all look the same, but it's moving slow, almost coming to a stop in the middle of West Avenue before speeding up again.

Billy has stepped into a doorway. When the van doesn't return, he starts walking again, always looking ahead for cover should it return. If they come back and see him, he's probably going to be dead. The closest thing he has to a weapon are the keys on his keyring. Unless, of course, Nick was playing straight with him all along. In that case he might get no more than a harsh tongue-lashing, but he has no intention of finding out. Either way, he has to keep going if he wants to get to the apartment building.

He pauses at the intersection, looking in the direction the Transit van went. He sees nothing but a few cars and a UPS truck. Billy trots across the street, head lowered, helpless not to think of Route 10 in Fallujah, also known as IED Alley.

He turns onto Pearson, jogs one final block, and there's his building. He has to cross the street to get to it, and he feels an insane itching on his right shoulderblade, as if someone – it would be Dana, of course – is zeroing the sight of a silenced pistol in on it. The near-constant wind that blows across the rubble-strewn vacant lot sends a coupon fold-in sheet from the local newspaper against one of his ankles and Billy gives a little skip of surprise.

He hurries along the frost-heaved walk of 658, then up the steps. He looks over his shoulder for the Transit van, sure he'll see it, but the street is deserted. The sirens are all behind him, like the rest of his David Lockridge life. He tries one key and it's wrong. He tries another and that one is wrong, too. He thinks of the phone he could have lost and the laptop he could have lost, the way he lost the baby shoe.

Easy, he thinks. Those are your Evergreen Street keys, you never took them off your keyring, so chill out. You're almost home free.

The next one opens the foyer door. He steps inside and closes it. He looks out through a ragged mesh of lace curtain, maybe Beverly Jensen's work. He sees nothing, sees nothing, sees a crow land on some of the jagged rubble across the street, sees the crow take off, sees nothing, sees a kid on a trike with his mother walking patiently beside him, sees another sheet of newspaper go cartwheeling across the patched pavement, has time to think *the patched pavement of Pearson Street*, and then he sees the Transit van, going slow. Billy holds perfectly still. He can see through the mesh, but Reggie in the passenger seat can't see in. He might notice a sudden movement behind the lace curtain, though. Billy thinks the other one certainly would.

The Transit van moves on. Billy waits for its brake lights to flash. They don't, and then it's out of sight. He's not sure he's safe, but he thinks he is. Hopes. He goes downstairs and lets himself into the apartment. Not home, just a place to hide, but for the time being that's good enough.

CHAPTER 11

1

The basement apartment's one window is covered by a length of burgundy cloth. Billy pushes it aside on its rod and sits down, thinking again that the apartment is like a submarine and this window is his periscope. He stays on the couch for fifteen minutes, arms folded across his chest, waiting for the Transit van to come back. It may even stop if Dana, who is no fool, decides the place might be worth checking out. Unlikely, when there are several rundown neighborhoods ringing the central city, but not impossible.

Billy has become more and more sure if they find him they mean to kill him.

Billy has no handgun, although it would have been simple enough to get one. There are gun sales in the area almost every day of the week, it seems. Not that he would have set foot in the building where the sale was being held when he could have bought a reliable piece in the parking lot for cash, no questions asked. Something simple, a .32 or .38 that could be easily concealed. It wasn't forgetfulness in that case, he just hadn't foreseen a situation where he might need one.

Although, he thinks, if you changed the plan without telling Nick, you must have foreseen *something*.

If they do come back – paranoid, but within the realm of possibility – what could Billy do about it? Not much. There's a butcher knife in the kitchen. And a meat fork. He could use the meat fork on the first one in, and he knows that would be Reggie. The easy one. Then Dana would do him.

When fifteen minutes have passed and the bogus DPW truck hasn't returned, Billy decides they have either moved on to another part of the city, maybe to check out the house on Evergreen Street, or have gone back to the McMansion to await further orders from Nick. He closes the curtain, shutting out the view, and looks at his watch. It's twenty to eleven. How the time flies when you're having fun, he thinks.

Channels 2 and 4 are broadcasting the usual morning drivel, but with crawls about the shooting and the explosions running across the bottom of the screen. The real motherlode is Channel 6, where they have trashed their morning shows to go live at the scene. They've got the goods to do that because someone in their news department dispatched a crew to the courthouse to cover Allen's arraignment, and didn't send them to Cody when the warehouse fire broke out. It might have been neglect or outright laziness, you didn't wind up as the head of news in a small border south city like Red Bluff because you were Walter Cronkite, but whoever was in charge is going to look mighty wise in retrospect.

ONE DEAD, NO REPORTED INJURIES IN COURTHOUSE CATASTROPHE, reads the chyron at the bottom of the screen. The correspondent in the red dress is still doing her thing, although she's now doing it on the corner of Main Street, because Court Street has been closed off. It looks to Billy like the city's entire police force is down there, plus two forensics vans, one from the state police.

'Bill,' the reporter says, presumably speaking to the anchor back in the studio, 'I'm sure there'll be a press conference later, but as of now we have no official word to pass on. We do have eyes on the scene, though, and I want to show you something that George Wilson, my incredibly brave cameraman, spotted just a few minutes ago. George, can you show that again?'

George raises the camera, centers it on Gerard Tower, then zeroes in on the fifth floor. There's hardly any shake in the image even at maximum zoom, and Billy can't help admiring that. Cameraman George stood his ground when the shit hit the fan, kept his head when those all about him were losing theirs, he got footage that will no doubt go national, and thanks to his sharp eyes he's probably just a step and a half behind the police at this point. He could have been a Marine, Billy thinks. Maybe he was. Just another jarhead bullet-sponge over there in the suck. For all I know, I could have passed him on what we called the Brooklyn Bridge, or hunkered down beside him in the Jolan graveyard while the wind blew and the shit flew.

The Channel 6 viewing audience, Billy among them, is treated to the image of a window with a shooter's loophole cut into it. The sunglare on the glass helps, just as Dana said it would.

'That is almost certainly where the shot came from,' the reporter says, 'and we should know very soon who was using that office. The police may know already.'

The picture switches to Bill in the studio. He's looking suitably grave. 'Andrea, we want to run your original story again, for people who may have just joined the broadcast. It's really extraordinary.'

They go to the video. Billy sees the SUV approaching with its blues alight. The door opens and the portly sheriff gets out. He has big ears, almost Clark Gable size. They seem to be anchoring his ridiculous Stetson. Andrea approaches, holding out the mic. The courthouse cops move in, but the sheriff holds up an imperious hand to stop them so she can ask her question.

'Sheriff, has Joel Allen confessed to the murder of Mr Houghton?'

The sheriff smiles. His accent is as southern as grits and collard greens. 'We don't need a confession, Ms Braddock. We've got all we need to get a conviction. Justice will be done. You can count on that.'

The reporter in the red dress – Andrea Braddock – steps back. George Wilson centers his camera on the opening door of the SUV. Out comes Joel Allen, like a movie star popping out of his trailer. Andrea Braddock steps forward to ask another question but backs off obediently when the sheriff raises his hands to her.

You'll never make the jump to the bigtime like that, Andrea, Billy thinks. You have to push, girl.

He leans forward. This is the moment, and it's fascinating to see it from another angle, a different perspective. He hears the shot, a liquid whipcrack of sound. He doesn't see the damage the bullet does, the editor in the Channel 6 video room has blurred it out, but he sees Allen's body fly forward and hit the steps. The picture joggles and dips as Cameraman George goes into his reflexive crouch, then steadies again. After holding on the body for a moment, the camera pans to the widebody cop who's looking up to find the source of the shot.

Then, *boom*! From up the street behind the Sunspot Café. There are screams. Wilson turns his magic eye in that direction to show fleeing pedestrians (Andrea Braddock among them, there's no way to miss that red dress) and the smoke billowing out from between the Sunspot and the neighboring travel agency. Andrea starts to come back – Billy has to give her points for that – and then the second flashpot goes off. She cringes, whirls in that direction, takes a look, then jogs back to her first position. Her hair is disheveled, her mic pack is hanging by its cord, and she's out of breath.

'Explosions,' she says. 'And someone has been shot.' She gulps. 'Joel Allen, who was to be arraigned for the murder of James Houghton, *has been shot on the courthouse steps!*'

Everything she's got to say from then on will be anticlimactic, so Billy zaps off the TV. By tonight there will be interviews on Evergreen Street with people he knew in his Dave Lockridge life. He doesn't want to see those. Jamal and Corinne won't allow cameras anywhere near the kids, but Jamal and Corinne would be bad enough. And the Fazios. The Petersons. Even Jane Kellogg, the boozy widow from down the street. Their anger would be bad, their hurt and bewilderment worse. They'll say they thought he was okay. They'll say they thought he was nice, and is it shame he's feeling?

'Sure,' he tells his empty apartment. 'Better than nothing.'

Will it help if Shan and Derek and the other kids find out that their Monopoly buddy shot a bad guy? It would be nice to think so, but then there's the fact that their Monopoly buddy shot the bad guy from cover. And in the back of the head.

2

He calls Bucky Hanson and gets voicemail. It's what Billy expects, because when UNKNOWN CALLER comes up on his screen (Bucky knows better than to put Dalton Smith in his contacts), Bucky won't answer even if he's there and thinks it's his client calling from a hick town in the border south.

'Call me back,' Billy tells Bucky's voicemail. 'ASAP.'

He paces the shotgun-style apartment, phone in hand. It rings less than a minute later. Bucky doesn't waste time, and he doesn't use names.

Neither of them do. It's an ingrained precaution, even if Bucky's phone is secure and Billy's is clean.

'He wants to know where you are and what the hell happened.'

'I did the job, that's what happened. He only needs to turn on the TV to see that.' Billy touches one of his back pockets with his free hand and feels a Dave Lockridge shopping list there. He has a tendency to forget them after he's finished Krogering.

'He says there was a plan. It was all set up.'

'I'm pretty sure a set-up is what it was.'

There's silence as Bucky chews this over. He's been in the brokerage business for a long time, never been caught, and he's not dumb. At last he says, 'How sure?'

'I'll know one way or another when the man pays the balance. Or when he doesn't. Has he?'

'Give me a break. This thing only went down a couple of hours ago.'

Billy glances at the clock on the kitchen wall. 'More like three, and how long does it take to transfer money? We're living in the computer age, in case you forgot. Check for me.'

'Wait one.' Billy hears clicking computer keys twelve hundred miles north of his basement apartment. Then Bucky comes back. 'Nothing yet. Want me to get in touch? I've got an email cutout. Probably goes to his fat sidekick.'

Billy thinks of Ken Hoff, looking desperate and smelling of mid-morning booze. A loose end. And he, Billy Summers, is another.

'You still there?' Bucky asks.

'Wait until three or so, then check again.'

'And if it's still not there, do I email then?'

Bucky has a right to ask. A hundred and fifty thousand of Billy's million-five payday belongs to Bucky. A very nice bundle, and tax free, but there's a drawback. You can't spend money if you're dead.

'Do you have family?' In all the years he's worked with Bucky, this is a question Billy has never asked. Hell, it's been five years since he was face to face with the man. Their relationship has been strictly biz.

Bucky doesn't seem surprised at the change of subject. This is because he knows the subject hasn't changed. He's the one link between Billy Summers and Dalton Smith. 'Two ex-wives, no kids. I parted company with the last ex twelve years ago. Sometimes she sends me a postcard.'

'I think you need to get out of the city. I think you need to catch a cab to Newark Airport as soon as you hang up.'

'Thanks for the advice.' Bucky doesn't sound mad. He sounds resigned. 'Not to mention for royally fucking up my life.'

'I'll make it worth your while. The man owes me one-point-five. I'll see you get the one.'

This time Billy reads the silence as surprise. Then Bucky says, 'Are you sure you mean that?'

'I do.' He does. He feels tempted to promise Bucky the whole fucking thing, because he no longer wants it.

'If you're right about the situation,' Bucky says, 'you could be promising me something your employer doesn't mean to deliver. Maybe never meant to deliver.'

Billy thinks again of Ken Hoff, who could almost have PATSY tattooed on his forehead. Did Nick think the same of Billy? The idea makes him mad, and he welcomes the feeling. It beats the hell out of feeling ashamed.

'He'll deliver. I'll make sure of it. In the meantime, you need to get over the hills and far away. And travel under a different name.'

Bucky laughs. 'Don't teach your grampy how to suck eggs, kiddo. I've got a place.'

Billy says, 'I guess I do want you to send a message through your email cutout. Write it down.'

A pause. Then: 'Give it to me.'

'"My client did the job and disappeared on his own, period. He's Houdini, remember, question mark. Transfer the money by midnight, period."'

'That it?'

'Yes.'

'I'll text you when I hear, okay?'

'Okay.'

3

He's hungry, and why not? He hasn't had anything but dry toast, and that was a long time ago. There's a package of ground beef in the fridge. He peels open the plastic wrap and smells it. It seems all right, so he dumps half a pound or so into a skillet with a little bit of margarine. While he stands at the stove, chopping up the meat and stirring it around, his hand happens on that shopping list in his back pocket again. He takes it out and sees it's not a shopping list at all. It's Shan's drawing of her and the pink flamingo, once named Freddy and now named Dave, although Billy guesses it won't stay Dave for long. It's folded up but he can see the red crayon ghosts of the hearts rising from the flamingo's head toward hers. He doesn't unfold it, just sticks it back in his pocket.

He's laid in supplies for his stay and the cupboard beside the stove is full of canned goods: soup, tuna fish, Dinty Moore Beef Stew, Spam, SpaghettiOs. He takes a can of Manwich and dumps it over the simmering beef, *sploosh*. When it starts to bubble, he sticks two slices of bread into the toaster. While he waits for them to pop up, he takes Shan's picture out of his pocket. This time he unfolds it. Ought to get rid of this, he thinks. Tear it up, flush it down the john. Instead he folds it and puts it in his pocket again.

The toaster pops. Billy puts the slices on a plate and spoons Manwich over them. He gets a Coke and sits down at the table. He eats what's on the plate, then goes back for the rest. He eats that, too. He drinks the Coke. Then, as he's washing out the skillet, his stomach knots up and he starts making a chugging sound. He runs to the bathroom, kneels in front of the bowl, and throws up until everything is in the toilet.

He flushes, wipes his mouth with toilet paper, flushes again. He drinks some water, then goes to his periscope window and looks out. The street is empty. So is the sidewalk. He guesses it's often that way on Pearson Street. There's nothing to see but the empty lot with the signs – NO TRESPASSING, CITY PROPERTY, DANGER KEEP OUT – guarding the jagged brick remnants of the train station. The abandoned shopping cart has disappeared but the men's undershorts are still there, now caught on a bunch of weeds. An old Honda station wagon passes. Then a Ford Pinto. Billy wouldn't have believed there were still any of those on the road. A pickup truck. No Transit van.

Billy closes the curtain, lies down on the couch, closes his eyes, and falls asleep. There are no dreams, at least that he can remember.

4

His phone wakes him up. It's the ringtone, so Bucky must have news too detailed to put in a text. Only it's not Bucky. It's Bev Jensen, and this time she's not laughing. This time she's . . . what? Not crying, exactly, it's more like the sound a baby makes when it's unhappy. Grizzling.

'Oh hi, hello,' she says. 'I hope I'm not . . .' A watery gulp. '. . . not bothering you.'

'No,' Billy says, sitting up. 'Not at all. What's wrong?'

At that the grizzling escalates into loud sobs. 'My mother is dead, Dalton! She really is!'

Well shit, Billy thinks, I knew that. He knows something else. She's drunk-dialed him.

'I'm very sorry for your loss.' In his muzzy state that's the best he can do.

'I called because I didn't want you to think I was a horrible person. Laughing and carrying on and talking about going on a cruise.'

'You're not going?' This is a disappointment; he was looking forward to having the house to himself.

'Oh, I guess we will.' She gives a morose sniff. 'Don wants to and I guess I do, too. We had a little bit of a honeymoon on Cape San Blas – that's on what they call the Redneck Riviera – but since then we haven't been anywhere. I just . . . I didn't want you to think I was dancing on Momma's grave, or anything.'

'I didn't,' Billy says. This is the truth. 'You had a windfall and you were excited. Perfectly natural.'

At this she lets go completely, crying and gasping and snorkeling and sounding like she's on the verge of drowning. 'Thank you, Dalton.' It comes out *Dollen*, like her husband. 'Thank you for understanding.'

'Uh-huh. Maybe you ought to take a couple of aspirin and lie down for awhile.'

'That's probably a good idea.'

'Sure.' There's a soft *bing*. It has to be Bucky. 'I'll just say goodb—'

'Is everything good there?'

No, Billy thinks. Everything is mega fucked up, Bev, thanks for asking. 'Everything's fine.'

'I didn't mean it about the plants, either. I'd feel terrible if I came back and found Daphne and Walter dead.'

'I'll take good care of them.'

'Thank you. Thank you so very, very, very, *very* much.'

'You're very welcome. I have to go, Bev.'

'Okay, Dollen. And thank you very, very, v—'

'Talk soon,' he says, and ends the call.

The text is from one of Bucky's many communication aliases. It's brief.

bigpapi982: No transfer of funds yet. He wants to know where you are.

Billy texts back under one of his own communication aliases.

DizDiz77: People in hell want ice water.

5

He scrambles some eggs and heats some tomato soup for supper, and this time he's able to keep it down. When he's finished he puts on the six o'clock news, tuning to the NBC affiliate because he doesn't want or need to watch the Channel 6 video again. An ad for Liberty Mutual is followed by his own picture. He's in his Evergreen Street backyard wearing a smile and an apron that says NOT JUST A SEX OBJECT, I CAN COOK! Others in the background have had their faces blurred out, but Billy knows them all. They were his neighbors. The photo was taken at the barbecue he had for the folks on the street, and he's guessing it came from Diane Fazio because she's always clicking pix, either with her phone or her little Nikon. He notes that his grass (he still thinks of it as his) looks damn good.

The super beneath the picture says WHO IS DAVID LOCKRIDGE? He's pretty sure the cops already know. Computer fingerprint searches are lickety-split these days, and his dabs are on file from his Marine days.

'This is the man police believe is responsible for the brazen assassination of Joel Allen on the courthouse steps,' one of the two anchors says. He's the one who looks like a banker.

The other anchor, the one who looks like a magazine model, picks up the narrative. 'His motive is a mystery at this point, and so is his method of escape. Police are certain of one thing: he had help.'

I didn't, Billy thinks. It was offered and I turned it down.

'Seconds after the rifle shot,' says the banker anchor, 'there were two explosions, one across from the shooter's location in the Gerard Tower, and the other from behind a building on the corner of Main and Court Streets. According to Chief of Police Lauren Conlee, these weren't high explosive devices but rather flash-bangs of the sort used at fireworks shows and by some rock and roll bands.'

Magazine model anchor picks it up. Why they go back and forth like that Billy doesn't know. It's a mystery. 'Larry Thompson is on the scene, or as close to it as he can get, because Court Street is still blocked off. Larry?'

'That's right, Nora,' Larry says, as if confirming he's really Larry. Behind him is yellow police tape, and around the courthouse the misery lights on half a dozen cop cars are still flashing. 'Police are now working under the assumption that this was a carefully planned mob hit.'

Nailed that one, Billy thinks.

'At her press conference today, Chief Conlee revealed that the suspected shooter, David Lockridge – probably an alias – has been in place since early summer, using a unique cover story. Here's what she had to say.'

Larry Thompson is replaced with a clip of the chief's press conference. Sheriff Vickery, he of the ridiculous Stetson, isn't in attendance. Conlee starts in with the story about how the shooter (she doesn't bother calling him the suspect) pretended to be writing a book, and Billy turns the TV off.

Something is gnawing at him.

6

Half an hour later, while Billy is in the Jensens' second-floor apartment, spritzing Daphne and Walter, he comes to a decision. He had no plans to leave his basement apartment on the day of the shooting, had in fact planned to stay there for several days, maybe even a week, but things have changed, and not for the better. There's something he needs to know, and Bucky can't help him with it. Bucky did his job, and if he's smart, he's now on a plane getting his ass out of the fallout zone. If there is fallout, that is. Billy still can't be sure he's not just jumping at shadows, but he has to find out.

He goes back downstairs and dons his Dalton Smith disguise, this time inflating the fake pregnancy belly almost to full and not neglecting the horn-rimmed glasses with the clear glass lenses, which have been waiting on the living room bookshelf with his copy of *Thérèse Raquin*. It's deep dusk now, he has that going for him. Zoney's is relatively close, and that's also on his side. What he doesn't have going for him is the possibility that Nick's guys are still combing the streets, Frankie Elvis and Paul Logan in one vehicle, Reggie and Dana in another, and it won't be the Transit van this evening.

But Billy feels it's a risk worth taking, because they'll certainly believe he's in hiding by now. They may even think he's left the city. And if they should happen to cruise by him, the Dalton Smith rig should work. Or so he hopes.

He's decided he needs a burner phone after all, and he doesn't beat himself up for having thrown away a perfectly good one that morning. Only God can foresee everything, and it's not on a level of stupidity like almost leaving that alley wearing his Colin White gear. In work like Billy's – wetwork, not to put too fine a point on it – you make your plan and hope the stuff you don't foresee won't show up to bite you in the ass. Or put you in a little green room with an IV in your arm.

I can't get nailed, he thinks. If I do, those fucking plants are going to die.

Everything in the sad little strip mall is closed except for the Zoney's convenience store, and Hot Nails is never going to re-open at all. The windows are soaped over and there's a legal notice of bankruptcy taped to the door.

Two Hispanic dudes checking out the Beer Cave are the only other customers. There's a stack of boxed FastPhones between the display of energy shots and the one holding fifty different varieties of snackin' cakes. Billy grabs a phone and takes it to the checkout. The woman who got stuck up, Wanda something, isn't behind the counter. It's a Middle Eastern-looking dude instead.

'That it?'

'That's it.' As Dalton Smith, he tries to speak in a slightly higher register. It's another way of reminding himself of who he's supposed to be.

The clerk rings him up. It comes to just under eighty-four dollars, with a hundred and twenty minutes thrown in. It would have been as much as thirty bucks cheaper at Walmart, but beggars can't be choosers. Besides, in Wally World you have to worry about face recognition. It's everywhere now. This place has video cams, but Billy's betting they recycle every twelve or twenty-four hours. He pays cash. When you're on the run – or in hiding – cash is king. The clerk wishes him a nice night. Billy wishes him the same.

It's now dark enough that the few cars he meets are running with headlights, so he can't see who's behind them. There's an urge, or maybe it's an instinct, to drop his head each time one approaches, but that would look furtive. He can't pull down the brim of the gimme cap, either, because he's not wearing it. He wants the blond wig to do its thing. He's not Billy Summers, the man both the police and Nick's hardballs are looking for. He's Dalton Smith, a small-time computer geek who lives on the po' side of town and has to keep pushing his hornrims up on his nose. He's overweight from eating Doritos and Little Debbies in front of a computer screen and if he puts on another twenty or thirty pounds, his walk will become a waddle.

It's a good disguise, not overdone, but he still breathes a sigh of relief when he closes the foyer door of 658 behind him. He goes downstairs, turns off the overhead light, and pushes back the curtain of his periscope window. No one is out there. The street is deserted. Of course if he's been spotted, they (it's Reggie and Dana he's thinking of, not Frankie and Paulie or the police) could be moving in from the back, but there's no sense worrying about what you can't control. Doing that is a good way to go crazy.

Billy closes the narrow curtain, turns the light back on, and sits in the room's single easy chair. It's ugly, but like many ugly things in life, it's also comfortable. He puts the phone on the coffee table and looks at it, wondering if he's thinking straight or just indulging in paranoia. In many ways paranoia would be better. Time to find out.

He frees the phone from its box, puts in the battery, and plugs it into the wall to charge. Unlike his previous burner, it's a flip phone. Kind of old-school, but Billy likes it. With a flip phone if you don't like what somebody is saying, you can actually hang up on them. Childish, maybe, but strangely satisfying. Charging doesn't take long.

Thanks to Steve Jobs, who got pissed when he couldn't use a device the second he took it out of the box, off-the-rack devices like this come with a fifty per cent charge already cooking inside.

The phone wants to know what language he prefers. Billy tells it English. It asks if he wants to join a wireless network. Billy says no. He plugs in the minutes he paid for, making the necessary call to FastPhone HQ to finish the transaction. His minutes are good for the next three months. Billy hopes by then he's on a beach somewhere and the only phone in his possession is the one that goes with his Dalton Smith credit cards.

Home and dry. That would be nice.

He tosses the phone from hand to hand, thinking about the day Frank Macintosh and Paul Logan took him to the house in Midwood, a trip he now wishes he had never taken. Nick was there to greet him, but not outside. Billy thinks of his first visit to the rented McMansion, Nick once more there to greet him with open arms, but again not outside. Next he thinks of the night Nick told him about the flashpots and pitched his getaway plan – *Just get in the back of the van, Billy, relax and take a ride to Wisconsin*. There had been Champagne to start and Baked Alaska to finish. A service couple, probably local and maybe married, cooked the meal and served it. Those two had seen Nick, but as far as they knew, he was a businessman from New York who was down here to do some kind of deal. He gave the woman some money and they were on their way.

Back and forth goes the burner phone. Right hand to left, left hand to right.

I asked Nick if Hoff was going to plant the flashpots, Billy thinks, and what did he say? What did he call him? A *grande figlio di puttana*, wasn't it? Which meant son of a bitch, or son of a whore, or maybe motherfucker. One of those, and the exact translation hardly mattered. What did matter was what Nick said next: *I'd be sad if that was your opinion of me*.

Because the *grande figlio di puttana* was the designated patsy. It was Hoff who owned the building the shot came from. Hoff who procured the gun and now the police had it and they'd already be trying to trace it back to the point of sale. And if they got there – make that *when* they got there – what would they find? Probably an alias if Hoff had any sense at all, but if the cops showed the seller Hoff's picture, there goes your ballgame. Ken winds up in a hot little interrogation room, willing to make a deal, *eager* to make a deal, because he believes that's what he does best.

Except Billy's betting that Ken Hoff is never going to get to the little room. He's never going to talk about Nikolai Majarian because he's going to be dead.

Billy got that far weeks ago, but the six o'clock news has taken him to a conclusion he should have reached sooner, and might have if he'd spent a little less time playing Monopoly with the Evergreen Street kids and taking care of his lawn and eating Corinne's cookies and schmoozing with his neighbors. Even now what he's thinking seems impossible, but the logic is undeniable.

Ken Hoff and David Lockridge weren't the only ones who were out front.

Were they?

7

Billy texts Giorgio Piglielli, aka Georgie Pigs, aka George Russo, the big literary agent. He uses an alias he knows Giorgio will recognize.

Trilby: Text me back.

He waits. There's no response, and that's fucked up because there are two things Giorgio always keeps close at hand: his phone and something to eat. Billy tries again.

Trilby: I need to talk to you right away. Billy considers, then adds: **The contract specified payment on publication day, right?**

No dots to say Giorgio is reading his texts or composing a reply. Nothing.

Trilby: Text me.

Nothing.

Billy flips the phone closed and puts it on the coffee table. The worst thing about Giorgio's silence is that Billy's not surprised. There really is a *dumb self*, it seems, and what it hasn't realized until the job has been done and it's too late to go back is that Giorgio has been out front right along with Ken Hoff. Giorgio was with Hoff when they entered the Gerard Tower to show Billy his writer's studio on the fifth floor. And it wasn't Giorgio's first visit to the building, either. *This is George Russo, you met him last week,* Hoff had said to Irv Dean, the security guy.

Is Giorgio back in Nevada? And if so, is he chowing down and drinking milkshakes in Vegas or buried somewhere in the surrounding desert? God knows he wouldn't be the first. Or the hundredth.

They'll trace Giorgio back to Nick even if he's dead, Billy thinks. The two of them have been a team since forever, Nick in charge and Georgie Pigs as his *consigliere*. Billy doesn't know if that's what they really call a guy like Georgie or just something the movies made up, but for sure that's what the fat man has been to Nick: his go-to guy.

Only not since forever, because the first time Billy worked for Nick – it was the third time he assassinated a man for pay – was in 2008, and Giorgio wasn't there. Nick handled that one by himself. He told Billy there was a rape-o working some of the smaller clubs and casinos on the edge of town. The rape-o liked older women, liked to hurt them, finally went overboard and killed one. Nick found out who he was and wanted a pro from out of town to take care of the guy. Billy, he'd said, had been recommended. Highly.

When Billy came to Vegas the second time, Giorgio was not only there, he did the deal. Nick came in while they were talking, gave Billy a manly hug and a few pats on the back, then sat in the corner sipping a drink and just listening. Until the very end, that was. That second job was less than a year after the first one, the rape-o. Giorgio said the target this time was an independent porno filmmaker named Karl Trilby. He showed Billy a picture of a man who looked eerily like Oral Roberts.

'Trilby like the hat,' Giorgio said, then explained when Billy pretended not to know what he was talking about.

'I don't shoot people just because they make movies of people fucking,' Billy had said.

'What about people who make movies of guys fucking six-year-olds?' Nick had said, and Billy had done the job because Karl Trilby was a bad person.

Billy did three more jobs for Nick, five in all not counting Allen, almost a third of his total. Excluding the dozens of hajis in Iraq he had taken down, that is. Sometimes Nick was there when the offer was made and sometimes he wasn't, but Giorgio always was, so him being on the scene for the Allen job at least part of the time hadn't struck Billy as odd. It should have. Only now does he realize it was *very* odd.

Nick has deniability as long as Giorgio keeps quiet; Nick can say sure I know the guy, but if he did this it was his own deal. I knew nothing about it. Even if the cook and the woman server from that first dinner put him with Giorgio and Billy, which is unlikely, Nick can shrug and say he was there to talk to Giorgio on casino business, the license on the Double Domino was coming up for renewal. And the other guy? As far as Nick knows, just a pal of Giorgio's. Or maybe a bodyguard. Quiet guy. Said his name was Lockridge but otherwise didn't say much at all.

When the cops ask where Nick was when Allen got hit, he can say he was in Vegas and produce plenty of witnesses to back his alibi. Plus casino security footage. That stuff doesn't get recycled every twelve or twenty-four hours; that stuff gets archived for at least a year.

If Giorgio keeps quiet. But would he stick to that *omertà* shit if *he* was the one getting extradited? If *he* was the one facing the possibility of lethal injection as an accessory to first-degree murder?

Georgie Pigs can't talk if he's under five feet of desert, Billy thinks. It's the great rule when it comes to things like this.

He stops tossing the phone from hand to hand and texts Giorgio one more time. Still no response. He could try texting or phoning Nick, but even if he reached him, could he trust anything Nick might say? No. The only thing Billy can trust is a million-five transferred to his offshore account, then transferred again, through electronic jiggery-pokery, to another one that Dalton Smith can access. Bucky would do that part when he gets to wherever he's decided to go, but only if the money is there to transfer.

Tonight Billy can do nothing more, so he goes to bed. It isn't even nine o'clock, but it's been a long day.

8

He lies with his hands beneath the pillow in that ephemeral cool pocket, thinking it doesn't make sense. No way does it.

Ken Hoff yes, okay. There's a certain breed of fast-dealing small-city sharpie who believes that no matter how deep the shit, someone will always throw him a rope. These are the broad-smiling, firm-handshaking hustlers in Izod polos and Bally loafers who could have come with *self-involved optimist* stamped on their birth certificates. But Giorgio Piglielli is different. He's eating himself to death, sure, but so far as Billy can tell, in most other ways he's a hard-eyed realist. And yet he's all over this thing. Why is that?

Billy lets it go. He drops into sleep and dreams of the desert. Not the one in the suck, though, where everything smells of gunpowder, goats, oil, and exhaust. The one in Australia. There's a huge rock out there, Ayers Rock it's called but its real name is Uluru, a word that's spooky even to say, one that sounds like wind around the eaves. A holy place for the aboriginal people who saw it first. Saw it, worshipped it, but never presumed to think they owned it. They understand that if there's a God, it's God's rock. Billy has never been there, but he's seen pictures of it in movies like *A Cry in the Dark* and magazines like *National Geographic* and *Travel*. He would like to go there, has even daydreamed about moving to Alice Springs, which is only a four-hour drive from Uluru, where the Rock raises its improbable head. Living there quietly. Writing, maybe, in a room filled with sunshine and a little garden outside.

His two phones are on the night table beside the bed. He has turned them off, but when he wakes up around three A.M., needing to empty his bladder, Billy touches the power button on each of them to see if anything's come in. There's nothing from Giorgio on the burner, which doesn't surprise him. He doesn't expect to hear from the fat man again, although he supposes that in a world where a conman can get elected president anything is possible. There is a message on the Dalton Smith phone, though. It's a news push from the local paper. *Prominent Businessman Commits Suicide.*

Billy uses the bathroom, then sits on the bed and reads the story. It's brief. The prominent businessman is, of course, Kenneth P. Hoff. One of his Green Hills neighbors was jogging by and heard a gunshot that seemed to have come from Hoff's garage. This was around seven P.M. The neighbor called 911. The police arrived and found Hoff dead behind the wheel of his car, which was running. There was a bullet hole in his head and a revolver in his lap.

There will be a longer, more detailed story later today or maybe tomorrow. It will recap Hoff's business career. There will be the usual shocked quotes from his friends and business associates. There will be references to 'current financial troubles' but no details, because other local movers and shakers, still very much alive, wouldn't care for that. His ex-wives will say nicer things about him than they surely told their divorce lawyers, and at the funeral they'll show up in black and dab their eyes with tissues – carefully, to protect their mascara. Billy doesn't know if the paper will say the car he was found in was a red Mustang convertible, but he's sure it was.

Hoff's connection to the Allen shooting, surely the motive for his suicide, will come later.

The story won't report the coroner's likely supposition, that the depressed man decided to kill himself by inhaling carbon monoxide, got impatient, and blew his brains out instead. Billy knows that isn't how it went down. The only thing he doesn't know is which of Nick's hardballs administered the killshot. It could have been Frank or Paulie or Reggie or someone he hasn't even met, possibly an import from Florida or Atlanta, but it's hard for Billy to see anyone but Dana Edison with his bright blue eyes and dark red manbun.

Did he march Hoff into the garage at gunpoint? Maybe he didn't need to, maybe he just told Hoff they were going to sit in his car and talk about how the situation was going to be resolved, and to Hoff's benefit. A self-involved optimist and designated patsy might buy that. He sits behind the wheel. Dana sits in the passenger bucket. Ken says *what's the plan*. Dana says *it's this* and shoots him. Then he turns on the engine, leaves through the back door, and rides away, silently, in a golf cart. Because that's what Green Hills is, a golf course with condos.

Maybe it didn't go down exactly that way, and maybe it wasn't Edison, but Billy's pretty sure he's got the picture in broad strokes. Which leaves Giorgio, the last piece of unfinished business.

Well, no, Billy thinks. There's me.

He lies down again, but this time sleep eludes him. Some of it is the way the old three-story house creaks. The wind has picked up, and without the railway station to block it, that wind blows straight through the vacant lot and across Pearson Street. Every time Billy starts to drift, the wind hoots around the eaves, saying *Uluru, Uluru*. Or there's another creak that sounds like a footstep on a loose board.

Billy tells himself a little insomnia doesn't matter, he can sleep the whole day away tomorrow if he so chooses, he won't be going anywhere for awhile, but the early morning hours are such long hours. There's too much to imagine, none of it good.

He thinks he will get up and read. He has no actual books except for *Thérèse Raquin*, but he can download something to his laptop and read in bed until he gets sleepy.

Then he has another idea. Maybe not a good idea, but he'll be able to sleep. He's sure of it. Billy gets up and takes Shan's drawing out of his pants pocket. He unfolds it. He looks at the smiling girl with the red ribbons in her hair. He looks at the hearts rising from the flamingo's head. He remembers Shan going to sleep next to him in the seventh inning of that playoff game. Her head on his arm. Billy puts the picture on the night table with his two phones and is soon asleep himself.

CHAPTER 12

1

Billy wakes up disoriented. The room is completely dark, not even a shred of light leaking in from around the shade of the window facing his backyard. For a moment he just lies there, still half asleep, then remembers there is no window, not in this room. The only window here is the one in his new living room. The one he calls his periscope. This isn't his large second-floor bedroom on Evergreen Street but the much smaller basement bedroom on Pearson Street. Billy remembers he's a fugitive.

He gets orange juice from the fridge, just a swallow or two to make it last, then showers off the sweat from yesterday. He dresses, pours milk over a bowl of Alpha-Bits, and turns on the six A.M. news.

The first thing he sees is Giorgio Piglielli. Not a photograph but an Identikit drawing that might as well be a photo, because it's amazingly good. Billy knows right away who worked with the police artist. Irv Dean, the Gerard Tower security guy, is an ex-cop, and it seems his observational skills are still intact, at least when he's not reading *Motor Trend* or examining breasts and butts in the *Sports Illustrated* swimsuit issue. There's nothing in the lead report about Ken Hoff. If the police have connected him to the Allen shooting, they haven't shared it with the news people. At least not yet.

The perky blonde weather girl gives a quick update, talking about how it's going to be unusually cold for this time of year. She promises a more detailed forecast later, then turns it over to the perky blonde traffic reporter, who warns commuters to expect a slow ride this morning 'because of a heightened police presence.'

That means roadblocks. The cops are assuming the shooter is still in the city, which is correct. They are also assuming that the fat man calling himself George Russo is also in the city. This, Billy knows, is incorrect. His former literary agent is in Nevada, possibly underground with his considerable bulk already beginning to decay.

After an ad for Chevy trucks, the anchors return with a retired police detective. He is asked to speculate on the possible reasons why Joel Allen was killed. The retired detective says, 'There's only one I can see. Someone wanted to shut him up before he could trade information for a reduced sentence.'

'What kind of sentence reduction could he possibly expect?' asks one of the anchors. She's a perky brunette. How can they all be so perky so early? Is it drugs?

'Life instead of the needle,' the detective returns, not even having to pause for thought.

Billy is sure this is also correct. The only question is what Allen knew, and why the killing had to be so public. As a warning to others who might share Allen's knowledge? Ordinarily Billy wouldn't care. Ordinarily he's just the mechanic. Only nothing about the situation in which he now finds himself is ordinary.

The anchors turn it over to a reporter who's interviewing John Colton, one of the Young Lawyers, and Billy doesn't want to see that. Just a week ago he and Johnny and Jim Albright were matching quarters to see who was going to pay for the tacos. They were on the plaza, laughing and having a good time. Now John looks stunned and woeful. He gets as far as 'We all thought he was a really decent—' before Billy kills the television.

He rinses out his cereal bowl, then checks the Dalton Smith phone. There's a text from Bucky, just three words: **No transfer yet**. It's what he expected, but that, added to the expression on Johnny Colton's face, is no way to start his first day in – might as well call it what it is – captivity.

If there's been no transfer yet, there probably isn't going to be any transfer at all. He was paid five hundred thousand up front, and that's a lot of cheese, but it's not what he was promised. Up to this morning Billy has been too busy to be really mad about getting stiffed by someone he trusted, but now he's not busy and he's pissed like a bear.

He did the job, and not just yesterday. He's been doing this job for over three months, and at far greater personal cost than he ever would have believed. He was promised, and who breaks their promises?

'Bad people, that's who,' Billy says.

He goes to the local newspaper. The headline is big – **COURTHOUSE ASSASSINATION!** – but it probably looks bigger and better in print than it does on his iPhone screen. The story tells him nothing he doesn't already know, but the lead photo makes it clear why Sheriff Vickery wasn't in attendance at Chief Conlee's press conference. The pic shows that absurd Stetson hat lying on the steps, with no county sheriff to hold it up. Sheriff Vickery beat feet. Sheriff Vickery skedaddled. This picture is worth a thousand words. For him it wouldn't have been a press conference, it would have been a walk of shame.

Good luck getting re-elected with that photo to explain, Billy thinks.

2

He goes upstairs to tend Daphne and Walter, then stops with the spray bottle in his hand, wondering if he's crazy. He's supposed to water them, not drown them. He checks the Jensens' fridge and sees nothing he wants but there's a package of English muffins on the counter with one left and he toasts it up, telling himself that if he doesn't use it, it will just get moldy. There are regular windows up here and he sits in a bar of sun, munching his muffin and thinking about what he's avoiding. Which is Benjy's story, of course. It's the only job he has to do now that he's finished the one that brought him here. But it means writing about the Marines, and there's so much, starting with the bus to Parris Island, basic . . . just so much.

Billy rinses off the plate he's used, dries it, puts it back in the cupboard, and goes downstairs. He looks out the periscope window and sees the usual not much. The pants he wore yesterday are on the bedroom floor. He picks them up and feels in the pockets, almost hoping he's lost the flash drive somewhere along the way, but it's there with his keys, one of them to Dalton Smith's leased Ford Fusion in the parking garage on the other side of town. Waiting until he feels it's safe to leave. *When the heat goes down*, as they say in those movies about the last job that always goes wrong.

The flash drive feels like it's gained weight. Looking at it, a marvelous storage device that would have seemed like science fiction only thirty years ago, there are two things he can't believe. One is how many words he's already put on it. The other is that there can possibly be any more. Twice as many. Four times as many. Ten, twenty.

He opens the laptop he thought he'd lost, a more expensive lucky charm than a battered baby shoe all grimy with dirt but otherwise about the same deal, and powers it up. He types in the password, plugs in the flash drive, and drags the single stored document to the laptop's screen. He looks at the first line – The man my ma lived with came home with a broke arm – and feels a kind of despair. This is good work, he feels sure of it, but what felt light when he started now feels heavy, because he has a responsibility to make the rest just as good, and he's not sure he can do it.

He goes to the periscope window and looks out at more nothing, wondering if he's just discovered why so many would-be writers are unable to finish what they have started. He thinks of *The Things They Carried*, surely one of the best books about war ever written, maybe *the* best. He thinks writing is also a kind of war, one you fight with yourself. The story is what you carry and every time you add to it, it gets heavier.

All over the world there are half-finished books – memoirs, poetry, novels, surefire plans for getting thin or getting rich – in desk drawers, because the work got too heavy for the people trying to carry it and they put it down.

Some other time, they think. Maybe when the kids are a little older. Or when I retire.

Is that it? Will it be too heavy if he tries writing about the bus ride and the jarhead haircut and the first time Sergeant Uppington asked him *Do you want to suck my cock, Summers? Do you? Because you look like a cocksucker to me.*

Ask?

Oh no, he didn't ask, Billy thinks, unless it was what you call a rhetorical question. He shouted in my face, his nose just an inch from mine, his spittle warm on my lips, and I said *Sir no sir, I do not want to suck your cock* and he said *Is my cock not good enough for you, Private Summers, you cocksucking poor excuse for a recruit?*

How it all comes back, and can he write it all, even as Benjy Compson?

Billy decides he can't. He pulls the curtain closed and goes back to the laptop, meaning to turn it off and spend the day watching TV. *Ellen DeGeneres*, *Hot Bench*, *Kelly and Ryan*, and *The Price Is Right* all before lunch. Then a nap and then some afternoon soap operas. He can finish with *John Law*, who tick-tocks his gavel like Coolio in the old music videos and takes no shit in his courtroom. But as he reaches for the off button, a thought comes from nowhere. It's almost as if someone has whispered in his ear.

You're free. You can do whatever you want.

Not physically free, God no. He'll be cooped up in this apartment at least until the police decide to lift their roadblocks, and even then it would be wise to stay a few days longer just to be sure. But in terms of his story, he's free to write whatever the fuck he wants. And *how* he wants. With no one looking over his shoulder, monitoring what he writes, he no longer has to pretend to be a dumb person writing about a dumb person. He can be a smart person writing about a young man (for that's what Benjy will be if Billy picks up the narrative again) who is poorly educated and naïve, but far from stupid.

I can let go of the Faulkner shit, Billy thinks. I can write *he and I* instead of *me and him*. I can write *can't* instead of *cant*. I can even use quotation marks for dialogue if I want to.

If he's writing strictly for himself, he can tell what's important to him and skip what isn't. He doesn't have to write about the jarhead haircut, even though he could. He doesn't have to write about Uppington screaming in his face, although he might. He doesn't have to write about the boy – Haggerty or Haverty, Billy can't remember which – who had a heart attack running and was taken away to the base infirmary, and Sergeant Uppington said he was fine and maybe he was and maybe he died.

Billy discovers that despair has given way to a kind of bullheaded eagerness. Maybe it's even arrogance. And so what if it is? He can tell whatever he wants. And will.

He begins by hitting global replace and changing Benjy to Billy and Compson to Summers.

3

I started my basic training at Parris Island. I was supposed to be there for three months but was only there for eight weeks. There was the usual shouting and bullshit and some of the boots quit or washed out but I wasn't one of them. The quitters and washouts might have had someplace to go back to, but I did not.

The sixth week was Grass Week, when we learned how to break down our weapons and put them back together. I liked that and was good at it. When Sergeant Uppington had us do what he called 'an arms race,' I always came in first. Rudy Bell, of course everybody called him Taco, was usually second. He never beat me, but sometimes he came close. George Dinnerstein was usually last and had to hit it and give Sergeant 'Up Yours' Uppington twenty-five, with Up's foot on George's ass the whole time. But George could shoot. Not as good as I could, but yes, he could put three out of every four in the center mass of a paper target at three hundred yards. Me, I could put four out of four center mass at seven hundred yards, almost every time.

There was no shooting during Grass Week, though. That week we just took our guns apart and put them back together again, chanting the Rifleman's Creed: 'This is my rifle. There are many like it, but this one is mine. My rifle is my best friend. It is my life.' And so on. The part I remember best is the part that says 'Without me, my rifle is useless. Without my rifle, I am useless.'

The other thing we did during Grass Week was sit on our asses in the grass. Sometimes for six hours at a stretch.

Billy stops there, smiling a little and remembering Pete 'Donk' Cashman. Donk fell asleep sitting in the tall South Carolina grass and Up Yours got down on his knees and screamed in his face to wake him up. *Is this boring you, Marine?*

Donk bolted to his feet so hard and fast he almost fell over, yelling *Sir no sir!* even before he was fully awake. He was George Dinnerstein's buddy and picked up the nickname Donk because he had a habit of grabbing his crotch and yelling *Honk my donk*. He never told Up to honk it, though.

The memories are piling in as Billy suspected they would – knew, really – but Grass Week isn't what he wants to write about. He doesn't want to write about Donk right now either, although he might later. He wants to write about Week 7, and all that happened after that.

Billy bends to it. The hours pass, unseen and unfelt. There's magic in this room. He breathes it in and breathes it out.

4

After Grass Week came Firing Week. We used the M40A, which is the military version of the Remington 700. Five-shot box, tripod mounted, NATO bottleneck rounds.

'You must see your target but your target must not see you.' Up told us that over and over. 'And no matter what you've seen in the movies, *snipers do not work alone.*'

Even though it wasn't Sniper School, Uppington put us in teams of two, spotter and shooter. I teamed with Taco and George teamed with Donk. I mention them because we ended up together in Fallujah, both Vigilant Resolve in April of '04 and Phantom Fury that November. Me and Taco

Billy stops, shaking his head, reminding himself the *dumb self* is in the past. He deletes and starts again.

Taco and I switched back and forth during Firing Week, me shooting and him spotting, then him shooting and me spotting. George and Donk started that way, too, but Up told them to quit it. 'You shoot, Dinner Winner. Cash, you just spot.'

'Sir I would also like to shoot sir!' Donk shouted. You had to shout when you addressed Up Yours. It was the Marine way.

'And I would like to tear your tits off and shove them up your sorry ass,' Up replied. So from then on, George was the shooter and Donk was the spotter in that pair. It stayed the same in Sniper School and in Iraq.

When Firing Week was almost over, Sergeant Uppington called me and Taco into his office, which wasn't much more than a closet. He said, 'You two are sorry fucking specimens, but you can shoot. Maybe you can learn to surf.'

That was how Taco and I found out we were being transferred to Camp Pendleton, and that's where we finished our basic, which by then was mostly shooting because we were in training to be snipers. We flew to California on United Airlines. It was my first time in an airplane.

Billy stops. Does he want to write about Pendleton? He doesn't. There was no surfing, at least not for him; how could there be when he never learned to swim? He did get himself a shirt that said CHARLIE DON'T SURF and wore it almost to tatters. He was wearing it the day he picked up the baby shoe and tied it to the belt loop on his right hip.

Does he want to write about Operation Iraqi Freedom? Nope. By the time he got to Baghdad, the war was over. President Bush said so, from the deck of the USS *Abraham Lincoln*. He said the mission was accomplished, and that made Billy and the jarheads in his regiment 'peacekeepers.' In Baghdad he had felt welcomed, even loved. Women and children threw flowers. Men yelled *nahn nihubu amerikaan*, we love America.

That shit didn't last long, Billy thinks, so never mind Baghdad, let's go right to the suck. He starts writing again.

By the fall of 2003 I was stationed in Ramadi, still peacekeeping up a storm, although sometimes by then there was shooting and the mullahs had started adding 'death to America' to their sermons, which were broadcast from the mosques and sometimes from storefronts. I was 3rd Battalion, also known as Darkhorse. My company was Echo. We shot a lot of target practice in those days. George and Donk were someplace else, but Taco and I were still a team.

One day a lieutenant colonel I didn't know stopped by to watch us shoot. I was using the M40, banging on a pyramid of beer cans at eight hundred yards, knocking them down one by one from top to bottom. You had to hit them low and kind of flip them, or the whole bunch would fall over.

This lieutenant colonel, Jamieson was his name, told me and Taco to come with him. He drove us in an unarmored Jeep to a hill overlooking the al-Dawla mosque. It was a very beautiful mosque. The sermon blaring from the loudspeakers wasn't so pretty. It was the usual bullshit about how the Americans were going to let the Jews colonize Iraq, Islam would be outlawed, the Jews would run the government and America would get the oil. We didn't understand the lingo, but *death to America* was always in English, and we'd seen translated leaflets, supposedly written by the leading clerics. The budding insurgency handed them out by the bale. *Will you die for your country?* they asked. *Will you die a glorious death for Islam?*

'How far is that shot?' Jamieson asked, pointing at the mosque's dome.

Taco said a thousand yards. I said maybe nine hundred, then added, being careful to address Jamieson respectfully, that we were forbidden to target religious sites. If, that was, the l-c had such a thing in mind.

'Perish the thought,' Jamieson said. 'I would never ask a soldier under my command to target one of their holy dungheaps. But the stuff coming out of those speakers is *political*, not religious. So which one of you wants to try knocking one of them off? Without putting a hole in the dome, that is? Which would be wrong and we'd probably go to muji hell for it.'

Taco right away handed the rifle to me. I had no tripod, so I laid the barrel on the hood of the Jeep and took the shot. Jamieson was using binoculars, but I didn't need them to see one of the speakers go tumbling to the ground, trailing its wire. There was no hole in the dome and the harangue, at least coming from that side, was noticeably less.

'Get some!' Taco yelled. 'Oh yeah, get summa *that* shit!'

Jamieson said we should bug the fuck out before someone started shooting at us, so that is what we did.

I look back on it and I think that day summed up everything that went wrong in Iraq, why 'we love America' changed to 'death to America.' The lieutenant colonel got tired of listening to that endless crap so he told us to shoot one of the speakers, which was stupid and meaningless when you considered there were at least six more pointing in other directions.

I saw men in doorways and women looking out of windows when we drove back to the base. Their faces were not happy *we love America* faces. No one shot at us – that day – but the faces said the day would come. As far as they knew, we weren't shooting at a loudspeaker. We were shooting at the mosque. Maybe there was no hole in the dome, but we were still shooting at their core beliefs.

Our patrols into Ramadi started getting more dangerous. The local police and the Iraqi National Guard were gradually losing control to the insurgents, but US forces weren't allowed to take their places because the politicians, both in Washington and Baghdad, were dedicated to the idea of self-rule. Mostly we sat out in camp, hoping we wouldn't end up doing protective duty while a repair crew worked on fixing a broken (or vandal-ized) watermain or a bunch of technicians, American and Iraqi, tried to get the broken (or sabotaged) power plant working again. Protective duty was just asking to get shot at, and we had half a dozen Marines KIA, many more wounded, by the end of 2003. The muj snipers were for shit, but their IEDs terrified us.

The whole house of cards tipped over on the last day of March, in 2004.

Okay, Billy thinks, this is where the story really starts. And I got here with a minimum of bullshit, as Up Yours would have said.

By then we had moved from Ramadi to Camp Baharia, also known as Dreamland. It was in the countryside about two miles outside of Fallujah, west of the Euphrates. Saddam's kids used to r&r there, we heard. George Dinnerstein and Donk Cashman were back with us in Echo Company.

The four of us were playing poker when we heard shooting coming from the other side of what we called the Brooklyn Bridge. Not just isolated shots, a regular barrage.

By nightfall the rumors had settled and we knew what had happened, at least in broad strokes. Four Blackwater contractors who were delivering food – including for our mess in Dreamland – decided to take a shortcut through Fallujah instead of going around, which was the normal protocol. They were ambushed just shy of the bridge over the Euphrates. I suppose they were wearing their armor, but nothing could save them from the concentrated fire that poured into the pair of Mitsubishi utes they were driving.

Taco said, 'What in God's name made them think they could drive right through the center of town, like it was Omaha? That was dumb.'

George agreed, but said that dumb or not, there had to be payback. We all thought the same. The killings were bad enough but killing wasn't enough for the mob. They dragged the dead from the 'Bishies, doused them with gasoline, and set them on fire. Two of them were pulled apart like rotisserie chickens. The other two were hung from the Brooklyn Bridge like Guy Fawkes dummies.

The next day Lieutenant Colonel Jamieson showed up while our squad was getting ready to go on patrol. He ordered me and Taco down from the back of the Hummer we were in and told us to come with him, because there was a man who wanted to see us.

The man was sitting on a pile of tires in an empty garage bay that stank of motor oil and exhaust. It was also hot as hell because all the doors were closed and those bays had no air conditioning. He stood up when we came in and looked us over. He was wearing a leather jacket, which was absurd in a stinky room that must have already been eighty-five degrees. It had the Darkhorse Battalion emblem on the breast: CONSUMMATE PROFESSIONALS on top and GET SOME on the bottom. But the jacket was just for show. I knew it right away and Taco said afterwards that he did, too. You only had to look at him to know he was 'fuckin'-A, CIA.' He asked which one of us was Summers and I said that was me. He said his name was Hoff.

Billy stops short, bemused. He has just crosswired his present life with his life in the suck. Was it Robert Stone who said the mind is a monkey? Sure it was, in *Dog Soldiers*. The one where Stone also said that men who shoot elephants with machine guns from Huey helicopters are just naturally going to want to get high. In Iraq it was camels the grunts and jarheads sometimes shot at. But yeah, while they were high.

He deletes the last line and consults the monkey that lives between his ears and behind his forehead. After a few seconds of thought, he comes up with the right name and decides the mistake is entirely forgivable. Hoff was at least close.

He said his name was Foss. He didn't offer to shake hands, just sat back down on the tires, which was sure to dirty up the seat of his pants. He said, 'Summers, I heard you were the best shot in the company.'

Since that wasn't a question I didn't say anything, just stood there.

'Could you make a twelve-hundred-yard shot across the river from our side?'

I took a quick look at Taco and saw he had heard it too, and knew what it meant. *Our side* meant anything outside of town. And if there were sides, that meant we were going in.

'Are you talking about hitting a human target, sir?'

'I am. Did you think I was talking about a beer bottle?'

A rhetorical question I didn't bother answering. 'Yes sir, I could make that shot.'

'Is that the Marine answer or your answer, Summers?'

Lieutenant Colonel Jamieson kind of frowned at that, as if he didn't believe there was any answer except the Marine answer, but he didn't say anything.

'Both, sir. Confidence maybe not so high on a windy day, but we—' I cocked a thumb at Taco. 'We can correct for wind. Blowing sand is something else.'

'The wind speed forecast for tomorrow is zero-to-ten,' Foss said. 'That wouldn't be a problem?'

'No, sir.' Then I asked a question I had no business asking, but I had to know. 'Are we talking about a bad haji, sir?'

The I-c said I was out of line, and would have said more, but Foss waved a hand at him and Jamieson closed his mouth.

'You ever tagged a man before, Summers?'

I told him I hadn't, and that was true. Tagging means sniping, and when I shot Bob Raines it was up close.

'Then this would be a very good way to start your career, because yes, this is a very bad haji. I'm assuming you know what happened yesterday?'

'We do, sir,' Taco said.

'Those contractors went through downtown Fallujah because they were told by what they considered to be a reliable source that it would be safe. They were told that goodwill was shifting toward the Americans. They were also given an escort by the Iraqi police. Only their escort was either insurgents in stolen uniforms, or renegade police, or real police who chickened out when they saw what a truly awesome raft of shit was coming their way. And they didn't do the killing, anyway. That was done by four dozen AK-wielding bad boys who . . . what do you think, fellas? Who just happened to turn up on the scene?'

I shrugged like I didn't know and let Taco carry the ball. Which he did. 'Doesn't seem likely, sir.'

'No, not likely at all. Those mujis were all in place. Waiting. A couple of pickup trucks were blocking the main drag. Someone planned that ambush, and we know who it was, because we were up on his cell phone. You follow?'

Taco said he did. I just shrugged again.

'That someone was a *shemagh*-wearing weasel named Ammar Jassim. In his sixties or seventies, nobody knows for sure, probably including him. He owns a computer and camera store that doubles as an Internet café and triples as a game room where the local young men can play Pac-Man and Frogger when they're not building IEDs and planting roadside bombs.'

'I know that place,' Taco said. 'Pronto Pronto Photo Photo. Seen it on patrol.'

Seen it? Hell, we'd been in there, playing Donkey Kong and Madden football. When we came in, the local boys all at once remembered they had business elsewhere and put on their boogie shoes. Taco didn't volunteer that and neither did I.

'Jassim's an old-line Ba'athist and new-line insurgent boss. We want him. Want him *bad*. Can't call in an LGB because we risk killing a bunch of kids playing video games, which will get us a fresh bunch of bad press on Al Jazeera. Can't afford that. Can't wait, either, because Bush is going to greenlight a clean-up operation within days, and if you tell anyone that, I'll have to kill you.'

'You won't get the chance,' Jamieson said. 'I'll do it first.'

Foss ignored him. 'Once the shit hits the fan, Jassim will be gone into the back streets with the rest of his gun-buddies. We need to get him before that can happen and make an example of that fucking Judas goat.'

Taco asked what a Judas goat was. I could have told him but kept my mouth shut and let Foss do the honors. Then he turned to me and asked again if I could do it and I said sir yes sir. I asked where I was supposed to shoot from and he told me. We'd been there before, carrying goods from resupply helicopters. I asked if I could swap the optics on my rifle for one of the new Leupold scopes or if I would have to make do with what I had. Foss looked at Jamieson, and Jamieson said, 'We'll make that happen.'

Going back to our barracks – the patrol had left without us – Taco asked me how sure I was that I could make the shot. I said, 'If I can't make it, I'll just blame my spotter.'

He thumped me on the shoulder. 'Fucking dickweed. Why do you always play dumb?'

'I don't know what you're talking about.'

'There you go again.'

'It's safer. What they don't know about you can't hurt you. Or come back to haunt you.'

He chewed that over for awhile. Then he said, 'Yeah, you can make the shot, okay, but that's not what I meant. This is an actual guy we're talking about. Are you sure you can do it? Shoot him stone-cold in the brainbox and take his life?'

I told Tac I was sure. I didn't tell him that I knew I could take a life because I'd done it before. I shot Bob Raines in the chest. It was Sniper School that taught me to always take the head shot.

5

Billy saves what he's written, gets up, and staggers a little because his feet feel like they're in another dimension. How long has he been sitting? He looks at his watch and is astounded to see it's been almost five hours. He feels like a man emerging from a vivid dream. He puts his hands in the small of his back and stretches, sending pins and needles down his legs. He walks from the living room to the kitchen to the bedroom, and finally back to the living room. He does it again, then a third time. The apartment seemed just the right size when he first saw it, the perfect place to hunker down in until things settled and he could drive his leased car north (or maybe west). Now it seems too small, like clothes that have been outgrown. He'd like to go out and walk, maybe even jog, but that would be a very bad idea even tricked out in his Dalton Smith gear. So he paces the apartment some more, and when that's not good enough he does pushups on the living room floor.

Drop and give me twenty-five, he thinks of Sergeant Up Yours saying. And don't mind my foot on your ass, you useless cumstain.

Billy has to smile. So much has come back to him. If he wrote it all, his story would be a thousand pages long.

The pushups make him feel calmer. He thinks about turning on the TV to see what's going on with the investigation, or checking his phone for newspaper updates (newspapers may be failing, but Billy has found they still seem to get the salient facts first). He decides against doing either. He's not ready to let the present back in. He thinks about getting something to eat, but he's not hungry. He should be, but he isn't. He settles for a cup of black coffee and drinks it standing up in the kitchen. Then he goes back to the laptop and picks up where he left off.

6

The next morning Lieutenant Colonel Jamieson himself drove me and Taco out to the intersection of Route 10 and the north–south road the Marines called Highway to Hell, after the AC/DC song. We went in the l-c's Eagle station wagon, which was special to him. Painted on the back deck was a decal showing a black horse with red eyes. I didn't like it, because I could imagine Iraqi spotters noting it, maybe even photographing it.

There was no sign of Foss. He had gone back to wherever those guys go after they set their plots in motion.

Parked out there on the hilltop in a dusty turnaround were two trucks from Iraqi Power & Light, or whatever was written in the pothooks on their sides. They looked just like American utility trucks, only smaller and painted apple green instead of yellow. The paint was much thicker on the sides, but even so it didn't completely obscure the smiling face of Saddam Hussein, like a ghost too stubborn to go away. There was also a Genie articulated boom lift with a bucket platform.

Two power poles stood at the intersection of the roads, with big transformers on them to step down the power-load to the residential neighborhoods of Fallujah and the surrounding suburbs. Guys in keffiyehs were scurrying around, plus a couple in those kufi hats. They were all wearing orange workmen's vests. No hardhats, though; I guess OSHA never made it to al-Anbar province. From across the river those men probably looked like any ragtag government work crew, but once you got closer than sixty yards, you could see they were all our guys. Albie Stark from our squad came over to me, flapping his headdress and singing that song about how you don't step on Superman's cape. Then he saw the l-c and saluted.

'Go someplace and look busy,' Jamieson told him. 'And please in the name of Jesus don't sing anymore.' He turned to me and Taco, but it was Taco he addressed, because he had decided Tac was the smart one. 'Give it to me again, Lance Corporal Bell.'

'Jassim comes outside most days around ten to have a smoke and talk to his adoring fans, probably some of the same guys that opened fire on the contractors. He'll be the one in the blue keffiyeh. Billy takes him out. End of story.'

Jamieson turned to me. 'If you make the kill, I'll put you in for a commendation. Miss, or hit one of the hanger-arounders, which would be worse, and I will transfer the boot that goes up my ass to yours, only harder and deeper. Do you understand that, Marine?'

'I think so, sir.' What I was thinking was that Sergeant Uppington could have delivered that line with far greater force and conviction. Still, I had to give the l-c props for trying. Months later he lost most of his face and all of his eyesight to a roadside bomb.

Jamieson motioned over Joe Kleczewski. He was another member of our squad, which we called the Hot Nine. Most of the 'utility workers' were. They volunteered for the job. They had to because Taco told them to.

'Sergeant, do you understand what must happen as soon as Summers takes the shot?'

Big Klew smiled, showing the gap in his front teeth. 'Get them down ASAP, then exfil like a motherfucker, sir.'

Although I could tell Jamieson was nervous – I think we all could – that made him smile. Most times Klew could coax a smile out of the stoniest face. 'That about covers it.'

'If he doesn't show, sir?'

'There's always tomorrow. Assuming the attack doesn't happen tomorrow, that is. Carry on, Marines, and none of that *oorah* shit, if you please.' He jerked his thumb at the Euphrates and the bear trap of a city on the other side. 'It's like the song says – voices carry.'

Albie Stark and Big Klew tried to cram into the bucket. It was supposed to be big enough for two, but not when one of them was Kleczewski's size. He almost knocked Albie over the side. Everybody but Jamieson laughed. It was as good as Abbott and Costello.

'Get out, you lummox,' the l-c told Klew. 'Jesus wept.' He motioned to Donk, whose brown combat boots were sticking out from beneath his pants, which were too short. This was also comical, because he looked like a kid clumping around the house in his daddy's shoes. 'You. Pipsqueak. Get over here. What's your name?'

'Sir, I am Pfc Peter Cashman, and I—'

'Don't salute, you dimwit, not in an op zone. Did your mother drop you on your head when you were a baby?'

'No sir, not that I remember, s—'

'Get in the bucket with what's-his-fuck, and when you get up there . . .' He looked around. 'Ah God, where's the fucking shroud?'

Maybe technically the right word for what he was talking about, but wrong in every other way. I saw Klew cross himself.

Albie, still in the bucket, looked down. 'Uh, I believe I'm standing on it, sir.'

Jamieson wiped his forehead. 'All right, okay, at least somebody remembered to bring it.'

That had been me.

'Get in there, Cashman. And deploy it with utmost haste. Time is marching.'

The bucket platform rose in a whine of hydraulics. At its maximum height, maybe thirty-five or forty feet, it shuddered to a stop beside one of the transformers. Albie and Donk danced around, yanking at the shroud and finally managing to get it out from under their feet. Then, aided by some inventive cursing – including some learned from the Iraqi kids who came out to beg candy and cigarettes – they got it deployed. The result was a canvas cylinder around the bucket and the transformer. It was held at the top by hooks on one of the pole's cross-arms and snapped together down one side, like the button-up fly on a pair of 501 jeans. The outside was emblazoned with a bunch of pothooks in bright yellow. I had no idea what they said and didn't care as long as it wasn't SNIPER TEAM AT WORK.

The bucket came back down, leaving the cylinder behind. It did look like a shroud once the waist-high rail of the bucket was no longer holding out the sides. Donk's hands were bleeding and Albie had a scratch on his face, but at least neither of them had taken a header out of the bucket. A couple of times it had looked close.

Taco was craning his neck to look up. 'What's that thing s'posed to be, sir?'

'Sand guard,' Jamieson said, then added, 'I believe.'

'Not exactly unobtrusive,' Taco said. Now he was looking across the river at the crammed-together houses and shops and warehouses and mosques on the other side. It was the southwestern part of town we'd come to call Queens. A hundred or so Marines came out of there in body bags. Hundreds more came out with fewer body parts than they had going in.

'When I want your opinion I'll give it to you,' the l-c said – an oldie but a goody. 'Grab your gear and get up there toot-sweet. Put on a couple of those orange vests before you get in the bucket so anyone looking sees them when you go up. The rest of you men kind of swirl around and look busy. The last thing we want is for anyone to see that rifle. Summers, keep your back to the river until you're under . . .' He stopped. He didn't want to say *until you're under the shroud* and I didn't want to hear it. 'Until you're under cover.'

I said roger that and up we went, me with my M40 held at port arms and my back to the city, Taco with his feet planted around his spotter stuff. Snipers are glamor boys, the ones they make movies about and the ones Stephen Hunter writes his novels about, but it's the spotters who really do the work.

I don't know how real shrouds smell, but the canvas cylinder stank like old dead fish. I undid three of the snaps down its seam to create a firing slit, but it was in the wrong place unless I wanted to shoot a goat wandering in the direction of Ramadi. The two of us managed to work it around, grunting and swearing and trying to keep the goddamned thing on at least two of the crossbar hooks as we did it. The canvas flapped in our faces. The dead fish smell got worse. This time I was the one who almost fell out of the bucket. Taco grabbed my orange vest with one hand and the strap of my rifle with the other.

'What are you men doing up there?' Jamieson called. From below, all he and the others could see were our feet shuffling around clumsily, like grammar school kids learning to waltz.

'Housework, sir,' Taco called back.

'Well, I suggest you stop the housework and get set up. It's almost ten.'

'Not our fault those nimrods put the slit facing the wrong direction,' Taco grumbled to me.

I checked the new scope and my rifle — there were many like it, but that one was mine — and used a square of chamois to wipe everything clean. In the suck, the sand and dust got into everything. I handed my piece to Taco for the mandatory recheck. He handed it back to me, licked his palm good and wet, then stuck it out through the firing slit.

'Wind speed nil, Billy-boy. I hope the bastard shows, because we'll never get a better day for it.'

Other than my rifle, the biggest piece of equipment we had in the bucket with us was the M151, also known as the Spotter's Friend.

Billy stops, startled out of his dream. He goes into the kitchen, where he splashes his face with cold water. He has come to an unexpected fork in what has been, up to now, a perfectly straight road. Maybe it makes no difference which of the diverging ways he takes, but maybe it does.

It's all about that M151. It's the optical scope the spotter used to calculate the distance from muzzle to target, and with eerie (it was to Billy, at least) accuracy. That distance is the basis for MOA, minute of angle. Billy needed none of that for the shot that took out Joel Allen, but the one he was responsible for making on that day in 2004, always assuming Ammar Jassim left his storefront to make it possible, was much longer.

Does he explain all that, or not?

If he does, that means he expects, or just hopes, that someday someone will read what he's writing. If he doesn't, it means he has given up that expectation. That hope. So which is it to be?

Standing there at the kitchen sink he flashes back to an interview he heard on the radio not long after he got out of the sand. Probably on one of those NPR shows where everyone sounds smart and full of Prozac. Some writer was getting interviewed, one of the oldtimers who was hot stuff back in the days when all the important writers were white, male, and borderline alcoholics. For the life of him Billy can't remember who that writer was, except it wasn't Gore Vidal – not snarky enough – and not Truman Capote – not quacky enough. What he *can* remember is what the guy said when the interviewer asked him about his process. 'I always keep two people in mind when I sit down to write: myself, and the stranger.'

Which brings Billy back full circle to the M151. He *could* describe it. He *could* explain its purpose. He *could* explain why MOA is even more important than distance, although the two are always joined together. He could do all of those things, but only needs to if he is writing for a stranger as well as himself. So is he?

Get real, Billy tells himself. I'm the only stranger here.

But that's okay. He can do it for himself if he has to. He doesn't need . . . what would you call it?

'Validation,' he murmurs as he goes back to the laptop. He once more picks up where he left off.

7

Other than my rifle, the biggest piece of equipment we had in the bucket with us was the M151, also known as the Spotter's Friend. Taco set up the tripod and I shuffled out of his way as best I could. The platform bounced a little and Taco told me to hold still unless I wanted to put a bullet in the sign over the shop door instead of in Jassim's head. I stayed as still as I could while Taco did his thing, making calculations and muttering to himself.

Lieutenant Colonel Jamieson had estimated the distance as 1,200 yards. Taco took his readings on a kid bouncing a ball in front of Pronto Pronto Photo Photo and called it 1,340 yards. A long shot for sure, but on a windless day like that one in early April, a high confidence one. I had made longer, and we had all heard stories of world-class snipers making shots at twice that distance. Of course I couldn't count on Jassim being perfectly stationary, like the head on a paper target. That concerned me, but the fact that he was a human being with a beating heart and a living brain didn't. He was a Judas goat who had lured four men into an ambush, guys guilty of nothing but delivering food. He was a bad guy and needed to be put down.

Around quarter past nine, Jassim came out of his store. He was wearing a long blue shirt like a dashiki and baggy white pants. Today he was wearing a knitted red cap instead of a blue topper. That was a wonderful sight marker. I started to line up the shot, but Jassim just shooed the ball-bouncing kid away with a swat on the butt and went back inside.

'Well doesn't that suck,' Taco said.

We waited. Young men went into Pronto Pronto Photo Photo. Young men came out. They were laughing and scuffling and grabassing around as young men do all over the world, from Kabul to Kansas City. Some of them had no doubt been shooting up those Blackwater trucks with their AKs just a couple of days before. Some of them were undoubtedly firing at us seven months later as we went from block to block, cleaning them out. For all I know, some of them were in what we called the Funhouse, where everything that could go wrong did go wrong.

Ten o'clock came, then ten-fifteen. 'Maybe he's taking his smoke break out back today,' Taco said.

Then, at ten-thirty, the door of Pronto Pronto Photo Photo opened and Ammar Jassim came out with two of his young men. I sighted in. I saw them laughing and talking. Jassim clapped one of them on the back and the two men strolled off with their arms around each other's shoulders. Jassim took a pack of cigarettes from his pants pocket. I was in the optics and could read Marlboro and see the two trademark gold lions. Everything was clear: his bushy eyebrows, his lips as red as a woman's wearing lipstick, his salt-and-pepper beard stubble.

Taco was sighting with the M151, now handheld. 'Fucker's a dead ringer for Yessir I'm-a Fat.'

'Shut up, Tac.'

I laid the crosshairs on the knitted cap and waited for Jassim to light up. I was willing to allow him one last drag before putting out his lights. He stuck a cigarette in his mouth. He put the pack back into his pocket and came out with a lighter. Not a cheap disposable Bic but a Zippo. He might have purchased it, either in a store or on the black market. It might also have been looted from one of the contractors who had been shot, burned, and hung from the bridge. He flipped it open and a tiny sunstar winked off the top. I saw that. I saw everything. Master Gunny Sergeant Diego Vasquez at Pendleton used to say that a Marine sniper lives for a perfect shot. This one was perfect. He also said, 'It's like sex, my little virgins. You will never forget your first.'

I drew in a breath, held it for a five-count, and squeezed the trigger. The recoil hit the hollow of my shoulder. Jassim's knitted hat flew off and at first I thought I had missed him, maybe only by an inch, but when you're sniping, an inch might as well be a mile. He just stood there with the cigarette between his lips. Then the lighter fell out of his fingers and the cigarette fell out of his mouth. They landed on the dusty sidewalk. In the movies, the person who gets shot flies back when the bullet hits. That's rarely how it happens in real life. Jassim actually took two steps forward. By then I could see that it wasn't just the hat that had come off; the top of his head was inside it.

He went to his knees, then full on his face. People came running.

'Payback's a bitch,' Taco said, and clapped me on the back.

I turned and yelled, 'Get us down!'

The platform started to descend. It seemed very slow, because the gunfire had begun on the other side of the river. It sounded like fireworks.

Taco and I ducked as we left the canvas sand-shield behind, not because ducking made us safer but because it was instinctive. I listened for bullets passing and tried to get ready to be hit, but I didn't hear anything or feel anything.

'Get out of there, get out!' Jamieson shouted. 'Jump! Time to didi mau!' But he was laughing, triumphant. They all were. I had my back slapped so often and so hard that I almost fell over as we ran back to the dirty Mitsubishi the I-c had used to drive us out. Albie, Donk, Klew, and the others ran for the little power trucks, a scam that we'd never be able to use again. We could hear yelling across the river, and now there was even more gunfire.

'Yeah, eat it!' Big Klew shouted. 'Eat it big, motherfuckers! Your man just got run over by the big dark horse!'

The I-c's old station wagon was parked behind the Iraqi power trucks in the turnaround. I opened the back to put in my rifle and Taco's gear.

'Hurry the fuck up,' Jamieson said. 'We're blocking those guys in.'

Well, you were the one who parked there, I thought but didn't say. I tossed in our stuff. When I slammed the hatchback shut, I saw something lying in the dirt. It was a baby shoe. It must have been a little girl's, because it was pink. I bent down to get it and as I did, some shooter's blind-luck round punched into the bulletproof glass of the hatchback's window. If I hadn't bent down, the round would have gone in the nape of my neck or the back of my head.

'Get in, get in!' Jamieson was screaming. Another blind-luck round pinged off the Eagle wagon's armored side. Or maybe not so blind; by then the shooters had to be all the way down by their side of the river.

I picked up the shoe. I got in the 'Bishi and Jamieson tore out of there, fishtailing and throwing up a cloud of dust the trucks would have to drive through. The I-c wasn't thinking about that; he was concentrating on saving his ass.

'They're shooting the shit out of that boom lift,' Taco said. He was still laughing, high on the kill. 'What have you got there?'

I showed it to him and said I thought it had saved my life.

'You keep that thing safe, brah,' Taco said. 'And keep it with you.'

I did. Until the Funhouse, that November. I looked for it just as we started to clear that house in the Industrial Sector and it was gone.

8

Billy finally shuts down and stands at the periscope window of his landlocked submarine, looking out across the little patch of lawn, to the street, to the vacant lot on the other side where the train station once stood. He doesn't know how long he's been standing here. Maybe quite awhile. His brain feels blasted, as if he's just finished taking the world's longest and most complicated test.

How many words did he write today? He could check the counter on his document — now Billy's story instead of Benjy's — but he's not that OCD. It was a lot, leave it at that, and he's still got a long way to go. There was the April assault that started less than a week after he killed Jassim, followed by the pullback when the politicians got cold feet. Then the final nightmare that was Operation Phantom Fury. Forty-six days of hell. He won't put it that way (if he even gets that far) because it's a cliché, but hell is what it was. Culminating in the Funhouse, which seemed to summarize all the rest. He might skim through some of it but not the Funhouse, because the Funhouse was the point of Fallujah. And what exactly was the point? That it was pointless. Just another house that had to be cleared, but the price they paid.

A few people walk by on Pearson Street. A few cars drive by. One is a police car, but it doesn't concern Billy. It's moving leisurely, heading nowhere special and in no hurry to get there. He is still amazed that this part of the city, which is so close to downtown, feels so deserted. On Pearson Street, rush hour is hush hour. He supposes that most people who work in the city's center haul ass to the suburbs when the workday is done — nicer places like Bentonville, Sherwood Heights, Plateau, Midwood. Even Cody, where he won a little girl a stuffed toy. The neighborhood of which he is now a part doesn't even have a name, at least that he knows of.

He needs to catch up. Billy flips on Channel 8, the NBC affiliate, wanting to stay away from 6, which will still be running the footage of Allen being shot. 8 comes on with a BREAKING NEWS logo and a soundtrack of ominous violins and thumping drums. Billy doubts that there's any serious news breaking with the assassin still at large. The assassin has spent the day writing a story that is in grave danger of becoming a book.

It turns out there have been developments, but nothing Billy hasn't expected and not anything that warrants the disaster soundtrack. One of the anchors says that local businessman Kenneth Hoff has been implicated in 'the widening assassination conspiracy.' The other anchor says that Kenneth Hoff's apparent suicide may have been murder. Holmes, your deductions astound me, Billy thinks.

The anchors hand it over to a correspondent standing across the street from Hoff's home, an expensive crib that is still several rungs below Nick's rented McMansion on the grandiosity ladder. The correspondent is a leggy blonde who looks like she might have gotten out of journalism school the week before. She explains that Kenneth Hoff has been 'positively linked' to the Remington 700 rifle that was used to kill Joel Allen. This is in addition to plenty of other links to the presumed assassin, who has now been 'positively identified' as William Summers, a Marine veteran of the Iraq war and winner of several medals.

Bronze Star and Silver Star, Billy thinks. Also a Purple Heart with a star on the ribbon, indicating not just one wound suffered in battle but two. He can understand them not wanting to do that particular rundown. He's the villain of the piece, so why muddle things up with a heroic background? Muddling things up is for novels, not news reports.

There are side-by-side pictures. One is the photo Irv Dean took of him at the Gerard Tower security stand on his first day as the building's resident writer. The other shows him as a new recruit, looking both solemn and goofy in his jarhead haircut. It was taken on Photo Day. In it he looks even younger than the blonde correspondent. Probably he was. They must have gotten it from some Marine archive, because Billy had no family to give a copy to on Family Day.

Local police believe that Summers may have fled the city, the correspondent says, and because he may also have fled the state, the FBI is now on the case. With that the blonde sends it back to the studio, where the anchors next display a picture of Giorgio Piglielli, and yes, they give his mob nickname, as if Georgie Pigs is an alias he might be traveling under. He's been linked to organized crime operations in Las Vegas, Reno, Los Angeles, and San Diego, but hasn't yet been apprehended. The subtext is that if you see a middle-aged Italian guy who goes 370, possibly wearing alligator shoes and drinking a milkshake, get in touch with your local law enforcement.

So, Billy thinks. Hoff is dead, Giorgio is almost certainly dead, and Nick's alibied up the ying-yang. Which makes me the last melon in the patch, the last pea in the pod, the last chocolate in the box, pick your metaphor.

After an ad for some wonder pill with about two dozen possible side effects, some lethal, there are more interviews with his neighbors on Evergreen Street. Billy gets up to turn off the TV, then sits down again. He flew under false colors and hurt these people. Maybe he deserves to watch and listen as they express that hurt. And their bewilderment.

Jane Kellogg, the block's resident alcoholic, doesn't seem a bit bewildered. 'I knew there was something wrong with him the first time I saw him,' she says. 'He had shifty eyes.'

Bullshit you did, Billy thinks.

Diane Fazio, Danny's mom, shares how horrified she was when she found out they had allowed their children to spend time with a cold-blooded killer.

Paul Ragland marvels about how smooth he was, how natural. 'I really thought Dave was the real deal. He seemed like a totally nice guy. It sort of proves that you can't trust anybody.'

It's Corinne Ackerman who says the one thing everyone else seems to have ignored. 'Of course it's terrible, but that man he shot wasn't going to court for shoplifting, was he? From what I understand he was a stone killer. If you ask me, David saved the county the cost of a trial.'

God bless you, Corrie, Billy thinks, and actually finds his eyes are welling up, as if it's the end of a Lifetime channel movie where everything comes out right. Always supposing your concept of right includes a dose of vigilante justice . . . and in cases like Joel Allen's, Billy has no problem with that.

Before moving on to the traffic (still slow because of police checkpoints, sorry folks) and the weather (turning colder), there's a final item in the courthouse assassination story, and Billy has to smile. The reason Sheriff Vickery was initially cut out of the investigation isn't because he skedaddled when his prisoner was shot, leaving only his ridiculous Stetson behind, or not just because of that. It's because he brought his prisoner up the courthouse steps instead of through the employees' door further down. There was initial suspicion that he might have been part of the plot. He has since convinced them otherwise, probably admitting that he wanted the press coverage.

And I could have made the shot either way, Billy thinks. Hell, I could have made it in the rain, unless it was a deluge out of Genesis.

He turns off the television and goes into the kitchen to inspect his stock of frozen dinners. He's already thinking about what he'll write tomorrow.

CHAPTER 13

1

Three days pass in a dream of Fallujah.

Billy writes about the Hot Nine: Taco Bell, George Dinnerstein and Albie Stark, Big Klew, Donk Cashman. He spends one morning writing about how Johnny Capps more or less adopted a bunch of Iraqi kids who came to beg candy and cigarettes and stayed to play baseball. Johnny and Pablo 'Bigfoot' Lopez taught them the game. One kid, Zamir, maybe nine or ten, used to chant – 'He was safe, mothafuckah!' over and over. Other than 'Gedda hit' it seemed to be the only English he had. Somebody would pop out to the shortstop and Zamir, sitting on the bench in his red pants and Snoop Dogg tee and Blue Jays cap, would scream, 'He was safe, mothafuckah!' Billy writes about how Clay Briggs, the corpsman they called Pillroller, kept up a lively and pornographic correspondence with five girls back in Sioux City. Tac said he couldn't understand how such an ugly guy got so much pussy. Donk said it was *fictional* pussy and Albie Stark said, 'He was safe, mothafuckah!' which had nothing to do with the issue of Pill's lively and pornographic correspondence, but which broke them up every time.

Billy exercises between stints at the laptop: pushups, situps, leg-lifts, squat thrusts. For the first two days he also runs in place, hands held out and down, smacking his palms with his knees. On the third day he suddenly remembers – duh! – that he has the house to himself, and instead of running in place he pelts up and down the stairs to the third floor until he's out of breath and his pulse is racing along at a hundred and fifty per. He's not exactly going stir-crazy, not after less than a week, but long spells of sitting and writing aren't what he's used to, and these bursts of exercise keep him from getting squirrelly.

Exercise also aids thinking, and on one of his sprints up the stairs Billy has an idea. He can't believe he hasn't thought of it before. Billy uses the Jensens' key to let himself into their apartment. He checks Daphne and Walter (both doing well), then goes into the bedroom. Don is a certain kind of guy, likes his football and NASCAR, likes his BBQ ribs and chicken, likes a few brewskis on Friday night with the boys. A man like that almost certainly has a gun or two.

Billy finds one in the nightstand on Don's side of the bed. It's a Ruger GP six-shooter, fully loaded. Beside it is a box of .38 centerfire cartridges. Billy sees no reason to take the gun downstairs; if the cops bust in on him, he's certainly not going to shoot it out with them. But you never know when a gun might come in handy, and it's good to know where he can lay his hands on one if the need arises. What need that might be he can't imagine, but there are many twists and turns as one hops down the bunny trail of life. No one knows better than he does.

He gives Bev's plants a squirt each with the vaporizer, then trots back downstairs. Outside he can hear the wind picking up, blowing across the vacant lot on the other side of the street. The forecast is for rain and even colder temperatures. 'You might not believe it,' the lady weatherperson chirped that morning, 'but there may actually be some sleet mixed in with it. I guess Mother Nature can't read the calendar!'

Billy doesn't care if it rains, sleets, snows, or shits bananas. He's going to be in this basement apartment no matter what the weather is. The story he's writing has taken over his life because for the time being it's the only life he has, and that's okay.

He's had two brief communications with Bucky Hanson. Last night he texted **Are u ok?** to which Bucky responded **Y**. He texted **Has the money been paid?** to which Bucky responded, as Billy expected, **N**. He can't call Giorgio, even with his burner, because the cops may be up on his phone. And what would he get if he took the risk? Almost certainly a female robot telling him that number is no longer in service. Because Giorgio is no longer in service. Billy is sure of it.

In the alternate world of his story, Billy has reached Operation Phantom Fury in November of 2004. He thinks that part may take ten days, possibly two weeks. When it's done, when he's put the story of the Funhouse to rest, he'll pack up his shit and get out of town. The checkpoints will be gone by then, may be gone already.

He sits at the laptop, looking at where he left off. Two days before the assault commenced, Jamieson ordered Johnny and Pablo to get the baseball kids off the base, and they all understood what that meant: they were going in again, and this time they'd be staying in until the job was done.

Billy remembers Zamir looking back at the gate and giving one final cry of 'He was safe, mothafuckah!' Then they were gone for good. All these years later they'd be grown men. If they're still alive.

He starts to write about the day the baseball kids got sent home, but it feels flat. The well is temporarily dry. He saves his copy, shuts down, then walks around to the other laptops, the cheapies. He boots each up in turn, checks that all clickbait is updated (MICHAEL JACKSON'S DYING WISH, ONE SIMPLE TRICK TO BEAT SCIATICA, WHAT THE ORIGINAL MOUSEKETEERS LOOK LIKE NOW), and shuts them down, too. All is well in his little world. He has a plan. He will finish the Iraq part of his story, the Funhouse serving as the natural climax. When that's done he'll pack up and get out of this bad luck town. He will drive west, not north, and at some point in the not-too-distant future, he will pay Nick Majarian a visit.

Nick owes him money.

2

Billy's plan lasts until quarter to midnight. He's been watching some action movie in his underwear, and although the plot is simple – something about a guy seeking revenge on the men who killed his dog – Billy has lost the thread. He decides to call it a day. He shuts off the idiot box and is heading for the bedroom when there's a loud squall of skidding tires and badly maintained brakes outside. He braces himself for the sound of the crash, that hollow slam-the-big-door boom as the vehicle goes head-on into a power pole. Instead he hears faint music and loud laughter. Drunken laughter, from the sound.

He goes to his periscope window and shoves back the curtain. There's a streetlight up the way and it casts just enough glow for him to see an old van with rusty sides. One set of wheels is on the sidewalk running beside the vacant lot. It's raining now, and hard enough so the van's headlights look like they're cutting through a gauze curtain. The long door on the passenger side rolls open on its track. The inside light goes on, but all Billy can make out through the blowing rain are shapes. Three at least, moving around. No, there are four. The fourth is slumped over, head low. Two of them are holding the shape under its arms, which hang down at the elbows like broken wings.

There's more laughter and talk. Two guys manhandle the slumped shape out of the van while a third stands behind them like he's supervising. The unconscious person has long dark hair. Probably a girl. The guys take her behind the van and let go of her. She folds up with her top half on the sidewalk and her bottom half in the gutter. The two guys hop back in. The cargo door rolls shut. For a moment the old van stays there, idling with its headlights cutting through the pelting rain. Then it pulls out with a squeal of tires and a belch of exhaust. There's a bumper sticker on the back, but no way can Billy read it. The light over the license plate is flickering, almost dead.

It's a girl for sure. She's wearing sneakers, a skirt hiked up high enough to show nearly all of one bent leg, and a leather jacket. The exposed leg is half submerged in running gutter water. It looks very white. Can she be dead? Would those men have been laughing if she was? After some of the things he's seen in the desert (and can never unsee), Billy knows it's possible.

He has to get her, and not just because she might die out there if he doesn't. This part of town is quiet even at noon on a weekday, but eventually someone will come along and spot her. They might not stop, good Samaritans are always in short supply, but they would surely call 911. Thank God it's late and thank God he didn't go to bed five minutes sooner. There would have come a knock on his door, cops canvassing the houses on this side of Pearson Street to find out if anyone had seen the girl dumped, and if the knock came at one or two in the morning, he'd have no chance to even put on the Dalton Smith wig, let alone the fake stomach. *Hey*, one of the cops might say. *You look familiar, buddy. I think you should come with us.*

Billy doesn't bother putting on his pants and shoes, just runs up the stairs in his boxers. He goes through the foyer and down the front steps, leaving the door open to bang back and forth in the wind. He's aware that he's gotten a pretty good splinter in the ball of one foot, run it in there deep, but more aware of how fucking *cold* it is. Not cold enough for the rain to turn to sleet, at least not yet, but close. His arms are covered in goosebumps. The part of his big toe that isn't there aches. If the girl is still alive, she might not stay that way for long.

Billy goes to one knee and picks her up, so cranked with adrenaline that he has no idea if she's heavy or light. He looks both ways with rain running down his face and bare chest. His boxers are soaked, hanging low on his hips. He sees no one. Thank God. He splashes back to the apartment side of the street, and as he's carrying her up the walk, she turns her head, makes a guttural sound, and spews a thin ribbon of vomit down his side and one of his legs. It's shockingly warm, almost like an electric heating pad.

Well, he thinks, she's alive all right.

He picks up another splinter on the steps, but then he's inside. He can't leave the outside door to bang in the wind, so he sets her down in the foyer and pulls it closed. When he turns back to her, the girl's eyes are half open. He can see a big purplish bruise on her cheek and the side of her nose. Can't be from the pavement because she didn't go down on her face. Besides, the bruising is too well established for that.

'Who're you?' the girl slurs. 'Where—' Then she vomits again. This time it backwashes down her throat and she starts to choke.

Billy kneels behind her and gets an arm around her midsection. He uses her breasts as a brace and hauls her up in front of him. Now his fucking boxers, wet with rainwater and a little too big to begin with, start sliding down his legs. He gets two fingers in her mouth, hoping to God she won't bite him. Infected cuts are the last thing he needs. He gets a wad of stuff out, flings it to the floor, then tightens his grip on her midsection. It does the trick. She hurls like a hero, a banner of puke that hits the foyer wall with a splat.

A car, one that would have spelled his doom just three minutes before, is coming. Billy can see its headlights brightening the rain-splattered glass of the front door. He drops to one knee, still holding the girl in front of him. His stupid boxers are now spread between his knees and he actually has time to wonder why he ever gave up Jockeys. Her head is lolling forward, but he thinks the rasping sounds he now hears are snores, not choking. She's out again.

The headlights brighten, then diminish without slowing. Billy gets to his feet, hauling the girl up with him. He gets an arm under her knees, the other around her shoulders. Her head lolls backward. He shimmies his legs and his shorts fall to his ankles. He steps out of them and kicks them aside. It's like some nightmarish vaudeville skit.

Her dank hair drips and pendulums back and forth as he sidesaddles down the stairs, trying not to overbalance and fall. Her upturned face is as pale as the moon. There's another bruise on her forehead, above her left eye.

And Jesus, his feet are killing him. Never mind his half-gone toe, those fucking splinters! He makes it to the foot of the stairs without falling and bumps open the door to his apartment with his butt. She starts to slither out of his grip, her body forming a limp U shape. He raises one leg into the small of her back, shoves her back up, and staggers inside. She starts to slide again. Ignoring the splinters digging into his cold-reddened feet, Billy sprints to the couch. He makes it just in time. She lands with a thump, gives out a fuzzy grunting noise, then resumes her snoring.

Billy bends forward with his hands braced above his knees to ease his back, which is trying to cramp up. The stink of puke rising from her almost makes him feel like puking himself. He can smell alcohol too, but it's faint.

Well, she offloaded it, he thinks, but if she really got her drink on he should still be able to smell it on her breath. He should have smelled it in the foyer. And—

He lifts his leg, smelling the mostly liquid vomit on his skin. He still gets only the faintest whiff of booze.

He looks her up and down. The skirt she's wearing is denim, frayed at the hem, and short. He could see her underpants if she was wearing any, but she's not. He sees something else. The outsides of her thighs are pale and white – like the moon – but the tops of the insides are speckled with drying blood.

3

The girl retches again, but weakly, and nothing comes out except for a dribble of cloudy drool down the side of her mouth. Then she starts to shiver. Of course she's shivering, she's soaked. Billy pulls off her sneakers. Tiny ankle socks come with them. There are hearts on the tops. He gets her to sit up, muttering 'Come on, little help here,' although he knows she can't help. Her eyelids flutter and she tries to talk. She may even think she *is* talking, that she's asking all the questions anyone might ask in a situation like this, but the only words he can make out are *who* and *you*. All the rest is just *huzzz* and *whaa*.

'That's right,' Billy says, 'all okay now, just don't die on me.'

Although even now, as he's trying to cope with this fucked-up situation, Billy realizes it might simplify things if she did. It's a rotten thought, but that doesn't make it untrue.

He gets her jacket − cheap, thin, and not real leather at all but some synthetic − off. Beneath is a T-shirt with BLACK KEYS NORTH AMERICAN TOUR 2017 on the front. He tries to pull it off over her head and it gets caught on her chin. She moans and he gets three words in the clear: 'No, don't *choke*.'

She starts to slide. He gets the shirt off just in time to catch her and keep her from falling onto the floor. Her plain white cotton bra is askew, one breast covered and one out because the strap that's supposed to go over her left shoulder is broken. He shoves the bra down, turns it around, and manages to get it unhooked.

Once her top half is undressed, he's able to lie her back down. He pulls off her soaked denim skirt and throws it on the floor with the rest of her clothes. Now she's naked except for one earring, the other gone God knows where. She's all over gooseflesh, still shivering. It's because she's cold, but it's also shock. He saw shivering like that in Fallujah, and saw it turn into convulsions. Of course she hasn't suffered multiple bullet wounds in the legs like poor old Johnny Capps, but there *is* blood on her, and now he sees three bruises on one of the girl's small breasts as well. Narrow bruises. Somebody grabbed her there and squeezed. Really hard. There are two more finger-shaped bruises on the left side of her neck and Billy thinks of her saying *No, don't choke.*

Mindful that she may not be done vomiting, Billy turns her on her side and then pushes her front-first to the back of the couch so she hopefully won't fall off. She's snoring again, the sound harsh but regular. And her teeth are chattering. She's one fucked-up American.

He hurries into the bathroom and gets one of his two bath towels. He kneels in front of the couch and rubs her back, her butt, her thighs and calves. He does it briskly, relieved to see a little faint color rise into her pallid skin. He takes one of her shoulders (another bruise there, but smaller), rolls her onto her back, and begins again: feet, legs, stomach, breasts, chest, shoulders. When he does her face she raises her hands in a weak warding-off gesture, then drops them as if it's too much work, just too much. He makes an effort to dry her hair but he's not going to get far with that because there's a lot of it, and the rainwater from the gutter soaked it to the scalp.

Billy thinks, I'm fucked. No matter how this goes, I'm fucked. He drops the towel and reaches for her, planning to roll her back onto her side so that she won't choke if she throws up again, then re-thinks. He takes her right leg and lowers it so her heel is on the floor and her vagina is revealed. The labia are enflamed bright red and split in several places, one of the splits still beading up fresh blood. The flesh between her vagina and her rectum – he knows the word for that part but can't think of it in this stressed-out moment – is torn worse than her labia, and God knows what damage there might be inside. He can see several dried splats of semen as well, most of it on her lower stomach and in her pubic hair.

The guy pulled out, Billy thinks, then remembers that there were three shapes in the van, and judging from the sound of their laughter, all male. One of them did, anyway.

This thought makes him aware of his own situation. Considering what has happened to the girl on his couch, it's not without irony: she's out cold with her legs open and both of them as naked as the day they were born. What would his Evergreen Street neighbors think if they could see this tableau? Not even Corrie Ackerman, kind heart that she is, would continue to defend him. He can see the headline in the *Red Bluff News*: COURTHOUSE ASSASSIN ALSO RAPED TEENAGER!

Fucked, he thinks. Fucked to the sky and back down to the ground.

Billy wants to get her into bed, but he has something else to attend to first. Now that things have settled down, he realizes his feet hurt like blue fuck. There's a lot of stuff he didn't buy when he stocked this place, and that includes tweezers, but there are Band-Aids and some leftover hydrogen peroxide in the bathroom from the last tenant. The disinfectant is probably long past the sell-by date, but beggars can't be choosers.

Walking on the sides of his feet as best he can, Billy gets a paring knife from the kitchen, then the bathroom stuff. The Band-Aids are decorated with *Toy Story* characters. He sits on the floor beside the snoring, shivering girl and uses the knife to lift the splinters enough so he can pull them out. There are five in all, including two big boys. He douses the bleeding wounds with peroxide. The sting makes him think the stuff may actually do some good. He covers the two biggest wounds with Band-Aids that probably won't stick very long. He guesses they're pretty old, maybe from two or even three tenants back.

He gets to his feet, rolls his shoulders to loosen them, then picks up the girl. Without the adrenaline to boost him, he guesses her weight at one-fifteen. Maybe one-twenty. Not much of a match for three men. Did they all rape her? Billy guesses that if they were together and one did, they all did. He will ask her when she comes around, for all the good it will do. He doubts if she'll be able to remember and what she'll want to know is why he didn't call the police or take her to the nearest ER.

She's sinking into a U shape again and Billy ends up dropping her onto the bed instead of putting her down on it gently, as he intended. She opens her eyes a bit, then closes them again and resumes snoring. He doesn't want to wrestle with her anymore, but he also doesn't want her lying there naked. She's going to be freaked out enough when she wakes up. He gets a T-shirt from the bureau, sits beside her, lifts her with his left arm and gets the shirt over her head with his right hand. Her fuzzy sounds of protest fade back into snores when he gets it past her face and over her shoulders.

'Help me now.' He lifts one of her arms and after a couple of failures manages to poke it through the short sleeve. 'Little help, okay?'

Some part of her must hear him because she raises her other arm and finally wavers it into the sleeve. He lays her back down, blows out a breath, and arms sweat from his forehead. The shirt is bunched above her breasts. He pulls it down in front, lifts her, pulls it down in back. She's shivering again and whimpering a little. Billy puts an arm under her knees, lifts her, and yanks the hem of the shirt down over her buttocks and thighs.

God, like dressing a baby, Billy thinks.

He hopes she won't piss the bed – he's only got this one set of sheets and the nearest laundromat is three blocks away – but he knows there's a good chance she will. At least most of the bleeding has stopped. He supposes it could have been worse. They could have torn her wide open, even killed her. That might even have been what they meant to do, dumping her the way they did, but Billy doubts it. He thinks they were all just really drunk. Or high on something mean, like crystal. The assholes probably thought she'd come around and walk home, sadder but wiser.

He stands, wipes his brow again, and pulls up the blanket. She clutches it at once, pulls it to her chin, and turns on her side. That's good because she might vomit again. He can't believe she has anything left to bring up, considering all she puked out in the foyer, but there's no way to tell.

Even with the blanket, she's shivering.

What am I supposed to do with you? Billy thinks. Just what the fuck am I supposed to do with you, tell me that.

It's a question he can't answer. All he knows is that he's in the mother of all messes.

4

He gets a fresh pair of boxers from the bureau, leaving just one. He goes out to the living room and lies down on the couch. He doubts he'll sleep, but if he does it will be thin and he'll hear her if she gets up and tries to leave the apartment. And do what? Stop her, of course, if only because it's cold and raining and damn near blowing a gale, from the sound. But that's tonight. When she wakes up in the morning, hungover and disoriented and in a stranger's apartment, clothes gone—

Her clothes. Still on the floor, in a sodden heap.

Billy gets off the couch and takes them into the bathroom. On the way he stops to look at his uninvited guest. She's stopped snoring but she's still shivering. A sodden clot of hair lies against one of her cheeks. He bends and pushes it away.

'Please, I don't want to,' she says.

Billy freezes, but when there's nothing more he goes into the bathroom. There's a hook on the door. He hangs the cheap jacket on it. There's a shower-tub combo of the sort found in cut-rate motels. He wrings out her shirt and skirt in the tub and drapes them over the shower curtain rod to dry. The jacket has three zip-style pockets, a little one above the left breast and two bigger diagonal ones on the side. There's nothing in the breast pocket. There's a man's wallet in one of the side pockets and a phone in the other.

He removes the SIM card and puts the phone back in the pocket it came from for the time being. He opens the wallet. The first thing he finds is her driver's license. Her name is Alice Maxwell and she's from Kingston, Rhode Island. She's twenty years old. No, check that, just turned twenty-one. DMV photographs are awful as a rule, something you're even embarrassed to show the cop who stops you for speeding, but hers is pretty good. Or maybe Billy only thinks that because he's seen her looking far worse than any DL photo. Her eyes are wide and blue. There's a little smile on her lips.

First license, he thinks. She hasn't even had it renewed yet, because it's still got the one A.M. restriction for teenagers.

There's one credit card, which she has signed Alice Reagan Maxwell with painstaking clarity. There's an ID card from Clarendon Business College here in the city, an AMC gift card (Billy can't remember if those were the late Ken Hoff's theaters or not), an insurance card which includes her blood type (O), and some pictures of a much younger Alice Maxwell with her high school friends, her dog, and a woman who's probably her mother. There's also a picture of a smiling teenage boy with his shirt off, maybe a high school boyfriend.

In the billfold he finds two tens, two ones, and a newspaper clipping. It's the obituary of one Henry Maxwell, services at Christ Baptist Church in Kingston, in lieu of flowers send contributions to the American Cancer Society. The picture shows a man in mid to late middle age. He has jowls and thinning hair painstakingly combed across his otherwise bald dome. He looks like anyone you would pass on the street without noticing, but Billy can see the family resemblance even in the grainy photo, and Alice Reagan Maxwell loved him enough to carry his wallet, with his obituary inside it. Billy has to like her for that.

If she's going to school here, and her father was buried there, her mother, almost certainly back in Kingston, won't wonder where she is, at least not immediately. Billy puts the wallet back in her jacket but takes the phone and puts it in the top drawer of his bureau, under his own supply of T-shirts.

He wonders if he should clean up her vomit in the foyer before it dries and decides against it. If she wakes up thinking he's the reason her female works feel like they're on fire, he'd like to have at least some evidence that he brought her in from the outside. Of course that won't convince her that he didn't help himself later, once he was reasonably sure she wasn't going to spew on him or wake up and fight while he was humping her.

She's still shivering. That's got to be shock, doesn't it? Or maybe a reaction to whatever those men put in her drink? Billy has heard about roofies but has no idea what the aftereffects might be.

He starts to leave. The girl – Alice – moans. She sounds desolate, bereft.

Well shit, Billy thinks. This is probably the worst idea ever, but what the hell.

He gets in bed with her. Her back is to him. He puts an arm around her and pulls her close. 'Snuggle up, kiddo. You're okay. Snuggle the fuck up, get warm, stop shaking. You'll feel better in the morning. We'll figure this out in the morning.'

I'm fucked, he thinks again.

Maybe the comfort is what she needed, or the extra heat from his body, or maybe all that shivering would have stopped on its own. Billy doesn't know and doesn't care. He's only glad when the shakes become intermittent, then finally quit. The snoring has quit, too. Now he can hear the rain pelting the building. It's an old structure, and when the wind gusts, its joints creak. The sound is oddly comforting.

I'll get up in a minute or two, he thinks. Just as soon as I'm sure she's not going to snap awake and start screaming bloody murder. In just a minute or two.

He falls asleep instead and dreams there's smoke in the kitchen. He can smell burned cookies. He needs to warn Cathy, tell her she needs to take them out of the oven before their mother's boyfriend comes home, but he can't speak. This is the past and he's only a spectator.

5

Billy jerks awake in the dark some time later, convinced he's overslept his appointment with Joel Allen and screwed up the job he's spent months waiting to do. Then he hears the girl breathing next to him – breathing, not snoring – and he remembers where he is. Her butt is socked into his basket and he realizes he has an erection, which is totally inappropriate under the circumstances. Downright grotesque, in fact, but so many times the body doesn't care about the circumstances. It just wants what it wants.

He gets out of bed in the dark and feels his way to the bathroom with one hand cupped over the front of his tented shorts, not wanting to whang his distended cock into the bureau and make this shit carnival of a night complete. The girl, meanwhile, doesn't stir. Her slow breathing suggests that she's gone deep, and that's good.

By the time he's in the bathroom with the door shut, his erection has deflated and he can piss. The toilet is noisy and has a tendency to keep running if you don't flap the handle a few times, so he just lowers the lid, turns off the light, and feels his way across back to the bureau, where he fumbles until he feels the elastic waistband of his one pair of workout shorts.

He closes the door to the bedroom and makes his way across the living room with a little more confidence, because the curtain across the periscope window is still pushed back and the nearby streetlight casts enough glow to see by.

He looks out and sees nothing but the deserted street. The rain is still coming down but the wind has let up a little. He pulls the curtain closed and checks his watch, which he never took off. It's quarter past four in the morning. He puts on the shorts, lies down on the couch, and tries to think what he should do with her when she wakes up, but what's jamming up the forefront of his mind, ridiculous but true, is that her unwelcome appearance in his life has probably put an end to his writing, and just when it was going well. He has to smile. It's like worrying if there's enough toilet paper when you hear the town's tornado siren go off.

The body wants what it wants, and so does the mind, he thinks, and closes his eyes. He means only to doze but falls fully asleep again instead. When he wakes up the girl is standing over him, wearing the T-shirt he got her into when he put her to bed. And holding a knife.

CHAPTER 14

1

'Where am I? Who are you? Did you rape me? You did, didn't you?'

Her eyes are red and her hair is every whichway. Her picture could be next to *hangover* in the dictionary. She also looks scared to death, and Billy can't blame her for that.

'You were raped, but I didn't rape you.'

The knife is just the little one he used to pry up the splinters in his feet. He left it on the coffee table. He reaches out and takes it from her. He does it gently and she makes no protest.

'Who are you?' Alice asks. 'What's your name?'

'Dalton Smith.'

'Where are my clothes?'

'Hanging from the shower rod in the bathroom. I undressed you and—'

'*Undressed* me!' She looks down at the shirt.

'And dried you off. You were soaking wet. Shivering. How's your head?'

'Aches. I feel like I drank all night, but I only had one beer . . . and I think maybe a g-and-t . . . where are we?'

Billy swings his feet to the floor. She backs away, hands coming up in a warding-off gesture. 'Would you like a cup of coffee?'

She considers it, but not for long. She lowers her hands. 'Yes. And do you have aspirin?'

2

He makes coffee. She swallows two aspirin while she waits for it, then slowly goes into the bathroom. He hears the door lock, but that doesn't concern him. A five-year-old could bust that lock, and a ten-year-old would probably bust the door off the hinges in the bargain.

She comes back to the kitchen. 'You didn't flush. Ugh.'

'I didn't want to wake you.'

'Where's my phone? It was in my jacket.'

'I don't know. Do you want some toast?'

She makes a face. 'No. I've got my wallet but not my phone. Did you take it?'

'No.'

'Are you lying?'

'No.'

'Like I should believe you,' she says with shaky contempt. She sits down, tugging at the hem of the T-shirt, although it's long and everything that needs to be covered is covered.

'Where's my underwear?' The tone is accusing, prosecutorial.

'Your bra is under the coffee table. One of the straps was broken. Maybe I can knot it together for you. As for underpants, you weren't wearing any.'

'You're lying. What do you think I am, a whore?'

'No.'

What he thinks is that she's a young girl away from home for the first time who went to a wrong place where there were wrong people. Bad people who loaded her up with something and took advantage of her.

'Well I'm not,' she says, and begins to cry. 'I'm a virgin. At least I was. This is a mess. The worst mess I've ever been in.'

'I can relate to that,' Billy says, and with absolute sincerity.

'Why didn't you call the police? Or take me to the hospital?'

'You were messed up but not circling the drain. By that I mean—'

'I know what it means.'

'I thought I'd wait until you woke up, let you decide what you want to do. Maybe a cup of coffee will help you figure it out. It can't hurt.

And by the way, what's your name?' Best to get that out, so he doesn't screw up and say it himself.

3

He pours the coffee, ready to dodge if she tries throwing it in his face and then running for the door. He doesn't think she will, she's settling down a little, but this is still a situation that could go bad. Well hey, it's bad already, but it could get worse.

She doesn't throw the coffee at him. She sips some and makes a face. Her lips press tight together and he can see the muscles in her throat moving even after it's gone down.

'If you're going to throw up again, do it in the sink.'

'I'm not going to . . . what do you mean again? How did I get here? Are you sure you didn't rape me?'

That isn't funny but Billy can't help smiling. 'If I did, I think I'd know.'

'How did I get here? What happened?'

He sips his own coffee. 'That would be the middle of the story. Let's start at the beginning. Tell me what happened to *you*.'

'I don't remember. Last night is your basic black hole. All I know is I woke up here, hungover and feeling like somebody stuck a fencepost up my . . . you know.' She sips her coffee and this time she gets it down without having to repress a gag reflex.

'What about before that?'

She looks at him, blue eyes wide, mouth moving. Then her head droops. 'Was it Tripp? Did he put something in my beer? My g-and-t? *Both*? Is that what you're telling me?'

Billy restrains an impulse to reach across the table and put his hand over hers. He's gained a little ground but if he touches her he'll almost certainly lose it. She's not ready to be touched by a man, especially one with nothing on but worn workout shorts.

'I don't know. I wasn't there. You were. So tell me what happened, Alice. Right up to when your memory drops out.'

So she does. And as she does, he can see the question in her eyes: if you didn't rape me, why did I wake up in your bed instead of a hospital bed?

4

It's not a long story, even with some background added in. Billy thinks he could tell it himself once she gets started, because it's an old story. Halfway through it she stops, her eyes widening. She begins to hyperventilate, her hand clutching her throat while the air goes whooping in and out.

'Is it asthma?'

He didn't find an inhaler, but it might have been in her purse. If she was carrying one, it's gone now.

She shakes her head. 'Panic . . .' *Whoop* '. . . attack.' *Whoop*.

Billy goes into the bathroom and wets a washcloth as soon as the tap runs warm. He wrings it out loosely and brings it back. 'Tip your head up and put this over your face.'

He would have thought it impossible for her eyes to get any wider but somehow they do. 'I'll . . .' *Whoop* '. . . choke!'

'No. It'll open you up.'

He tips her head back himself – gently – and drapes the washcloth over her eyes, nose, and mouth. Then he waits. After fifteen seconds or so, her breathing starts to ease. She takes the washcloth off her face. 'It worked!'

'Breathing the moisture makes it work,' Billy says.

There might be some truth in that, but probably not much. It's breathing the *idea* that makes it work. He saw Clay Briggs – Pillroller, their corpsman – use it several times on newbies (and a few vets, like Bigfoot Lopez) before they went back for another bite of the rotten apple named Phantom Fury. Sometimes there was another trick he used if the wet washcloth didn't work. Billy listened carefully when Pill explained both of these tricks to soothe the mental monkey. He's always been a good listener, storing up information like a squirrel storing up nuts.

'Can you finish now?'

'Can I have some toast?' She asks almost shyly. 'And is there any juice?'

'No juice, but I've got some ginger ale. Want that?'

'Yes, please.'

He makes toast. He pours ginger ale into a glass and adds an ice cube. He sits down across from her. Alice Maxwell tells her timeworn story. It's one Billy has heard before and read before, most recently in the works of Émile Zola.

She spent a year after high school waitressing in her hometown, saving up money for business school. She could have gone in Kingston, there were two there that were supposed to be good, but she wanted to see a little more of the world. And get away from Mom, Billy thinks. He might be starting to understand why she's not demanding he call the police immediately. But the question of why 'seeing a little more of the world' meant coming to this nondescript city . . . about that he has no idea.

She works part time as a barista at a coffee shop on Emery Plaza, not three blocks from Billy's writing nest in Gerard Tower, and that was where she met Tripp Donovan. He struck up casual conversations with her over a week or two. He made her laugh. He was charming. So of course when he invited her out for a bite after work one day, she said yes. A movie date followed, and then – fast worker, that Tripp – he asked if she'd like to go dancing at a side-of-the-road place he knew out on Route 13. She told him she wasn't much of a dancer. He of course said neither was he, they didn't have to dance, they could just buy a pitcher of beer and stretch it out while they listened to the music. He told her it was a Foghat cover band, did she like Foghat? Alice said she did. She had never heard of Foghat, but she downloaded some of their music that very night. It was good. A little bluesy, but mostly straight-ahead rock and roll.

The Tripp Donovans of the world have a nose for a certain kind of girl, Billy thinks. They are shy girls who make friends slowly because they aren't very good at making the first move. They are mildly pretty girls who have been bludgeoned by beauty on TV, in the movies, on the Internet, and in the celebrity magazines so that they see themselves not as mildly pretty but as plain, or even sort of ugly. They see their bad features – the too-wide mouth, the too-close-set eyes – and ignore the good ones. These are girls who have been told by the fashion mags in the beauty shops, and often by their own mothers, that they need to lose twenty pounds. They despair over the size of their boobs, butts, and feet. To be asked out is a wonder, but then there is the agony of what to wear. This certain kind of girl can call girlfriends to discuss that, but only if she has them. Alice, new in the city, does not. But on their movie date, Tripp doesn't seem to mind her clothes or her too-wide mouth. Tripp is funny. Tripp is charming. Tripp is complimentary. And he's a perfect gentleman. He kisses her after the movie date, but it's a wanted kiss, a *desired* kiss, and he doesn't spoil it by sticking his tongue in her mouth or grabbing at her breasts.

Tripp is a student at one of the local colleges. Billy asks how old he is, thinking she probably won't know, but thanks to the wonders of Facebook, she does. Tripp Donovan is twenty-four.

'Little old to still be going to college.'

'I think he's a grad student. He's doing advanced studies.'

Advanced studies, Billy thinks. Right.

Of course Tripp suggested Alice come by his crib for a drink before heading out to the Bucket, and of course she agreed. The aforementioned crib was in one of those Sherwood Heights condos near the Interstate. Alice took the bus because she doesn't have a car. Tripp was waiting for her outside, the perfect gentleman. He kissed her on the cheek and took her up to the third floor in the elevator. It was a big apartment. He could only afford it, Tripp said, because he and his roommates split the rent. The roommates were Hank and Jack. Alice doesn't know their last names. She tells Billy that they seemed perfectly nice, came out to the living room to meet her, then went back into one of the bedrooms where some sports show was playing on TV. Or maybe it was a video game, she's not sure which.

'So that's where your memory starts to get foggy?'

'No, they just shut the door when they went back in.' Alice is using the washcloth to dab at her cheeks and forehead.

Tripp asked if she wanted a beer. Alice tells Billy she doesn't care for beer but took one to be polite. Then, when Tripp saw she was going slow on the Heinie, he asked if she wanted a gin and tonic. The door to Jack's room opened and the sound from the TV went off and Jack said, 'Did I hear someone mention gin and tonic?'

So they all have g-and-t's, and that's when Alice says things started to get fogged-in. She thought it was because she's not used to alcohol. Tripp suggested she have another. Because, he said, the second drink will fight the first. He said it's a known fact. One of the roommates put on some music and she thinks she remembers dancing in the living room with Tripp, and that's where her memory pretty much runs out.

She picks up the washcloth and breathes through it again for a little while. Her bra is still underneath the coffee table, looking like a small animal that died.

'Now it's your turn,' she says.

Billy tells her what he saw and did, beginning with the screech of brakes and tires and ending with putting her to bed. She thinks it over, then says, 'Tripp doesn't own a van. He has a Mustang. He picked me up in it when we went to the movies.'

Billy thinks of Ken Hoff, who also had a Mustang. And died in it. 'Nice car,' he says. 'Was your roommate jealous?'

'I'm on my own. It's just a small place.' As soon as the words are out, Billy can see she thinks she's made a mistake telling him she's on her own. He could point out that Tripp Donovan probably also knew this but doesn't. She puts the washcloth over her face again and breathes, but this time her breath keeps whooping.

'Give me that,' Billy says. This time he wets it under the kitchen tap, keeping an eye on her while he does it, but he doesn't think she'll break for the door wearing nothing but a thin T-shirt. He comes back. 'Try again. Slow deep breaths.'

When her respiration eases, he says 'Come with me. I want to show you something.'

He takes her out of the apartment, up the stairs, into the foyer. He points to the vomit drying on the wall. 'That's from when I brought you in.'

'Whose underwear is that? Is it yours?'

'Yes. I was getting ready to go to bed. It was falling down while I was trying to keep you from choking. It was actually kind of comical.'

She doesn't smile, only repeats that Tripp doesn't drive a van.

'I imagine it belongs to one of his roommates.'

Tears begin to spill down her cheeks. 'Oh my God. Oh my God. My mother can never find this out. She never wanted me to come.'

Billy thinks he already knew that. 'Let's go back downstairs. I'll make you some real breakfast. Eggs and bacon.'

'No bacon,' she says, grimacing, but she doesn't say no to the eggs.

5

He scrambles two eggs and sets them before her with two more slices of toast. While she eats, he goes into the bedroom and closes the door. If she bolts, she bolts. He has been gripped by the fatalism he felt during Operation Phantom Fury, clearing the city of insurgents street by street and block by block. Checking for the baby shoe on his belt loop before stacking to go in each house. Each day he wasn't wounded or killed increased the odds that the next day he would be. You could only roll so many sevens or make so many points before you crapped out. That fatalism became sort of a friend. *What the fuck*, they used to say. *What the fuck, let's get some.* Same thing now: what the fuck.

He dons the blond wig, the mustache, the glasses. He sits on the bed and checks a couple of things on his phone. Once he's got the info he needs, he goes into the bathroom and spreads a handful of baby powder on his stomach. He's found it helps with the chafing. Then he takes the fake belly into the kitchen.

She looks at him with wide eyes, the last forkful of eggs suspended above the plate. Billy holds the Styrofoam appliance against his stomach and turns around. 'Would you tighten the strap for me? I always have a hard job doing it for myself.'

He waits. A lot depends on what happens next. She might refuse. She might even stick him with the knife he gave her to butter her toast. It's not exactly a lethal weapon, she could have done more damage with the paring knife if she'd decided to use it on him while he was sleeping, but she could put a hurt on him even with a butter knife if she put her arm into it and got it in the right place.

She doesn't stick him. She pulls the strap tight instead. Tighter than he's ever managed even when he starts by turning the fake belly around to the small of his back so he can see the plastic buckle.

'When did you know I knew?' she asks in a small voice.

'While you were telling me your story. You were looking right at me and I saw it click. Then you had the panic attack.'

'You're the man who killed—'

'Yes.'

'And this is . . . what, your hideout?'

'Yes.'

'The wig and mustache is your disguise?'

'Yes. And the fake potbelly.'

She opens her mouth, then closes it. She seems to have run out of questions to ask, but she's not whooping for breath and Billy thinks that's another step in the right direction. Then he thinks, Who am I kidding? There *is* no right direction.

'Have you looked at your—' He points at her lap.

'Yes.' Small voice. 'Just before I got up to see where I was. There's blood. And it hurts. I knew that you . . . or somebody . . .'

'It isn't just blood. You'll see when you clean yourself up. At least one of them didn't use protection. Probably none of them did.'

She puts the forkful of eggs down uneaten.

'I'm going out. There's a twenty-four-hour drugstore about half a mile from here, back toward the city. I'll have to walk because I don't have a car. You can buy the morning-after pill over the counter in this state, I just checked on my phone to make sure. Unless you have religious or moral objections to taking it, that is?'

'God, no.' In that same small voice. She's crying again. 'If I got pregnant . . .' She just shakes her head.

'Some drugstores also sell ladies' underwear. If they do, I'll buy some.'

'I can pay you back. I have money.' This is absurd and she seems to know it because she looks away, flushing.

'Your clothes are hanging in the bathroom. Once I'm gone you could put them on and get out of here. I can't stop you. But listen, Alice.'

He reaches out and turns her face back to him. Her shoulders stiffen, but she looks at him.

'I saved your life last night. It was cold and it was raining and you were unconscious. Drugged to the gills. If you didn't die of exposure you would have choked on your own vomit. Now I'm going to put my life in your hands. Do you understand me?'

'It was those men who raped me? You swear?'

'I couldn't swear to it in court because I didn't see their faces, but three men dumped you out of that van and you were with three men in that apartment when your memory went dark.'

Alice puts her hands over her face. 'I'm so ashamed.'

Billy is honestly perplexed. 'Why? You trusted and you were tricked. End of story.'

'I saw your picture on the news. You shot that man.'

'I did. Joel Allen was a bad man, a hired killer.' Like me, Billy thinks, but there's at least one difference. 'He waited outside a poker game and shot two men because he lost big and wanted his money back. One of them died. I want to go now while it's still early and there aren't too many people on the streets.'

'Do you have a sweatshirt?'

'Yes. Why?'

'Wear it over that.' She points to the fake belly. 'It will look like you're trying to hide your stomach. It's what fat people do.'

6

The rain has let up but it's still cold and he's glad for the sweatshirt. He waits for a car to pass, splashing up water, then crosses the street to the vacant lot side. He sees the skid marks from the van. They're not as long and dark as they would have been if the pavement had been dry. He drops to one knee, knowing what he's looking for but not really expecting to find it. He does, though. He puts it in his pocket and re-crosses Pearson Street because the sidewalk on the vacant lot side was damaged by the machines the city brought in to demolish the train station. That was a year ago or more, judging by the way the vegetation has grown up, but nobody has bothered to fix the concrete.

He touches her lost earring as he walks. When the police take him, it will go in an evidence envelope, as will the rest of his possessions, and she'll probably never get it back. Billy's pretty sure she'll drop a dime on him. Whether she believes he saved her life or not, she knows he's a wanted killer, and she may also believe that she could be charged with aiding and abetting for not turning him in as soon as she gets a chance.

But no, Billy thinks. She's a shy girl, a scared girl, and a confused girl, but she's not a dumb girl. She could claim he kidnapped her and they'd believe her. Her phone won't work even if she searches and finds it, but the Zoney's convenience store is close and she can call the police from there. She's probably there already and they'll take him as he walks back from the drugstore. Cop cars with their misery lights flashing, one of them bouncing up over the curb in front of him, doors flying open even before the cruiser stops, cops getting out with guns drawn: *Show your hands, get on the ground, face down, face down.*

Then why did he do it?

Something about the dream he had last night, maybe – the smell of burned cookies. Something about Shan Ackerman, maybe, and the picture she drew for him of the flamingo. Maybe it even has something to do with Phil Stanhope, who will have told the police she went out with him because he seemed like such a nice man. A writer, maybe even one with a future, a star to which a working girl could hitch her wagon. Would she tell them she slept with him? If she leaves that part out, Diane Fazio won't. Diane saw them leaving the house, even gave Billy a thumbs-up.

Maybe it has to do with all those things, but probably it just comes back to the simple fact that he couldn't kill her. No way could he. That would make him as bad as Joel Allen, or the Las Vegas rape-o, or Karl Trilby, who made movies of men fucking kids. So he put on his fake wig and fake belly and plain glass spectacles and here he is, walking to a drugstore in the rain. Alice Maxwell not only knows he's William Summers, she knows about Dalton Smith, the clean identity he had spent years building up.

Those assholes could have dumped her on another street, Billy thinks, but they didn't. They could have dropped her further down Pearson Street, but they didn't do that, either. He could blame fate, except he doesn't believe in fate. He could tell himself everything happens for a reason, but that's goofy bullshit for people who can't face plain unpainted truth. Coincidence is what it was, and everything followed from that. From the moment they dumped the girl he might as well have become a cow in a chute, with nothing to do but trot with the others onto the killing floor. But it is what it is, as they also used to say in the sand, so what the fuck.

And there is one tiny glimmer of hope: she told him to put on the sweatshirt. It probably means nothing, just something she said to make him feel like she was a little bit on his side, but maybe it does.

Maybe it does.

7

The drugstore's a CVS. Billy finds the morning-after pill in the family planning aisle. It costs fifty dollars, which he supposes is cheap compared to the alternatives. It's on the bottom row (as if to be as hard to find as possible for bad girls who need it) and when he straightens up he gets a glimpse of wiry red hair two rows over. Billy's heart jumps. He bends down again and straightens up again slowly, peering over the boxes of Vagisil and Monistat. It's not Dana Edison, who he's decided is the hardest of Nick's hardballs. It's not even a man. It's a woman with her wiry red hair yanked into a ponytail.

Easy, he tells himself. You're jumping at nothing. Dana and the others are long gone back to Vegas.

Well, maybe.

The women's underwear is on the back wall. Most of it is for ladies who are leaky, but there's a few other kinds as well. He thinks about the bikinis but decides that would be a little suggestive. It's funny, in a way; he's still operating on the assumption that she'll be there when he gets back. But what other assumption is there? He *will* go back, because he has no other place to go.

He grabs a three-pack of Hanes cotton boy-leg shorts and takes them to the counter, looking for police cars outside, but doesn't spot any. Of course they wouldn't park in front, anyway. He'd clock them and maybe hole up with hostages. The clerk is a woman in her fifties. She rings up his purchases with no comment, but Billy is good at reading faces and knows she's thinking that someone had a busy night. He pays with a Dalton Smith credit card and walks back out into the rain, now just a fine drizzle, waiting to be taken. There's no one there but three women, chatting amiably together. They don't look at him as they go into the drugstore.

Billy walks back to 658 Pearson. It seems like a very long walk because it's more than a glimmer of hope now, and hope may be the thing with feathers, but it's also the thing that hurts you. They could be waiting around back or in the apartment, he thinks. But no blue boys come rushing around the old three-decker, and there's no one in the apartment but the girl. She's watching *Today* on his television.

Alice looks at him and something passes between them. He shifts the pharmacy bag and digs in his righthand pocket. He holds his hand out to her and sees her flinch a little, as if she thinks he means to strike her. The bruises on her face are at their most colorful. They shout assault and battery.

'I found your earring.'

He opens his hand and shows her.

8

Alice goes into the bathroom to put on a pair of the new underpants but stays in the shin-length T-shirt because her skirt is still damp. 'Denim takes forever to dry,' she says.

She takes the pill with water from the kitchen tap. He tells her the side effects may include vomiting, dizziness—

'I can read. Who else lives in this building? It's as quiet as the . . . it's quiet.'

He tells her about the Jensens and how they went on a cruise, neither of them knowing that in another six months the cruise lines will be shut down, along with just about everything else. He takes her upstairs – she comes willingly enough – and introduces her to Daphne and Walter.

'You're watering them too much. You want to drown them?'

'No.'

'Give them a couple of days off.' She pauses. 'Will you be here for a couple of days?'

'Yes. It's safer to wait.'

She looks around the Jensens' kitchen and living room, sizing it up the way that women do. Then she astounds him by asking if she can stay with him. Maybe stay in the basement apartment even after he's gone.

'I don't want to go out until the bruises get better,' she says. 'I look like I was in a car accident. Also, what if Tripp comes looking for me? He knows where I go to school, and he knows where I live.'

Billy thinks that Tripp and his friends will want nothing more to do with her now that they've had their fun. Oh, they might cruise Pearson Street to make sure the place where they threw her out isn't a crime scene, and when they sober up – or come down from whatever high they were riding – they will surely check the local news to make sure she's not a part of it, but he doesn't point these things out. Having her stay solves a lot of problems.

Back downstairs she says she's tired and asks if she can take a nap in his bed. Billy tells her that would be fine unless she's feeling dizzy or nauseated. If she is, it would be better for her to stay awake for awhile.

She says she's okay and goes into the bedroom. She's doing a good job of pretending she's not afraid of him, but Billy is pretty sure she still is. She'd be crazy if she wasn't. But she's also still in shock, still humiliated by what has happened to her. And ashamed. He told her she didn't have to be, but that bounced right off. Later on she'll undoubtedly decide that asking to stay with him was a bad call, really bad. But right now all she wants is sleep. It's in her slumped shoulders and shuffling bare feet.

Billy hears the creak of bedsprings. He looks in five minutes later and she's either zonked out or doing a world-class acting job.

He boots up his laptop and goes to where he left off. You can't write today, he thinks, not with everything that's going on. Not with that girl in the other room, the one who may wake up and decide she wants to get the hell away from here, and me.

Only he's also thinking about Pill's wet washcloth treatment for panic attacks, and how it worked on Alice. Sort of a miracle, really. But that wasn't Clay Briggs's only miracle cure, was it? Smiling, Billy begins to write. The prose seems flat at first, ragged, but then he starts to get the rhythm. Soon he's not thinking of Alice at all.

9

Clay Briggs – Pill – was a Corpsman 1st Class. He worked on everyone who needed working on, but he was Hot Nine from top to toe. He was small and wiry. Thinning hair, beaky nose, little rimless glasses that he was always polishing. He had a peace sign on the front of his helmet and for a week or so, before the CO made him take it off, a sticker on the back that said NEVER MIND THE MILK, GOT PUSSY?

Panic attacks were common as Phantom Fury went on (and on, and on). Marines were supposed to be immune from things like that, but of

course weren't. Guys would start rasping for breath, doubling over, sometimes falling down. Most were good little jarheads who wouldn't admit to
being scared so they said it was the smoke and dust, because those things
were constant. Pill would agree with them – just the dust, just the smoke
– and wet a washcloth to put over their faces. 'Breathe through that,' he'd
say. 'It'll clear the crap out and you'll be able to breathe fine.'

He had cures for other things, too. Some were bullshit and some were
not, but they all worked at least some of the time: thumping wens and
swellings with the side of a book to make them disappear (he called it
the Bible cure), pinching your nose shut and singing *Ahhhh* for hiccups and
coughing fits, breathing Vicks VapoRub steam to stop up bloody noses, a
silver dollar rubbed on eyelids to cure keratitis.

'Most of this shit is pure hill-country folk medicine I learned from my
grammaw,' he told me once. 'I use what works, but mostly it works because
I *tell* 'em it works.' Then he asked me how my tooth was, because I had
one in back that had been giving me trouble.

I said it hurt like blue fuck.

'Well, I can take care of that, my brother,' he said. 'I've got a rattlesnake
rattle in my pack. Bought it on eBay. You go on and stick it between your
cheek and gums back there, suck on it awhile, and your tooth is going to
quiet right down.'

I told him I would pass and he said that was good, because the rattle
was way at the bottom of his pack, and he'd have to dump all his shit out
to get it. If it was even still there, that was. All these years later I wonder
if it would have worked. I eventually had that tooth pulled.

Pill's most amazing cure – that I saw, anyway – was in August of '04. It
was the slack time between Operation Vigilant Resolve in April and Phantom
Fury, the big one, in November. During those months, the American politicians had their own panic attack. Instead of letting us go in full-bore,
they decided to give the Iraqi police and military one more chance to
clean out the muj themselves and restore order. The big Iraqi politicians
said it would work, but they were all in Baghdad. In Fallujah, a lot of the
police and military *were* muj.

During that period, we mostly stayed out of the city. For six weeks in
June and July we weren't even there, we were in Ramadi, which was relatively quiet. Our job, when we did go into Fallujah, was to win 'hearts and
minds.' This meant our translators – our terps – made nice on our behalf

with the mullahs and community leaders instead of bawling 'Come out, you pig-fuckers' through loudspeakers as we drove rapidly through the streets, always expecting to get shot at or blown up or RPGd. We gave out candy and toys and Superman comic books to the kids, along with fliers for them to take home, talking about all the services the government could provide and the insurgency couldn't. The kids ate the candy, traded the comics, and threw away the fliers.

During Phantom Fury we stayed in what came to be known as Lalafallujah (after Lollapalooza) for days at a time, sleeping when we could on rooftops with overwatch on the four main corners of the compass, keeping an eye out for muj creeping up on other rooftops, ready to do damage and inflict hurt. It was like the death of a thousand cuts. We took in hundreds of RPGs and other weaponry, but the hajis never seemed to run out.

During that summer, though, our patrols were almost like a 9-to-5 job. On days when we went in to win 'hearts and minds,' we'd leave when the sun was up and head back to base before it got dark. Even with the fighting in a lull, you didn't want to be in Lalafallujah after dark.

One day when we were coming back we saw Mitsubishi Eagle station wagon overturned on the side of the road, still smoking. The front end was blown off, the driver's door was open, and there was blood on what was left of the windshield.

'Fuck me, that's the lieutenant colonel's ride,' Big Klew said.

There was a CSH tent set up at the base – the Combat Surgical Hospital. Without sides, it was actually more of a pavilion with a couple of big fans set up at either end. It was over a hundred degrees that day. About like usual, in other words. We could hear Jamieson screaming.

Pill went running, slipping off his pack as he went. The rest of us followed. There were two other patients in the tent, clearly fucked up with their own shit but not as divinely fucked up as Jamieson, because they were on their feet. One had his arm in a sling, the other had a bandage wound around his head.

Jamieson was lying on a cot with stuff, I think they call it Ringer's lactate, running into his arm. The place where his left foot used to be had a pressure bandage on it, but the foot was gone and the bandage was already bleeding through. His left cheek was torn open and that eye was bleeding and all crooked in its socket. A couple of grunts were holding him down while a medic tried to get him to swallow some morphine tabs, but the lieutenant colonel was having none of it. He kept twisting his head from side to side, his good eye bulging and terrified. It landed on Pill.

'Hurts!' he yelled. There was nothing of the old bossy (but sometimes funny) l-c in him. The pain had swallowed all that. 'Hurts! Oh my fucking God it fucking *hurts!*'

'Dustoff's on the way,' one of the medics said. 'Take it easy. Swallow these. You'll feel bet—'

Jamieson raised one bloody hand and swatted the pills away. Johnny Capps chased after them and picked them up.

'Hurts! Hurrts! HURRRRTS!'

Pill dropped to his knees beside the cot. 'Listen to me, sir. I got a cure for the pain, better than the morph.'

Jamieson's remaining eye rolled toward Pill, but I didn't think it was seeing anything. 'Briggs? Is that you?'

'Yessir, Corpsman Briggs. You gotta sing.'

'This hurts so bad!'

'You gotta sing. It bypasses the pain.'

'It's true, sir,' Taco said, but he gave me a look that said *What the fuck?*

'Here we go,' Pill said. He started to sing. He had a good voice. 'If you go down to the woods today . . . now you.'

'Hurts!'

Pill took him by the right shoulder. Jamieson's shirt was shredded on the other side and blood was oozing through. 'Sing it and you'll feel better. Guaranteed. I'll give it to you one more time. If you go down to the woods today . . .'

'If you go down to the woods today,' the l-c croaked. Then: '"The Teddy Bears' Picnic"? You have to be fucking shitting m—'

'No, sing it.' Pillroller looked around. 'Somebody help me. Who knows the fucking song?'

It so happened I knew it, because my mother used to sing it to my sister when she was just a baby. Over and over until Cathy went to sleep.

I couldn't sing for shit, but I sang. 'If you go down to the woods today you're sure of a big surprise. If you go down to the woods today—'

'Better go in disguise,' Jamieson finished. Still croaking.

'Fucking right you better,' Pill said, and sang: 'For every bear that ever there was will gather there for certain . . .'

The man with the bandage around his head joined in. He had a lovely strong baritone. 'Because today's the day the teddy bears have their piiiic-nic!'

'Give it to me, Lieutenant Colonel,' Pill said, still kneeling beside him. 'Because today's the day . . .'

'The teddy bears have their piiic-nic.' Jamieson said most of it but sang the first syllable of *picnic* the way the man with the bandage on his head had sung it, drawing it out long, and Johnny Capps dropped the morphine tabs into his mouth, bombs away.

Pill turned his head to look at the rest of the Hot Nine. He was like a fucked-up bandleader encouraging audience participation. 'If you go down to the woods today . . . come on, *everybody!*'

So the members of the Hot Nine sang the first verse of 'Teddy Bears' Picnic' to Lieutenant Colonel Jamieson, most of them just faking it until about the third time around. By then they had the words. The two wounded men joined in. The corpsmen joined in. On the fourth repetition, Jamieson sang it right through with sweat pouring down his face. People were running toward the tent to see what was going on.

'Pain's less,' Jamieson gasped.

'Morphine's kicking in,' Albie Stark said.

'Not that,' Jamieson said. 'Again. Please. Again.'

'One more time,' Pill said, 'and put some feeling into it. It's a picnic, not a fucking funeral.'

So we sang: *If you go down to the woods today you're sure of a big surprise!*

The jarheads who'd come to see what was going on also joined in. By the time Jamieson passed out, there must have been four dozen of us singing that foolish fucking song at the top of our lungs and we didn't hear the Black Hawk coming in to take Lieutenant Colonel Jamieson uprange until it was swopping up dirt and practically on top of us. I never forgot

10

'What are you doing?'

Billy looks around, startled out of this dream, and sees Alice Maxwell standing in the bedroom door. Her bruises are stark against her white skin. Her left eye is puffed half-shut, making him think of the l-c, lying in that hot tent where the fans did jack shit even running at top speed. Her hair is all bed head.

'Nothing. Playing a video game.' He hits save, then turns off the laptop and shuts the lid.

'That was a lot of typing for a video game.'

'Do you want something to eat?'

She considers the idea. 'Do you have any soup? I'm hungry, but I don't want to eat anything too chewy. I think I bit the inside of my cheek. It must have been while I was blacked out, because I don't remember doing it.'

'Tomato or chicken noodle?'

'Chicken noodle, please.'

That's a good call, because he has two cans of chicken noodle soup in the pantry nook and only one of tomato. He heats the soup and ladles out a bowl for each of them. She asks for seconds, and maybe a piece of buttered bread? She sops it in the chicken broth, and when she sees him looking at her over his own empty bowl, she offers a guilty smile. 'I'm a pig when I'm hungry. My mother always said so.'

'She's not here.'

'Thank God. She'd call me crazy. I probably am crazy. She told me I'd get in trouble if I went away and she was right. First I date a rapist, now I'm in an apartment with a . . .'

'Go on, you can say it.'

But she doesn't. 'She wanted me to stay in Kingston and go to hairdressing school, like my sister. Gerry makes good money, she said I could, too.'

'Why did you want to go to business school here? I don't get that.'

'It was the cheapest that was still good. Are you done?'

'Yes.'

She takes their bowls and spoons to the sink, self-consciously pulling the T-shirt away from her bottom as soon as her hands are free. He can tell by the way she walks that she's still in a fair amount of pain. He thinks he should get her to sing the first verse of 'Teddy Bears' Picnic.' Or they could sing it together, a duet.

'What are you smiling about?'

'Nothing.'

'It's how I look, isn't it? Like I was in a prize fight.'

'No, just something I remembered from when I was in the service. Your clothes might be dry now.'

'Probably.' But she sits down again as she is. 'Did someone pay you to shoot that man? They did, didn't they?'

Billy thinks of the half a million – minus his walking-around money – that's safe in an offshore bank. Then he thinks of the million and a half that hasn't been paid. 'It's complicated.'

Alice offers a thin smile: tight lips and no teeth. 'What isn't?'

11

She flicks through the cable channels on his TV, working her way up. She stops for a bit on TCM, where Fred Astaire is dancing with Ginger Rogers, then moves on. She watches an infomercial for beauty products for a little while, then turns it off.

'What are *you* doing?' she asks.

Waiting, Billy thinks. Nothing else *to* do. He can't work on his story with her in the room. He'd feel self-conscious, and besides, she'd want to know what he was writing. He thinks that of all the strange events in his life – there have been quite a few – this time on Pearson Street may be the strangest.

'What's out back?'

'A little yard, then a drainage ditch with some scrappy trees growing around it, then some buildings that might be storage sheds. Maybe from when the trains still stopped over there.' He gestures to the periscope window, now curtained. The rain is coming down in buckets again and there's nothing to see out there. 'The sheds are abandoned now, I think.'

She sighs. 'This has got to be the deadest neighborhood in the whole city.'

Billy thinks of telling her that *dead*, like *unique*, is a word that cannot, by its nature, be modified. He doesn't because she's right.

She stares at the blank TV. 'I don't suppose you have Netflix?'

As a matter of fact he does, on one of his cheapie laptops, but then he realizes there's something better. 'The Jensens do. The people upstairs? And there's popcorn, unless they ate it all. I bought it myself.'

'Let me see if my skirt is dry.'

She goes in the bathroom and shuts the door. He hears the lock turn, which tells Billy that he is still very much on probation. When she comes out she's wearing the denim skirt and the Black Keys tee.

They go upstairs. While he figures out how to find Netflix on the Jensens' television, which is four times as big as the one Billy has downstairs, Alice peers out their bedroom window at the backyard.

'There's a barbecue,' she says, coming back. 'It's uncovered and sitting in a puddle. The whole backyard is a puddle.'

Billy gives her the controller. She spends a few minutes spinning through the choices, then asks Billy if he likes *The Blacklist*.

'Never seen it.'

'Then we'll start at the beginning.'

The premise of the show is ridiculous, but Billy gets into it because the main character, Red Reddington, is amusing and resourceful. Always one step ahead, as Billy wishes he were. They watch three episodes while the rain pelts down outside. Billy makes popcorn in the Jensens' microwave and they both pig out on it. Alice washes the bowl and puts it in the drainer.

'I can't watch any more or I'll get a headache,' she says. 'You can if you want to. I think I'll go back downstairs.'

Casual. No big deal. Like we're roommates sharing a duplex, Billy thinks. We could be sitcom people. *The Existential Couple*. He tells her he's also had enough for now, although he thinks he wouldn't mind going back for more Red another time.

He locks the Jensens' apartment and they go back to Billy's. After the popcorn, neither of them wants dinner. They watch the news and eat pudding cups instead. 'Total junk food a-thon,' Alice says. 'My mother—'

'Don't start,' Billy tells her.

The assassination of Joel Allen is no longer the lead story. There's been a gas explosion in Senatobia, across the border in Mississippi, three dead and two more badly injured. Also, the turnpike west of Red Bluff has been temporarily closed because of flooding.

'How long are you going to stay here?' Alice asks.

Billy has been mulling this over himself. If the people looking for him – local cops, FBI, possibly Nick's hardballs – think he's gone to ground in the city, they may think he'll stay hidden for five or six days, maybe a week. He needs to stay on Pearson Street long enough to make them believe that he slipped out right after the shot after all. If Alice doesn't complicate things by running away, that is.

'Four more days. Maybe five. Can you do that, Alice?' Is it the first time he's used her name? He can't remember.

'I saw how much that pill cost,' she says. 'If I stay, can we call it square?'

She might be deking him, but he doesn't think so. She has wounds to lick, and she's decided he's not dangerous. At least not to her. Although she *did* lock the bathroom door when she was putting on her clothes, so there's still a trust issue. If he tries to persuade himself otherwise he'd be kidding himself.

'Yes,' Billy says. 'We can call it square.'

12

They have their first fight at ten-thirty that night. It's over who's going to sleep in the bed and who's going to sleep on the couch. Billy insists that she take the bed, says he'll be fine on the couch.

'That's sexist.'

'Sleeping on the couch is sexist? Are you kidding me?'

'Being a manly man is sexist. You're too long for it. Your feet will hang out on the floor.'

'I'll put them here.' He pats the arm of the couch.

'Then all the blood will run out of your legs and they'll go to sleep.'

'You were . . .' He hesitates, looking for the right word. '. . . attacked. You need to rest. You need *sleep*.'

'You want the couch because you think if I'm out here in the living room, I can run away. Which I'm not going to do. We've got a deal.'

Yes, Billy thinks, and if she keeps to it, we need to talk about how she's going to handle the questions once I'm gone. He wonders if Alice knows what Stockholm Syndrome is. If she doesn't, he'll have to explain it.

'We'll flip a coin.' He takes a quarter out of his pocket.

Alice holds out her hand. '*I'll* flip it. I don't trust you, you're a criminal.'

That makes him laugh. She doesn't, but at least she smiles a little. Billy thinks it would be a good one if she really let it go.

He hands her the quarter. She tells him to call it in the air, then flips it like someone with experience. He calls tails (he always calls tails, learned it from Taco) and tails it is.

'You take the bed,' Billy says, and she doesn't argue. In fact, she looks relieved. She's still walking very carefully.

She closes the bedroom door. The light beneath goes out. Billy takes off his shoes, pants, and shirt, and lies down on the couch. He reaches behind him and turns out the lamp.

Very quietly, from the other room, she calls, 'Goodnight.'

'Goodnight,' he calls back. 'Alice.'

CHAPTER 15

1

Billy's back in Fallujah and the baby shoe is gone.

He and Pill and Taco and Albie Stark are behind an overturned taxi, the rest of the Nine behind a burned-out bakery truck. Albie is lying with his head in Taco's lap while Pill tries to patch him up, which is a fucking joke, all the doctors in the Mayo Clinic couldn't patch him up. Tac's lap is a pond of blood.

It's nothing, just clipped me, Albie said when the hajis ambushed them and the four of them ducked behind the overturned Corolla. His hand was pressed against the side of his neck, but he was smiling. Then the blood began spurting through his fingers and he started gasping.

Heavy fire is pouring at them from a house two down from the corner, there are muj in the upstairs windows and more on the roof, bullets going *ponk ponk ponk* into the taxi's undercarriage. Tac has called in air support and he shouts to the others behind the bakery truck that a gunship is inbound, a couple of Hellfire missiles will shut those fucks up, two minutes, maybe four, and Pill's on his knees with his dusty ass up and his hands pressed to the side of Albie's neck, but the claret keeps flowing, a fresh squirt with every beat of Albie's heart, and Billy sees the truth in Taco's wide eyes.

George, Donk, Johnny, Bigfoot, and Klew are returning fire from behind the truck because they can see that those guys on the roof have almost got the angle on Billy and the others behind the taxi; it's scant cover and lethal geometry. Maybe they can hold out until the Cobra arrives with the Hellfires, maybe not.

Billy looks around for the baby shoe, thinking he might have lost it just a minute ago, thinking it might be close, thinking if he can grab it everything will be magically okay, it'll be like singing 'The Teddy Bears' Picnic,' but it's not close and he knew it wouldn't be close but looking means he doesn't have to look at Albie, who is now breathing his final rasping gasping breaths, trying to take in all the world he can before he leaves it, and Billy wonders what he's seeing and what he will see when he makes it to the other side, pearly gates and golden shores or just black nothing, and Johnny Capps is yelling from behind the truck, yelling *Leave him, leave him, leave him and get back here*, but they won't leave him because you don't do that, you leave none behind, that was Drill Sergeant Uppington's biggest fucking rule, and the shoe isn't there, the shoe is nowhere, he lost it and their luck went with it, and Albie's going, almost gone, those terrible gasps for breath, and there's a hole in his boot and Billy realizes it's bleeding, he got shot in the fucking fo—

2

Billy bolts up so fast he almost falls off the couch. It's Pearson Street, not Fallujah, and that's not Albie Stark gasping for breath.

He hurries into the bedroom and finds Alice sitting up in bed with one hand grasping her throat, horribly like Albie when Albie at first thought the bullet just clipped him. Her eyes are wide and full of panic.

'Wash . . .' *Whoop!* '. . . cloth!' *Whoop!*

He goes into the bathroom and gets one. Wets it down without waiting for the tap to run warm, comes back and drapes it over her face, glad to cover eyes so wide they look ready to fall out of their sockets and dangle on her cheeks.

She keeps gasping.

He sings the first line of 'Teddy Bears' Picnic' to her.

Whoop! Whoop! is his answer.

'Give it back to me, Alice! Sing! It'll open you up! If you go down to the woods today . . .'

'If you . . . go down . . . to the woods today . . .' A gasp after every two or three words.

'You're sure of a big surprise.'

Under the washcloth, Alice shakes her head. He grasps her shoulder, the bruised one, knowing he's hurting her but doing it anyway. Anything to get through to her. 'All in one breath, you're sure of a big surprise.'

'You're sure . . . big surprise.' *Whoop!*

'Not perfect but not bad. Now both lines together, and put some feeling into it. If you go down to the woods today, you're sure of a big surprise. With me. *À deux.*'

She does it with him, her half of the duet muffled by the wet washcloth where a crescent of mouth-shaped shadow appears each time she inhales.

He sits beside her as her breathing finally begins to ease. He puts an arm around her shoulders. 'You're all right. You're okay.'

She takes the washcloth off her face. Locks of damp dark hair are stuck to her forehead. 'What's that song?'

'"Teddy Bears' Picnic."'

'Does it always work?'

'Yes.' Unless, that is, half of your throat has been blown out.

'I need to have it on my phone.' Then she remembers. 'Shit, my phone is gone.'

'I'll put it on one of the laptops,' Billy says, and points to the living room.

'Why do you have so many? What are they for?'

'Verisimilitude. That means—'

'I know what it means. Part of your disguise. Like the wig and the fake belly.' She uses the heel of her hand to brush the damp locks off her forehead. 'I dreamed he was choking me. Tripp. I thought he was going to choke me to death. He was saying "Get them panties down" in this funny growling voice that wasn't like his regular voice. Then I woke up—'

'—and you couldn't breathe.'

She nods.

'Have you ever seen a movie called *Deliverance*? Guys on a canoe trip?'

She looks at him as if he's gone crazy. 'No. What's that got to do with the price of tea in China?'

'Get them panties down is a line from the movie.' He touches the marks on the side of her neck, very lightly. 'Your dream was a recovered memory. That's possibly the last thing you heard before you went all the way out, not just from whatever he put in your drink but because he choked you. Lucky he didn't kill you. It probably wouldn't have been on purpose, but you'd have been just as dead.'

'If you go down to the woods today, you're in for a big surprise. Okay, what's the rest of it?'

'I don't remember the whole song, but the first verse goes like this: If you go down to the woods today, you're in for a big surprise. If you go down to the woods today, you better go in disguise. Your mother never sang that to you?'

'My mother didn't sing. You have a good voice.'

'If you say so.'

They sit together for a little bit. She's breathing okay again, and now that the crisis has passed, Billy becomes aware that she's wearing only her Black Keys T-shirt (which she somehow missed throwing up on) and he's in his boxers. He gets up. 'You'll be okay now.'

'Don't go. Not yet.'

He sits down again. She moves over. Billy lies down beside her, tense at first, his arm behind him for a makeshift pillow.

'Tell me why you killed that guy.' A pause. 'Please.'

'It's not exactly a bedtime story.'

'I want to hear. To understand. Because you don't seem like a bad guy.'

I've always told myself I'm not, Billy thinks, but recent events have certainly called that into question. He glances guiltily at the picture of Dave the Flamingo on the nightstand.

'What gets said here stays here.' She gives him a tentative smile.

It's a fucked-up bedtime story but he tells it to her, starting with Frank Macintosh and Paul Logan coming to pick him up at the hotel. He thinks about changing the names (as he did at first in the story he's been writing) and then decides there's little point. She knows Ken Hoff's from the news, ditto Giorgio's. He makes one exception: Nick Majarian becomes Benjy Compson. Knowing his name might make life dangerous for her later on.

He thought saying everything out loud might clarify things in his own mind. That didn't happen, but her breathing is easy again. She's calm. The story did that much, anyway. After thinking it over she says, 'This guy Benjy Compson hired you, but who hired him?'

'I don't know.'

'And why get the other guy, Hoff, involved? Couldn't one of these gangsters have found you a gun? And not get caught doing it?'

'Because Hoff owns the building, I suppose. The one I took the shot from. Well, he did own it.'

'The building where you had to wait for however long. Embedded, like.'

Embedded, he thinks. Yes. Like the reporters who came and went in Iraq, putting on armor and helmets and then taking them off when their stories were filed and they could go back home.

'It wasn't too long.' It was though.

'Still, it seems awfully complicated.'

It does to Billy, too.

'I think I can go back to sleep now.' Without looking at him she adds, 'You can stay if you want.'

Billy, wary that his body might betray him again below the waist, says he thinks he better go back to the couch. Maybe Alice understands, because she gives him a look and a nod, then turns on her side and closes her eyes.

3

In the morning Alice tells him they're almost out of milk and Cheerios are no good dry. Like I didn't know that, Billy thinks. He suggests eggs and she says there's only one left. 'I don't know why you only bought half a dozen.'

Because I wasn't expecting company, Billy thinks.

'I know you weren't expecting to feed two,' she says.

'I'll go down to Zoney's. They'll have milk and eggs.'

'If you went to the Harps on Pine Plaza, you could get some pork chops or something. We could grill them on the barbecue out back if it ever stops raining. And some salad, the kind that comes in bags. It isn't that far away.'

Billy's first thought is that she's trying to get rid of him so she can do a runner. Then he looks at the yellowing bruises on her cheek and forehead, her swollen nose just beginning to go down, and thinks no, just the opposite. She's settling in. Means to stay. At least for the present.

It would seem crazy to someone on the outside, but in here it makes sense. She might have died in the gutter if not for him, and he's showed no signs of wanting to re-rape her. On the contrary, he went out and got her the emergency pill in case one of those assholes impregnated her. Also, there's the leased Ford Fusion to think about. It's waiting for him on the other side of town. It's time to bring it over here so he can leave for Nevada as soon as he feels it's safe.

Besides, he likes Alice. He likes the way she's coming back. She's had a couple of panic attacks, sure, but who wouldn't have panic attacks after being drugged and gang raped? She hasn't talked about going back to school, she hasn't mentioned friends or acquaintances who might be concerned about her, and she hasn't fretted about calling her mother (or maybe her sister, the hairdresser). He thinks that Alice is in a space of hiatus. She has put her life on pause while she tries to figure out what should come next. Billy is no psychiatrist, but he has an idea that might actually be healthy.

Those fucks, Billy thinks, and not for the first time. Assholes who'd rape an unconscious girl. Who does that?

'Okay, groceries. You'll stay here, right?'

'Right.' As if it's a foregone conclusion. 'I'm going to have cereal with the last of the milk. You can have the egg.' She gives him an uncertain look. 'If that's all right. We can do it the other way around if it's not. They're your supplies, after all.'

'That's fine. Will you help me with my stomach again after breakfast?'

That makes her laugh. It's the first one.

4

While they eat, he asks if she knows what Stockholm Syndrome is. She doesn't, so he explains. 'If I get spotted by the police and picked up, they'll come here. Tell them you were afraid to leave.'

'I am,' Alice says, 'but not because I'm afraid of you. I don't want people to see me like this. I don't want people to see me at all, at least for awhile. Besides, you won't get picked up. With that stuff on you look a lot different.' She raises an admonitory finger. '*But.*'

'But what?'

'You need an umbrella, because a wig always looks like a wig in the rain. Water beads up on it. Real hair just gets wet and kind of tamps down.'

'I don't have an umbrella.'

'There's one in the Jensens' closet. By the door as you go in.'

'When did you look in their closet?'

'While you were making the popcorn. Women like to see what other people have.' She looks at him across the kitchen table, her with her Cheerios, him with his egg. 'Did you really not know that?'

5

The umbrella does more than keep the rain off his blond wig; it shields his face and makes him feel a little bit less like a bug on a microscope slide as he leaves the house and starts walking toward the nearest bus stop. He can completely relate to how Alice feels, because he feels the same. Going to the drugstore was nerve-racking, but this is worse because he's going farther. He could walk to Pine Plaza, it's fairly close and the rain has slacked off again, but he can't walk all the way across town. And something else – the closer he gets to leaving this city, the more he dreads being captured before he can do it.

Never mind the cops and Nick's men, what if he meets someone from his David Lockridge life? He imagines rounding a corner in Harps with his little shopping basket over his arm and coming face to face with Paul Ragland or Pete Fazio. They might not recognize him, but a woman would. Never mind what Alice said about him looking different with his wig and fake belly, Phil would. Corinne Ackerman would. Even tipsy Jane Kellogg would, even if she was drunk. He's sure of it. He understands such a meeting is statistically unlikely, but such things happen all the time. Journeys end in lovers meeting, every wise man's son doth know.

He examined the online bus schedule before leaving, and waits for the Number 3 at Rampart Street, standing under the bus shelter with three others, collapsing the umbrella because leaving it open would look weird. None of the others look at him. They are all looking at their phones.

He has a bad moment in the parking garage when the Fusion won't start, then remembers he has to have his foot on the brake pedal. Duh, he thinks.

He drives to Pine Plaza, both enjoying the feeling of being behind the wheel again and paranoid about getting in a fender-bender or attracting the attention of the police (two cruisers pass him on the three-mile trip) in some other way. At Harps he buys meat, milk, eggs, bread, crackers, bag salad, dressing, and some canned goods. He doesn't meet anyone he knows, and really, why would he? Evergreen Street is in Midwood, and people who live in Midwood shop at Save Mart.

He pays for his groceries with his Dalton Smith Mastercard and drives back to Pearson Street. He parks in the crumbling driveway beside the house and goes downstairs with his groceries. The apartment is empty. Alice is gone.

6

He purchased a couple of cloth shopping bags to put his groceries in – HARPS and HOMETOWN FRESH printed on them – and they sag almost to the floor as he looks at the empty living room and kitchen. The bedroom door is open and he can see that's empty too, but he calls her name anyway, thinking she might be in the bathroom. Except that door is also open and if she was in there she'd close it, even with him gone. He knows this.

He isn't scared, exactly. It's more like . . . what? Is he hurt? Disappointed?

I guess I am, he thinks. Stupid, but there it is. She reconsidered her options, that's all. You knew it could happen. Or you should have.

He goes into the kitchen, puts the bags on the counter, sees their breakfast dishes in the drainer. He sits down to think about what he should do next and sees a paper towel anchored by the sugar bowl. On it she's written two words: OUT BACK.

Okay, he thinks, and lets out a long breath. Just out back.

Billy puts away the stuff that needs to go in the fridge, then goes out the front door and around the house, once more using the umbrella. Alice has moved the barbecue out of the puddle. She's scrubbing away at the grill, her back to him. She must have raided the Jensens' front closet again, because the green raincoat she's wearing has to belong to Don. It goes all the way down to her calves.

'Alice?'

She yells and jumps and almost knocks the grill over. He reaches out to steady her.

'Scare a person, why don't you?' she says, then whoops in a big breath.

'I'm sorry. Didn't mean to creep up on you.'

'Well . . .' *Whoop!* '. . . you did.'

'Give me the first line of "Teddy Bears' Picnic."' Only half-joking.

'I don't . . .' *Whoop!* '. . . remember it.'

'If you go down to the woods today . . .' He raises his hands and wiggles his fingers in a come-on gesture.

'If you go down to the woods today, you're in for a big surprise. Did you get some stuff?'

'I did.'

'Pork chops?'

'Yes. At first I thought you were gone.'

'Well I'm not. I don't suppose you got any Scrubbies, did you? Because this is the last one from upstairs, and it's pretty well done-in.'

'Scrubbies weren't on the list. I didn't know you were going on a cleaning binge in the rain.'

She closes the lid on the barbecue and looks at him with a hopeful expression. 'Want to watch some more *Blacklist*?'

'Yes,' he says, so that's what they do. Three more episodes. Between the second and third, she goes to the window and says, 'It's stopping. The sun's almost out. I think we can barbecue tonight. Did you remember the salad?'

This is going to work, Billy thinks. It shouldn't, it's crazy, but it's going to work for as long as it has to.

7

The sun comes out that afternoon, but slowly, as if it doesn't really want to. Alice grills the chops, and although they're a little burned outside and a little pink in the middle ('I'm not much of a cook, sorry,' she says), Billy eats all of his and then gnaws the bone. It's good, but the salad is better. He doesn't realize how starved he's been for greens until he starts in on them.

They go upstairs and watch some more *Blacklist*, but she's restless, moving from the couch to the seat-sprung easy chair that must be Don Jensen's roost when he's home, then back to the couch again. Billy reminds himself that she's seen all these episodes before, probably with her mother and sister. He's getting a little bored with it himself now that he's figured out Red Reddington's schtick.

'You ought to leave some money,' she says when they turn the TV off and get ready to go back downstairs. 'For the Netflix.'

Billy says he will, although he guesses that thanks to their windfall, Don and Bev don't exactly need financial help.

She tells him it's his turn for the bed, and after a night on the couch he doesn't argue the point. He's asleep almost at once, but some deep part of his brain must have already trained itself to listen for her panic attacks, because he comes wide awake at quarter past two, hearing her whoop for breath.

He's left the door ajar in case of this. He reaches it, then stops with his hand on the knob. She's singing, very softly.

'If you go down to the woods today . . .'

She goes through the first verse twice. Her gasps for breath come further apart, then stop. Billy goes back to bed.

8

Neither of them knows – no one does – that a rogue virus is going to shut down America and most of the world in half a year, but by their fourth day in the basement apartment, Billy and Alice are getting a preview of what sheltering in place will be like. On that fourth morning, a day before Billy has decided to set sail into the golden west, he is doing his sprints up to the third floor and back. Alice has neatened up the apartment, which hardly needed it since neither of them is particularly messy. With that done she subsided to the couch. When Billy comes in, out of breath from half a dozen stair-sprints, she's watching a cooking show on TV.

'Rotisserie chicken,' he says. 'Looks good.'

'Why make it at home when you can buy one just as good at the supermarket?' Alice turns off the TV. 'I wish I had something to read. Could you download a book for me? Maybe a detective story? On one of the cheap laptops, not yours.'

Billy doesn't answer. An idea, audacious and frightening, has come into his head.

She misreads his expression. 'I didn't look or anything, I just know it's yours because the case is scratched. The others look brand new.'

Billy isn't thinking she tried to snoop in his computer. She'd never get past the password prompt, anyway. He's thinking of the M151 spotter scope, and how he didn't explain its purpose because what he was writing was only for himself. No one else would ever read it. Only now there is someone, and what harm can it do, considering what she knows about him already?

But it could do harm, of course. To him. If she didn't like it. If she said it was boring and asked for something more interesting.

'What's going on with you?' she asks. 'You look weird.'

'Nothing. I mean . . . I've been writing something. Kind of a life story. I don't suppose you'd want to—'

'Yes.'

9

He can't bear to watch her sitting with his Mac Pro on her lap, reading the words he wrote here and in Gerard Tower, so he goes upstairs to the Jensens' to spritz Daphne and Walter. He puts a twenty on the kitchen table, with a note that says *For Netflix*, and then just walks around. Paces around, actually, like an expectant father in an old cartoon. He looks at the Ruger in the drawer of Don's nightstand, picks it up, puts it back, closes the drawer.

It's ridiculous to be nervous, she's a business school student, not a literary critic. She probably sleepwalked through her high school English courses, happy with Bs and Cs, and very likely the only thing she knows about Shakespeare is that his name rhymes with kick in the rear. Billy understands he's downplaying her intelligence to protect his ego in case she doesn't like it, and he understands that's stupid because her opinion shouldn't matter, the story itself shouldn't matter, he's got more important things to deal with. But it does.

Finally he goes back downstairs. She's still reading, but when she looks up from the screen he's alarmed to see her eyes are red, the lids puffy.

'What's wrong?'

She wipes her nose with the heel of her hand, a childish gesture, oddly winning. 'Did that really happen to your sister? Did that man really . . . *stomp* her to death? You didn't make that up?'

'No. It happened.' Suddenly he feels like crying himself, although he didn't cry when he wrote it.

'Is that why you saved me? Because of her?'

I saved you because if I'd left you in the street the cops would have eventually come here, he thinks. Except that's probably not all the truth. Do we ever tell ourselves all of it?

'I don't know.'

'I'm so sorry that happened to you.' Alice begins to cry. 'I thought what happened to me was bad, but—'

'What happened to you *was* bad.'

'—but what happened to her is worse. Did you really shoot him?'

'Yes.'

'Good. *Good!* And you got put in a home?'

'Yes. You can stop if it's upsetting you.' But he doesn't want her to stop and he's not sorry for upsetting her. He's glad. He reached her.

She grips the laptop as if afraid he might pull it away. 'I want to read the rest.' Then, almost accusingly: 'Why haven't you been doing this instead of watching a stupid TV show upstairs?'

'Self-conscious.'

'All right. I get that, I feel the same, so stop looking at me. Let me read.'

He wants to thank her for crying, but that would be weird. Instead he asks what her sizes are.

'My *sizes?* Why?'

'There's a Goodwill store close to Harps. I could get you a couple of pairs of pants and some shirts. Maybe a pair of sneakers. You don't want me to watch you reading and I don't want to watch you do it. And you have to be tired of that skirt.'

She gives him an impish grin and it makes her pretty. Or would, if not for the bruises. 'Not afraid to go out without the umbrella?'

'I'll take the car. Just remember if the cops come back instead of me, you were afraid to leave. I said I'd find you and hurt you.'

'You'll come back,' Alice says, and writes down her sizes.

He takes his time in the Goodwill, wanting to give *her* time. He sees no one he knows, and no one pays particular attention to him.

When he gets back, she's finished. What took him months to write has taken her less than two hours to read. She has questions. None are about the spotter scope; they're about the people, especially Ronnie and Glen and 'that poor little one-eyed girl' in the House of Everlasting Paint. She says she likes how he wrote like a kid when he was a kid but changed it up when he got older. She says he should keep writing. She says she'll go upstairs while he does it, watch TV and then take a nap. 'I'm tired all the time. It's crazy.'

'It's not. Your body is still working to get over what those fucks did to it.'

Alice stands in the doorway. 'Dalton?' It's what she calls him, even though she knows his real name. 'Did your friend Taco die?'

'A lot of people did before it was over.'

'I'm sorry,' she says, and closes the door behind her.

10

He writes. Her reaction lifts him. He doesn't spill many words on the slack time between April and November of 2004, when they were supposed to be winning hearts and minds and won neither. He gives it a few more paragraphs, then goes to the part that still hurts.

They were pulled back for a couple of days after Albie's death because there was talk of a ceasefire, and when the Hot Nine (now the Hot Eight, each of them with ALBIE S. written on his helmet) got back to base, Billy looked everywhere for the baby shoe, thinking he might have left it there. The others also looked, but it was nowhere to be found and then they went back in, back to the job of clearing houses, and the first three were okay, two empty and one inhabited only by a boy of twelve or fourteen who raised his hands and screamed *No gun Americans, no gun love New York Yankees no shoot!*

The fourth house was the Funhouse.

Billy stops there for exercise. He thinks maybe he and Alice will stay on Pearson Street a little longer, maybe three more days. Until he finishes with the Funhouse and what happened there. He wants to write that losing the baby shoe made no difference one way or the other, of course it didn't. He also wants to write that his heart still doesn't believe it.

He does a few stretches before running up and down the stairs, because he can't go to a walk-in clinic if he pops a hamstring. He hears no TV behind the Jensens' door, so Alice is probably sleeping. And healing, he hopes, although Billy doubts that any woman ever heals completely after being raped. It leaves a scar and he guesses that on some days the scar aches. He guesses that even ten years later – twenty, thirty – it still aches. Maybe it's like that, maybe it's like something else. Maybe the only men who can know for sure are men who have been raped themselves.

As he runs the stairs, he thinks about the men who did it to her, and they *are* men. She said that Tripp Donovan is twenty-four, and Billy guesses Jack and Hank, Donovan's rapin' roomies, must be about the same age. Men, not boys. Bad ones.

He comes back into the basement apartment out of breath, but feeling loose and warm, ready to get back at it for another hour or maybe even two. Before he can get going, his laptop bings with a text message. It's from Bucky Hanson, now hunkered down in the Great Wherever. **No money has been transferred. Don't think it's going to happen. What are you going to do?**

Get it, Billy texts back.

11

That night he sits beside Alice on the couch. She looks good in her black pants and striped shirt. When he turns off the TV and says he wants to talk to her she looks frightened.

'Is it something bad?'

Billy shrugs. 'You tell me.'

She listens to him carefully, her wide eyes steady on his. When he finishes, she says, 'You would do that?'

'Yes. They need a payback for what they did to you, but that's not the only reason. What men like that have done once they'll do again. Maybe you're not even the first.'

'You'd be taking a risk. It could be dangerous.'

He thinks of the gun in Don Jensen's nightstand and says, 'Probably not very.'

'You can't kill them. I don't want that. Tell me you won't kill them.'

The idea hasn't even crossed Billy's mind. They need to pay, but they also need to learn, and those who are obliterated are beyond lessons. 'No,' he says. 'No killing.'

'And I really don't care about Jack and Hank. They weren't the ones who pretended to like me and got me to come to that apartment.'

Billy says nothing, but he does care about Jack and Hank, assuming they participated, and based on what he saw when she was undressed, he's sure that at least one of them did. Probably both.

'But I care about Tripp,' she says, and puts a hand on his arm. 'If he was hurt that would make me happy. I suppose that makes me a bad person.'

'It makes you human,' Billy says. 'Bad people need to pay a price. And the price should be high.'

CHAPTER 16

1

We could hear heavy small-arms fire and explosions in other parts of the city, but until the shit hit the fan, our area in the Jolan was relatively quiet. We cleared the first three houses in our section, Block Lima, with no trouble. Two were empty. There was a kid in the third one, not armed and not wired up to explode. We made him take off his shirt to be sure. We sent him to the police station with a couple of army guys who were headed that way with their own prisoners. We knew that kid would probably be back on the street by nightfall, because the cop shop was basically a turnstile. He was lucky to be alive at all, because we were still red-assed about losing Albie Stark. Din-Din actually raised his gun, but Big Klew pushed the barrel down and said to leave the kid alone.

'The next time we see him he'll have an AK,' George said. 'We ought to just kill them all. Fucking roaches.'

The fourth house was the biggest on the block, a regular estate. It had a domed roof and a courtyard with palms on the inside to give it shade. Some rich Ba'athist's crib, no doubt. The whole thing was surrounded by a high concrete wall painted with a mural of children playing ball and skipping rope and running around while several women looked on. Probably with approval, but it was hard to tell because they were so bundled up in their abayahs. There was also a man standing off to the side. Our terp, Fareed, said he was the *mutawaeen*. The women watched the children, Fareed said, and the *mutawaeen* watched the women to make sure they did nothing that might incite lust.

We all got a kick out of Fareed, because his accent made him sound like a Yooper from Traverse City. Lots of the terps sounded like Michiganders, who knows why. 'Dat picture means dis house, the *al'atfal*, da kiddies, can come und play.'

'So it's a funhouse,' Donk said.

'No, dey don't allow fun in da house,' Fareed said. 'Just in da yard.'

Donk rolled his eyes and snickered, but no one laughed outright. We were still thinking of Albie, and how it could have been any one of us.

'Come on, you guys,' Taco said. 'Let's get some.' He handed Fareed the bullhorn that had GOOD MORNING VIETNAM printed on the side in Sharpie and told him

2

Billy is snapped back from Fallujah by the sound of Alice running down the stairs. She bursts into the apartment, hair flying out behind her. 'Someone's coming! I was spritzing the plants and saw the car turn into the driveway!'

One look at her face tells Billy not to waste time asking if she's sure. He gets up and goes to the periscope window.

'Is it them, do you think? The Jensens coming back early? I turned off the TV but I had coffee, the place smells of it, and there's a plate on the counter! Crumbs! They'll know somebody's been—'

Billy pushes the curtain back a few inches. He couldn't see the new car if it was able to pull all the way up, the angle is wrong, but because his leased Fusion is in the driveway, he can. It's a blue SUV with a scratch running down the side. For a moment he doesn't know where he's seen it before, but it comes to him even before the driver gets out. It's Merton Richter, the real estate agent who rented him the apartment.

'Did you lock the door?' Billy jerks his chin upward.

Alice shakes her head, her eyes big and scared, but maybe that's okay. It might be even if Richter tries the door and peeks in when there's no answer to his knock. The Jensens asked him to water their plants, after all. But he may be coming here, and Billy isn't wearing the wig, let alone the fake stomach. He's in a T-shirt and his workout shorts.

The front door opens and they hear Richter step inside. The puke has been cleaned up, but will he detect the smell? It's not like they opened the door to air out the foyer.

Billy wants to wait and see if Richter goes up to the Jensens' but knows he can't afford to. 'Turn on the computers.' He sweeps his hand around, indicating the AllTechs. And Christ, Richter *isn't* going up there, he's coming down here. 'You're my niece.'

It's all he has time for. He slams down the lid of the Mac Pro, runs for the bedroom, and shuts the door. As he crosses to the bathroom, where the fake belly is hanging on the back of the door, he hears Richter knock. She'll have to open it because he'll know from the car in the driveway that someone is home. When she does he'll see a young woman half Billy's age, bruised and still flushed from her run down the stairs. Only that's not the exercise Richter will think of first. This is bad.

Billy puts the belly in the small of his back so he can cinch the strap, but he misses the buckle and the belly falls to the floor. He picks it up and tries again. This time he gets the strap in the buckle, but he pulls it too tight and can't turn the belly to his front even when he sucks in his gut. When he loosens the strap, the fucking thing falls down again. Billy bumps his head on the washbasin, picks up the appliance, tells himself to calm down, and buckles the strap. He rotates the belly into position.

Back in the bedroom, Billy can hear the murmur of voices. Alice giggles. It sounds nervous rather than amused. Fuck, fuck, *fuck*.

He yanks on chinos and then the sweatshirt, both because it's quicker than a button-up and because Alice was right, fat guys think baggy clothes make them look less fat. The blond wig is on the bureau. He grabs it and jams it on over his black hair. In the living room Alice laughs again. He reminds himself not to say her name because for all Billy knows, she's given their visitor a false one.

He takes two big breaths to calm himself, puts on a smile that he hopes will look embarrassed — as if he's been caught doing the neces-sary — and opens the door. 'We have company, I see.'

'Yes,' Alice says. She turns to him with a smile on her lips and an expression of naked relief in her eyes. 'He says he rented you the apartment.'

Billy frowns, trying to remember, then smiles as it comes to him. 'Oh yes, right. Mr Ricker.'

'Richter,' he says, and extends his hand. Billy shakes it, still smiling, trying to read what Richter is thinking. He can't. But Richter will have noticed the bruises on her face and her nervousness. Those are impossible to miss. And is Billy's hand sweaty? Probably.

'I was in the . . .' Billy points vaguely toward the bedroom and the bathroom beyond.

'Quite all right,' Richter says. He looks at the screens of the AllTech laptops, which are cycling through all sorts of pre-loaded clickbait: the wonders of acai berries, two weird little tips for erasing wrinkles, doctors plead with you not to eat this vegetable, see what these ten child stars look like now.

'So this is what you do?' Richter asks.

'As a sideline. I earn most of my beer and skittles doing IT work. Travel around a lot, don't I, dear?'

'Yes,' Alice says, and gives another of those jagged giggles. Richter slips her a quick side-glance, and in it Billy sees that whatever Alice may have told Richter while Billy was fumbling with the fucking fake stomach, the man believes that she's Dalton Smith's niece like he believes the moon is made of green cheese.

'Fascinating stuff,' Richter says, bending to squint at the screen that's just changed from the dangerous vegetable (corn, as it happens, which isn't even a real vegetable) to ten famous unsolved murders (JonBenét Ramsey leading the pack). 'Just fascinating.' He straightens up and looks around. 'I like what you've done to the place.'

Alice has neatened it up a bit, but otherwise it's the same as it was when he moved in. 'What can I do for you, Mr Richter?'

'Well, I just came to give you a little heads-up.' Richter, recalled to business, smooths his tie and puts on a professional smile. 'A consortium called Southern Endeavor has bought up those storage sheds back there on Pond Street and the houses, the few that remain, here on Pearson Street. Which includes this one. They're planning on a new shopping mall that should revitalize this whole section of town.'

Billy doubts that malls can revitalize anything in the age of the Internet, including themselves, but he says nothing.

Alice is calming down, and that's good. 'I'll just go in the bedroom and let you men talk,' she says, and does just that, closing the door behind her.

Billy puts his hands in his pockets and rocks back and forth on his feet, making the fake stomach bulge a bit against the sweatshirt. 'The storage sheds and houses are going to be knocked down, is that what you're telling me? Including this one, I assume.'

'Yes, but you'll have six weeks to find new accommodations.' Richter says it as if conveying a great gift. 'Six weeks is firm, I'm afraid. Give me a forwarding address before you move out, Cuz, and I'll be happy to refund any rent that's owing.' Richter sighs. 'I'll have to tell the Jensens when I leave here. That could be harder, because they've been here longer.'

It's not for Billy to tell him that Don and Beverly will be looking for a new place anyway, maybe to buy instead of to rent, when they get back from their cruise. But he does tell Richter that the Jensens will be gone for awhile and he's been taking care of their plants. 'Me and my niece, that is.'

'Very neighborly of you. And she's a lovely girl.' Richter licks his lips, perhaps just to moisten them, perhaps not. 'Do you have a phone number for the Jensens?'

'I do. It's in my wallet. Will you excuse me for just a sec?'

'Of course.'

Alice is sitting on the bed and looking at him with big eyes. Most of the color has left her face, making the bruises even more prominent. *What?* those eyes say. And *How bad?*

Billy raises a hand and pats the air with it: *Be cool, be cool.*

He gets his wallet and goes back into the living room, remembering to walk fat. Richter is bent over one of the AllTechs, hands on knees, tie hanging down like a stopped pendulum, looking at the wonders of the avocado, nature's most perfect vegetable (it's actually a fruit). For one moment Billy actually considers lacing his fingers together and bringing the hammer down on the back of Richter's neck, but when Richter turns, Billy just opens his wallet and holds out a slip of paper. 'Here it is.'

Richter takes a little pad from his inner pocket and jots down the number with a silver pencil. 'I'll give them a ringy-dingy.'

'I can do it, if you want.'

'By all means, by all means, but I'll still have to call them myself. Part of the job. Sorry to trouble you, Mr Smith. I'll let you go back . . .' His eyes flick briefly to the bedroom door. '. . . to whatever you were doing.'

'I'll see you out,' Billy says. Pitching his voice lower, he says 'I want to talk to you about . . .' He tilts his head to the bedroom.

'None of my business, Cuz. This is the twenty-first century.'

'I know, but it's not like that.'

They walk up the stairs to the foyer. Billy brings up the rear, puffing a little. 'Got to lose some weight.'

'Join the club,' Richter says.

'That poor kid's my sister Mary's girl,' Billy says. 'Mary's husband left her a year ago and she picked up this loser, I think in a bar. Bob somebody. He's been after the girl and beat her up when she wouldn't come across for him, if you know what I mean.'

'I get it.' Richter is looking out the foyer door like he can't wait to get back to his car. Maybe the story makes him uncomfortable, Billy thinks. Or maybe he just wants to get away from me.

'Here's the other piece. Mary's got quite the temper, doesn't like anyone telling her her business.'

'Know the type,' Richter says, still looking out the door. 'Know it very well.'

'I'll keep my niece for a week, maybe ten days, let Sis cool down a bit, then take her back and talk to her about Bob.'

'Got it. Wish you luck.' He turns to Billy and offers a hand with a smile to go with it. The smile looks genuine. Richter may believe his story. On the other hand, he may be acting as if his life depends on it, which he might think it does. Billy gives him a good firm shake.

Richter exclaims, 'Women! Can't live with em and can't shoot em outside the state of Alabama!'

It's a joke, so Billy laughs. Richter lets go of his hand, opens the door, then turns back. 'I see you shaved off your mustache.'

Startled, Billy raises two fingers to his upper lip. What he did was forget to put it on in his haste, and maybe that's for the best. The mustache is tricky, it needs spirit gum to hold it, and if he applied it crooked, or the spirit gum showed, Richter would have known it was fake and wondered what the fuck.

'Got tired of picking food out of it,' Billy says.

Richter laughs. Billy can't tell if it's forced. It might be. 'I hear that, Cuz. Loud and clear.'

He trots down the steps to his scratched SUV, shoulders a bit hunched, maybe because it's chilly this morning, maybe because he's expecting Billy to put a bullet in the back of his neck.

He gives a wave before getting in. Billy waves back. Then he hurries downstairs.

3

Billy says, 'I'm going to visit your bad date today. Tomorrow I'm getting out of Dodge.'

Alice puts a hand to her mouth but drops it when her index finger brushes against her swollen nose. 'Oh God. Did he recognize you?'

'My instinct says no, but he's observant, noticed I didn't have my mustache anymore—'

'Jesus!'

'He assumed I shaved it off, so it's okay. At least I think so. I'm willing to push my luck one more day. Did you give him a name?'

'Brenda Collins. My best friend in high school. Did you—'

'Give him a different one? No, just called you my niece. I told him your mother's boyfriend beat you up because you wouldn't go to bed with him.'

Alice nods. 'That's good. It covers everything.'

'Which doesn't mean he'll believe it. Stories are one thing, seeing is another. What he saw was a middle-aged fat man with a banged-up underage girl.'

Alice draws herself up, looking offended. Under other circumstances it might have been funny. 'I'm twenty-one! A legal adult!'

'Do you get carded in bars?'

'Well . . .'

Billy nods, case closed.

'Maybe,' Alice says, 'if you really mean to . . . well . . . *confront* Tripp, we shouldn't wait until tomorrow. Maybe we should go right now.'

4

He stares at her, simultaneously believing that pronoun and not believing it. And what's worse, she's looking at him like it's a foregone conclusion.

'Holy shit,' Billy says. 'You really *do* have Stockholm Syndrome.'

'I don't because I'm not a hostage. I could have walked out anytime from the Jensens' apartment, as long as I was quiet on the stairs. You would never have noticed because you'd've been all wrapped up in your writing.'

Probably true, Billy thinks. And furthermore—

Alice says it for him. 'If I was going to run away, I could have done it the first time you went out. For the morning-after pill.' She pauses, then adds, 'Plus I gave him a false name.'

'Because you were scared.'

Alice shakes her head vehemently. 'You were in the other room. I could have whispered that you were William Summers, who killed that man at the courthouse. We would have been upstairs and in his car before you finished putting on *that*.' She pokes him in the fake belly.

'You can't go with me. It's nuts.'

Still, the idea is starting to seep down, like water in dry earth. She can't go with him all the way to Vegas, but if they can work out a story that protects the Dalton Smith identity, which is now in dire peril, then maybe . . .

'Maybe you could go by yourself if you leave Tripp and his friends alone. Because if anything happens to them, they'd connect it to me. Tripp and his friends, I mean. They wouldn't want to go to the police, but they might decide to hurt me.'

Billy has to hide a smile. She is playing him, and doing a good job of it on short notice. This is quite a change from the puking semi-conscious girl he fished out of the rain, the one who sometimes has panic attacks in the night. Billy thinks it's a change for the better. Plus, she's right – anything he does to those three they would connect to her. Assuming, that is, she's the only woman they date-raped last week, which seems likely.

'Yes,' Alice says, watching him from under her eyebrows and still playing him for all she's worth. 'I guess you better leave them unpunished.' Then she asks him what he's smiling about.

'Nothing. Just that I like you. My friend Taco would have said you've got some gimme to you.'

'I don't know what that means.'

'It doesn't matter. But yeah, those guys need a payback for what they did. I need to think about this.'

Alice says, 'Can I help you pack while you think?'

5

It's Billy who does the packing. It doesn't take long. There's no room for her new clothes in his suitcase, but he finds a plastic Barnes & Noble bag, the kind with handles, on the top shelf of the bedroom closet and dumps her stuff into that. He carries the AllTechs out to the Fusion in a stack.

While he does that, Alice goes through the Jensens' apartment with a dish towel and a spray bottle of Lysol and water, wiping down surfaces. She pays special attention to the TV remote, which they've both used, and doesn't neglect the light switches. When she goes downstairs, Billy helps her wipe down the basement apartment, paying particular attention to the bathroom: fixtures, shower head, mirror, the toilet's flush handle. It takes them about an hour.

'I think we're done,' she says.

'What about the key to the Jensens' apartment?'

'Oh glory,' she says. 'I've still got it. I'll wipe it down and . . . what? Slip it under the door?'

'I'll do it.' He does, but goes in first to get Don Jensen's Ruger. He sticks it in his belt, beneath the pregnancy belly. The XL sweatshirt covers it. The revolver is a pricey item, five or six hundred dollars, and Billy doesn't have that much cash. He leaves two fifties and a C-note on the nightstand, along with a quick scribble that says *Took your gun. Will send the balance when I can.* More like if he can. Meanwhile, what about Daphne and Walter? Will they die of thirst on their windowsill? Romeo and Juliet of the plant world? Stupid to even wonder, given everything else he has to worry about.

It's because Bev gave them names, he thinks. He treats each to one final spray for good luck. Then he touches his back pocket, where Shan's flamingo drawing is folded up and stowed away.

Back downstairs, he takes Alice's phone out of his hip pocket and holds it out to her. He's replaced the SIM card.

She takes it with an accusing look. 'It wasn't lost. You had it all along.'

'Because I didn't trust you.'

'And now you do?'

'Now I do. And at some point you need to call your mother. Otherwise she's going to get worried.'

'I suppose she would,' Alice says. Then, with a trace of bitterness: 'After a *month* or so.' She sighs. 'Okay, and tell her what? I made a friend, we bonded over chicken noodle soup and *The Blacklist?*'

Billy considers, but comes up empty.

Alice, meanwhile, breaks into a smile. 'You know what, I'm going to tell her I quit school. She'll believe that. And I'm going to Cancun with some friends. She'll believe that, too.'

'Will she really?'

'*Yes.*'

Billy thinks there's a whole mother–daughter relationship in that single word, complete with tears, recriminations, and slammed doors. 'You need to work on that a little,' he says. 'Right now it's time to go.'

6

There are two Sherwood Heights exits off the Interstate, both with clusters of fast-food restaurants, gas-em-up quick-stops, and motels. Billy tells Alice to look for a motel that isn't part of a chain. While she's busy checking out the signs, he slips the Ruger out of his belt and stows it under the seat. At the second exit she points out the Penny Pines Motel and asks what he thinks. Billy says it looks good. Using one of his Dalton Smith credit cards, he gets them a pair of adjoining rooms. Alice waits in the car, making Billy think of that old song by the Amazing Rhythm Aces, 'Third Rate Romance.'

They bring in their stuff. He takes the Mac Pro out of the carrybag, puts it on the room's single table (shaky and needing a shim under one leg), re-zips the bag, and slings it over his shoulder.

'What do you need that for?'

'Supplies. I need to do some shopping. And it's got a good look. Professional. What's your phone number?'

She gives it to him and he puts it into his contacts.

'Do you have an address for the condo where these guys live?' It's a question he should have asked before, but they've been a little busy.

'I don't know the number, but it's Landview Estates, on Route 10. It's the last stop the bus makes before it gets to the airport and turns around.' Alice takes him by the sleeve and leads him to the window.

She points. 'Pretty sure that's Landview Estates, those three on the left. Tripp lives – *they* live – in building C.'

'Third floor.'

'That's right. I don't remember the apartment number, but it's the one at the end of the hall. You have to push a code to get in the front door, and I didn't see what he put in. It didn't seem important at the time.'

'I'll get in.' Billy hopes he's right about that. His expertise is guns, not entering buildings with security doors.

'Will you come back here before you go there?'

'No, but I'll stay in touch.'

'Are we staying in these rooms tonight?'

'I don't know. It depends on how things go.'

She asks if he's sure he wants to do this. Billy says he is, and it's the truth.

'Maybe it's a bad idea.'

It might be, but Billy means to go through with it anyway, if he can. Those men owe.

'Tell me no and I'll back off.'

Instead of doing that, Alice takes one of his hands and squeezes. Hers is cold. 'Be safe.'

He gets halfway down the hall, then turns back. There's another question he forgot to ask. He knocks and she opens the door.

'What does Tripp look like?'

She takes out her phone and shows him a picture. 'I took this the night we went to the movies.'

The man who drugged her drink and raped her and, along with his two friends, tossed her out of the old van like a piece of trash, is holding up a bag of popcorn and smiling. His eyes sparkle. His teeth are white and even. Billy thinks he looks like an actor in a toothpaste ad.

'Okay. What about the other two?'

'One was short and had freckles. The other was much taller, with an olive complexion. I don't remember which one was Jack and which one was Hank.'

'It doesn't matter.'

7

The Airport Mall is just up the road from the motel. It's anchored by a Walmart even bigger than the one in Midwood. Billy locks his car, mindful of the gun under the driver's seat, and does his shopping. The mask is easy. Halloween is still weeks away, but the stores always put out their holiday shit well ahead of time. He also picks up a cheap pair of binoculars, a package of heavy-duty zip-ties, a pair of thin gloves, a Magic Wand hand mixer, and a can of Easy-Off oven cleaner. Outside, a couple of cops – real ones, not Wally World security guards – are drinking coffee and discussing outboard motors. Billy gives them a nod. 'Afternoon, officers.'

They nod back and go on with their conversation. Billy walks fat until he's well into the parking lot, then hurries to the Fusion. He transfers the gun and his purchases to his laptop case and drives the mile and a half to Landview Estates. It's pretty upscale, the perfect place for swinging singles, but not upscale enough for a security booth manned by a rent-a-cop, and at this time of day the parking lot in front of Building C is fairly empty.

Billy pulls into a spot facing the door, takes off the fake stomach, and waits. After twenty minutes or so a sporty Kia Stinger pulls in and two young women get out with shopping bags. Billy raises the binoculars. They go to the door and push some buttons on the keypad, but one of them is in the way and Billy gets nothing. The next arrival, twenty minutes later, is a man . . . but not one Billy is looking for. This guy is in his fifties. He also stands between Billy and the pad, rendering the binocs useless.

This isn't going to work, he thinks.

He could try going in with a legitimate resident ('Would you hold the door a second? Thanks!'), but that probably just works in the movies. Also, this is a slack time of day. Only two people have entered in forty minutes, and no one at all has come out.

Billy shoulders his computer bag and walks around to the back of the building. The first thing he sees in the smaller auxiliary parking lot is the van. Now he can read the bumper sticker: DEAD-HEADS SUCK. Unless the van's broken down, always a possibility, at least one of these fuckwits is home.

There are two big garbage dumpsters on the left of what must be a service door. On the right is a lawn chair and a rusty little table with an ashtray on it. The door is propped open a few inches with a brick, because this is the kind of door that locks as soon as you shut it, and whoever comes out here to smoke doesn't want to bother unlocking it each time he goes back in.

Billy goes to the door and peeks through the gap. He sees a dim hallway, no one in it. There's music, Axl Rose wailing 'Welcome to the Jungle.' Thirty feet or so along are open doors on the left and right. The music is coming from the one on the right. Billy enters and walks briskly down the hall. When you're in a place where you don't belong, you have to act like you do. The room on the left is a laundry, with a few coin-op washers and driers inside. The one on the right goes down to the basement.

Someone is down there, singing along with the music. And not just singing. Billy can't see him but he can see his shadow, and the shadow is dancing. Someone, probably the building super, has taken a pause in whatever chore he came down to do – re-setting a breaker, hunting out a can of touch-up paint – to fantasize that he's on *Dancing with the Stars*.

There's an oversized freight elevator at the end of the hall, doors open, sides hung with furniture pads, but Billy doesn't even think about using it. The machinery will be in the basement and if the elevator starts up, the shadow dancer will hear it. There's a door to the left of the elevator marked STAIRS. Billy climbs to the third-floor landing. There he unzips his laptop case. He puts on the gloves and the mask. He puts the zip-ties in his pants pocket. He has the Ruger in his left hand and the can of oven cleaner in his right. He cracks the stairway door and peeks out into a little lobby. It's empty. So is the hallway beyond. There's one apartment door on the left, one on the right, and one at the end. That will be the one where the rapin' roomies live.

Billy walks down the hall. There's a bell, but instead of using it he knocks good and loud. He gives it a pause, then knocks even louder.

Footsteps approach. 'Who is it?'

'Police, Mr Donovan.'

'He's not here. I'm just one of his roommates.'

'You don't get a prize for that. Open up.'

The man who opens the door is olive-skinned and at least six inches taller than Billy. Alice Maxwell is five-four at most, and the thought of this big man hulking over her infuriates Billy.

'What—' The guy's face goes slack as he beholds a man in a Melania Trump mask with a laptop bag slung over his shoulder.

'Get them panties down.' Billy says, and sprays him in the eyes with Easy-Off.

8

Jack or Hank, whichever one it is, stumbles backward, pawing at his eyes. Foam drips off his cheeks and plops from his jaws. He stumbles over a hassock in front of a wicker chair with a hood – what Billy thinks is called a 'bungalow chair' – and goes sprawling. It's a swinging singles living room for sure, with a curving two-person couch – Billy knows that one, it's a 'love-seat' – facing a big-screen TV. There's a round table with a laptop on it and a bar in front of a wide window that looks toward the airport. Billy can see a plane taking off, and he's sure if the fuckwit could see it, he'd wish he was on it. Billy slams the hall door shut. The guy is yelling that he's blind.

'No, but you will be if you don't get your eyes rinsed out pretty fast, so pay attention. Hold out your hands.'

'I can't see! I can't see!'

'Hold out your hands and I'll take care of you.'

Jack or Hank is rolling around on the wall-to-wall carpet. He's not holding out his hands, he's trying to sit up, and this guy is too big to fool with. Billy drops the laptop bag and kicks him in the stomach. He lets out a whoof of air. Splatters of foam fly and land on the carpet.

'Did I stutter? Hold out your hands.'

He does it, eyes squeezed shut, cheeks and forehead bright red. Billy kneels, holds his wrists together, and secures him with one of the zipties before the man on the floor knows what's happening.

'Who else is here?' Billy's pretty sure there's no one. If there was, this man's bellowing would have brought them in a hurry.

'Nobody! Ah Christ, my eyes! They *burn!*'

'Get up.'

Jack or Hank blunders to his feet. Billy grabs him by the shoulders and turns him toward the passthrough that gives on the kitchen. 'March.'

Jack or Hank doesn't march, but he stumbles forward, waving his arms in front of him for obstacles. He's breathing fast and hard but not whooping for breath the way Alice was; there's no need to teach him the first verse of 'Teddy Bears' Picnic.' Billy shoves him until the buckle of his pants hits the front of the sink. The faucet has a sprayer attachment. Billy turns on the water and points the spray at Jack or Hank's face. He also gets wet in the process, but that's all right. It's actually refreshing.

'It burns! It still burns!'

'It'll go away,' Billy says, and it will, but hopefully not too soon. He's betting Alice's works burned plenty. Maybe still do. 'What's your name?'

'What do you want?' Now he's crying. Got to be in his mid to late twenties, tall and at least two-twenty, but he's crying like a baby.

Billy jams the Ruger into the small of the guy's back. 'That's a gun, so don't make me ask you again. What's your name?'

'Jack!' he almost screams. 'Jack Martinez! Please don't shoot me, *please*!'

'Let's go in the living room, Jack.' Billy pushes Jack ahead of him. 'Sit in the wicker seat. Can you see it?'

'A little,' Jack weeps. 'It's all fucking *blurry*. Who are you? Why—'

'Sit down.'

'You can have my wallet. There's not much but Tripp keeps a couple of hundred in his bedroom, in the top drawer of the desk, just take it and go!'

'Sit down.'

He takes Martinez by the shoulders, turns him, and pushes him into the bungalow chair. It's suspended on a hook-and-rope combo from the ceiling and starts a mild rocking motion when the man's weight hits it. Martinez peers at Billy through bloodshot eyes.

'Just sit there a minute and get yourself together.'

There are napkins on the bar next to the ice bucket. Cloth ones, not paper, very nice. Billy takes one and goes to Martinez.

'Don't move.'

Martinez sits still and Billy wipes his face, getting rid of the last runnels of foam. Then he steps back. 'Where are the other two?'

'Why?'

'You don't ask, Jack. I do. Your job is to answer, unless you want another shot of foam. Or a bullet in the knee if you really irritate me. Understand?'

'Yes!' The crotch of Martinez's chinos has gone dark.

'Where are they?'

'Tripp went to RBCC to see his advisor. Hank's at work. He's a salesman at JossBank.'

'What's JossBank?'

'Joseph A. Bank, it's a men's—'

'Okay, I know what it is. What's RBCC?'

'Red Bluff Community College. Tripp's a graduate student. Part time. History. He's writing a paper on the Australian and Hungarian War.'

Billy thinks of telling this idiot that Australia had nothing to do with the Hungarian revolution of 1848, but why would he? He's here to teach a different lesson.

'When will he be back?'

'I don't know. I think he said his meeting was at two. He might stop for coffee after, sometimes he does that.'

'Chat up a barista, maybe,' Billy says. 'That is if she's new in town and hoping to meet someone nice.'

'Huh?'

Billy kicks him in the leg. It's not hard, but Martinez cries out and the bungalow chair starts swinging again. It's a swinging chair for three swinging roommates.

'What about Hank? When does he get back?'

'He gets off at four. Why do you—'

Billy raises the can of Easy-Off. It must still look blurry to Martinez, but he knows what it is and subsides.

'What about you, Jack? How do you earn your beer and bagels?'

'I'm a day trader.'

Billy goes over to the laptop on the round table. Numbers are flowing across it, most of them green. It's Saturday, but someone is trading somewhere, because money never sleeps.

'Is that your van out back?'

'No, Hank's. I've got a Miata.'

'Is the van broken down?'

'Yeah, blew a head gasket. He's been taking my car to work this week. The store he works at is in the Airport Mall.'

Billy pulls a regular chair over to the hanging bungalow chair. He sits in front of Martinez. 'I can be done with you, Jack. If you behave. Can you behave?'

'Yes!'

'That means when your roomies come home, you keep perfectly quiet. No yelling out a warning. It's Tripp I mostly want to deal with, but if you alert him, or Hank, I will give you what I was going to give Tripp. Do you understand me? Are we clear?'

'Yes!'

Billy takes out his phone and calls Alice. She asks if he's all right and Billy says he is. 'I'm with a guy named Jack Martinez. He has something he wants to say to you.' Billy holds the phone out to Jack. 'Tell her you're a worthless piece of shit.'

Jack doesn't protest, perhaps because he's cowed, perhaps because that's how he feels just now. Billy is hoping for that. He's hoping even day traders can learn.

'I'm . . . a worthless piece of shit.'

'Now say you're sorry.'

'I'm sorry,' Martinez says into the phone.

Billy takes the phone back. Alice sounds like she's crying. She tells him to be careful and Billy says he will. He ends the call and turns his attention to the red-faced man in the bungalow chair. 'Do you know what you were apologizing for?'

Martinez nods and Billy decides that's good enough.

9

They sit there and time passes. Martinez says his eyes still burn, so Billy wets another bar napkin in the bar sink and wipes his face, paying particular attention to his eyes. Martinez thanks him. Billy thinks the man may regain his MAGA swagger eventually, but that's okay because he also thinks Martinez will never rape another woman. He has been rehabilitated.

Around three-thirty someone comes to the door. Billy stands behind it after first looking at Martinez with a finger to the lips of the Melania mask. Martinez nods. It's got to be Tripp Donovan because it's too early for Hank. The key rattles in the lock. Donovan is whistling. Billy holds the Ruger by the barrel and raises it to the side of his face.

Donovan comes in, still whistling. He's looking very young-man-about-town in his designer jeans and short leather coat, the picture finished off to perfection by the monogrammed briefcase in his hand and the scally cap perched jauntily on his dark hair. He sees Martinez in the bungalow chair with his hands bound together and stops whistling. Billy steps forward and clubs him with the butt of the gun. Not too hard.

Donovan stumbles forward but doesn't go down like the guys on TV do when they get pistol-whipped. He turns around, eyes wide, hand to the back of his head. Now Billy is pointing the business end of the gun at him. Donovan looks at his hand. There's a smear of blood on it.

'You hit me!'

'Better than what I got,' Martinez says in a grumbly tone that's almost funny.

'Why are you wearing that mask?'

'Put your hands together. Wrist to wrist.'

'Why?'

'Because I'll shoot you if you don't.'

Donovan puts his hands together wrist to wrist with no further argument. Billy tucks the Ruger into his belt at the front. Donovan rushes at him, which Billy expected. He steps aside and aids Donovan's forward motion with a hearty push into the closed door. Donovan cries out. Billy grabs him by the collar of his trendy leather coat – perhaps purchased at Joseph A. Bank – and pulls him backward, tripping Tripp over one outstretched leg. He falls on his back. His nose is bleeding.

Billy kneels beside him, first putting Don Jensen's gun in his belt at the back so Donovan can't make a grab for it, then holding out one of the ties. 'Put your hands together, wrist to wrist.'

'No!'

'Your nose is bleeding but not broken. Put your hands together or I'll fix that.'

Donovan puts his hands together. Billy binds his wrists and then calls Alice to tell her two down and one to go. He doesn't put Donovan on the phone because Donovan doesn't seem like he's ready to apologize. At least not yet.

10

Tripp Donovan, sitting on the love-seat, keeps trying to engage Billy in conversation. He says he knows why Billy is here, but whatever that girl Alice told him is total self-protecting bullshit. She was horny, she wanted it, she got it, everyone parted friends, end of story.

Billy nods agreeably. 'You took her home.'

'That's right, we took her home.'

'In Hank's van.'

Donovan's eyes shift at that. He's got that magic mixture of charm and bullshit, it's worked for him his whole life and he even expects it to work on the home invader in the Melania Trump mask, but he doesn't like that question. It's a *knowing* question.

'No, the Love Machine's broken down in the back parking lot.'

Billy says nothing. Martinez says nothing, and Donovan doesn't see his roomie's *you fucked up* look. Donovan is concentrating on Billy.

'That a Pro?' Nodding at the computer bag on the floor. 'Sweet cruncher, man.'

Billy says nothing. He's sweating inside the plastic shell of the mask and he can't wait to get it off. He can't wait to finish his business and get out of this swinging bachelor pad.

At quarter to five another key rattles in the lock and in comes the third little pig, a small and dapper porker in a black three-piece suit set off by a tie as red as the blood on Alice Maxwell's thighs. Hank makes no trouble. He sees the blood on Donovan's face and Martinez's swollen eyes and when Billy tells him to hold out his hands he does so with only token protest and allows Billy to zip-tie his wrists. Billy leads him to the round table.

'Here we are,' Billy says. 'All in our places with bright shiny faces.'

'There's money in my desk,' Donovan says. 'In my room. Also some dope. World-class coke, man. An eightball.'

'I've got some cash, too,' Hank says. 'Only fifty, but . . .' He gives a what-can-you-do shrug. Billy can almost like this one. Stupid considering what he did but true. The flesh under his eyes and around his mouth is white with terror, but he's behaving and putting up a good front.

'Oh, you know this isn't about money.'

'I told you—' Donovan begins.

'He knows the whole thing, Tripp,' Martinez says.

Billy turns to Hank. 'What's your last name?'

'Flanagan.'

'And the van out back, the Love Machine . . . that's yours, right?'

'Yes. But it's broken down. The head gasket—'

'Blew, I know. But it was running last week, yeah? You guys took Alice home in it after you were done with her?'

'Don't say anything!' Donovan barks.

Hank ignores him. 'What are you? Her boyfriend? Her brother? Oh boy.'

Billy says nothing.

Hank lets out a sigh. It sounds wet. 'You know we didn't take her home.'

'What did you do with her?'

Donovan: 'Don't say anything!' This seems to be his scripture.

'Bad advice, Hank. Just say it and spare yourself a lot of grief.'

'We dropped her off.'

'Dropped her off? Is that what you want to call it?'

'Okay, we dumped her,' he says. 'But man . . . she was *talking*, okay? And we knew she had her phone and money for an Uber. She was *talking*!'

'And making perfect sense?' Billy asks. 'Holding a conversation? Tell me that if you fucking dare.'

Hank doesn't tell him that. He starts to cry, which tells Billy something else.

Billy calls Alice. He doesn't make Hank tell her he's a worthless piece of shit, because the man's tears make it clear he already knows that. He only asks Hank to say he's sorry. Which he does and sounds like he means it. For whatever that's worth.

Billy turns to Donovan. 'That leaves you.'

11

The swinging roommates are cowed. No one's going to run for the door because they know the intruder in the mask would clothesline them if they tried. Billy goes to his computer bag and takes out the

Magic Wand hand mixer. It's a slim stainless steel cylinder about eight inches long. Its electrical cord has been bound into a neat bow by two twist ties.

'Here's what I've been thinking about,' Billy says. 'That men don't know what it's like to be raped unless they've been raped themselves. You, Mr Donovan, are about to have a reasonable facsimile of that experience.'

Donovan tries to lunge up from the love-seat and Billy pushes him back. When he lands the cushion makes a farting sound. Martinez and Flanagan don't move, only stare at the mixer with big eyes.

'What I need you to do is stand up, push down your pants and undershorts, then lie on your stomach.'

'No!'

Donovan has gone white. His eyes are even bigger than those of his roommates. Billy hardly expected instant compliance. He takes the Ruger from his belt. He remembers Pablo Lopez, one of the squad's Funhouse casualties. Bigfoot Lopez had that Dirty Harry speech down pat, the one that ends with Harry saying *You've got to ask yourself one question: Do I feel lucky? Well do you, punk?* Billy can't remember it all, but he has the gist.

'This isn't my gun,' he says. 'I borrowed it. I know it's loaded, but I don't know what the loads are. I didn't check them. If you don't drop trou and lie on your stomach, I'm going to shoot you in the ankle. Point blank. So you've got to ask yourself one question – ball or hollow point? If they're hard point, you'll probably walk again, but only after a lot of pain and therapy and you'll limp for the rest of your life. If they're softnose, most of your foot is going to say *adios*. So here's the deal. Roll the dice on the bullet or get cornholed. Your choice.'

Donovan begins to blubber. His tears don't make Billy feel pity; they make him want to hit the man in the mouth with the butt of the Ruger and see how many of those toothpaste-ad teeth he can knock out.

'Let me put it to you another way. Either you can endure short-lived pain and humiliation or you can drag your left foot around for the rest of your life. Assuming the doctors don't amputate. You have five seconds to decide. Five . . . four . . .'

On three, Tripp Donovan stands up and drops trou. His cock has shriveled to a noodle and his balls are barely visible at all.

'Mister, do you have to—' Martinez begins.

'Shut up,' Hank says. 'He deserves it. Probably we all do.' To Billy he says, 'Just so you know, I didn't put it in, just on her belly.'

'Did you come?' Billy knows the answer to that question.

Hank lowers his head.

Donovan is lying down on the carpet. His ass is white, the buttocks clenched.

Billy takes a knee beside the prone man's hip. 'You want to stay still, Mr Donovan. Still as you can, anyway. You can be grateful I'm not going to plug this thing in. I considered it, believe me.'

'I'll fuck you up,' Donovan sobs.

'No one is getting fucked up today but you.'

Billy sets the base of the hand mixer on Donovan's right asscheek. Donovan jerks and gasps.

'I thought about picking up some goo while I was shopping – you know, body lotion, massage oil, even Vaseline – but I decided against it. Alice didn't get any lube, did she? Unless maybe you spit on your hand before you went in.'

'Please don't,' Donovan sobs.

'Did Alice say that? Probably not, she was probably too roofied out to say much of anything. One thing she did say was "Don't choke me." She probably would have said more if she could. Here we go, Mr Donovan. Hold still. I won't tell you to relax and enjoy it.'

12

Billy doesn't draw it out as he thought he might. He doesn't have the heart for it. Or the stomach. When he's finished he takes pictures of Tripp and the other two with his phone. Then he pulls the mixer out of Tripp, wipes his prints, and tosses it away. The cylinder rolls under the round table with Martinez's laptop on it.

'Each of you stay right where you are. This is almost over, so don't fuck it up on the homestretch.'

Billy goes into the kitchen and grabs a paring knife. When he comes back, none of them have moved. Billy tells Hank Flanagan to hold out his hands. Hank does, and Billy cuts the zip-tie holding him. 'Mister?' Hank says, sounding timid. 'You lost your wig.'

He's right. The blond wig is lying against the baseboard like a small dead animal. A rabbit, maybe. It must have come off when Donovan rushed him and Billy threw him against the door. Did he remember to glue it on before leaving the basement apartment? Billy can't remember but guesses he didn't. He doesn't try putting it on because he has the mask to contend with, just holds it in the hand not holding the Ruger GP.

'I have pictures of all of you, but because Mr Donovan is the only one with a hand mixer sticking out of his ass, he's the star of the show. I don't think you're going to call the police, because then you'd have to explain why I broke in but left without taking any money or valuables, but if you *should* decide to whomp up some kind of story that doesn't involve gang rape, this picture is going on the Internet. With an explanation. Any questions?'

There are no questions. It's time for Billy to go. He can stow the mask and don the wig on the way to the third-floor lobby. But he wants to say something else before he goes. He feels he has to. The first thing that comes to mind is a question: don't any of you have sisters? And surely they have mothers, even Billy had one of those, although she wasn't very good at the job. But such a question would be rhetorical. Preaching, not teaching.

Billy says, 'You should be ashamed of yourselves.'

He leaves, taking off the mask as he hurries down the hall and putting it in the unzipped computer bag. He's thinking that he's not much better than those guys, really, pot calling the kettle black, but thinking that way is no good. What he tells himself as he puts on the wig and trots down the stairs is that he's stuck with himself and must make the best of it. It's cold comfort, but cold is better than none.

CHAPTER 17

1

Alice must have been waiting just inside the door of her room, because when Billy knocks she opens up at once. And hugs him. He's startled for a moment and starts to pull away, but when he sees the hurt look on her face he hugs her back. Other than meaningless bro-hugs from people like Nick and Giorgio, he hasn't had a real hug in a long time. Then he realizes that's not true, he got hugs from Shanice Ackerman. They were good and this one is, too.

They go inside. He told her he was okay when he called from the car after leaving Landview Estates, but she asks again now and he tells her again that he is.

'And you . . . dealt with them?'

'Yes.'

'All three of them?'

'Yes.'

'Do I want to know how?'

'None of them is going to need a hospital visit but all of them paid a price. Let's leave it at that.'

'Fine, but can I ask a question I asked before?'

Billy says she can.

'Did you do it for me or your sister?'

He thinks it over and says, 'I think both.'

She gives a case-closed nod. 'That wig looks like a hurricane blew through it. Do you have a comb?'

He does, in his shaving bag. Alice tents the wig over her spread fingers and starts combing it out in brisk strokes. 'Are we staying here tonight?'

Billy has thought about this on the short drive back. 'I think we should. I don't believe we have to worry about the Three Stooges calling the cops.' He's thinking of the pictures on his phone. 'And it's getting late.'

She stops combing and looks at him dead-on. 'Take me with you when you go. Please.' She mistakes his silence for reluctance. 'There's nothing for me here. I can't go back to business school and serving cappuccinos. I can't go home, either. I won't. Not after all this. I need to get out of this town. I need to start over. Please, Dalton. *Please*.'

'All right. But there's going to be a point where we go our separate ways. You understand that, right?'

'Yes.' She holds out the wig. 'Better?'

'It is. And my friends call me Billy. Okay?'

She smiles. 'Okay.'

2

There's a Slim Chickens a quarter mile down the service road. Billy drives through and brings back food and shakes. The way she keeps her eyes on her chicken-and-bacon sandwich, planning the next bite even while she's chewing the one in her mouth, pleases him. He has no idea why, but it does. They watch the local news. There's just one item about the courthouse assassination. It's nothing new, just a two-minute filler piece before the weather. The world is moving on.

'Are you going to be okay tonight?'

'Yes.' She steals one of his fries, as if that proves it.

'If you start getting short of breath—'

'"Teddy Bears' Picnic," I know.'

'And if that doesn't work, knock on the wall. I'll come.'

'Okay.'

He gets up and tosses his trash. 'Then I'll say goodnight. There's some stuff I have to do.'

'Are you going to work on your story?'

Billy shakes his head. 'Other stuff.'

Alice looks troubled. 'Billy . . . you wouldn't run out on me in the middle of the night, would you?'

This is such a perfect turnaround that he has to laugh. 'No, I'm not going to do that.'

'Promise.'

He crooks his little finger as he sometimes did with Shan and often did with Cathy. 'Pinky-swear.'

She crooks her own, smiling, and they link up.

'Go to bed early because we're going to leave early. Long drive.'

All he has to do now is find out where they're going.

3

In his room on the other side of the wall, he texts Bucky Hanson.

Can I come to where you are? Actually it's we, I have someone with me. She's safe but going to need new ID. Not staying long. When I get the balance of what's owed to me, you'll get what I promised.

He sends and waits. He and Bucky go back almost to the beginning. Billy trusts him completely and thinks Bucky trusts him. Also, a million dollars is a lot of cheese.

Five minutes later his phone bings.

SCOTS live show Skipper's Smokehouse 2007 69 El Camino YT. Delete and DTA.

They haven't communicated like this in several years, but Billy remembers what DTA means: *Don't text again.* For Bucky to go to such lengths means he's being very, very cautious. He may have heard something. If so, it was nothing good.

Billy also knows SCOTS. It stands for Southern Culture on the Skids, Bucky's favorite band. ''69 El Camino' is one of their songs. Billy goes to YouTube and types out *SCOTS live at Skipper's Smokehouse.* Southern Culture on the Skids must have played that particular venue a lot over the years because there are over forty vids of various songs. Five of them are of ''69 El Camino,' but there's only one from 2007. Billy selects it but doesn't hit play. It's smeary cell phone video, the sound will suck, and it's not music he came for.

It's had a little over four thousand views and hundreds of people have left comments. Billy scrolls down to the last one, which is tagged Hanson 199. It was posted two minutes ago.

Great tune, the comment reads. **Saw them play a kick-ass 10-minute version at Edgewood Saloon in Sidewinder.**

Billy adds his own post, tagging himself Taco04. It's brief. **Hope to see them soon!**

He deletes his text to Bucky and Bucky's reply about the SCOTS video, then goes to Google. There's only one town named Sidewinder in the continental United States. It's in Colorado. There's no Edgewood Saloon, but there is a thoroughfare called Edgewood Mountain Drive.

He texts Alice: **Leaving at 5 AM, OK?**

The reply – **roger** – comes back immediately.

Billy downloads an app to one of the AllTech laptops. It takes awhile because the Penny Pines WiFi is weak as shit. When the download is complete he reads for an hour, then takes a long hot shower. He sets the alarm on his phone before going to bed even though he knows he won't need it. He dreams of Lalafallujah. No surprise there.

4

It's still dark when they stow their few belongings in the back seat of the Fusion. Billy sets one of the cheap AllTechs on the console between the front seats and plugs it into the power outlet. 'I knew one of these cheapies would come in handy sooner or later.'

'Did you really?' Alice looks still half-asleep.

'Nope, but sometimes you get lucky.'

While she fastens the seatbelt, Billy opens the app he downloaded last night. There's a shrill sound, like an old-fashioned modem connecting. He squelches the volume.

'What's that for?'

Billy bends over and points to an unobtrusive panel down low and to the left of the glove compartment. 'That's the OBD. On-board diagnostic. It does all sorts of things, and because this is a lease car, one of the things it does is pinpoint our location if anyone at the dealership wants to check. Which they would as soon as we cross the state line, because it's programmed to send a notification. The app is a jammer. If anyone checks, they'll think the OBD is on the fritz.'

'You hope they'll think that.'

'Confidence is high,' Billy says. 'You ready? Don't want to dummy-check the room?'

'I'm ready.' She's wide awake now. 'Where are we going?'

'Colorado.'

'Colorado, my God.' She sounds very young. 'How far?'

'Over a thousand miles. Two-day drive.'

She smiles. 'Then we better get going.'

Billy says 'Roger that,' and drops the Fusion's transmission in drive. Five minutes later they're on the turnpike and headed west.

5

They stop for gas and food in Muskogee, the town made famous by Merle Haggard. Alice has been busy on the AllTech, and directs Billy to the Arrowhead Mall. When they get there, she points out a building with bright orange awnings.

'What's Ulta?' Billy asks.

'Makeup store. You go in. I don't want to with my face looking like this.'

Billy can't blame her. She's young, she's healthy, and the bruises have started to fade, but it's still pretty clear that someone tuned up on her in the recent past. She tells him what to get and he gets it. The basic product is called Dermablend Cover Creme. It's less expensive than the morning-after pill, but once he adds in the brush and the setting powder, he's closing in on eighty bucks.

'You're an expensive date,' he says when he gives her the bag.

'Wait 'til you see the results.'

She sounds pert. Billy likes that. She has come a long way back from the girl who couldn't bear to look at herself in the mirror . . . but not all the way back. She falls asleep that afternoon as they continue to drive northwest, and after an hour or so he hears her moaning. She puts out her hands in a warding-off gesture. One of them strikes the dashboard and she wakes up with a gasp. Then another. And a third, this time with her hand on her throat.

'"Teddy Bears' Picnic," stat!' Billy says. He's already slowing, moving over into the breakdown lane.

'I'm okay, keep going. I'm all right now. Bad dream is all.'

'What was it?' Billy asks, turning off his blinker and swerving the Fusion back into the travel lane.

'I don't remember.'

She's lying, but that's okay.

6

They stop for the night in the little town of Protection, Kansas, because it's almost halfway to where they're going but also because they both like the idea of staying at a place called the Protection Motel. This time Alice goes in with him when he registers, and the guy at the desk barely gives her a glance. A woman might have, Billy thinks. The makeup is good and she applied it skillfully, but it's not quite perfect. He asks if she wants him to get takeout and Alice shakes her head. She's ready to go public, and that's also good. They eat at Don's Place, which is just about the only place in Protection when it comes to food. The menu consists mostly of burgers and corn dogs.

'This guy we're going to see,' Alice says. 'What's he like?'

'Bucky's sixty-five or seventy now. Skinny as hell. Ex-Marine. Pretty much lives on beer, cigarettes, Slim Jims, and rock and roll. He's good with computers, he has a lot of contacts, and he helps put strings together.'

'Strings?'

'Pro stickup guys. Not kids, not junkies, not trigger-happy hot-heads. He's part agent, part talent scout.'

'For the underworld.'

Billy smiles. 'I don't know if there's really an underworld anymore. I think the Computer Age pretty much killed it.'

'And he finds jobs for people like you.' She lowers her voice. 'Hired killers.'

So far as Billy knows, he's the only hired killer Bucky does business with, but he doesn't disagree. How could he when it's true? He could tell her again that he only kills people who deserve to be killed, but why bother? Either she believes it or she doesn't. In any case it's a moot point. He can't change his past but he means to change his future. He also intends to have his payday. He earned it.

'Bucky will have ID for you, I think. It's one of the things he does. You can be a new person. If you want to.'

'I do.' She doesn't pause to think about it. 'Although at some point I suppose I'll want to call my mother again.' She gives a little laugh and a small shake of the head. 'You know, I can't remember the last time she called me. I really can't.'

'But you did talk to her?'

'Yes. While you were . . . um, visiting Tripp and his roommates.'

'You didn't really tell her you were going to Cancun, did you?'

She smiles. 'I was tempted, but no. I said I had a boyfriend, and we broke up when I quit school, and I needed some time to think about what comes next.'

'She was okay with that?'

'It's been a long time since she was okay with anything I do. Can we talk about something else, please?'

7

The next day is nothing but driving, most of it on I-70. Alice, still recovering from physical and mental trauma, sleeps a lot. Billy thinks about the Fallujah part of his story, which is now stored on a thumb drive in his computer bag. That leads him to Albie Stark, who used to talk about getting his Harley out of storage when he got home and taking a road trip from New York to San Francisco. *None of that blue highways shit, either*, he said. *I be turnpikin' the whole way. Crank it up to eighty and pull the knobs off.* Albie never had a chance to do that. Albie died behind a rusty old Fallujah taxi and his last words were *It's nothing, just clipped me.* Only then he started gasping, the way Alice did when she had her panic attacks, and he never got a chance to sing even the first line of 'Teddy Bears' Picnic.'

They stop for gas and food in the little town of Quinter, Kansas. It's a Waffle Delite and when they get out of the Fusion and approach, they see a couple of state cops sitting at the counter. Alice hesitates, but Billy keeps going and it turns out fine. The cops hardly give them a glance.

'If you act right, most times they don't even notice you,' Billy says as they walk back to the car.

'Most times?'

Billy shrugs. 'Anything can happen to anybody. You play the odds and hope for the best.'

'You're a fatalist.'

Billy laughs. 'I'm a realist.'

'Is there a difference?'

He stops with his hand on the Fusion's doorhandle and looks at her. She has a way of surprising him.

'You're maybe too smart for business school,' he says. 'I think you could do better.'

8

Alice sleeps again, full of waffles and bacon. Billy glances at her from time to time. He likes her looks more and more. He likes who she is. To just slam the door on one life and open the door on a new one? How many people would do that even if they got the chance?

Around four o'clock she wakes up, stretches, then gasps. She's looking through the windshield with wide eyes. 'My sainted hat!'

Billy laughs. 'Never heard that one before.'

'It's the Rockies! Oh my God, *look* at them!'

'They're something, all right.'

'I've seen pictures, but it's not the same. I mean, they just *start*.'

It's true. They have driven through hundreds of miles of flatlands and then all at once there they are.

'I thought we might get to Bucky's today, and I guess we still could, but I don't want to drive Route 19 into the mountains after dark. It's probably twisty.' What he doesn't tell her is that he wouldn't want Bucky seeing headlights pulling into his driveway between ten and midnight. Not after Bucky was so careful about giving out his location. 'See if you can find us an off-brand motel east of Denver.'

She uses his Dalton phone with the dexterity of the very young. 'There's a place called the Pronghorn Motor Rest. That sound off-brand enough for you?'

'It does. How far?'

'Looks like about thirty miles.' She does some more typing and swiping. 'It's in a town called Byers. They have a turkey shoot with a big dance after, but it's not until November. Guess we'll miss it.'

'Too bad.'

'Well,' she says, 'shit happens. Life is a party, and parties weren't meant to last.'

He looks sideways at her, a little startled. 'Is that F. Scott Fitzgerald?'

'Prince,' she says. 'I can't get over how gorgeous those mountains are. When the sun goes down I don't think I'll look. My heart might break. And the only reason I'm here is because those men raped me and threw me out in the rain. I guess everything happens for a reason.'

Billy has heard the saying many times before and it always makes him mad. 'I don't believe that. I *won't* believe that.'

'Okay. I'm sorry.' She sounds a little scared. 'I didn't mean to—'

'Believing that would mean believing that someone or something up the line was more important than my sister. Same with Albie Stark. Taco. Johnny Capps, who'll never walk again. There's nothing *reasonable* about any of that.'

She doesn't answer. When he looks at her she's looking down at her tightly clasped hands and there are tears on her cheeks.

'Jesus, Alice, I didn't mean to make you cry.'

'You didn't,' she says, brushing away the evidence on her cheeks.

'It's just that if there's a God, he's doing a piss poor job.'

Alice points ahead, at the blue teeth of the Rockies. 'If there's a God, He made those.'

Well, Billy thinks, girl's got a point.

9

There's no problem getting adjoining rooms at the Pronghorn Motor Rest; based on the number of cars in the parking lot, Billy thinks they could've had every room on the hallway to themselves. They eat at a nearby Burger Barn. Back at the motel, Billy plugs in the thumb drive with his story on it. He opens the document and goes to where he left off: Taco handing Fareed their GOOD MORNING VIETNAM bullhorn. Then he closes it again. He's not afraid to write about what happened in the Funhouse, exactly, but he doesn't want to do it in installments, either. He wants to be in a quiet place where he can pour it out like poison from a bottle. He doesn't think it will take long, but those hours will be *intense*.

He goes to the window and looks out. There are a couple of cheap lawn chairs in front of each unit. Alice is sitting in one of them, staring up at the stars. He looks at her looking for a long time. He doesn't need a psychiatrist to tell him what she means to him; she's a version of Cathy only grown up. A psychiatrist might try to argue that she is also Robin Maguire, aka Ronnie Givens, from the House of Everlasting Paint, but that wouldn't be true because he wanted to fuck Robin, many was the night he jacked off to that fond fantasy, and he doesn't want to fuck Alice. He cares for her, and that means more than fucking.

Is caring for her dangerous? Of course it is. Is the way Alice has come to care for him – to trust him, to depend on him – equally as dangerous? Of course it is. But to see her sitting there and looking up at the stars, that means something. It might not if things go wrong, but right now it does. He gave her the mountains and the stars, not to own but at least to look at, and that means a lot.

10

They get an early start and are skirting Denver at eight in the morning. It's flat. They drive through Boulder at quarter of nine. Also flat. Then boom, they're in the mountains. The road is every bit as twisty as Billy thought it would be. Alice sits up straight, her head on a swivel, her eyes wide as she looks from deep gorges on her right to the steep wooded upslopes on her left. Billy gets it. She's a New England girl who's made one short and ultimately unpleasant side trip to the mid-South and this is all new to her, all amazing. He will never believe she had to get raped in order to be here in the Rocky Mountain foothills, but he's glad she can be. He likes her amazement. No, loves it.

'I could live here,' she says.

They drive through Nederland, a little town that seems to be a mere adjunct to the sprawling shopping center on the outskirts. The parking lot is jammed. Billy, who can believe almost anything, would be hard-pressed to believe that in the early spring of the following year that parking lot will be almost deserted on a business day, with most of the stores closed.

'I need to go in there,' Alice says, and points. There are spots of color in her cheeks. 'To the drugstore.'

He pulls in and finds a parking space. 'Is something wrong?'

'No, but I'm going to have a visit from my friend. It's two weeks early, but I can feel it coming. Cramps.'

He remembers the flier that came with the morning-after pill. 'Are you sure you don't want me to—'

'No, I'll do it. I won't be long. God, I hope I don't make a mess in these pants.'

'If you do, we'll buy—' *Some new ones* is how he means to finish, but she's already out of the car and hurrying toward the Walgreens, almost running. She comes back a few minutes later with a bag.

He asks if she's okay. She tells him, almost curtly, that she's fine. Outside of town they come to a scenic turnout and she asks him to stop and park away from the few other cars. Then she asks him to look the other way. He does so and sees a hang-gliding fool soaring over a ravine as deep as a stab wound. From this distance the guy hardly appears to be moving. He hears her shifting around, her zipper going down, the rattle of the bag, more rattling as she strips the paper from what she needs – a pad he assumes, she wouldn't want to try a tampon, not yet – and then her zipper again.

'You can look now.'

'No, *you* look,' Billy says, and points out the hang-glider. The guy is wearing a bright red singlet and a yellow helmet which will do exactly jack shit if he crashes into the side of the mountain.

'Oh . . . my . . . *God!*' Alice is shading her eyes.

'Not to mention your sainted hat.'

Alice grins. A real grin. Very good to see. She repeats, 'I could live here.'

'And do *that*?' Billy points.

'Maybe not that.' She pauses, thinking it over. 'But maybe.'

'Ready to roll? You all high and tight?'

'Roger that,' Alice replies, smart as you please.

11

Billy is glad he decided not to drive on through yesterday, because it takes them another two hours to reach Sidewinder. There's no shopping center here, just a one-street downtown crammed with souvenir shops, restaurants, clothing stores featuring western apparel, and bars. Plenty of those, with names like Rough Rider Saloon, Boots 'N Spurs, Homestead, and 187. There's no Edgewood Saloon, but Billy didn't expect one.

'Funny name for a bar,' Alice says, pointing to 187.

'It is,' Billy agrees, but based on the rank of motorcycles parked out front, he doesn't think the name is funny at all. 187 is the California Penal Code designation for murder.

Alice is using his phone to navigate because the Fusion's GPS is jammed along with the locator. 'Another mile, maybe a little more. On the left.'

A mile takes them out of town. Billy slows and sees the sign for Edgewood Mountain Drive. He makes the turn. They pass nice-looking homes and Swiss-style chalets set back from the street, many with their driveways chained off because ski season is still six weeks away. Beyond 108 Edgewood, the paving ends. The previously smooth road becomes first bouncy and then downright jouncy. Billy negotiates a tight S-curve and bulls the Fusion over a washed-out culvert. This time the car bounces so hard their seatbelts lock.

'Are you sure this is right?' Alice asks.

'It's right. We're looking for 199.'

She consults the phone. 'This says there's no such number.'

'I'm not surprised.'

Half a mile further on, the dirt runs out and they find themselves on a grassy track with wildflowers growing on the hump between the ruts. Billy thinks it might be the remains of an old logging road. The trees crowd in. Branches whip the Fusion's sides. The track goes steeper. Billy steers his way around protruding rocks left over from the last ice age. Alice looks increasingly uneasy.

'If this just ends, you're going to have to back up for two miles, because there's no place to—'

Billy hauls the Fusion around the tightest curve yet, and the road *does* end. Dead ahead is a log house jutting its long length over a steep slope, supported by posts that look like cut-off telephone poles. A Jeep Cherokee is parked underneath an open porch. Billy can hear a generator somewhere out back, the sound low but strong and steady.

Billy and Alice get out and look up at the porch, shading their eyes.

Bucky Hanson rises from the rocking chair he's been sitting in and comes to the shakepole railing. He's wearing a New York Rangers gimme cap and smoking a cigarette.

'Yo, Billy. I thought you got lost.'

'She did, too. Bucky, this is Alice Maxwell.'

'It's a pleasure to meet you, Alice. And Billy, look at you. How long has it been since we were face to face?'

'Got to be four years at least,' Billy says. 'Maybe five.'

'Well, come on up. Steps are on the side. Are you hungry?'

12

Billy was afraid his long-time fixer and agent might resent him bringing a stranger to this place, which is pretty clearly an emergency bolthole, but Bucky treats Alice kindly. He doesn't come right out and say that any friend of Billy's, etc., but he makes it clear, and after her initial shyness (or maybe it's wariness), she relaxes. Still, she's careful to stay near Billy.

The kitchen is neat, roomy, sunshiny. Bucky heats up macaroni and cheese in the microwave. 'I'd love to make you huevos rancheros, I'm not half-bad at it, but I'm still not completely situated here. Need to finish getting supplied. Then I'll just hunker down until this business comes to a conclusion. A happy one would be nice.'

'I got you into a mess and I'm sorry,' Billy says.

Bucky flaps a hand at him. 'I brokered the deal and knew the risks.' He sets a steaming bowl before each of them. 'What about you, Alice? How'd you meet this vet of Georgie Bush's war?'

Alice looks down at her mac and cheese as if she finds it especially fascinating. Her cheeks turn pink. 'I guess you could say he picked me up off the street.'

'Is that so? Huh. Has he shown you his stupid act yet? That is something to see. Give it to her, Billy.'

Billy doesn't want to, Alice is different from mugs like Nick and Giorgio, but Bucky has given them a place to stay for awhile and he doesn't want to refuse such a simple request. Only he doesn't have to do it.

'I've seen it already.' Alice pauses, then adds, 'In a manner of speaking.'

She gives Billy a look before addressing her food again, just a quick one, but it's enough to make him feel sure she's talking about the first part of his story. The part he wrote knowing Nick or Giorgio was probably reading over his shoulder.

'Great, isn't it?' Bucky says, fetching his own bowl and sitting down. 'Billy reads all the hard books, but he can also tell you every kid at Riverdale High and how Batman got his cape.'

Billy thinks what the hell, a little won't hurt. He makes his eyes big and slows his speech. 'I actually don't know that part.'

Bucky laughs and points his fork, a macaroni noodle still caught on one of the tines, at Billy. 'Man, you haven't lost a step.'

He turns to Alice.

'Just picked you up off the street, huh? What's that mean exactly?'

'That he saved my life.'

Bucky raises his eyebrows. 'Did he now? I want to hear all about it. In fact I want to hear everything. Especially what went wrong.'

Billy considers this carefully. 'Everything but Alice,' he says, and starts laughing. He can't help it.

13

He again starts with Frank Macintosh and Paulie Logan picking him up at the hotel and goes through it to the end, skimping only on the last part, just saying some guys roughed Alice up and he took care of them.

Bucky doesn't ask how. He only collects their dishes, takes them over to the sink, and starts running hot water. The little house at the ass end of Edgewood Mountain Drive has a microwave and a satellite dish on the roof, but there's no dishwasher.

'I'll do those,' Alice says, getting up.

'No you won't,' Bucky says. 'There's only a few and I'll leave the casserole dish to soak. That baked-on cheese is a bitch. Billy, how long do you want to stay? I only ask because if you're gonna be here long, I'll have to make a run to King Soopers.'

'I don't know, but I'm happy to get the groceries.'

'I'll go, too,' Alice says. 'Just give me a list.' She looks in the fridge. 'You need some vegetables.'

Bucky ignores that. From the sink, back turned, he says, 'They're after you, Billy. Not just Nick's organization, four other brands of competition plus God knows how many independents. One of those occasions, rare but not unheard-of, where everybody's on the same page. You're a big topic of conversation in certain chat rooms where you're referred to as Mr Summerlock.'

'As in Billy Summers and David Lockridge,' Billy says.

'Right.'

'Is anybody chatting about Dalton Smith?' Please God no, he thinks.

'So far as I know Dalton Smith is still good, but these guys have access to all the best investigative agencies, outfits that make the FBI look like rubes, and if you left any loose ends, any at all, Dalton Smith is a goner.'

Bucky turns from the sink, and as he wipes his reddened hands on a dish towel, he looks directly at Alice. He doesn't have to say anything to make his point.

Billy says, 'She's not a loose end. When I leave here, she goes her own way as someone else. If you can put together the documentation, that is.'

'Oh, I can do that. Did one thing already. There's nothing like the Internet when it's hooked up to state-of-the-art equipment.' He comes back to the table and sits down. 'How do you feel about being Elizabeth Anderson?'

Alice looks startled, then gives a tentative smile. 'Fine, I guess. I don't get to pick my own name?'

'It's better that you don't. Too easy to pick one that links to your past. I didn't pick it, either. Computer did. A site called Name Generator.' He looks at Billy. 'If you trust her, that's good enough. What about these Jensens? Or the real estate guy? They have any idea you were someone other than Dalton Smith?'

Billy shakes his head.

'So you're clean and that's good, because there's a bounty on your head.'

'How much?'

'Chat rooms say six million dollars.'

Billy gapes. 'Are you shitting me? Why? They were only paying me two to do the job in the first place!'

'I don't know.'

Alice is turning her head from one to the other as if watching a tennis match.

Bucky says, 'Nick's handling the contract, but I don't think it's his money any more than the money you were promised was his.'

Billy props his elbows on the table and his loosely closed fists on the sides of his face. 'Who pays six million dollars to kill a shooter who shot another shooter?'

Bucky laughs. 'Save that one. It's right up there with she sells seashells down by the seashore.'

'Who? And why? Joel Allen was *nobody*, as far as I can tell.'

Bucky shakes his head. 'Don't know. But I bet Nick Majarian does. Maybe you'll get a chance to ask him.'

'Who's Nick Majarian?' Alice asks.

Billy sighs. 'Benjy Compson. The guy who got me into this mess.'

Which is sort of a lie. He got into it all by himself.

14

In the end, Billy decides he and Alice will stay with Bucky for three days, maybe four. He wants to finish writing about the Funhouse. That won't take long, but he also needs time to think about his next move. Does he need another long gun, scope-equipped, to go with the Ruger? He doesn't know. Does he need another handgun, maybe a Glock that holds seventeen rounds instead of a measly six? He doesn't know. But a potato-buster for the Ruger might come in handy, little as he likes them. Would he have occasion to use such a thing? He doesn't know that either, but Bucky tells him that a jam-and-lock silencer for the GP should be no problem. If, that is, he doesn't mind something homemade that might break apart after a few shots were fired through it. Bucky says in the high country all sorts of accessories are available.

'I could get you an M249, if you wanted. I'd have to ask around, but I know some people to ask. Safe people who can keep their mouths shut.'

A SAW, in other words. Billy has a brief but brilliant memory of Big Joe Kleczewski standing outside the Funhouse with that very same gun. He shakes his head. 'Let's stick with the silencer for now.'

'Silencer for a Ruger GP, got it.'

Alice will have her paperwork in three days as well, but when she and Billy go for groceries in Sidewinder, Bucky wants her to pick up some hair dye. 'I think you should go blonde for your driver's license. But leave the eyebrows dark. That would be a good look for you.'

'You think?' She sounds doubtful but looks interested.

'I do. You were in business school, so I'll give you some background to go with that. Can you take shorthand?'

'Yes. I took a summer course in Rhode Island and picked it up fairly fast.'

'And you can answer a phone? "Dignam Chevrolet, how may I direct your call?"'

Alice rolls her eyes.

'Okay, entry-level skills at least, and the way the economy is roaring, that should be enough. Add nice clothes, good shoes, and a cheery smile and there's no reason why Beth Anderson can't find her niche.'

But Bucky doesn't like it. Alice doesn't pick up on it, but Billy does. He just doesn't know why.

15

They go for groceries, Billy wearing his wig and a pair of dark glasses Bucky finds for him in the clutter of stuff – what he calls Irish luggage – he hasn't unpacked yet. At King Soopers Billy pays cash. They go back up Edgewood Mountain Drive, the Fusion thudding and bumping and forging grumpily ahead over the last two miles.

Alice helps Bucky put the things away. He looks at the plantains she purchased doubtfully but says nothing. When that chore is done, she says she's tired of being cooped up and asks if it would be okay for her to take a walk. Bucky tells her that if she goes out the back door, she'll find a path into the woods. 'Steep slope, but you look young and strong. Might want to put on some bug dope. Check the bathroom.'

Alice comes back with her sleeves rolled up trucker style, slathering on Cutter. Her cheeks are shiny with it.

'Don't mind the wolves,' Bucky says. Then, seeing her alarmed expression: 'Kidding, kiddo. The oldtimers say there haven't been wolves around here since the 1950s. All hunted out. Bears, too. But if you can make it a mile, you're going to come to one hell of a view. You can look across I don't know how many miles of gulch and ravine to a big old flat clearing on the other side. Used to be a resort hotel there, but it burned flat many a moon ago.' He drops his voice. 'It was reputed to be haunted.'

'Watch your step,' Billy says. 'You don't want to break an ankle.'

'I'll be careful.'

When she's gone, Bucky turns to Billy with a smile. '"Watch your step, you don't want to break an ankle." What are you, her daddy? God knows you're old enough to be.'

'Don't get Freudian. She's just my friend. I couldn't tell you exactly how that happened, but it did.'

'You said they roughed her up. Does that mean what I think it does?'

'Yes.'

'All of them?'

'Two out of three. One of them just jizzed on her belly. That's what he said, anyway.'

'Jesus Christ, she seems so . . . you know, okay.'

'She's not.'

'No. Of course she's not. Probably never will be, not completely.'

Billy thinks that, like too many depressing ideas, it's probably true.

Bucky gets two beers and they go out on the front porch. Billy has parked the Fusion beneath, nose-to-nose with the Cherokee.

'She seems to be coping, at least,' Bucky says when he's resumed his rocking chair. Billy has taken another one. 'Got some guts.'

Billy nods. 'She does.'

'And she can read a room, as they say. Maybe she did want to go strolling, but she mostly left so we could talk.'

'You think?'

'I do. She can have the spare room while you stay here. A bunch of my stuff's in it now, but I'll clear it out. The bed's stripped and I don't know if there's sheets, but I saw a couple of blankets on the shelf in the closet. That'll do for three or four nights. Since you're not sleeping with her, you get the attic. Most times of year you'd freeze or boil up there, but right now it should be just about perfect. I've got a sleeping bag somewhere. Maybe still in the back of the Cherokee.'

'Sounds good. Thanks.'

'Least I can do for a guy who's promising me a million dollars. Unless you've changed your mind about that.'

'I haven't.' Billy gives Bucky a sideways look. 'You don't think I'll get it.'

'You might.' Bucky pulls a pack of Pall Mall straights out of his shirt pocket – Billy didn't know they still made those – and offers it to Billy, who shakes his head. Bucky lights his smoke with an old Zippo, the Marine emblem and *Semper Fi* embossed on the side. 'I learned a long time ago not to sell you short, William.'

They sit for awhile without talking, two men in porch rockers. Billy thought Pearson Street was quiet, but this place makes Pearson Street sound like downtown. Somewhere far off someone is using a chainsaw, or maybe it's a wood-chipper. That and a light breeze sighing through the pines and aspens is the whole soundtrack. Billy watches a bird go stiff-wing gliding across the blue sky.

'You should take her with you.'

Billy turns to him, startled. Bucky has an old tin ashtray loaded with filterless butts sitting on his lap. 'What? Are you crazy? I thought she could stay here with you while I track Nick down in Vegas.'

'She could, but you really should take her along.' He stubs out his cigarette, sets the ashtray aside, and leans forward. 'Hear me now, because I'm not sure you did before. *Guys are looking for you.* Hard guys like this Dana Edison you mentioned. They know the cops didn't catch you, they know Nick stiffed you, and they know there's a damn good chance that you'll be on your way to get what's owing. That you'll take it out of his hide if you can't get it any other way.'

'Like Shylock,' Billy murmurs.

'I don't know about that, never saw the movie, but if you think *that* will fool them—' He flicks the blond wig, which really has become bedraggled and needs to be replaced. '—you're taking dumb pills. They know you've changed your appearance, you never would have gotten out of Red Bluff otherwise. And if you're driving, there are only so many ways into Vegas. They'll be watching all of them.'

He's making sense, but Billy doesn't like the idea of bringing Alice into danger. The idea was to get her out of it.

'The first thing you might want to think about is the license plates on that ride of yours.' He points down at the deck and the vehicles beneath. 'There are cars with Dixieland plates in this part of the country, but not that many.'

Billy doesn't reply. He's struck dumb by his own stupidity. He set up the jammer to block the Fusion's onboard computer, but he's been flashing those blue-diamond plates all the way across the Midwest. Like a sign saying HERE I AM.

Bucky doesn't have to read his mind because everything Billy's thinking is on his face. 'Don't beat yourself up about it. You did most stuff right, especially for someone moving fast.'

'It only takes one thing wrong to put your head in the noose.'

Bucky doesn't disagree, just lights another cigarette and says he doubts if they're looking for Billy in places like Oklahoma and Kansas. 'They'll want to concentrate out west. Keep it tight. Idaho, Utah, maybe Arizona, but most of all in Nevada. Until you get to Vegas, things stand out there.'

Billy nods.

'Besides, if they'd seen you and tracked you, they'd be here already.' Bucky gestures with his hand, leaving a trail of smoke in the air. 'Isolated spot. Fine place for a shooting party. I think you're okay, the odds in your favor. Which is good in another way, because the paperwork on that leased car is in the Dalton Smith name, right?'

'Yes.'

'Do you have ID in any other name?'

Billy still has his David Lockridge DL and Mastercard, for all the good it will do him. 'None that's not burned.'

'I can make you some, enough to get by. I'll use Name Generator. Just, if I make you a credit card, don't try using it. It'll only be for show. And never mind switching the plates, you need to switch vehicles. That lease car can stay here for the time being, it's butt-ugly anyway.'

'Comfy, though,' Billy says, and drinks some beer.

'You've got money? You wired me my ten per cent of your advance, so I'm thinking you do.'

'Forty thousand or so, but not in cash. Money Manager accounts back in Red Bluff.'

'But in Dalton Smith's name, yeah?'

'Yes.'

Bucky's cigarette is down to a roach. He butts it. 'There's a place on

the east side of Sidewinder called Ricky's Good Used Cars. Kind of a
fly-by-night operation. You can buy something there. No, better, *I* buy
something there. I can pay cash and you can give me a Dalton Smith
check for the amount. I'll wait to cash it until you've finished this
fucktub of an operation.'

'And if I get killed, you'll be stuck.'

Bucky flaps a hand at him. 'I'm not talking about a BMW, just
something that'll roll for as long as you need it to roll. Fifteen hundred
dollars, maybe two grand. Maybe not a car at all. Maybe an old pickup
truck would be better, something rusted out with bad springs but a
worthwhile motor.' He looks up into the sun, calculating. 'And maybe
pulling one of those little open trailers like landscape guys use to tote
their mowers and blowers and shit.'

Billy can see it in his mind's eye. A truck with paint cracking on
the doors, rust on the rocker panels, and Bondo around the headlights.
Clap a beat-up old cowboy hat on his head and yes, it could be good
camouflage. He'd look like any day-wage drifter.

'They'll still be looking for a man alone,' Bucky says, 'and that's
where Alice comes in. You two pull into some roadside café where a
couple of bounty hunters are drinking coffee and keeping an eye out
on Highway 50, they're going to see nothing but some fella and his
daughter or niece in a broke-down old Dodge or F-150.'

'I'm not taking Alice into a situation that might get bloody.' The
worst thing about it is that she might go.

'Did you take her with you when you dealt with those dinks who
raped her?'

Of course he didn't, he left her in a nearby motel, but before he
can say so, the back door opens and Alice is back.

16

When she comes out on the porch her color is high, she's smiling, her
hair is blown into a haystack, and Billy sees, with only minimal surprise,
that, today at least, she's actually kind of gorgeous.

'It's beautiful up there!' she says. 'So windy it almost blew me off
my feet but oh my God, Billy, you can see *forever*!'

'On a clear day,' Billy agrees, smiling.

Alice either doesn't get the reference or is too full of what she's seen to give it even a token smile. 'There were clouds in the sky above me, but also some *below* me. I saw this huge bird . . . it couldn't have been a condor, but—'

'Yes it could,' Bucky tells her. 'We get them up here now, although I've never seen one myself.'

'And way across, on the other side, this is *crazy*, but I thought I saw that hotel you talked about. Then I blinked my eyes – the wind was so strong they were tearing up – and when I looked again, it was gone.'

Bucky doesn't smile. 'You're not the only person who's seen that. I'm not a superstitious man, but I wouldn't go anywhere near where the Overlook Hotel used to stand. Bad stuff happened there.'

Alice ignores that. 'It was a beautiful view and a beautiful walk. And guess what, Billy? There's a little log cabin about a quarter of a mile up the path.'

Bucky is nodding. 'Kind of a summerhouse type of thing, I guess. Once upon a time.'

'Well, it looks clean and dry and there's a table and some chairs. With the door open, it gets some sun. You could work on your story there, Billy.' She hesitates. 'If you wanted to, I mean.'

'Maybe I will.' He turns to Bucky. 'How long have you owned this place?'

Bucky thinks about it. 'Twelve years? No, I guess it's more like fourteen. How the time slides by, huh? I make sure to come up for a week or a weekend once or twice every year. Get seen around town. It's good to be a familiar face.'

'What name do you go by?'

'Elmer Randolph. My real first name and my middle.' Bucky gets up. 'I see you got eggs, and I think the time is just about right for huevos rancheros.'

He goes in. Billy gets up to follow, but before he can, Alice takes his arm just above the wrist. He remembers how she looked when he carried her across Pearson Street through the pouring rain, her eyes dull marbles peeping out between slitted lids. This is not that girl. This is a better girl.

'I could live here,' she says again.

CHAPTER 18

1

In deference to his guests, Bucky has taken to smoking on the porch, although the whole house holds the olfactory ghosts of the hundreds of Pall Malls he's smoked since relocating from New York. Billy joins him the next morning while Alice is in the shower. And singing in there, which might be the best sign of recovery yet.

'She says you're working on a book,' Bucky says.

Billy laughs. 'I doubt if it will mount up to that.'

'Says you might like to work on it in the summerhouse today.'

'I might.'

'She says it's good.'

'I don't think she has much to compare it to.'

Bucky doesn't chase that. 'I thought she 'n I might do some shopping this morning, give you a chance to get after it. You need a new wig and she needs some lady things. Not just hair dye.'

'You've already discussed this?'

'As a matter of fact we have. I usually get up around five – or rather my bladder gets me up – and after I took care of that business I came out to have a smoke and she was already here. We watched the sun come up together. Talked a little bit.'

'How did she seem?'

Bucky tilts his head toward the sound of the singing. 'How does she sound?'

'Pretty good, actually.'

'I think so, too. We might take a ride all the way to Boulder, better selections there. Stop at Ricky Patterson's used car lot on the backswing. See what he's got. Maybe have lunch at Handy Andy's.'

'What if they're looking for you, too?'

'You're the one in the crosshairs, Billy. I imagine they took a look for me in New York, maybe checked out my sister's place in Queens, then gave me up for a lost cause.'

'I hope you're right.'

'Tell you what, the first stop we make will be either Buffalo Exchange or Common Threads. I'll buy a cowboy hat and yank it down to my ears. Yeehaw.' Bucky puts out his current Pall Mall. 'She thinks the world of you, you know. Thinks you're the tomcat's testicles.'

'I hope she didn't put it like that.'

In the bathroom, the shower keeps on. She's still singing, which is good, but Billy thinks she may be having a hard job getting clean enough to suit her.

'Actually,' Bucky says, 'she called you her guardian angel.'

2

Half an hour later, after the steam has cleared out of the bathroom, Alice comes to the door while Billy is shaving.

'You don't mind if I go?'

'Not a bit. Have fun, keep your eyes open, and don't be afraid to tell him to turn the radio down when your fillings start to rattle. He always had a tendency to blast it when Creedence or Zep came on. I doubt if he's changed.'

'I want to get a couple of skirts and tops as well as the dye for my hair and a wig for you. A pair of cheap tennies. Also some underwear that's not so . . .' She trails off.

'The kind of stuff your clueless uncle might pick up for you in a pinch? Don't spare my feelings. I can take it.'

'What you got me was fine, but I could use a little more. And a bra that doesn't have a knot holding one of the straps together.'

Billy forgot about that. Like the Fusion's license plates.

Although Bucky is back on the porch, smoking and drinking orange juice (Billy doesn't know how he can bear the combination), Alice lowers her voice. 'But I don't have much money.'

'Let Bucky take care of that, and I'll take care of Bucky.'

'Are you sure?'

'Yes.'

She takes the hand not holding the razor and gives it a squeeze. 'Thank you. For everything.'

Her thanking him is simultaneously crazy and perfectly reasonable. A paradox, in other words. He keeps this to himself and tells her she's welcome.

3

Bucky and Alice leave in the Cherokee at quarter past eight. Alice has done her face and there's no sign of the bruises. They wouldn't show much even without the makeup, Billy thinks. It's been over a week since her date with Tripp Donovan, and the young are fast healers.

'Call me if you need to,' he says.

'Yes, Dad,' Bucky says.

Alice tells Billy she will, but he can see that in her mind she's already on the road, talking with Bucky the way normal people talk (as if any of this is normal) and thinking about what she will see in stores that are new to her. Maybe trying stuff on. The only sign he's gotten this morning of the girl who was raped is the way the shower ran and ran.

Once they're gone, Billy walks the path Alice took yesterday. He stops at the little cabin Bucky calls the summerhouse and looks inside. There's an unpainted plank floor and the only furniture is a card table and three folding chairs, but what else does he need? Just his word-cruncher and maybe a Coke out of the fridge.

Oh for the life of a writer, he thinks, and wonders who said that to him. Irv Dean, wasn't it? The security guy at Gerard Tower. That seems long ago, in another life. And it was. His David Lockridge life.

He walks up to where the path ends and looks across the gorge to the clearing, wondering if he might see Alice's phantom hotel. He doesn't, just a few charred uprights where it once stood. There's no condor, either.

He goes back to the house for his Mac Pro and that can of Coke. He sets them on the card table in the summerhouse. With the door wide open, the light is good. He sits in one of the folding chairs gingerly at first, but it seems solid enough. He boots up his story and scrolls down to where Taco was handing the squad bullhorn to Fareed, their terp. He's about to pick up where he left off when Merton Richter interrupted him, then notices there's a picture on the wall. He gets up for a closer look, because it's in the far corner – weird place for a painting – and the morning light doesn't quite reach there. It appears to show a bunch of hedges that have been clipped into animal shapes. There's a dog on the left, a couple of rabbits on the right, two lions in the middle, and what might be a bull behind the lions. Or maybe it's supposed to be a rhinoceros. It's a poorly executed thing, the greens of the animals too violent, and the artist has for some reason plinked a dab of red in the lions' eyes to give them a devilish aspect. Billy takes the painting down and turns it to face the wall. He knows that if he doesn't his eyes will be continually drawn to it. Not because it's good but because it isn't.

He cracks the can of Coke, takes a long swallow, and gets going.

4

'Come on, you guys,' Taco said. 'Let's get some.' He handed Fareed the bullhorn that had GOOD MORNING VIETNAM on the side and told him to give the house the usual loudhail, which came down to come out now and you come out on your feet, come out later and you'll be in a body bag. Fareed did it and nobody came out. That was usually our cue to go in after chanting *We are Darkhorse, of course of course*, but this time Taco told Fareed to give it to them again. Fareed shot him a questioning look but did as he was told. Still nothing. Tac told him to go one more time.

'What's up with you?' Donk asked.

'Don't know,' Taco said. 'Just feels wrong somehow. I don't like the fucking balcony running around the dome, for one thing. You see it?' We saw it, all right. It had a low cement railing. 'There could be muj behind it, all crouched down.' He saw us looking at him. 'No, I'm not freaking out, but it feels hinky.'

Fareed was halfway through his spiel when Captain Hurst, the new company commander, came by, standing up in an open Jeep, legs spread like he thought he was George S. Fucking Patton Esquire. On the other side of the street from him were three apartment buildings, two finished and one half-built, all spray painted with a big C, meaning they had been cleared. Well, supposedly. Hurst was green, and maybe not aware that sometimes the hajis crept back, and through even bad optics his head would look as big as a Halloween pumpkin.

'What are you waiting for, Sergeant?' he bawled. 'Daylight's wastin'! Clear that fucking hacienda!'

'Sir, yes, sir!' Taco said. 'Just giving them one more chance to come out alive.'

'Don't bother!' Captain Hurst shouted, and on he sped.

'The dingbat has spoken,' Bigfoot Lopez said.

'All right,' Taco said. 'Hands in the huddle.'

We grouped in tight, the Hot Eight that used to be the Hot Nine. Taco, Din-Din, Klew, Donk, Bigfoot, Johnny Capps, Pillroller with his medical bag of tricks. And me. I saw us as if I was outside myself. It happened to me that way sometimes.

I remember sporadic gunfire. A grenade went off somewhere behind us in Block Kilo, that low *crump* sound, and an RPG banged somewhere up ahead, maybe in Block Papa. I remember hearing a helo off in the distance. I remember some idiot blowing a whistle, *fweet-fweet-fweet*, Christ knows why. I remember how hot it was, the sweat cutting clean trails down our dirty faces. And the kids up the street, always the kids in their rock n rap T-shirts, ignoring the gunfire and the explosions like they didn't exist, bent over their scabbed knees and picking up spent shell casings to be reloaded and redistributed to the fighters. I remember feeling for the baby shoe on my belt loop and not finding it.

Our hands all together for the last time. I think Taco felt it. I sure did. Maybe they all did, I don't know. I remember their faces. I remember the smell of Johnny's English Leather. He put on a little every day, rationing it out, his own private lucky charm. I remember him once saying to me that no man could die smelling like a gentleman, God wouldn't let it happen.

'Give it to me, kids,' Taco said, so we did. Stupid, childish – like so many things in war are stupid and childish – but it pumped us up. And maybe if there were muj waiting for us in that big domed house it gave them a moment's pause, time to look at each other and wonder what the fuck they were doing and why they were probably going to die for some elderly half-senile imam's idea of God.

'*We are Darkhorse, of course of course! We are Darkhorse, of course of course!*'

We gave our knotted hands a shake, then stood up. I had an M4 and my M24 slung over my shoulder, as well. Next to me, Big Klew held the SAW over one arm, twenty-five pounds or so fully loaded and the belt slung over one massive shoulder like a necktie.

We clustered at the gate in the outer courtyard. Crisscross shadows from the unfinished apartment building across the street made the mural on the wall into a checkerboard – children in some squares, the watching women and the *mutawaeen* in others. Bigfoot had his M870 breaching tool, a doorbuster shotgun meant to blow the lock on the gate to smithereens. Taco stood aside so Foot could do his thing, but when Pablo gave the gate an experimental push, it swung open with a horror movie creak. Taco looked at me and I looked at him, two lowly jarhead bullet-sponges with but a single thought: how fucking dinky-dau is this?

Tac gave a little shrug as if to say it is what it is, then led us across the courtyard at a run, head down and bent at the waist. We followed. There was a single lonely soccer ball on the cobbles. George Dinnerstein gave it a sidefoot kick as he went by.

We crossed without a single shot fired from the house's barred windows and finished against the cement wall, four on either side of the double doors, which were heavy wood and at least eight feet high. Carved into each were crossed scimitars over a winged anchor, the symbol of the Ba'athist Battalions. Another hoodoo sign. I looked around for Fareed and saw him back by the gate. He saw me looking and shrugged. I got it. Fareed had a job and this wasn't it.

Taco pointed to Donk and Klew, signaling them to go left and check the window there. Me and Bigfoot went to the right. I snuck a peek in the window on my side, hoping to pull back in time if some muj decided to blow my head off, but I saw no one and no one shot at me. I saw a big circular room with rugs on the floor, a low couch, a bookcase now containing just one lonely paperback book, a coffee table on its side. There was a tapestry of running horses on one wall. The room was almost as high as the nave of a smalltown Catholic church, rising at least fifty feet to that dome, which was lit by lasers of sunlight made almost solid by dancing dust motes.

I ducked back for Bigfoot to take my place. Since I hadn't gotten my head blown off, he looked a little longer.

'Can't see the doors from here,' Foot said to me. 'Angle's wrong.'

'I know.'

We turned back to Tac. I rocked my hands back and forth in a gesture that meant maybe okay, maybe not. From beside the window on the other side, Donk conveyed the same message with a shrug. We heard more gunfire, some distant and some closer, but there was none on Block Lima. The big domed house was quiet. The soccer ball Din-Din kicked had come to rest in the corner of the courtyard. The place was probably deserted, but I kept feeling my belt loop for that fucking shoe.

The eight of us drew back together, flanking the door. 'Gotta stack,' Taco said. 'Who wants some?'

'I do,' I said.

Taco shook his head. 'You went first last time, Billy. Quit grubbing for tin and give someone else a chance.'

'I want some,' Johnny Capps said, and Taco said, 'You're it, then,' and that's why I'm walking today and Johnny isn't. Simple as that. God doesn't have a plan, He throws pickup sticks.

Taco pointed to Bigfoot, then at the double doors. The one on the right had an oversized iron latch sticking out like an impudent black tongue. Foot tried it, but the latch stayed firm. The courtyard had been open, maybe because kids came in there to play in better times, but the house was locked. Taco gave Bigfoot the nod and Foot shouldered his shotgun, which was loaded with special door-busting shells. The rest of us moved into a line – the ever-popular stack – behind Johnny. Klew was second, because he had the SAW. Taco was behind Klew. I was fourth in line. Pill was at the back of the stack, as he always was. Johnny was hyperventilating, psyching himself up. I could see his lips moving: *Get some, get some, fucking get some.*

Foot waited for Taco, and when Tac signaled, Foot blew the lock. A good chunk of the righthand door went with it. It shuddered inward.

Johnny didn't hesitate. He hit the lefthand door with his shoulder and burst into the room, yelling '*Banzai, motherfuck—*'

That was as far as he got before the muj who had been waiting behind the door on that side opened fire with an AK aimed not at Johnny's back but at his legs. His pants rippled as if in a breeze. He gave a shout. Surprise, probably, because the pain hadn't hit yet. Klew backed into the room, shouting '*Get back Marines!*' We did and when we were clear he opened fire with the SAW. He had it set for rapid-fire rather than sustained and the door blew back against the guy behind it, splinters flying, the crossed scimitars vaporizing. The muj fell out with nothing but his clothes holding him together.

And still he was grabbing for one of the grenades taped to his belt. He got it, but it fell from his fingers with the spoon still in. Klew kicked it away. I could see Johnny over Taco's shoulder. Now he was feeling the pain. He was screaming and weaving around, blood pouring onto his boots.

'Get him,' Taco said to Klew, and then he yelled, *'Corpsman!'*

Johnny took one more step and then went down. He was screaming *'I'm hit oh my God I'm hit bad!'* Klew started forward with Taco right behind him, and that was when they opened up on us from above. We should have known. Those dusty rays of sunlight high in the dome should have told us, because we had observed no windows from the outside. Those were loopholes busted in the concrete, down low, where the waist-high wall around the outside balcony hid them.

Klew was hit in the chest and staggered backward, holding onto the SAW. His body armor stopped that one, but the next round took him in the throat. Taco looked up at the sunbeams, then grabbed for the SAW. A bullet hit him in the shoulder. Two more pinged off the wall. The fourth hit him in the lower face. His jaw turned as if on a hinge. He spun toward us spraying out a fan of blood, waving us back, and then the top of his head came off.

Someone thumped me and for just a second I thought I'd been shot from behind and then Pill ran past, his medical pack now off his back and dangling from his hand by one strap.

'No, no, they're up top!' Bigfoot shouted. He grabbed the pack's other strap and yanked our corpsman back, which is the only reason Clayton 'Pillroller' Briggs is still in the land of the living.

Bullets hit the big room's floor, sending chips of tile flying. Bullets hit the rugs, raising puffs of dust and fiber. A bullet hole appeared in the tapestry, taking one of the running horses in the chest. A bullet hit the coffee table and sent it spinning. The mujahedeen on the balcony were firing steadily now. I saw the bodies of Taco and Klew jerk again and again as they shot them some more, maybe to make sure, maybe venting their rage, probably both. But they stayed away from Johnny, who lay in the middle of the floor in a spreading pool of blood. And screaming his head off. They could have taken him out easily, but that wasn't what they wanted. Johnny was their staked goat.

All of this, from Foot blowing the door to the muj on the balcony pouring fire into the bodies of Tac and Klew, happened in a minute and a half. Maybe less. When things go wrong, they don't waste time.

'We have to get Cappsie,' Donk said.

'That's what they want,' Din-Din said. 'They ain't stupid, don't you be.'

'He'll bleed to death if we leave him,' Pill said.

'I got him,' Foot said, and ran in the door, bent almost double. He grabbed the back-hook on Johnny's body armor and started dragging, bullets hitting all around him. He made it as far as the body of the dead muj, then he took one in the face and that was the end of Pablo Lopez of El Paso, Texas. He went over on his back and the insurgents above switched to him for their target practice. Johnny continued to scream.

'I can reach him,' Din-Din said.

'That's what Foot thought,' Donk said. 'Those assholes can shoot.' He turned to me. 'What do we do, Billy? Call for air?'

We all knew that a Hellfire missile could take care of the hajis on the balcony, but it would end Johnny Capps in the process.

I said, 'I'm going to take them out.'

I didn't wait for any discussion. We were way past that. I ran back across the courtyard, dropping my M4 on the cobbles. 'You guys pull back now, boss?' Fareed asked.

I didn't answer, just ran across the street to the unfinished apartment building. There was no door. Inside it was shadowy and smelled of wet cement. The lobby was a treasure trove of canned goods, snack packs, and Hershey bars. There was a pallet of Coca-Cola and a pile of magazines with a *Field & Stream* on top. Some enterprising Iraqi *tajir* had been using this as his trading post.

I started running up the stairs. There was a lot of trash scattered on the first flight. On the second landing someone had spray painted YANKEE GO HOME, an old favorite that never loses its charm. I could still hear fusillades of gunfire from across the street and Johnny Capps screaming. I didn't hear Pete Cashman get it, but he surely did. Din-Din said Donk's last words were 'I can get him no problem, he's so close now.'

The walls stopped on the fourth floor and sunlight hit me like a fist. I dodged around a wheelbarrow filled with hardened cement, shoved aside a pile of boards, and kept going up. I was panting like a dog and sweat was pouring off of me. The stairs ended at the sixth floor and that was okay because I was even with the top of the dome across the street and able to look down on the balcony.

There were three of them. They were on their knees with their backs to me. I looped the strap of the M24 over my right shoulder nice and tight and laid the barrel on a handy piece of rebar jutting out of an unfinished wall. All three were laughing and cheering each other on like it was a soccer match and their side was winning. I aimed for the middle guy's head. It wasn't as big as a Halloween pumpkin, but it was plenty big enough. I squeezed the trigger and presto, the head was gone. Nothing but blood and brains running down the curved side of the dome where it had been. The other two looked at each other, bewildered – *what just happened?*

I took out the second one and the third threw himself against the cement railing, maybe thinking it would give him cover. It didn't. It was too low. I shot him in the back. He lay still. No body armor. He probably believed that Allah had his six but Allah was busy elsewhere that day.

I ran back down the stairs and across the street. Fareed was still standing there. Din-Din and Pill were in the Funhouse, Pill on his knees beside Johnny. He had already cut away the legs of Johnny's pants. Bone fragments were stuck to the fabric and poking out of Johnny's skin. Din-Din was yelling into Pill's walkie, telling someone that we had casualties, many casualties, Block Lima, big domed house, evac, evac, need a dustoff, etc.

'Hurts!' Johnny screamed. '*Oh Christ it hurts SO FUCKING BAD!*'

'Take these,' Pill said. He had the morphine tablets.

'*Oh God I wish I was dead I wish they killed me OH MY GOD MAKE IT STOP!*'

Pill two-fingered Johnny's mouth open and dumped in the tabs. 'Chew those and you're gonna see God.'

'What happened here, Marines?'

I looked around and saw Hurst. Still standing spread-legged, trying his best to do the General Patton thing, but he looked pretty fucking green around the gills.

'What does it look like?' Din-Din said. 'Fallujah happened. *Sir.*'

Pill said, 'If he doesn't get some blood ASAP, he's going to

5

What brings Billy back from Iraq could have *been* in Iraq, part of Lalafallujah's endless soundtrack: Angus Young's guitar snarling its way through 'Dirty Deeds Done Dirt Cheap.' Bucky and Alice must be back from their shopping trip. Billy looks at his watch and sees it's quarter past three in the afternoon. He's been here for hours, with no sense of passing time at all.

He finishes that dangling last sentence, saves his work, cases up his lappie, and is about to leave when he happens to glance at the picture he took down, not neglecting to turn it to the wall so he wouldn't be distracted by those bright primitive colors. He puts it back up on its hook, maybe (probably) because he's still in Marine mode and remembering Sergeant 'Up Yours' Uppington's dictum: *leave no trace when you leave the space.*

He studies the painting, frowning. The hedge dog is on the right, the hedge rabbits on the left. Weren't they the other way around before? And aren't the lions closer?

I got it wrong, that's all, he thinks, but before leaving the summerhouse he takes the picture down again. Not neglecting to turn it so it faces the wall.

6

The music gets louder as he approaches the house. With no neighbors, Bucky can really crank it if he wants to. It must be a mixtape, because as Billy approaches the house AC/DC gives way to Metallica.

They've brought back a new vehicle – new to them, at least – and Billy pauses before going up the steps to look it over. There not being any more space under the porch, they've parked it at the end of the driveway. It's a Dodge Ram, the Quad Cab model from early in the twenty-first century, once blue, now mostly gray. There's no Bondo around the headlights, but the bench seat has been mended with a strip of black tape and the rocker panels are mighty rusty. So is the bed of the pickup, which contains a Lawn-Boy mower maybe older than the truck itself. There's a trailer hooked up behind, a two-wheeler, pretty battered, nothing in it.

By the time Billy starts up the steps to the porch, Metallica has been replaced by Tom Waits croaking '16 Shells from a Thirty-Ought-Six.' Billy stops in the doorway. Bucky and Alice are dancing in the middle of the big room. She's wearing a new shell top, her color is high and her eyes are bright. With her hair in a ponytail – really a horsetail, it goes all the way down to the middle of her back – she looks like a teenager. She's laughing, having a ball. Maybe because Bucky is a pretty fucked-up dancer, maybe just because she's having a good time.

Bucky gives Billy a double V and keeps shuffling off to Buffalo. He does a twirl and Alice spins the other way. She sees Billy leaning in the doorway and laughs some more and gives a hip-shake that makes her tied-back hair flip from side to side. Tom Waits ends. Bucky goes to the stereo and turns off Bob Seger before he can get a grip on that song about Betty Lou. Then he collapses on the couch and pats his chest. 'I'm too bushed to boogaloo.'

Alice, years from being too bushed to boogaloo, turns to Billy, almost popping with excitement. 'Did you see the truck?'

'I did.'

'It's perfect, isn't it?'

Billy nods. 'Nobody would remember it five minutes after it passed them by.' He looks at Bucky over her shoulder. 'How does it run?'

'Ricky says it's fine for an old girl that's already made one trip around the clock. Burns a little oil is all. Well, maybe a little more than a little. Alice and me took it for a test drive and it seemed okay. Suspension's rough, but you gotta expect that in a truck that's been around as long as this one. Ricky let it go for thirty-three hundred.'

'I drove it back,' Alice says. She's still high on the shopping or the dancing or both. Billy is so glad for her. 'It's a standard, but I learned on a standard. My uncle taught me. Three on the tree, up to the side when you want a backwards ride.'

Billy has to laugh. He learned to drive at the House of Everlasting Paint, so he could be more help with the chores after Gad – Glen Dutton in his story – left to go in the service. Mr Stepenek – Mr Speck in his story – taught him those same two rhymes.

'I got you something,' she says. 'Wait until you see.'

She runs into the other room to get it, and Billy looks at Bucky. Bucky nods and makes a quick thumbs-up sign: A-OK.

Alice comes back with a box that has SPECIALTY COSTUMERS embossed on the top in scrolly letters. She holds it out to him.

Billy opens it and lifts out a new wig, probably twice as expensive as the one he mail-ordered from Amazon. This one isn't blond, it's black threaded with plenty of gray, and longer than the Dalton Smith wig. Thicker, too. His first thought is that if he's wearing it and gets stopped by a cop, it won't match his DL photo. Then another thought comes, a much bigger one that drives all other thoughts from his mind.

'You don't like it,' Alice says. Her smile is fading.

'Oh, but I do. Very much.'

He risks a hug. She hugs him back. So that's all right.

7

The day Billy and Alice came was like summer, but their second night at Bucky's is cooler, and the wind hooting around the house is downright cold. Billy brings up some split chunks of maple from under the porch and Bucky fires up the little Jøtul stove in the kitchen. Then they sit at the table looking at the pictures Bucky has printed, some from Google Earth and others from Zillow. They show the exterior grounds and the interior rooms and amenities of a house at 1900 Cherokee Drive in the town of Paiute, which is actually a northern suburb of Las Vegas. It is the residence of one Nikolai Majarian.

The house backs up against the Paiute Foothills. It's snow white and built on four levels, each one stepped back from the one below so it looks like a giant's staircase. The view of downtown Vegas must be pretty spectacular at night, Billy thinks, especially from the roof.

On Google Earth they can see a high wall surrounding the property, the main gate, and the driveway – actually a road, it's got to be almost a mile long – leading to the compound. There's a barn about two hundred yards from the house. A paddock and an exercise ring for horses nearby. Three other outbuildings, one big and two smaller. Billy thinks the help must stay in the biggest one, which would have been called a bunkhouse in the old days and maybe still is. The other two are probably for maintenance and storage. He sees nothing that could be a garage and asks Bucky about it.

'Built into this first slope would be my guess,' Bucky says, tapping the wooded rise behind the house. 'Only it's probably more like a hangar. Room for a dozen cars. Or more. Nick's got a taste for the classics, or so I heard. I guess everybody's got an itch that only money can scratch.'

There are plenty that money can't scratch, Billy thinks.

Alice is examining the pix from Zillow. 'God, there has to be twenty rooms. And look at the pool out back!'

'Nice,' Bucky agrees. 'All the mods and cons. And he might have added more, because these pictures have to be from before Nick bought it. He paid fifteen mil. I saw it on Zillow.'

And stiffed me out of a measly million-five, Billy thinks.

The Zillow photos of the exterior show what Google Earth can't. The vistas of lawn, for instance, brilliant green and dotted with flower-beds. The paddock is equally green. There are groves of palms, some with groupings of outdoor furniture in their kindly shade. How many hundreds of thousands of gallons of water must it take to keep that estate looking like Eden in the desert? How many groundskeepers? How many on the domestic staff? And how many hardballs are hanging out on the off chance that a hired assassin named Billy Summers might come looking for the rest of his blood money?

'He calls it Promontory Point,' Bucky says. 'I did some digging, it's amazing what you can find with a computer these days if you know how to dip into the darker regions. Nick's been there since 2007, and with his back to the mountains nobody's ever bothered him. Maybe he's gotten a little careless, but I wouldn't count on that.'

No, Billy thinks, it wouldn't do to count on it. Someone who could get rid of a valued long-time associate like Giorgio Piglielli can't be taken lightly. The only assumption he can make is that Nick is looking for him. Waiting for him. What Nick maybe doesn't understand is how angry Billy is. There was a bargain. He held up his end of it. Instead of holding up the other end, Nick stiffed him. Then tried to kill him. Face to face Nick might deny that, but Billy knows. They both do.

Bucky taps a spot on the Google Earth aerial photo of the grounds. 'This little square is the gatehouse, and it'll be manned. Guarded. You can count on that.'

Billy has no doubt. He wonders again how many men Nick will have guarding his little kingdom. In a Sylvester Stallone or Jason Statham movie there would be dozens, armed with everything from gas-powered light machine guns to shoulder-mounted missile launchers, but this is real life. Maybe five, maybe only four, carrying automatic pistols or shotguns or both. But there's only one of him, and he's no Sylvester Stallone.

Alice pulls one of the photos from Google Earth to the middle of the table. 'What's this? I don't see it on any of the Zillow pix.'

Bucky and Billy look. It's where the west side of the wall ends against a rocky rise. After a bit Bucky says, 'I think it must be a service entrance. You wouldn't bother showing that on a real estate site, any more than you'd show the shed where the trash gets stored for pickup. Real estate sites stick to the glamour. What do you think, Billy?'

'I don't know.' But he's starting to. The more he thinks about that beat-up old truck, the more he likes it. And the new wig. That, too.

8

After supper, Alice commandeers the bathroom to dye her hair. When Bucky offers her a beer ('Just to keep up your strength'), she accepts. They both hear her lock the door behind her. Billy's not surprised. He doubts if Bucky is, either.

Bucky gets two more bottles of beer from the fridge. After Bucky puts on a light jacket and tosses Billy a sweatshirt, they go out on the porch and settle side by side in the rockers. Bucky clinks the neck of his bottle against the neck of Billy's. 'Here's to success.'

'Good toast,' Billy says, and takes a drink. 'I want to thank you again for having us. I know you didn't expect guests.'

'You serious about wanting a silencer for the Ruger?'

'Yes. Can you also get me a Glock 17 and ammunition for both?'

Bucky nods. 'Shouldn't be a problem, not around here. What else do you need?'

'A mustache to match the wig she bought me. I don't have time to grow one.' There's more, but Alice will have ideas about finding the rest.

'What are you thinking of doing? Maybe it's time to tell me so I can try to argue you out of it.'

Billy tells him. Bucky listens closely and after awhile starts to nod. 'Going out to his place is risky, bearding the lion in his den type of thing, but it could work. Any bounty hunters looking for you are apt to be downtown, especially around Nick's casino. Double Deuce, or whatever.'

'Double Domino.'

Bucky leans forward, looking at him. 'Look, if you're worried about the money you promised me—'

'I'm not.'

'—you can let it go. I'm doing all right for money, and I'm glad to be out of the city. I have no idea why I stayed so fucking long in the first place. Someday someone's going to blow up a dirty bomb on Fifth Avenue, or a communicable disease will come along that turns everything from Manhattan to Staten Island into a giant Petri dish.'

Billy thinks Bucky has been listening to too much talk radio but doesn't say so. 'It's not about your money or mine, although I'll take it if he has it. He cheated me. He *fucked* me. He's a bad person.' Billy hears himself falling into the speech patterns of the *dumb self* and doesn't care. 'He killed Giorgio, or had him killed. He meant to do the same to me.'

'All right,' Bucky says quietly. 'I get it. A matter of honor.'

'Not honor, *honesty*.'

'I stand corrected. Now drink your beer.'

Billy takes a swig and tilts his head toward the house where the shower is running. Again. 'How was she on the shopping trip? Okay?'

'Mostly. Before we went into Common Threads to buy you a cowboy hat – forgot to show it to you, it's a fuckin beaut – she had a little bit of a breathing problem and sang something under her breath. I couldn't make out what it was, but after that she was all right again.'

Billy knows what it was.

'At the used car lot she rocked the house. Spotted that truck and bargained Ricky down from forty-four hundred to thirty-three. When he tried to hold steady at thirty-five she grabbed me and said "Come on, Elmer, he's nice but he's not serious." You believe that?'

'Actually I do,' Billy says. He laughs, but Bucky doesn't laugh with him. He's grown serious. Billy asks him if something's wrong.

'Not yet, but there could be.' He puts his beer bottle down and turns to look Billy square in the face. 'The two of us are outlaws, okay? People don't use that word so much these days, but that's what we are. Alice isn't, but if she keeps running with you, she will be. Because she's in love with you.'

Billy puts his own bottle down. 'Bucky, I'm not . . . I don't . . .'

'I know you don't want to jump in the sack with her and maybe she doesn't want to jump in the sack with you, not after what she's been through. But you saved her life and put her back together—'

'I didn't put her back—'

'Okay, maybe you didn't, but you gave her the time and space to start doing it herself. That doesn't change the fact that she's in love with you and she'll follow you as long as you let her and if you let her you'll ruin her.'

Having delivered himself of what Billy now believes he came out here to say, Bucky pauses for breath, picks up his beer, downs half of it, and gives a ringing belch.

'Argue me back if you want. Giving you a place to stay for a few days doesn't give me the right not to hear opposing arguments, so go on and argue me back.'

But Billy doesn't.

'Take her to Nevada with you, sure. Find a cheap place to stay outside the city and leave her there while you take care of your business. If you get out clean and with your money, give her a bunch of it and send her back east. Tell her to stop and see me and remind her those false papers are just short-term camouflage. She can go back to being Alice Maxwell again.'

He raises a finger, which is starting to show the first twists and gnarls of arthritis. '*But only if you keep her out of it.* Capisce?'

'Yes.'

'If you don't get out clean you probably won't be getting out at all. That will be hard for her to hear, but she has to know. Agreed?'

'Agreed.'

'Tell her that if a few days go by and she hasn't heard from you, you pick how many, she should come back here. I'll give her some money. A thousand, fifteen hundred maybe.'

'You don't have to—'

'I want to. I like her. She's not a whiner, and given what happened to her she'd have a right to whine. Besides, it'd be money you made for me. You're my only client now. Have been for the last four years. No more bankrolling stickups for this kid. Too easy for one of them to come back on me if something went wrong, and I'm too old for prison.'

'All right. Thank you. Thank you.'

The shower goes off. Bucky leans toward Billy again over the arm of his rocker.

'You know, a baby kitten will take to a dog that decides to groom it instead of chasing it or eating it. Hell, a baby duck will. They imprint. She's imprinted on you, Billy, and I don't want her to get hurt.'

The bathroom door opens and Alice comes out on the porch. She's wearing an old blue bathrobe that must be Bucky's; it's so long it brushes the tops of her bare feet. Her hair is put up, held with what looks like a dozen barrettes, and covered in transparent plastic. She's not going to be even close to platinum, maybe because her hair was so dark to begin with, but it's still a big change.

'What do you think? I know it's hard to tell right now, but . . .'

'Looks good,' Bucky says. 'I was always partial to a dirty blonde. My first ex was a dirty blonde. I saw her hanging by the jukebox and knew I had to have her. More fool me.'

She gives that a distracted smile but it's Billy she's looking at, his opinion that matters. Billy knows exactly what Bucky was talking about. He remembers a video he saw on YouTube, one that showed a bird taking a bath in a dog's water dish while the dog – a Great Dane – sat and watched. And he thinks of that old saying about how if you save someone's life, you are responsible for them.

'You look terrific,' he says, and Alice smiles.

CHAPTER 19

1

Billy and Alice stay with Bucky for five days. On the morning of the sixth day – the one where God reputedly created the beasts of the field and the fowls of the air – they pack up the Dodge Ram and get ready to leave. Billy is wearing the blond wig and the fake glasses. Because the truck is the Quad Cab model, they can stow their scant luggage behind the bench seat. The ancient mower is still in the truckbed. It has been joined by a hedger, a leaf-blower, and an old Stihl chainsaw. The trailer, empty when Billy first saw it, now contains four cardboard barrels purchased at Lowe's. The two men kicked them around awhile to give them the right battered look and filled them with hand tools bought for a song at a bank foreclosure auction in Nederland. The barrels have been secured to the sides of the trailer with bungee cords.

'You want to look like the twenty-first-century version of a saddle bum,' Bucky said while they were playing kick-the-barrels. 'God knows there are plenty of them in the West Nine. They drift around, find a little work, then move on.'

Alice asked him what the West Nine were, and Bucky named them off: Colorado, Wyoming, Montana, Utah, Arizona, New Mexico, Idaho, Oregon, and – of course – Nevada. Billy thinks the truck is okay. It might be a needless precaution on their road trip, anyway; Bucky's right, any bounty hunters will be concentrated in the Vegas metro area. Later, though, when it comes to Promontory Point, the way the truck looks could be vital.

'This has been a good visit,' Bucky says. He's wearing biballs and an Old [97s] T-shirt. 'I'm glad you came.'

Alice gives him a hug. Her new blonde hair looks good in the morning sun.

'Billy?' Bucky holds out his hand. 'You be safe now.'

Billy almost hugs him, that's the way things are done these days, but he doesn't. He's never been much for bro-hugs, even in the sand.

'Thanks, Bucky.' He takes Bucky's hand in both of his and squeezes lightly, mindful of Bucky's arthritis. 'For everything.'

'Welcome.'

They get in. Billy fires up the engine. It's rough at first but smooths out. Bucky has agreed to find someone to drive the Fusion back to its home base, thus protecting the Dalton Smith name. Something else on my tab, Billy thinks.

He gets the old truck's nose pointed down the road. Just as he puts it in first gear, Bucky makes a *whoa, whoa* gesture and comes over to the passenger side. Alice rolls down her window.

'I want to see you back here,' he tells her. 'In the meantime, stay out of his business and stay clean, you hear?'

'Yes,' she says, but Billy thinks she may only be telling Bucky what Bucky wants to hear. Which is okay, Billy thinks. She'll listen to me. I hope.

He gives a final blip of the horn and gets rolling. An hour and a half later they turn west on 1-70 toward Las Vegas.

2

They stop for the night in Beaver, Utah. It's another motel of the no-tell variety, but not too bad. They get chicken baskets at the Crazy Cow and a couple of cans of Bud at Ray's 66 on the way back. Later they sit outside their adjoining rooms, draw the obligatory lawn chairs close, and drink the cold beer.

'I read the rest of your story while we were driving,' Alice says. 'It's really good. I can't wait to read more.'

Billy frowns. 'I hadn't planned on going on after Fallujah.'

'*Lala*fallujah,' she says, and smiles. Then: 'But aren't you going to write about how you got into the business of killing people for money?'

That makes him wince because it's so bald. And of course so true. She sees it.

'Bad people, I mean. And how you met Bucky, I'd like to know that.'

Yes, Billy thinks, I could write about that, and maybe I should. Because dig, if that muj hiding behind the door had shot Johnny Capps to death instead of just blowing his legs apart, Billy Summers wouldn't be here now. Neither would Alice. It comes to him as sort of a revelation – although maybe it shouldn't – that if Johnny Capps hadn't lived, Alice Maxwell might well have died of shock and exposure on Pearson Street.

'Maybe I will write it. If I get a chance. Tell me about you, Alice.'

She laughs, but it's not the free and easy one he's come to like so much. This one's a warding-off laugh. 'There isn't much to tell. I've always been a fade-into-the-woodwork person. Being with you is the only interesting thing that's ever happened to me. Other than getting gang raped, I guess.' She utters a sad little snort.

But he's not going to let it go at that. 'You grew up in Kingston. Your mother raised you and your sister. What else? There must be more.'

Alice points to the darkening sky. 'I've never seen so many stars in my life. Not even at Bucky's place.'

'Don't change the subject.'

She shrugs. 'Okay, just prepare to be bored. My father owned a furniture store and my mother was his bookkeeper. He died of a heart attack when I was eight and Gerry – she's my sister – was nineteen and going to beauty school.' Alice touches her hair. 'She'd say I did this all wrong.'

'Probably she would, but it looks fine. Go on.'

'I was a B student in high school. Had a few dates but no boyfriend. There were popular kids, but I wasn't one of them. There were unpopular kids – you know, the ones who always get pranked and laughed at – but I wasn't one of them, either. Mostly I did what my mom and my sister said.'

'Except about going to beauty school.'

'I almost said yes to that too, because I sure wasn't going to a smart-peoples' college. I didn't take many of the courses you need for that.' She thinks about it. Billy lets her. 'Then one night I was lying in bed, almost asleep, and I all at once came full awake. *Snapped* awake. Almost fell out of bed. Did that ever happen to you?'

Billy thinks about Iraq and says, 'Many times.'

'I thought, "If I do that, if I do what they want, it will never end. I'll be doing what they want for the rest of my life and one day I'll wake up old right here in little old Kingston."' She turns to him. 'And do you know what my mom and Gerry would say if they knew what happened to me in Tripp's apartment, and what I'm doing now, being here with you? They'd say "See what it got you."'

Billy puts out a hand to touch her shoulder. She turns to him before he can and he sees the woman she might be, if time and fate are kind.

'And do you know what I'd say? I'd say I don't care, because this is my time, I *deserve* to have my time, and this is what I want.'

'Okay,' he says. 'Okay, Alice. That's fine.'

'Yes. It is. You bet it is. As long as you don't get killed.'

That's something he can't promise, so he says nothing. They look at the stars awhile longer and drink their beer and she says nothing until she tells him she thinks she'll go to bed.

3

Billy doesn't go to bed. He has a pair of texts from Bucky. The first says the landscaping company that does the work at Promontory Point is called Greens & Gardens. The man who runs the crew might be Kelton Freeman or Hector Martinez, but it might be someone else entirely. It's a high-turnover business.

The following text says that Nick often stays at the Double during the week but always tries to get back to his estate in Paiute for the weekend. Especially for Sundays. **Never misses the Giants during football season**, Bucky adds. **Everybody who knows him knows that.**

You can take the boy out of New York, Billy thinks, but you can't take New York out of the boy. He texts back, **Any luck with the garage?**

Bucky's response is quick: **No.**

Billy has brought the pictures, both Google Earth and Zillow. He studies them for awhile. Then he opens his laptop and looks up a handful of Spanish phrases. He won't have to say them when and if the time comes but he says them now, over and over, committing them to memory. He almost certainly won't need all of them. He might need none of them. But it's always best to be ready.

> *Me llamo Pablo Lopez.*
> *Esta es mi hija.*
> *Estos son para el jardín.*
> *Mi es sordo y mudo:* I am a deafmute.

4

They go back to the Crazy Cow for breakfast, then get on the road. Billy wouldn't want to push the old truck, and he doesn't have to. It's only a couple of hundred miles to Vegas, and he won't move against Nick until Sunday, when the pros play football and the compound at the end of Cherokee Drive is apt to be at its most quiet. No grounds-keepers or landscapers and hopefully no hardballs. He checked the schedule and the Giants play the Cardinals at four P.M. eastern, which will be one P.M. in Nevada.

To pass the time, he tells Alice how he got into the business from which he now considers himself retired. Johnny Capps was the first link in the chain that ends – so far, there's at least one more link still to be forged – on Interstate 70 heading west.

'He's the one who got shot in the legs in that house. The one they left alive to try and lure the rest of you in.'

'Yes. Clay Briggs – Pillroller – got him stabilized and he was airlifted out. Johnny spent a long time in a shitty VA hospital and got hooked on dope while they were trying to rehab what couldn't be rehabbed. Eventually Uncle Sam sent him back to Queens in his wheelchair, hooked through the bag.'

'That's so sad.'

Well, Billy tells her, at least the dope addict part of Johnny's story had a happy ending. His cousin Joey reached out to him, a guy who'd kept the Italian family name of Cappizano, although he was of course called Joey Capps. With permission from one of the larger

New York organizations – and of course the Sinaloa Cartel, who controlled the dope business – Joey Capps ran his own little organization, one so modest it was really more of a posse. Joey offered his wounded warrior cousin a job as an accountant, but only if he could get clean.

'And he did?'

'Yes. I got the whole story from him when we reconnected. He went into a rehab – his cousin paid – and then went to NA meetings three and four times a week until he died a few years ago. Lung cancer got him.'

Alice is frowning. 'He went to NA meetings to get off dope, but his day job was *pushing* dope?'

'Not pushing it, counting and washing the money from the trade. But yeah, it comes to the same thing, and once I pointed that out to him. You know what he said? That there are recovered alcoholics tending bar all over the world. He sponsored people, he said, and some of them got clean and resumed their lives. That's how he put it, they resumed their lives.'

'God, talk about the left hand not knowing what the right hand is doing.'

Billy tells her that he almost signed up for another tour in the suck, decided he'd be crazy to do it – suicidal-crazy – and took off the uniform. Kicked around, trying to decide what came next for a guy whose job for a lot of years had been shooting other guys in the T-box. That was when Johnny got in touch.

There was a Jersey guy, he said, who liked to pick up women in bars and then beat them up. He probably had some kind of childhood trauma he was trying to work out, Johnny said, but fuck a bunch of childhood trauma, this was a very bad guy. He put the last woman in a coma, and this woman happened to be a Cappizano. Only a second cousin or maybe a third, but still a Cappizano. The only problem was this guy, this beater of women, was part of a larger and more powerful organization headquartered across the river in Hoboken.

Joey took Johnny Capps along for a sit-down with the head of this organization, and it turned out the New Jersey guys didn't have much use for this shitpoke, either. He was trouble, a nasty *stronzo madre* with rings on the fingers of both hands, the better to beat the living crap out of women instead of taking them home to fuck them as any natural man would want to do, or even *fottimi nel culo*, which some men liked and even some women. But no woman likes getting her face beat off.

The upshot was that the *capo* couldn't give Joey Capps permission to off the *stronzo madre*, because there would have to be retribution. But if an outsider did it, and if both outfits – the Hoboken organization and the much smaller Queens crew – paid for it, the thorn could be pulled. Call it mob diplomacy.

'So Johnny Capps called you.'

'He did.'

'Because you were the best?'

'The best he knew, anyway. And he knew my history.'

'The man who killed your little sister.'

'That, yes. I looked into the guy before I agreed to take the job, got a little of his history. Even went to see the woman he put into a coma. She was on life-support machinery, and you could tell she was never coming back. The monitor . . .' Billy draws a straight line above the steering wheel. 'So I did him. It really wasn't much different from what I did in Iraq.'

'Did you like it?'

'No.' Billy says it with no hesitation. 'Not in the sand and not back here. Never.'

'Johnny's cousin got you other jobs?'

'Two more, and there was one I turned down because the guy . . . I don't know . . .'

'Didn't seem bad enough?'

'Something like that. Then Joey introduced me to Bucky, and Bucky introduced me to Nick, and that's where we are.'

'I'm guessing there's quite a lot more to it.'

She's guessing right, but Billy doesn't want to say any more, let alone go into the details of the jobs he did for Nick and for others. He has never said any of this, not to anyone, and he's appalled to hear that part of his life told out loud. It's sordid and stupid. Alice Maxwell, business school student and rape survivor, is sitting in an old truck with a man who killed people for a living. It was his fucking *job*. And is he going to kill Nick Majarian? If he gets the chance, very likely. So, a question: is killing for honor better than killing for money? Probably not, but that won't stop him.

Alice is silent for a bit, thinking it over. Then she says, 'You told me that because you think you might never get a chance to write it down. Isn't that right?'

It is, but he doesn't want to say so out loud.

'Billy?'

'I told you because you wanted to know,' he says finally, and turns on the radio.

5

They register at another off-brand motel. There are a lot of them in a rough ring around the outskirts of Vegas. While Billy registers them as Dalton Smith and Elizabeth Anderson, Alice plugs four dollars in one of the lobby slots. On the fifth, ten fake cartwheels drop into the trough with a clatter and she squeals like a kid. The desk clerk offers her a choice: ten bucks or motel credit in that amount.

'How's the restaurant here?' Alice asks.

'Buffet's pretty good.' Then he lowers his voice and says, 'Take the money, honey.'

Alice takes the money and they get to-go at the Sirloin Super Burger down the road. She insists that it be her treat and Billy doesn't argue.

Back in Billy's room, she sits at the window and watches the endless traffic streaming toward downtown, and the lights of the hotels and casinos coming on. 'Sin City,' she marvels, 'and here I am in a motel room with a good-looking guy who happens to be twice my age. My mother would just *shit*.'

Billy throws back his head and laughs. 'And your sister?'

'Wouldn't believe it.' She points. 'Are those the Paiute Mountains?'

'If that's north, those are them. I think they're actually called foothills. If it matters.'

She turns to him, no longer smiling. 'Tell me what you're going to do.'

He does, and not just because he needs her help with the prep. She listens carefully. 'It sounds awfully dangerous.'

'If it looks hinky, I'll back off and reconsider.'

'Will you *know* if it's hinky? The way your friend Taco knew outside that house in Fallujah?'

'You remember that, huh?'

'Will you?'

'I think so, yes.'

'But you'll probably go in anyway. The way you went into the Funhouse and look what happened there.'

Billy says nothing. There's nothing to say.

'I wish I could go with you.'

He says nothing to that, either. Even if the idea didn't fill him with horror, the plan wouldn't work if she were with him and she knows it.

'How badly do you need that money?'

'I could get along without it, and most of it's going to Bucky anyway. The money's not the reason I'm going. Nick treated me badly. He needs to pay a price, just like the boys who raped you needed to pay a price.'

It's Alice's turn to be silent.

'There's something else. I don't think it was Nick's idea to kill me after the job was done, and I *know* it wasn't his idea to put a six-million-dollar price on my head. I want to know who that person is.'

'And why?'

'Yes. That too.'

6

The first thing Billy does the next morning is to check the back of the old Dodge truck, because the tools were only tied down, not locked down. Everything is present and accounted for. He's not surprised, partly because everything in the truckbed and trailer is old and pretty clapped-out, but also because his experience over the years has taught him that the great majority of people are honest. They don't take what isn't theirs. People who do – people like Tripp Donovan, Nick Majarian, and whoever is behind Nick – piss him off mightily.

He almost texts Bucky to ask if Bucky can find out what car Nick is currently driving – it would probably be in the VIP area of the Double Domino's parking garage, undoubtedly something fancy with a vanity plate – then doesn't do it. Bucky probably *could* find out, and it might raise a red flag. That's the last thing Billy wants. He hopes that by now Nick has started to relax.

Once the stores are open, he and Alice go to the nearest Ulta Beauty. This time he's the one who needs makeup, but he lets Alice do the buying. After that she wants to go to a casino. It's a bad idea, but she looks so excited and hopeful that he can't say no. 'But not the big hotels and not the Strip,' he says.

Alice consults her phone and directs them to Big Tommy's Hotel and Gambling Hall in East Las Vegas. She's carded before she's allowed in and flashes her new Elizabeth Anderson DL with aplomb. As she wanders around, gawking at the roulette, craps, blackjack, and the ever-spinning Money Wheel, Billy checks around him for guys with a certain look. He doesn't see any. Most of them out here in the boonies are moms and pops that could stand to lose a few.

He reflects again that Alice is a different girl from the one he brought in out of the pouring rain. On the way to being a better girl, and if what he's planning goes wrong and she's damaged more than she has been already, that's on him. He thinks, I should just quit this shit and take her back to Colorado. Then he remembers Nick pitching him on the so-called 'safe house,' all the time knowing the ride to Wisconsin was going to last about six miles until Dana Edison put a bullet in his head. Nick needs to pay. And he needs to meet the real Billy Summers.

'It's so *noisy*!' Alice says. Her cheeks are bright and her eyes are trying to look everywhere at once. 'What should I do?'

After checking out the roulette table, Billy guides her there and buys her fifty dollars' worth of chips, all the while telling himself bad idea, bad idea. Her beginner's luck is phenomenal. In ten minutes she's up two hundred dollars and people are cheering her on. Billy doesn't care for that, so he guides her to a bank of five-dollar slots where she spends half an hour and wins another thirty bucks. Then she turns to him and says, 'Push the button and look, push the button and look, rinse and repeat. It's kinda stupid, isn't it?'

Billy shrugs but can't help smiling. He remembers Robin Maguire saying it's only a grin when your teeth show, and then it's nothing else.

'You said it, not me,' he says. And shows his teeth.

7

After the casino they go to the Century 16 and see not one movie but two, a comedy and an action flick. When they come out of that one, it's almost dark.

'How about something to eat?' Alice asks.

'Happy to stop somewhere if you want, but I'm full of popcorn and Sour Patch Kids.'

'Maybe just a sandwich. Want to hear something nice about my mom?'

'Sure.'

'Every now and then, if I was good, we'd have what she called a special day. I could have pancakes with chocolate chips for breakfast and then do almost anything I wanted, like have an egg cream at the Green Line Apothecary, or get a stuffed animal – if it was cheap – or ride the bus to the end of the line, which I liked to do. Stupid kid, huh?'

'No,' Billy says.

She takes his hand, natural as anything, and swings it back and forth as they walk to the truck. 'This day has been like that. Special.'

'Good.'

Alice turns to him. 'You better not get killed.' She sounds absolutely fierce. 'You just better not.'

'I won't,' Billy says. 'Okay?'

'Okay,' she agrees. 'All okay.'

8

But that night she isn't. Billy is sleeping just below the surface of wakefulness, or he never would have heard Alice's knock. It's light and tentative, almost not there at all. For a moment or two he thinks it's part of the dream he's having, something about Shanice Ackerman, then he's back to the motel room on the outskirts of Vegas. He gets up, goes to the door, and looks through the peephole. She's standing there in the baggy blue pajamas she bought on her shopping trip with Bucky. Her feet are bare and her hand is at her throat and he can hear her gasping. The gasping is louder than her knock was.

He opens up, takes her by the hand that's not clasping her throat, and leads her into the room. As he closes the door he sings, 'If you go down to the woods today . . . sing it with me, Alice.'

She shakes her head and tears in another breath. '—can't—'

'Yes you can. If you go down to the woods today . . .'

'You better go . . .' *Whoop.* '. . . in dis . . . dis . . .' *Whoop!*

She's swaying on her feet, close to fainting. Billy thinks it's a wonder she didn't pass out in the hall.

He gives her a shake. 'Nope, that's wrong. Try again. Next line.'

'You're sure of a big surprise?' She's still gasping but looks a little less likely to collapse.

'Right. Now let's do it together. And don't talk it, sing it. If you go down to the woods today . . .'

She joins him. 'You're sure of a big surprise. If you go down to the woods today you better go in disguise.' She pulls in a deep breath and lets it out in a series of jerks: *huh . . . huh . . . huh.* 'Need to sit down.'

'Before you fall down,' Billy agrees. He still has her hand. He leads her to the chair by the window, the drape now drawn.

She sits, looks up at him, brushes her newly blonde hair off her forehead. 'I tried in my room and it didn't work. Why did it work now?'

'You needed someone to duet with.' Billy sits on the edge of the bed. 'What was it? Bad dream?'

'Horrible. One of those boys . . . those *men* . . . was stuffing a dishrag in my mouth. To make me stop yelling. Or maybe I was screaming. I think it was Jack. I couldn't breathe. I was sure I was going to choke to death.'

'Did they do that?'

Alice shakes her head. 'I don't remember.'

But Billy knows they did, and she does, too. He has experienced this sort of thing himself, although not as badly or as often as some. He didn't keep up with the jars he knew in Iraq – Johnny Capps was the exception – but there are websites and sometimes he checks them out.

'It's natural, how the minds of combat survivors deal with the trauma. Or try to.'

'Is that what I am? A combat survivor?'

'That's what you are. The song may not work every time. A wet cloth across your face may not work every time. There are other tricks to getting through panic attacks, you can read about them on the Internet. Sometimes, though, you just have to wait it out.'

'I thought I was better,' Alice whispers.

'You are. But you're also under stress.' And I put you there, Billy thinks.

'Can I stay here tonight? With you?'

He almost tells her no, then looks at her pale pleading face and thinks again, I put you there.

'Okay.' He wishes he was wearing more than just a pair of loose boxers, but they will have to do.

She gets in and he gets in next to her. They lie on their backs. The bed is narrow and their hips touch. He looks up at the ceiling and thinks, I am not going to get an erection. Which is like telling a dog not to chase a cat. Their legs are also touching. Hers is warm and firm through the cotton. He hasn't been with a woman since Phil and he doesn't want to be with this one, but oh God.

'Can I help you?' Her voice is quiet but not timid. 'I can't make love to you . . . you know, the real way . . . but I could help you. I'd be glad to help you.'

'No, Alice. Thank you, but no.'

'Are you sure?'

'Yes.'

'All right.' She rolls on her side, away from him and toward the wall.

Billy waits until her breathing grows long and mild and steady. Then he goes in the bathroom and helps himself.

9

Days go by, just a few, almost like a vacation, and then it's almost time. There's a Target down the road, and after breakfast they shop there. Alice buys a big plastic jug of moisturizer and a spray bottle. Also bathing suits. Hers is a modest blue tank. His are billowy trunks with tropical fish on them. She also buys him a pair of pre-washed bib overalls, yellow work gloves, a denim barn coat, and a T-shirt with a very Vegas slogan on it.

They swim in the motel pool, which they discover is the best part of their current accommodation. Alice plays water volleyball with some kids while Billy lies on a chaise, watching. It all feels natural. They could be a father and daughter on their way to Los Angeles, maybe looking for work, maybe looking for relatives they can touch up for a long-term loan or a place to stay.

The motel clerk was right about the buffet – it's heavy on mac and cheese and prehistoric roast beef *au jus* – but after almost two hours in the pool, Alice eats everything on her heaped plate and goes back for more. Billy can't keep up with her, although there was a time – basic training, for instance – when he could have eaten her under the table. After lunch, she says she wants a nap. Billy isn't surprised.

Around four o'clock they go shopping again, this time at a farm-and-garden store called Grow Baby Grow. Alice's great mood of the morning has darkened, but she makes no effort to change his mind about the next day. Billy is grateful. Persuasion might lead to argument and arguing with Alice is the last thing he wants. Not on what could be their last day together.

When they park at the motel, Billy reaches into his back pocket and brings out a folded piece of paper. He unfolds it, smooths it gently, and then attaches it to the dashboard with Scotch tape from Target. Alice looks at the little girl hugging the pink flamingo.

'Who is that?'

Shanice's careful crayon work has blurred a little, but the hearts rising from the flamingo's noddy head to Shanice's are still clear enough. Billy touches one of them. 'The little girl who lived next door to me in Midwood. But tomorrow she's going to be my daughter. If I need her to be.'

10

Billy trusts people not to steal, but only so far. The old tools and dirty barrels are safe enough, but someone might see the stuff they bought at Grow Baby Grow and decide to filch some, so they carry the bags inside and store them in Billy's bathroom. There are four 50-pound sacks of Miracle-Gro potting soil, five 10-pound sacks of Buckaroo Worm Castings, and a 25-pound sack of Black Kow fertilizer.

Alice lets Billy tote the Black Kow. She wrinkles her nose and says she can smell it even through the bag.

They watch TV in her room and she asks him if he will stay the night with her. Billy says it would be better if he didn't.

'I don't think I can sleep alone,' Alice says.

'I don't think I can, either, but we're both going to try. Come here. Give me a hug.'

She gives him a good one. He can feel her trembling, not because she's afraid of him but because she's afraid for him. She doesn't deserve to be afraid at all, but if she has to be, Billy thinks, this way is better. A lot.

'Set your phone alarm for six,' he says when he lets her go.

'I won't have to.'

He smiles. 'Do it anyway. You might surprise yourself.'

In his room next door, he texts Bucky: **Have you heard anything about N?**

Bucky's reply is immediate. **No. He's probably there but I don't know for sure. Sorry.**

It's okay, Billy texts back, then sets his own phone alarm for five. He doesn't expect to sleep, either, but *he* might surprise himself.

He does, a little, and dreams of Shanice. She's tearing up the picture of Dave the Flamingo and saying *I hate you I hate you I hate you*.

He wakes up at four, and when he goes outside with the new gloves in one hand, Alice is sitting in the eternal motel lawn chair, bundled up in an I LOVE LAS VEGAS sweatshirt and looking up at a rind of moon.

'Hey,' Billy says.

'Hey.'

He goes to the edge of the cement walk and scrubs the new gloves in the dirt. When he's satisfied that they look right, he claps the dust off them and stands up.

'Cold,' Alice says. 'That will be good for you. You can wear the coat.'

Billy knows it will warm up fast once the sun rises. It may be October, but this is the desert. He'll wear the barn coat anyway.

'You want something to eat? Egg McMuffin? The Mickey D's down the road is twenty-four-hour.'

She shakes her head. 'Not hungry.'

'Coffee?'

'Sure, that would be great.'

'Cream and sugar?'

'Black, please.'

He goes down to the deserted lobby and gets them each a cup from the eternal motel Bunn. When he comes back, she's still looking at the moon. 'It looks close enough to reach out and touch. Isn't it beautiful?'

'It is, but you're shivering. Let's go inside.'

She sits in his chair by the window and sips her coffee, then sets it on the little table and falls asleep. The sweatshirt is too big and the neck slips to the side, baring one shoulder. Billy thinks it's at least as beautiful as the moon. He sits and drinks his coffee and watches her. He likes her long slow breaths. The time passes. It's got a knack for that, Billy thinks.

11

When he wakes her up at seven-thirty she scolds him for letting her sleep. 'We need to get you sprayed up. That goo takes at least four hours to work.'

'It's okay. The game starts at one and I'm not going to move on him until at least one-thirty.'

'Still, I wish we'd done this an hour ago, just to be safe.' She sighs. 'Come in my room. We'll do it there.'

A few minutes later his shirt is off and he's rubbing moisturizer over his hands, forearms, and face. She tells him not to neglect his eyelids and the back of his neck. When he's done, she goes to work with the tanning spray. The first coat takes five minutes. When she's done, he goes into the bathroom and takes a look. What he sees is a white man with a desert tan.

'Not good enough,' he says.

'I know. Moisturize again.'

She uses the spray a second time. When he goes into the bathroom for another look it's better, but he's still not satisfied. 'I don't know,' he tells Alice when he comes out. 'This might have been a bad idea.'

'It's not. Remember what I said? For the next four to six hours, it will continue to darken. With the cowboy hat and the bib overalls . . .'

She gives him a critical look. 'If I didn't think you could pass for Chicano, I'd tell you.'

This is where she asks me again to just give it up and come back to Colorado with her, Billy thinks. But she doesn't. She tells him to get dressed in what she calls 'your costume.' Billy goes back to his room and puts on the dark wig, T-shirt, bib overalls, barn coat (work gloves stuffed in the pockets), and the battered cowboy hat Bucky and Alice bought in Boulder. It comes down to his ears and he reminds himself to raise it up a little when the time comes, to show that long black hair streaked with gray.

'You look fine.' All business, red-rimmed eyes notwithstanding. 'Got your pad and pencil?'

He pats the front pocket of the biballs. It's capacious, with plenty of room for the silenced Ruger as well as the writing stuff.

'You're getting darker already.' She smiles wanly. 'Good thing the PC Police aren't here.'

'Needs must,' Billy says. He reaches into the side pocket of the biballs, the one that doesn't hold the Glock 17, and brings out a roll of bills. It's everything he has left except for a couple of twenties. 'Take this. Call it insurance.'

Alice pockets it without argument.

'If you don't get a call from me this afternoon, wait. I have no idea what kind of cell coverage they have north of here. If I'm not back by eight tonight, nine at the outside, I'm not coming back. Stay the night, then check out and get a Greyhound to Golden or Estes Park. Call Bucky. He'll pick you up. All right?'

'That would not be all right, but I understand. Let me help you carry those bags of fertilizer out to the truck.'

They make two trips and then Billy slams the tailgate. They stand there looking at each other. A few sleepy-eyed people – a couple of salesmen, a family – are toting out their luggage and preparing to move on.

'If you don't need to be there until one, you can stay another hour,' she says. 'Two, even.'

'I think I better go now.'

'Yeah, maybe you better,' Alice says. 'Before I break down.'

He hugs her. Alice hugs back fiercely. He expects her to say be careful. He expects her to tell him again not to die. He expects her to ask him one more time, maybe plead with him, not to go. She doesn't. She looks up at him and says, '*Get what's yours.*'

She lets go of him and walks back toward the motel. When she gets there, she turns to him and holds up her phone. 'Call me when you're done. Don't forget.'

'I won't.'

If I can, he thinks. I will if I can.

CHAPTER 20

1

An hour north of Vegas on Route 45, Billy comes to a Dougie's Donuts mated to an ARCO gas station and a convenience store with the unlikely name of Terrible Herbst. It's a truck stop surrounded by great expanses of parking, big rigs on one side snoring like sleeping beasts. Billy gasses up, grabs a bottle of orange juice and a cruller, then parks around back. He thinks about calling Alice, only because he'd like to hear her voice and thinks she might like to hear his. My hostage, he thinks. My Stockholm Syndrome hostage. Only that's not what she is now, if she ever was. He remembers how she said *Get what's yours*. Not fearless, she hasn't morphed into some comic book warrior queen (at least not yet), but plenty fierce. He has his phone in his hand before remembering she got as little sleep as he did last night. If she's gone back to bed with the DO NOT DISTURB sign hanging on the door, he doesn't want to wake her.

He drinks his juice and eats his cruller and lets the time pass. There's enough of it for doubts to creep in. In some ways – many, actually – it's like the Funhouse all over again, only with no squad to back him up. He can't be sure Nick went to Promontory Point for the weekend. He has no idea how many men he may have brought back with him if he did. Some for sure, not bounty hunters from some other outfit but his own guys, and Billy has no idea where they might be placed. He has an idea of the interior layout from the Zillow photographs, but there might have been changes made after Nick bought the place. If Nick *is* there, rooting on the Giants, Billy doesn't know where he'll be watching. He doesn't even know if he can get in through the service entrance. Maybe *sí*, maybe *no*.

There's a line of Porta-Johns, and he uses one to offload his coffee and juice. When he comes out, a black chick in a halter and a denim skirt short enough to show the edges of her panties is standing nearby. She looks like she's been up all night and the night was a hard one. The mascara around her eyes reminds Billy – *dumb self* Billy – of the Beagle Boys in the old Donald Duck and Uncle Scrooge comics he sometimes picks up at rummage and yard sales.

'Hey, good-looking man,' the lot lizard says. 'Want to date me?'

This is as good a chance as any to try out his cover story. He takes his pad and pencil from the front pocket of his biballs and writes *mi es sordo y mudo.*

'What the fuck does that mean?'

Billy touches his ears with both hands, then pats his mouth with the other.

'Forget it,' she says, turning away. 'I ain't sucking no wetback cock.'

Billy watches her go, delighted. No wetback cock, huh? he thinks. Doesn't exactly make me John Howard Griffin, but I'll take it.

2

He stays parked behind the donut shop until eleven. During that time he sees the black chick and a few of her co-workers chatting up truck drivers, but none of them come near him. Which is fine with Billy. Every now and then he gets out of the truck, pretending to check his goods, actually just wanting to stretch his legs and stay loose.

At quarter past eleven he starts up the truck (the starter doesn't catch at first, giving him a scare) and continues north on 45. The Paiute Foothills draw closer. From five miles out he can see Promontory Point. It's different from the house Nick rented in the city where Billy did his job, but every bit as ugly.

As his GPS is informing him that his turn onto Cherokee Drive is a mile ahead, Billy comes to another rest area, this one just a turnout. He parks in the shade and uses another Porta-John, thinking of Taco Bell's dictum: *Never neglect a chance to piss before a firefight.*

When he comes out, he checks his watch. Twelve-thirty. In his big white hacienda, Nick is probably settling in to watch the pregame show with a couple of his hardballs. Maybe eating nachos and drinking Dos Equis. Billy punches up Siri, who tells him he's forty minutes from his destination. He forces himself to wait a little longer and forces himself not to call Alice. Instead he gets out, grabs a crowbar from one of the dirty barrels, and punches a couple of holes in the Ram's muffler, which is already distressed. If he comes up to the service entrance with his old truck farting and backing off, so much the more in character.

'Okay,' Billy says. He thinks of giving the Darkhorse chant and tells himself not to be ridiculous. Besides, the last time they all chanted that, their hands in the huddle, things didn't work out so well. He turns the key. The starter spins and spins. When it starts to lag, he clicks it off, waits, gives the gas pedal a single pump, then tries again. The Dodge fires right up. It was loud before. It's louder now.

Billy checks for traffic, merges onto 45, then turns off at Cherokee Drive. The grade grows steeper. For the first mile or so there are other, more modest houses on either side of the road, but then they're gone and there's only Promontory Point, looming ahead of him.

I was always coming here, Billy thinks, and tries to laugh at the thought, which is not just omenish but pretentious. The thought won't go, and Billy understands that's because it's a true thought. He was always coming here. Yes.

3

The air is bell-clear outside the smog bowl of Las Vegas, and maybe even has a slight magnifying effect, because by the time Billy is closing in on the compound's main gate the house looks like it's rearing back so it won't fall on him. The wall is too high to see over, but he knows there's a lookout post just inside and if it's manned, his old beater is probably already on video.

Cherokee Drive ends at Promontory Point. Before it does, a dirt track splits off to the left. There are two signs flanking this track. The one on the left says MAINTENANCE & DELIVERY. The other says AUTHORIZED VEHICLES ONLY. ONLY is in red.

Billy turns onto the track, not neglecting to set his hat a little higher on his head. He also pats the front pocket of the overalls (silenced

Ruger) and side pocket (Glock). Sighting the guns in would be a joke, handguns are really only good for close work, but he realizes he hasn't test-fired either of them or examined the loads. It would be a fine joke on him if he had to use the Glock and it jammed. Or if the Ruger's silencer, maybe made in the garage of some guy with a taste for meth, plugged the gun's barrel and caused it to blow up in his hand. Too late to worry about any of that now.

The compound's wall is on his right. On the left, piñons grow close enough for their branches to thwap the sides of his truck. Billy can imagine bigger vehicles – trash haulers, propane gas delivery, a septic pumper – waddling their way along, their drivers cursing a blue streak every time they have to make this trip.

Then the wall makes a right angle turn and the trees end. The 20-degree grade does, too. He's now on a plateau, probably bulldozed flat especially for the house and grounds. The maintenance road loops out, then curves back toward the much humbler gate Billy is looking for. Beyond the wall he can see the upper fifteen feet or so of the barn, painted rustic red. The roof is metal, heliographing the sun. Billy keeps his eyes off it after one quick look, not wanting to compromise his vision.

The gate is open. There are flowerbeds on either side of it. There's a security camera mounted on the wall, but it's hanging down like a bird with a broken neck. Billy likes it. He thought Nick might be relaxing, letting down his guard a bit, and here's proof.

In the flowerbed on the left, a Mexican woman in a big blue dress is down on her knees, digging in the dirt with a trowel. A wicker basket half-filled with cut flowers is nearby. Her yellow gloves might have been purchased in the same place Billy bought his. She's wearing a straw sombrero so big it's comical. Her back is to him at first, but when she hears the truck – how can she miss it? – she turns to look and Billy sees she's not Mexican at all. Her skin is tanned and leathery, but she's Anglo. An old lady Anglo, at that.

She gets to her feet and stands in front of the truck with her feet spread, blocking the way forward. She only moves to the driver's side when Billy slows to a stop and powers down the window.

'Who the fuck are you and what do you want?' And then, another good thing to go with the broken security camera: '*Qué deseas?*'

Billy holds up a finger – wait one – and takes the pad from the front pocket of his biballs. For a moment he blanks, but then it comes to him and he writes *Estos son para el jardín*. These are for the garden.

'Got it, but what are you doing here on Sunday? Talk to me, Pedro.'

He flips a page and writes *mi es sordo y mudo*. I am a deafmute.

'You are, huh? Do you understand English?' Moving her lips with exaggerated care.

Her eyes, dark blue in her narrow face, are studying him. Two things come to Billy. The first is that Nick may have let his guard down . . . but not all the way. The security camera is broken and his guys may be in the house watching the football game with him, but this woman is here with her trowel and her basket of blooms. Maybe that's what his old friend Robin used to call a coinkydink, but maybe it's not, because there's a bottle of water and a sandwich wrapped in waxed paper in the shade of a nearby tree. Which suggests she might be meaning to stay for awhile. Maybe until the game is over and she's relieved.

That's one thing. The other is she looks familiar. Goddamned if she doesn't.

She reaches into the cab and snaps her fingers in front of his nose. They stink of cigarettes. '*Lo entiendes?*'

Billy holds his thumb and forefinger a smidgen apart to indicate that yes, he understands, but only a little.

'Bet if I asked to see your green card, you'd be shit out of luck.' She gives a laugh as raspy as her speaking voice. 'So why you here on Sunday, *mi amigo?*'

Billy shrugs and then points at the barn looming over the wall.

'Yeah, I didn't think you came for tea and cookies. What have you got to put in the barn? Show me.'

Billy likes this less and less. Partly because she could look in the truckbed herself and see the bags of gardening stuff, mostly because of that troubling sense that he's seen her before. Which can't be true. She's too old to be one of Nick's guard dogs, and he'd never hire a woman for that kind of job anyway. He's old-school and she's just old, a domestic they shoved out here to keep an eye on the service gate while they watch the game, and she decided to pass the time by cutting some flowers for the house. But he still doesn't like it.

'*Ándale, ándale!*' More finger-snapping in front of his face. Billy doesn't like that, either, although her assumption of superiority – her very Trumpian prejudice, if you like – is another sign that his disguise is working.

Billy gets out, leaving the door open, and walks her to the back of the truck. She ignores that and goes on to the little trailer. She looks in the barrels, gives a disdainful sniff, then comes back to look in the truckbed. 'How come you've only got one bag of Black Kow? What good is that gonna do?'

Billy shrugs that he doesn't understand.

The woman stands on tiptoes and slaps the bag. Her sombrero flops. 'Only one! One! *Solo uno!*'

Billy shrugs that he's only the delivery guy.

She sighs and flicks a hand at him. 'Well, what the fuck. Go on. I'm not going to call Hector on Sunday afternoon and ask him why he sends a deafmute out to deliver a piddling load of shit, he's probably watching the fucking game, too. Or a different one.'

Billy shrugs that he still doesn't *entender*.

'Take that crap in. *Tómalo!* Then fuck off to the nearest *cantina*, maybe you'll be in time for the second half.'

That is when he should have known. Something in her eyes. But he doesn't. He only gets lucky. He sees her coming in the driver's side mirror as he climbs into the cab and slides behind the wheel. He pulls back just in time, dipping his shoulder, and the trowel only scrapes his upper arm below the T-shirt he's wearing under the overalls. He slams the door, catching her arm in it, and the trowel drops to the floorboards beside his left foot.

'*Ow, fuck!*'

She pulls her arm free so fast and hard that it flies up and knocks off the sombrero, revealing gray hair piled high and pinned that way. That's when Billy understands where he's seen her before.

She's reaching into one of the big side pockets of her gardening dress. Billy gets out of the truck in a hurry and roundhouses her on the left side of her face. She goes sprawling on her back in the flower-bed. The thing she was reaching for falls out of her pocket. It's a cell phone. It's the first time in his life he's hit a woman and when he sees the bruise rising on her cheek he thinks of Alice but doesn't regret the blow. It could have been a gun.

And she recognized him. Not at first but yeah, she did. Covered it up well, too, until the end. So much for the biballs, tanning spray, wig, and cowboy hat. So much for Shan's picture taped to the dashboard, the one he could write (with a fatherly smile of pride) was his daughter's work. Was it because the woman has seen and studied his picture as well as meeting him once in Red Bluff? Or because she's a woman and they tend to see past disguises quicker? That could be sexist bullshit, but Billy kind of doubts it.

'You fucking fuck. You're him.'

He thinks, She seemed so nice at Nick's rented house. Almost refined. Of course then she was in serving mode. He remembers now that Nick gave her a wad of cash for Alan, the chef who lit up their Baked Alaska, but none for her. Because she was on the payroll. She was, in fact, family. Pretty funny.

She looks dazed, but that could be another shuck and jive. Either way he's glad the trowel is in the truck. He puts an arm around her shoulders and helps her sit. Her cheek is puffing up like a balloon, making him think of Alice again, but Alice never looked at him like this woman is looking at him now. If looks could kill, and all that.

With the hand not supporting her, Billy takes the Ruger out of his coat pocket and presses the muzzle lightly against her wrinkled forehead. Frank Macintosh is known (never to his face) as Frankie Elvis, sometimes Solar Elvis. Hair piled up high in front, like hers. Same hair, same narrow face, same widow's peak. Billy thinks he might have made the connection sooner and saved himself a lot of trouble, if not for the oversized sombrero.

'Hello, Marge. You're not as polite as you were when you were serving us our dinner that night.'

'You fucking traitor,' she says, and spits in his face.

Billy feels a well-nigh insurmountable urge to hit her again, but not because she spat on him. He arms it off his face, leaving her to support herself. She looks perfectly able to do so. She may be in her seventies and a lifelong smoker, but there's no quit in her, Billy has to give her that much.

'You've got it backwards. Nick's the fucking traitor. I did the job and instead of paying me he stiffed me and planned to kill me.'

'Nick would never do that. He stands up for his people.'

That might be true, Billy thinks, but I'm not one of them and never was. I'm your basic independent contractor.

'Let's not argue, Marge. Time is tight.'

'I think you broke my fucking arm.'

'And you tried to open up my jugular vein. As far as I'm concerned that makes us even. How many men are in there watching the game?'

She doesn't answer.

'Is Frank in there?'

She doesn't reply, but the flicker he sees in those dark eyes tells him what he needs to know. He picks up her cell phone, knocks off the dirt, and holds it out to her. 'Call him and tell him a guy from Greens & Gardens is dropping off some fertilizer and potting soil. Nothing to worry about. Say—'

'No.'

'Say you told the guy to go ahead and put it in the barn.'

'No.'

Billy has lowered the muzzle of the Ruger. Now he puts it back between her eyes. 'Tell him, Marge.'

'No.'

'Tell him or I'll blow your brains out, then Frank's.'

She spits in his face again. At least tries to, there isn't much to it. Because her mouth is dry, Billy thinks. She's scared, but she's still not going to do it. Even if she does, she'll either tip them off by how she sounds or just go whole hog and scream *It's him, it's that fucking fuck of a traitor Billy Summers.*

Helpless not to think of Alice but reminding himself this isn't her and never could be, he hits Marge in the temple. Her eyes roll up to whites and she flops back into the flowers. He stands over her for a minute to make sure she's still breathing, then tosses her phone into the truck. He starts to get in himself, then re-thinks and dumps the cut flowers out of her basket. Under them is a walkie-talkie and a short-barreled .357 King Cobra revolver. So she wasn't just gardening. And they didn't just put her out here as an afterthought. This one's got a lot of hard bark on her. He tosses the gun and the walkie in the truck.

The starter turns over without catching for ten long seconds and Billy thinks why now, oh Lord, why now. At last the engine fires up and he drives onto the estate. He stops ten feet inside the wall, leaving the truck in neutral, and closes the gate. There's a huge steel bolt. He runs it through the double catch and heads back to the truck, which is bellowing through its perforated muffler. Doing that seemed like a good idea at the time. Not so much now.

As he climbs into the cab, Marge Macintosh starts pounding on the gate and shouting. *'Hey! Hey! It's Summers! It's Summers in the truck!'* Billy can't believe anyone could hear her even if the Dodge's muffler was intact, but he's amazed by her vitality. He hit her as hard as he could and she's already back for more.

Except you *didn't* hit her as hard as you could, he thinks. You thought of Alice and held back a little.

Too late now and he doesn't think it matters. She'd have to run all the way around the wall, shoving her way through the pines, to alert anyone in the little guardhouse by the main gate . . . assuming anyone is actually in there.

And of course there is. As Billy drives past the barn and the paddock, a guy comes out. He's got a rifle or a shotgun but for the time being it's slung over his shoulder. He looks relaxed. He raises his hands to his shoulders with the palms out: *Qué pasa?*

Instead of heading toward the house as he had intended, Billy reaches out the driver's side window, gives the guy a thumbs-up, and turns down the main driveway toward the guardhouse.

He pulls up. The guy walks toward him with the gun – it's a Mossberg – still slung over his shoulder. Billy realizes he knows him. Billy has never been here, but he's been in Nick's penthouse suite at the Double Domino three or four times, and on a couple of them this guy was there. Sal something. But unlike Frank's sharp-eyed mother, Sal doesn't recognize him.

'What's up, partner?' he says. 'Old lady let you through?'

'She did.' Billy makes no attempt at a Spanish accent, he'd sound like Speedy fucking Gonzalez. 'I got something for someone to sign. Can you do it?'

'I don't know,' Sal says. He's starting to look troubled. Billy thinks, too late, amigo, too late. 'Let's see what you got.'

Billy's deafmute pad is sticking up from the front pocket of his overalls. He pats it and says, 'It's right here.'

He reaches past the pad and grabs Don Jensen's Ruger. For a wonder it comes out smoothly, even with the bulb-shaped silencer on the end. He fires. A hole appears between two of the pearl buttons up the front of Sal's Western-style shirt. There's a bursting balloon sound and wouldn't you know it, the silencer falls in two smoking pieces, one half on the ground and the other in the cab.

'You shot me!' Sal says, staggering back a step. His eyes are wide.

Billy doesn't want to shoot the guy again because the second one will be a lot noisier, and he doesn't have to. Sal folds up, knees on the ground and head lowered. He looks like he's praying. Then he falls forward.

Billy thinks about taking the Mossberg but decides to leave it. As he told Marge, time is tight.

4

He drives up to the main house. There are three cars parked on the apron, a sedan, a compact SUV, and a Lamborghini that must belong to Nick. Billy remembers Bucky saying Nick has a thing for cars. Billy turns off the noisy truck and walks up the main steps. He has his deafmute pad in one hand. He's holding the Glock behind it. He just killed a man, and Sal was probably a bad guy who has done many bad things at Nick's behest, but Billy doesn't know that for a fact. Now he will kill more, assuming he doesn't get killed himself. He'll think about it later. If there is any later.

He puts his finger on the bell, then hesitates. Suppose a woman comes to the door? If that happens, Billy doesn't think he'll be able to shoot her. Even if everything turns to shit as a result, he doesn't believe he'll be able to. He'd like a chance to go around the house instead, scope it out a little, but there's no time. Mommy Elvis is on the warpath.

He tries the door. It opens. Billy is surprised but not shocked. Nick has decided he's not coming. Also it's Sunday afternoon, the sun is out, and it's football day in America. Billy believes the Giants have just scored. The crowd is whooping and so are several men. Not close but not far away.

Billy puts the pad back in the front pocket of the overalls and walks toward the sound. Then, just what he was afraid of. Down the main hall comes a pretty little Latina maid with a tray of steaming franks in buns balanced on top of an Igloo cooler that's probably full of beer. Billy has time to think of an old Chuck Berry lyric, *She's too cute to be a minute over seventeen.* She sees Billy, she sees the gun, her mouth opens, the Igloo tilts, the tray of franks starts to slide. Billy pushes it back to safety.

'Go,' he says, and points at the open door. 'Take that and get out of here. Go far.'

She doesn't say a word. Carrying the tray, she walks down the hall and out into the sunlight. Her posture, Billy thinks, is perfect and the sunlight on her black hair suggests that God may not be all bad. She goes down the steps, back straight and head up. She doesn't look back. The crowd cheers. The men watching do, too. Someone shouts, *'Fuck 'em up, Big Blue!'*

Billy walks partway down the tiled corridor. Between two Georgia O'Keeffe prints – mesas on one side, mountains on the other – a door is standing open. Through the gap between the hinges, Billy can see stairs going down. There's a commercial on for beer. Billy stands behind the open door, waiting for it to end, wanting their attention back on the game.

Then, Nick, from the foot of the stairs: 'Maria! Where are those dogs?' When there's no answer: 'Maria! Hurry up!'

Someone says, 'I'll go see.' Billy isn't sure, but it sounds like Frank.

Footsteps thumping up the stairs. Someone comes out into the hall and turns left, presumably toward the kitchen. It's Frank, all right. Billy recognizes him even with his back turned: the pomp trying to cover the solar sex panel. Billy steps out from behind the door and follows him, walking on the sides of his feet, glad he wore sneakers. Frank goes into the kitchen and looks around.

'Maria? Where are you, honey? We need—'

Billy hits him in the bald spot with the butt of the Glock, raising it high and giving it everything he has. Blood flies and Frank collapses forward, smacking his forehead on the butcher block table in the middle of the room on his way down. His mother's head was hard, and maybe Frank has inherited that from her along with the widow's peak, but Billy doesn't think he's coming back from this. Not for awhile, anyway, and maybe never. Guys are always getting clonked on the head in films and getting up a few minutes later with little or no damage done, but that's not the way it works in real life. Frank Macintosh could die of a cerebral edema or a subdural hematoma. It could happen five minutes from now or he could linger in a coma for five years. He might also come back sooner, but probably not before Billy finishes his day's work. Still, he bends and frisks him. No gun.

Billy walks quietly back down the hall. The game must have resumed, because the crowd is roaring again. One of the men down there in Nick's man-cave yells, *'Fucking clothesline him! Yeah! That's what I'm TALKIN' about!'*

Billy descends the stairs, not fast and not slow. Three men are watching a TV screen that's beyond big. Two of them are in bucket chairs. A third bucket chair – probably Frank's – is empty. Nick is sitting in the middle of the couch with his legs spread. He's wearing shorts that are too short, too tight, and too loud. His belly is bulging out the front of a New York Giants shirt and supporting a bowl of popcorn. The other two also have popcorn bowls, which is good because it keeps their hands occupied. Billy knows both of them. One he's seen in Nick's suite and in the Domino's main offices. An accountant, maybe, a numbers guy for sure. Billy doesn't remember his name, Mikey or Mickey or maybe Markie. The other was one of the fake Department of Public Works guys with the Transit van. Reggie something.

'Well it took you long enough,' Nick says. The other two have seen Billy, but Nick only has eyes for the play in progress on the television. 'Just set it on the—'

He finally registers the shocked expressions of his companions, turns his head, and sees Billy standing two steps from the carpeted floor. The look of fear and amazement that dawns on Nick's face gives Billy a great deal of satisfaction. It isn't payback for the last five months of his life, not even close, but it's a step in the right direction.

'Billy?' The bowl balanced on Nick's stomach overturns and popcorn goes pattering to the rug.

'Hello, Nick. You're probably not glad to see me, but I'm glad to see you.' He gestures with the Glock at the accountant guy, who has already raised his hands. 'What's your name?'

'M-Mark. Mark Abromowitz.'

'Get down on the floor, Mark. You too, Reggie. On your stomachs. Arms and legs spread. Like you're making snow angels.'

They don't argue. They set aside their popcorn bowls – carefully – and get down on the floor.

'I've got a family,' Mark Abromowitz says.

'That's good. Behave yourself and you'll see them again. Are either of you armed?' He doesn't have to ask about Nick, because in that ridiculous game-day outfit he's got no place for a hidden weapon, not even an ankle gun.

The two men, face down, shake their heads.

Nick says Billy's name again, this time not as a question but as an exclamation of delight. He's striving for his old lord of the manor *bonhomie* and not finding very much of it. 'Where the hell have you been? I've been trying to get in touch with you!'

Billy wouldn't bother to answer this ridiculous lie even if he didn't have a more pressing concern. There's a fourth chair, and a half-empty bowl of popcorn beside it.

'*They keep it on the ground with Barkley,*' the play-by-play announcer is saying, '*with Jones leading the way, and—*'

'Turn it off,' Billy says. Nick is king of the house and king of the couch, so of course the controller is beside him.

'What?'

'You heard me, turn it off.'

As Nick points the remote at the television, Billy is happy to see a slight tremble in his hand. The game goes away. Now it's just the four of them, but that fourth empty chair with the popcorn bowl beside it says there's an unaccounted-for fifth.

'Where is he?' Billy asks.

'Who?'

Billy points at the empty chair.

'Billy, I have to explain why I had to wait to get in touch with you. There was a problem at my end. It—'

'Shut up.' What a pleasure to say that, and what a pleasure not to have to play dumb. 'Mark!'

The accountant jerks his legs, as if he's just had an electric shock.

'Where is he?'

Mark replies promptly, which is wise. 'He went to the bathroom.'

'Shut up, asshole,' Reggie says, and Billy shoots him in the ankle. He doesn't know he's going to do it until it's done but his aim is as good as ever and he regrets it no more than he regrets cold-cocking Frank in the kitchen. Reggie was part of the plan to get rid of dumb old Billy Summers. Get him in the back of the fake DPW van, drive him a few miles out of town, put a bullet in his head, case closed. Besides, this little man-cave trio needs to know who is in charge.

Reggie screams and rolls on his back, trying to clutch his ankle. 'You fuck! You fucking shot me!'

'Shut up or I'll shut you up. If you don't believe me, give it a try.' He turns the gun on Abromowitz, who's looking at him with bulging eyes. 'Where's the bathroom? Point.'

Abromowitz points behind the couch. Three pinball machines are lined up against the wall, their lights flashing but all the boops and beeps silenced because of the game. Just beyond them is a closed wooden door.

'Nick. Tell him to come out.'

'Come on out, Dana!'

So that's who the missing man is, Billy thinks. Reggie's DPW partner. The little redhead with the dork knob who talked smack to me in the Gerard Tower. Maybe not the guy who got rid of Ken Hoff, but Billy thinks there's a good chance that he was. Of course it's Edison, because every character in a story must be used at least twice: Dickens's rule. And Zola's.

He doesn't come out.

'Come on, Dana!' Nick calls. 'It's okay!'

No answer.

'He armed?' Billy asks Nick.

'What, are you kidding? You think when I invite friends over to watch a football game they come strapped?'

Billy says, 'I think we're going to find out about that. Nick, do your two friends there on the floor understand that I can shoot? That it's what I *do?*'

'He can shoot,' Nick says. His normal olive complexion has gone yellow. 'He learned it in the Marines. Sniper.'

'I'm going to go over to the bathroom and convince Dana to come out. I guess you can't run, Reggie, but you still could, Mr Abromowitz. Do it and I'll kill you. Same goes for you, Nick.'

'I'm not going anywhere,' Nick says. 'We'll work this out. I just have to explain why—'

Billy tells him again to shut up and goes around the couch. Nick is now back to him, an easy head shot if Billy needs to take it. Reggie and the accountant are blocked by the couch, but Reggie has a shattered ankle and he doesn't think Abromowitz the family man is going to be a problem. It's Dana Edison he's concerned with.

He stands beside the pinball machine closest to the closed door. He says, 'Come on out, Dana. If you do that, you might live. Otherwise, no.'

Billy doesn't expect a reply and doesn't get one.

'Okay, coming in.'

Like hell I am, he thinks, but he bends, reaches forward, and grabs the doorknob. The second he rattles it Edison fires four times, the shots so rapid Billy can hardly differentiate them. It's a thin door and there are no holes, only wood flying in big splinters. Billy senses movement behind him but doesn't look. Nick and Abromowitz may be on the run, but neither is going to run into Edison's field of fire to tackle him, any more than that pair of mokes would have run into the Funhouse to try and rescue Johnny Capps.

Edison will expect Billy to hesitate if he's still alive so he doesn't. He steps in front of the splintered door and pumps half a dozen rounds into it. Edison shrieks. There's a clatter and then – only reality can serve up such absurdities – the toilet flushes.

From the corner of his eye, Billy sees Abromowitz heading to the first floor in a series of gazelle-like leaps. Billy has no idea what Nick is up to but he's not following Abromowitz up the stairs and this is the wrong time to check further. He raises a foot and kicks the remains of the door beside the lock. It flies open. Dana Edison is lying across the toilet, bleeding from the head and throat. His own Glock is lying in the shower along with his little rimless spectacles. He apparently struck the toilet's flush lever when he went down. His eyes roll up to look at Billy.

'Doc . . . tor . . .'

Billy looks at the blood spilling down the side of the toilet. A doctor isn't going to help Dana. Dana has bought that place they call the farm. Billy bends over him, gun in hand. 'Do you remember the last thing you said to me when you came to my office in the Gerard Tower?'

Edison makes a hoarse huffing sound. A spray of blood comes out with it.

'I do.' Billy puts the muzzle of the Glock against Edison's temple. 'You said "Don't miss."'

He pulls the trigger.

5

When he comes out Reggie is on his knees in front of the couch. Billy can see the top of his head. He sees Billy and raises a small silver pistol that must have been stashed under one of the cushions. Nick wasn't unarmed after all. Billy puts two rounds through the back of the couch before Reggie can fire and Reggie flops backward out of sight. Billy goes to the couch in three running steps and peers over. Reggie is on his back, the gun on the rug beside one of his outstretched hands. His eyes are open and starting to glaze.

You should have settled for the shattered ankle, Billy thinks. Doctors might have been able to fix that.

Something falls over deeper in the man-cave. Glass shatters and there's a curse – 'M'qifsh Karin!' Billy hurries that way, bent low. The lights in the area beyond the TV room are off, but Billy can see Nick in the gloom. His back is turned. He's pushing buttons on a lighted keypad beside a steel door. There's a billiards table in this adjoining room, and a few vintage slot machines, and a rolling bar that's lying on its side in a glitter of broken glass and the eye-watering smell of spilled whiskey.

Nick stabs frantically at the buttons, still cursing in Albanian or whatever language he learned as a child and has otherwise forgotten. He only stops when Billy tells him to quit it and turn around.

Nick does as he's told. He looks like a man on the precipice of death, which is fair because that's where he is. But he's smiling. Just a little, but yeah, that's a smile. 'I went the wrong way. I should have taken the stairs like Markie, but . . .' He shrugs.

'That your safe room?' Billy asks.

'Yeah. And do you know what? I forgot the fucking combination.' Then he shakes his head. 'Nah, that's bullshit. I *blanked* on the combination. Just four numbers and all I could remember is the second one's a two.'

'What about now?' Billy asks.

'6247,' Nick says, and actually laughs.

Billy nods. 'It happens to the best of us and it happens to the rest of us.'

Nick studies him. He wipes his lips, which are shiny with spit. 'You sound different. You even *look* different. You were never as stupid as you made out, were you? Giorgio told me that and I didn't believe him.'

'Before you had him killed,' Billy says.

Nick's eyes widen with what Billy could swear is genuine surprise. 'Giorgio isn't dead, he's in Brazil.' He studies Billy's face. 'You don't believe me?'

'After the shit you pulled, why would I believe a word that comes out of your mouth?'

Nick shrugs as if to say point taken. 'Can I sit down? My legs are all weak.'

Billy gestures with the barrel of the Glock to the three spectators' seats beside the pool table. Nick walks unsteadily to the one in the middle and sits down. He reaches behind him and flips a switch that turns on the three hanging lights over the green felt.

'I never should have taken the contract. But all that money . . . it blinded me.'

Billy reckons he has some time. It would be a mistake to push it too far, but he may do so anyway. Because he wants answers. The money seems secondary. Not to mention unlikely. It's only in movies that the gangster has a wall of cash in his safe room. These days it's all computer transfers. Money hardly exists at all. Money has become the ghost in the machine.

'Pigs has got liver disease. You would've put money on his heart going, fat as he is, but it was his liver that turned out to be the problem. He needs a transplant. Doctors said no way unless he loses some weight, like two hundred pounds. If he doesn't, he'll die on the operating table. So he went to Brazil.'

'A fat farm?'

'A special clinic. The kind where once you sign in you can't sign out until you reach your target weight and they *let* you sign out. He knew that's the only way it could work, otherwise he'd be gone the first time he got a yen for a Triple Whopper with Cheese.'

Billy is starting to believe it. Nick is talking about Giorgio mostly in the present tense, and he hasn't slipped up. In a way it's like Edison flushing the toilet as he fell, mortally wounded. Some things are too bizarre not to be true. Georgie Pigs in a fat farm gulag is surely one of those things.

'Giorgio knew he'd be ID'd after you killed Joel Allen, he's a fucking whale, but he was okay with that. He said it was a way of making sure he wouldn't back out at the last minute, new liver or no new liver. Plus he wanted to retire.'

'Really?' Billy would have believed Giorgio was one of those guys who would die in harness.

'Yeah.'

'Sunset years in Brazil?'

'I think Argentina.'

'Sounds expensive. What kind of a retirement bonus did he get for helping to set me up?'

Nick hesitates, then says, 'Three million.'

'Three for Giorgio and six for bringing me down.'

Nick's eyes widen and he sags in the chair. He's thinking that if Billy knows that, any chance he might have had of getting out of this alive just flew away. He's probably right.

'But you stuck at paying me the lousy million and a half you owed? I knew you were cheap, Nick, but I didn't peg you for a chiseler.'

'Billy, we were never going to—'

'You were. I want to hear you say it or I'll kill you right now.'

'You're going to kill me anyway,' Nick says, and although his voice is steady enough, a single tear rolls down one plump and beautifully shaved cheek.

Billy doesn't reply.

'Okay, yeah. We were going to kill you. That came with the deal. Dana was going to do it.'

'I was going to be your Oswald.'

'It wasn't my idea, Billy. I told the client you'd stand up no matter what. He insisted, and like I said, the money blinded me.'

Billy could ask how much Nick got, but does he want to know? He does not. 'Who's the client?'

Instead of answering, Nick points to the door leading to the panic room. '*I've* got money. Not a million-five but at least eighty thousand, probably more like a hundred. I'll give it to you and I'll get you the rest.'

'I believe that completely,' Billy says. 'I also believe that we won in Vietnam and the moon landing was staged.' Something else occurs to him. 'Did you know about the fire?'

Nick blinks at the change of subject. 'Fire? What fire?'

'Those flashpots weren't the only diversion that day. There was a warehouse fire in a nearby town not long before I took the shot. I knew about it ahead of time because Hoff told me.'

'Hoff told you? That *budalla?*'

'You sure you didn't know about it?'

'No.'

Billy believes him, but he wanted to hear him say it, and watch his face as he did. It doesn't matter, anyway. He's downriver from all that. 'Who was the client?'

'Are you going to kill me?'

I should, Billy thinks. You richly deserve it.

'Who was the client?'

Nick raises a hand to his face and brings it down slowly, wiping away sweat from his brow and more spit from his lips. His eyes say he has given up hope, and he never had much to begin with. 'If I tell you, will you at least let me pray before you do it? Or is killing me not enough, do you want me in hell for eternity, too?' Now there are more tears.

'You can pray. Client's name first.'

'Roger Klerke.'

At first Billy thinks he's saying Clerk, like the guy who takes your money in a convenience store, but then Nick spells it. The name has a slightly familiar ring, but it's not one he associates with Nick's world. Or Bucky Hanson's, for that matter. More like a name Billy has seen in the newspapers or blogs or heard on a podcast. Maybe on TV. Politics? Business? Billy has little interest in either.

'World Wide Entertainment,' Nick says. 'It's okay if you don't recognize it, WWE's only one of the four biggest media conglomerates in the world.'

Nick tries to smile – a man on his deathbed telling a feeble joke – but Billy hardly notices. He's rewinding, almost all the way to the beginning. To his first meeting with Ken Hoff, who is certainly not looking forward to retirement in South America.

'Tell me.'

Nick does, and Billy is so totally amazed by what he hears – and horrified, that too – that he loses track of time. He doesn't remember that not everyone at Promontory Point has been neutralized until he hears a desolate howl from upstairs. It is the sound only a mother can make when she discovers her son stretched out unconscious and maybe dying. Maybe already dead.

'Do you want to live, Nick?' A rhetorical question.

'Yes. *Yes!* If you let me, I'll see that you get your money. Every cent of it. That's my solemn promise.' His tears stopped while he was telling his tale, but at the possibility of a reprieve they start again.

Billy's not interested in Nick's promises, solemn or otherwise. He points to the unadorned steel door to the safe room. Upstairs there's another howl, then words: '*Help me! Somebody help me!*'

'Are there guns in there?'

Nick is no longer the guy in charge, no longer the host with the most who welcomed Billy with outstretched arms five months ago, no longer the drinker of Champagne who just wanted to help Billy with his getaway. He has been broken down to his basic humanity, which is a desire to continue drawing breath, and so Billy accepts his look of surprise as genuine. 'In the safe room? Why would I have guns in there?'

'Go in. Close the door. Look at your watch. Wait an hour. If you come out before then, I might be gone or I might still be here.' As if, Billy thinks. 'If I'm here, I'll kill you.'

'I won't. I won't! And the money—'

'I'll be in touch about that.'

Maybe, Billy thinks. Or maybe I no longer want any of it, considering what I did and who I did it for. Not knowing at the time may be an excuse, but not a good one.

'Call off the bounty hunters. Tell them I came here, there was a shootout, and I got killed. If there's still guys on the prod for me, you better hope they kill me because if they don't, I'll come back here and kill you. Tell Klerke the same thing. I'll ask him, and if he says anything different, I'll come back and kill you. Got it?'

'Yes. Yes!'

Billy gestures toward the TV part of the man-cave. 'And clean up this mess. Make it go away. Do you understand?'

'*Help me, he won't wake up!*' From upstairs.

'Do you understand?'

'Yes. What are you planning to—'

'Get in there.'

Nick has no trouble with the combo this time. The door must be sealed as tight as the airlock of a spaceship, because there's a faint *whoosh* when it opens. Nick goes in. He gives Billy a final look from eyes that no longer believe they are master of all they survey, and maybe that's revenge enough. Or would be, if it were to last. Billy knows it won't.

'For once in your life be honorable,' Billy says.

Nick closes the door and there's a thud as it re-locks. Billy sees a cheesecloth bag full of billiard balls hanging from a hook beside the chairs. He takes it and spills the balls onto the green felt of the table. He gets Edison's Glock from the bathroom and Nick's hideout gun from where it lies next to Reggie's dead hand. He puts both guns in the bag. Then he searches Reggie's pants pockets, an unpleasant task that has to be done because he has no intention of driving out of here in the old pickup with its unreliable starter. He finds the key to Reggie's vehicle.

Billy has tucked his own Glock in the bib pocket of his overalls. As he mounts the stairs he takes it out. Now he can hear Frank's mother – who Billy has started to think of as the Bride of Terminator – on the telephone. 'Nick's! *Yes*, you idiot, Nick's! Why do you think I'm calling you instead of the hospital?'

Billy goes down the hall to the kitchen, once more walking on the sides of his feet. He can't see Marge, aka Mommy Elvis, but he can see her shadow pacing back and forth, and the shadow of the landline's cord. He can also see a Mossberg shotgun lying beside Frank Macintosh's splayed feet. It's got to be the one Sal, the gate guard, had slung over his shoulder.

Should have taken it when I had the chance, Billy thinks.

'Get here fast! He's barely breathing!'

Billy drops to his knees and leans forward, hand outstretched. She has used a towel to sop up the blood from the back of Frank's head and left it on the nape of his neck. Billy snags the shotgun by the trigger guard and pulls it toward him slowly, hoping she won't hear it and turn. He wants no more to do with Marge.

He feels a sudden cold prickling along the back of his neck and knows it's Nick. He had a gun in the safe room after all. He came out, he climbed the stairs, and now he's aiming the gun at the back of Billy's head. Billy turns, hearing his neck creak, sure it will be the last sound he ever hears, at least in this world. No one is there.

He gets to his feet. His knees pop. Frank's mother hears it and comes around the fridge (not as big as the TV but almost) and stares at him. Her face is one big bruise and Billy thinks of Alice again. Marge is still holding the phone, but the cord has reached its limit, all its curls now straight. Her lips part in a snarl.

Billy points the Glock at the prone figure of her son, then raises the barrel to his lips: *Shhhh.*

The snarl stays, but she nods.

Billy leaves, backing down the hall until he gets to the front door.

6

The SUV parked on the tarmac has a triple-diamond logo on the grill that matches the one on Reggie's key. When he gets inside it still has that new car smell, although it's fighting a losing battle against the smell of its late owner's cigarettes. There's an aluminum Table Talk pie tin on the console full of butts. Billy rolls down the window and tosses it out. Something else for Nick to clean up.

Marge comes out the door. In bright sunlight she looks like death on a cracker. '*If my son dies I'll get you!*' she hollers. '*If he dies I'll follow you to the ends of the earth!*'

And she probably would, Billy thinks, but Frank got what was coming to him and so did you, ma'am.

He never got a chance to show Nick the slogan on his T-shirt, but now he calls it out to her.

He drives past Sal's body and through the open gate. Once he's on Route 45 he phones Alice and tells her he's all right. Against all odds, this is true. His only wound is a scrape from Marge's trowel.

'Thank God,' Alice says. 'Are you . . . did you . . .'

'I'll be there in a couple of hours, maybe sooner. I've upgraded my ride. I'm driving a green Mitsubishi Outlander now. I want you to pack up. We're leaving. I'll tell you everything on the way.'

Nor will he omit anything. She deserves to know the whole thing, especially if he's going to ask for her help with the rest. He hasn't completely made up his mind about that, has only the vaguest intimations of a plan, but he's leaning in that direction. It will be her decision, but there are powerful reasons for wanting her in on the rest. And she'll know it, he thinks.

'Are we going back to . . . you know, your friend's place?'

'To start with. You can stay there, or you can come back east with me to finish this business. Your choice.'

Her reply is instant. 'I'll come.'

'Don't decide now. Wait until you hear where I'm going. And why.'

He ends the call. Ahead of him is the Las Vegas smog bowl, which he will be happy to leave behind. The slogan on his shirt, the very Vegas slogan that he didn't get to show Frank but called out to Frank's mom, is IF YOU WANT TO PLAY, YOU HAVE TO PAY. Someone else needs to pay: Roger Klerke.

He's a very bad man.

CHAPTER 21

1

When he pulls in, Alice is waiting for him at the head of the space where the old truck was parked. She hugs him as soon as he's out of the car, really throws herself into it. No hesitation. He hugs back the same way. When that's done, he's partly amused and partly saddened by her first question, because it comes from a young woman who is now living in an outlaw frame of mind.

'Is that car safe to drive? We won't be stopped by the police?'

'It's safe. The vehicle tracker was already disabled. Which didn't surprise me.' Also the owner is dead and Nick isn't going to call the cops. He would have far too much to explain. And Billy now has information that could blow him and his whole operation sky-high.

'I packed everything. There wasn't much.'

'Okay. Let's go. While we're driving, you can make us a reservation at a motel in Wendover. That's just over the Utah state line.'

Alice looks around at their current lodgings. 'I'm not sure the kind of places we've been staying have websites. Maybe, but . . .' She shrugs.

'Book us into a chain. The Dalton Smith name is still clean and the pressure's off. Nobody is going to be looking for us.'

'Are you sure?'

Billy thinks about it and decides he is. The last thing he said to Nick was *for once in your life be honorable*, and he thinks that Nick, who was sure he was going to die in his man-cave, will do that. At least for awhile. There's something else, as well. If Billy succeeds in getting to Klerke, Nick Majarian will be off the hook, and quite possibly with the six-million-dollar bounty in one of his numbered accounts.

Meanwhile, Alice is looking up at him and waiting.

'I'm sure. Let's go.'

2

It's a long story, but it's a five-hour drive to Wendover and that will be plenty of time for Billy to tell her what he knows and what he's deduced. But before they roll, he powers up his phone and googles Roger Klerke. The thumbnail biography says he was born in 1954, which makes him sixty-five, but in the accompanying photo he looks at least ten years older. He's pasty, balding, wrinkled, jowly. His eyes are bright little animals living in sagging pockets of flesh. It's the face of hard living and indulgence.

'He's the man behind this whole shit-show,' Billy says, and hands her his phone.

She types and sweeps with her finger as Billy pulls out and heads for the 15. She bends over the phone, brushing her hair impatiently away from her face. 'Holy crap. According to Wikipedia, he practically owns the world, at least media-wise.'

Billy again thinks back to his first meeting with Ken Hoff, the two of them sitting at an umbrella-shaded table outside the Sunspot Café, right across from the building where Billy would eventually take the shot. Hoff with a glass of wine, Billy with a diet soda, Hoff broadcasting a slightly desperate vibe even then. Although along with it, like a fraternal twin, was the mindset that had gotten him in so much trouble and was about to get him in even more. It was the core belief, maybe inculcated in childhood, that he was the star of a movie called *The Fabulous Life of Ken Hoff*, and no matter how bad things got, in the end he would come out with the girl, the gold watch, and everything.

'Newspapers, websites, a movie studio, *two* streaming services . . .'

'And TV,' Billy says. 'Don't forget that. Including Channel 6 in Red Bluff, the only station that got footage of the courthouse killing.'

'Are you thinking—'

'Yes.'

'Fuck,' Alice says softly.

I'm a little bit tight this year, wasn't that what Hoff said? *Cash flow problems since I bought into WWE, but three affils, how could I say no?*

'He owns World Wide Entertainment,' Alice says. 'That's a network plus about twelve cable channels. One of them is that news station that loves Trump. There's this bunch of rabid commentators—'

'I know the ones you're talking about.'

He's seen WWE News 24, everybody has. It plays all the time in hotel lobbies and airport terminals. Billy sometimes stops for a few minutes to absorb some rightwing pundit's bilge, then either moves on or changes to one of the movie channels if he has access to the controller. He had no idea they franchised local TV stations, though. Had no idea (at least at first) what Hoff was talking about and didn't care. He hadn't thought it was important. But it was. Very. It was how Hoff got into this. It was why the Channel 6 news crew didn't go chasing the fire in Cody. It was how Ken Hoff ended up dead in his own garage.

'This guy wanted you to kill Joel Allen? *This* guy? He's *old*. And *rich*.'

Yes, Billy thinks. Old and rich and used to being emperor. Ken Hoff had only thought he was starring in a movie. Roger Klerke really has been. He's the man who thinks he deserves everything, and that it should not just be brought to him but that it should be served to perfection. Which included film footage of Joel Allen's death.

And I was the waiter, Billy thinks.

'Tell me what happened at Promontory Point.'

Billy does as she asks, skipping over only what Nick told him before Billy sent him into his safe room like a bad kid grounded and confined to his bedroom. When he finishes, she says, 'You did what you had to do.'

This is true, but it's the verdict of a young woman barely old enough to buy a legal drink. He's sure Ken Hoff thought the same. 'Yes, but it was wrong choices that got me to the *point* where I had to do it.'

'That old lady,' Alice says, and shakes her head. 'Amazing. Do you think she'll be all right?'

'Not if her son dies.'

She gives Billy a look he's actually glad to see. If she feels safe enough to be pissed at him, she's probably still getting down the road to being all right. 'Don't you think she bears some of the responsibility for the job he was doing? Working for a gangster?'

Billy can't answer that.

'Now tell me what you're leaving out. What the gangster told you. Tell me *why*.'

They're on the Interstate now. The shadows are starting to lengthen. The game between the Giants and the Cardinals will be over. One team won and the other team didn't. A clean-up crew will be on its way to Promontory Point. Billy's got the cruise control pegged just below seventy.

'Nick hired Joel Allen to do a killing, but Nick was just the go-between. He even told me that, although he called himself the agent. It was Roger Klerke who wanted the job done, and paid millions for it. They met on an island in Puget Sound and struck the deal there.'

'Who did he want killed?'

'His son.'

3

Alice jumps like a person startled by a slamming door. 'Peter, Paul, something like that! He was supposed to take over from his father!'

'It was Patrick,' Billy says. 'You knew?'

'Just kinda-sorta. Because my mother has News 24 on all the time.'

Alice's mom and probably seventy per cent of the cable-watching news junkies in America, Billy thinks.

'I'd mostly leave the room, I hate that drivel but it's not worth arguing about with her. Only it was like their top story for almost a week, even ahead of Trump.' She looks at him. 'Now I know why. Klerke *owns* News 24.'

'Correct.'

'They said it was a gang thing and Patrick Klerke got mistaken for somebody else.'

'It was no gang thing and no mistake. Klerke's apartment was in a building with all sorts of security. A gangbanger never could have gotten past the gate guard, let alone into the building. Plus no one heard the shot. Allen must have used a potato-buster.'

'A what?'

'A silencer.'

'24 was all over the cops to catch the guy but they never did. Because by then Allen was probably out of town.'

'Sure, over the hills and far away,' Billy agrees. 'And if he hadn't shot those two men because he lost big at poker, he'd probably still be over the hills and far away. Maybe even then, if he hadn't gone back to LA and mistaken some lady writer for a hooker.'

'Why would Klerke . . . his own son? *Why*?'

'I can only tell you what Nick told me. There's probably more to it, but I didn't have a whole lot of time.'

'Because of that man's mother. Marge.'

'Yes, Marge. I knew she'd head for the main gate, I had to believe she knew the code to open it, and I left the gate guard—'

'Sal.'

'Right, him. I left him with his shotgun. So I only had time for the abridged version.'

'Then tell me that.'

'Klerke was old. Not *old* old, but old for his age and with a host of medical problems. He needed to name a successor – to keep his board happy, I guess – and most people expected it would be Patrick, the elder son. But Patrick was a heavy drug user and a party animal who used to get through his yearly stipend before the end of April and come to daddy on the first of May, begging for more.'

Alice smiles. 'He maybe should have gone to his mother. They can be a softer touch.'

'Patrick's mother died of an overdose. Pills. Or maybe it was suicide. Maybe even murder. Klerke's divorced from the younger son's mother. That's Devin.'

'I think he was on TV, too. Made a statement or something.'

Billy nods. 'What Nick told me reminded me of the story of the grasshopper and the ant, with the addition of a father smart enough to tell the difference. Patrick was the grasshopper. Devin, his younger brother by four years, was the ant. Industrious and smart. Nose to the grindstone. Shoulder to the wheel. Klerke called his sons together and told them his decision. Patrick was furious. As far as he was concerned, *he* was the one with the brilliant ideas to move WWE forward and his brother was nothing but an office drone.'

Billy thinks of the mean little eyes in the photograph and imagines Klerke saying something delicate like *You picked up most of your brilliant ideas from your libtard hip-hop wannabe friends while you were snorting dope.*

However he put it, he'd driven his older son into a rage. In most cases it would have been an impotent rage, but Roger Klerke had an Achilles heel, and Patrick either knew about it then or found out shortly thereafter.

'I don't know *how* he knew about it, Nick didn't tell me. Maybe he didn't know, either. Maybe Patrick got a clue from someone in his lifestyles-of-the-rich-and-foolish circle of friends. Maybe he overheard something. But he wasn't entirely dumb, because he was able to follow the dots to a certain small house outside of Tijuana.'

'A whorehouse.'

'Not exactly. It was privately funded by Klerke himself, Nick said, for his exclusive use. He paid tribute money, a lot of it, each year to the Félix brothers, who basically run the Tijuana Cartel. There may have been certain other inducements, as well. Money laundering would be my guess. It doesn't matter. Nick said Klerke never brought friends, because word gets around.'

'Was Patrick doing business with the cartels?' Alice asks. 'Moving dope for them? There's a word for it.'

'Muling,' Billy says. 'He might have been.'

'He could have heard about it from one of them. That might have been his loose end.'

Billy pats her shoulder. 'That's good. We'll never know for sure, but it makes more sense than the hearing-it-from-a-friend idea.'

She smiles at the compliment, but only a little. She knows where this is going, Billy thinks. A girl a little less intelligent might not, a girl who hadn't been recently raped might not, but this girl checks both boxes.

'Klerke has a taste for young girls.'

'How young?' she asks.

'Nick said thirteen or fourteen.'

'Jesus.'

'It gets worse. Do you want to hear?'

'No, but tell me anyway.'

'There was at least one occasion – he told Nick it was only one, for what that's worth – when there was a girl who was a lot younger.'

'Twelve?' Her face says that no matter how much of a shit that jowly old lizard may be, she wants to believe that's the limit of his depravity.

'According to Klerke she was no more than ten, and Patrick had the pictures to prove it. What Roger Klerke told Nick at their meeting on that island was that he was "pretty drunk and just wanted to see what it was like."'

'Dear God.'

'The rest of it is as simple as dominos falling over. Patrick had the pictures on a thumb drive. Swore they existed nowhere else, that the man who took them was dead and buried in the desert. He told his father that he wanted to be CEO. He also wanted a transfer of most of his father's voting stock, which would render meaningless any objections the board might have to the new direction he wanted to take WWE in. He wanted his brother – "my asshole brother" is what he called him, according to Nick – transferred to the Chicago offices, which I guess in the media business is like Siberia. He wanted those changes effective as of January 1, 2019, and he wanted it all in writing. Then and only then would he turn over the flash drive with the pictures.'

'How could Klerke be sure there weren't more pictures?'

Billy shrugged. 'Maybe there were. In any case, what choice did he have? And Patrick must have been at least bright enough to know that if the pictures came out, the company stock would tank no matter who was CEO.'

Alice thinks that over and says, 'Like mutually assured destruction. In a way.'

'I guess. What I know from Nick is that Klerke agreed, and once his lawyer had a letter announcing his intentions to basically retire and turn the company over to his older son, and once that letter was published in the board minutes, Patrick gave the thumb drive to his father. Who destroyed it. Patrick never foresaw his father going to Nick Majarian and hiring a man to kill him. His imagination just didn't stretch that far.'

'It isn't the grasshopper and the ant. More like a Shakespeare play. One of the bloody ones.'

'With Patrick dead, when Klerke steps down – given his health it won't be long – Devin will take over.'

He pulls into a service area, because the Mitsubishi needs gas and because his throat is dry and he wants a cold drink. Alice checks out the Quik-Pik shelves and uses the restroom while he pays. When she gets back into the car she's crying.

'I'm sorry.' Her purchases are in a little white bag. She takes out a pack of Kleenex, wipes her nose, and tries on a smile. 'But while I was in the bathroom I made us a reservation at the Ramada Inn in Wendover. It's supposed to be nice.'

'Good. And you don't have to be sorry.'

'I keep thinking about that horrible man with a child. He deserves to die.'

Billy thinks, that's the plan.

4

By the time he finishes – again weaving what he knows from Nick into what he deduced on his drive back from Promontory Point – some of the cars on the highway are showing headlights.

'Klerke told Nick he wanted the best man for the job, a guy who'd do it and get away clean and not talk about it afterward. Nick said he knew a guy—'

'You?'

'He said he thought of me first, but never even went to Bucky with it. He said he was pretty sure I wouldn't do it because Patrick Klerke was maybe not bad enough to fit my scruples. He put it to Allen as an ordinary cleaning job.'

'That's what he called it? *Cleaning?*'

'Yes. The figure they settled on was eighty thousand dollars, twenty before and the rest after. Basically the same method of payment I was promised, but on a smaller scale.'

Alice is nodding. 'He didn't want Allen to know what a big deal this was. How much was involved.'

'Sure. Nick felt okay about it, because Allen was what I always pretended to be, just your basic mechanic who fixed problems with a gun instead of socket wrenches and a timing computer. He gave Allen photos of Patrick's apartment building, photos of the apartment itself, the code to the service entrance, the car exchange after the job was done, anything he might need to do the job clean and quick.' Billy pauses. 'Nick didn't tell me all that, but I've worked for him before. I knew the drill. What he didn't tell Allen was why and Allen didn't ask.'

'But he asked Patrick, didn't he? Before he killed him.'

Billy thinks that over. 'It's possible, but it seems unlikely for a guy like Joel Allen. He'd be a lot more likely to just do the job. No conversation, just point and shoot.'

'Maybe Patrick offered him the thumb drive in exchange for . . .' Alice stops. 'Except he couldn't, could he? He didn't have it. Thought he was home free once his appointment was announced to the board.'

'Nick doesn't know what happened, and Allen can't tell us how he found out about Roger Klerke and the kid in Tijuana, but I have an idea. Allen was told to make it look like a robbery, maybe committed by some fellow user who met Patrick along the Los Angeles drug trail. He was told to take any money or jewelry he found. He was supposed to toss the jewelry, watches and gold chains and shit like that, but he could keep the money as a little bonus. So after he killed Patrick he searched the place and might have found a picture, maybe more than one, that Patrick kept in reserve. At least one that showed his father's face nice and clear while he was . . . doing what he was doing. Does that make sense?'

Alice nods hard enough to make her hair bounce. 'I bet it happened just that way. Even if the picture or pictures were in a safe, Allen could have been given the combination with the rest of his background info. Would he really have recognized the man in the picture?'

Based on what he knows about Joel Allen, Billy doesn't see him as the sort of guy who watched the WWE business channel or read the Bloomberg report. 'Probably not at first, but it wouldn't have taken him long to find out. A few Google searches would have shown him that he'd killed the son of a billionaire who also happened to be a pedophile.'

Alice's eyes are intent. She's totally into this now. Billy thinks again that a rinky-dink business school in Red Bluff would have wasted a lot of potential. And hairdressing school? Forget it.

'So this paid killer, this mechanic, this *cleaner*, had two things worth money — that the father was almost certainly the one who paid to have the son killed, and the father also raped a child. Because he "just wanted to see what it was like."' Some of the light goes out of her eyes when she says that.

'I doubt if he tried to turn what he knew into cash, although he might have down the line. He would've known that blackmailing someone as rich and powerful as Roger Klerke would be a tremendous risk. I think he kept it as a hole card. Which he eventually had to play not for money but because of his own stupidity.'

Double stupidity, Billy thinks, if you count in the lady writer.

'Almost like he wanted to be caught,' Alice says. 'Some repeat killers do.' She rewinds what she's said and puts a hand on his wrist. 'Ones without a moral code, I mean.'

Is that what you call it? Billy wonders.

'I doubt if Allen wanted to get caught. And if he was able to figure out what made that picture such a valuable commodity, I guess he wasn't completely stupid, either.'

'If he wasn't completely stupid, why kill that man over a poker game? And why attack that woman in LA?'

Well, Billy thinks, Allen believed the poker game guy was cheating. And the lady writer pepper-sprayed him. But neither of those things goes to the heart of Alice's question.

'My guess? Simple arrogance. Do you want to stop somewhere for dinner?'

She shakes her head. 'Let's drive straight through and eat when we get there. I want to hear the rest.'

5

Billy feels surer about this part even though it's still mostly guesswork. After Allen was arrested for assault and attempted rape in LA, he must have known he'd be connected almost immediately with the murder and attempted murder back east in Red Bluff. There was a lively trade in cell phones in the county lockup, most of them burners. Allen could have gotten hold of one, called Nick, and said that if he had to go back to Red Bluff and stand trial for murder in a death penalty state, a very rich man, initials RK, was probably going to spend the rest of his life in jail, possibly getting buggered by Harvey Weinstein. And if anything happened to Allen in LA lockup, RK was going to be very, very sorry.

'Nick got in touch with Roger Klerke. Klerke – almost certainly through an intermediary – hired an expensive lawyer to fight extradition.

Nick and Klerke had another meeting at that island and laid out any number of possible scenarios. I imagine they had the expensive legal talent on speed-dial. If so, he would have told them what Nick probably knew already, that he could draw out the extradition fight for quite awhile, but in the end Allen was going to be put on a plane and sent back to face trial. Because first-degree murder trumps aggravated assault.'

'That's when Majarian hired you.'

'Around then, yes. To get me placed where I could eventually take the shot. By then Allen was out of gen-pop because he'd been attacked. By arrangement, I'd guess. Maybe his idea, probably his lawyer's. Either way he wound up having his own private accommodation while the extradition fight was ongoing. He met regularly with the expensive lawyer, who told him everything was under control. Or would be, once he was back east. Either an escape would be arranged, along with a completely new identity, or certain wheels would be greased, certain witnesses would be bribed, certain key evidence would disappear, and Allen would walk free as himself.'

'And he had no reason to doubt it.'

Billy shakes his head. 'Guys like Allen doubt everything. But he had no choice.'

'What about the picture? Or pictures? His hole card?'

'I think both Nick and Klerke had people looking for that all the time the extradition fight was going on. That was one reason *why* the extradition fight was going on. And I think they eventually found it, or them. All I know for sure is that no federal marshals have turned up to arrest Roger Klerke.'

'Maybe we'll turn up first,' Alice says.

Billy hates that pronoun, but he doesn't correct it. He only has a ghost of a plan, and when it comes more into focus, maybe he can leave Alice out of it. He remembers what Bucky said: *She's in love with you and she'll follow you as long as you let her and if you let her you'll ruin her.*

6

'Ohhh, look – it's a palace!' So says Alice when they pull into the Wendover Ramada Inn at quarter of nine that Sunday night. 'I mean, compared to the last three motels.'

Their adjoining rooms are far from palatial, but they're nice, and the hallway carpet looks as if it's been vacuumed recently.

'Will you be able to sleep?' she asks.

'Yes.' He doesn't actually know if that's true.

Her eyes are fixed on his. 'I'll sleep with you, if you want.'

Billy thinks of Roger Klerke's taste for the young ones – on at least one pestiferous occasion a *very* young one – and shakes his head. 'It's a kind offer and much appreciated, but better not.'

'Are you sure?'

Still looking directly at him, and is he tempted? Of course he is.

'Thank you, Alice, but no. Will *you* be able to sleep?'

'Will we be back at Bucky's tomorrow?'

'Should be.'

'Then I'll be able to sleep. I like him. He's, you know, safe.'

Billy isn't sure she'd feel that way if she knew even half the deals Elmer 'Bucky' Hanson has been involved in over the years, but he knows what she means and thinks she's right. She and Bucky have made a connection.

'Goodnight.' He kisses her for the first time, on the corner of the mouth.

'Goodnight. Oh, and here.' She hands him the white Quik-Pik bag. 'Baby oil and Handi Wipes. Clean off as much of that goop as you can, then get in the shower. You won't get it all, but you can get most of it.' She goes to the door, uses her keycard, then turns back. 'And leave a good tip, because more of it will come off on the sheets.'

'Okay.' He wouldn't have thought of that himself, although he probably would have tomorrow, when he looked at the bed.

She starts to go in, then looks at him over her shoulder. Her face is solemn but calm. 'I love you.'

Billy doesn't even think of lying. He tells her he loves her, too, then goes into his room.

7

He calls Nick. He's not sure Nick will answer, but he does.

'Who's this?' And then, without waiting for a reply: 'Is it you?'

'It's me. Are you getting things right there?'

'They will be by tomorrow.'

'I didn't cool anybody that I didn't have to.'

A long pause with just the sound of breathing. Then Nick says, 'I know.'

'What's up with Frank?'

'In the hospital. His mother called my pet medic. Doc Rivers sent a private ambulance. She went with him.'

'That's a hard woman.'

'Marge?' Nick gives a short laugh. 'You don't know the half of it.'

I believe I do, Billy thinks. If I'd hit her in the back of the head with that Glock instead of Frank, it probably would have bounced right off.

'Is our fat friend still in the land of the living?'

'He was as of an hour ago when I called to tell him about what happened. He said I should have taken you more seriously. I said I thought four made guys – plus Marge – was pretty serious. Why do you ask?'

'Did he procure for Mr K when he came to Vegas? It seems like the kind of job you'd delegate to him.'

'You are a *lot* smarter than I thought,' Nick says, as if talking to himself. 'Smarter than *anybody* thought. Except maybe for Pigs.'

'Did he or didn't he?'

'Well, yeah. Kinda. Pigs'd get with Judy Blatner when he knew K was coming. They'd go over her picture books, try to find one he'd like. Ten, twelve years ago he woulda wanted two, but his stamina's declined. He ain't what you'd call a gentleman, but he does prefer blondes.'

'And they have to be young.'

'Well duh,' Nick says. 'But the girls he went with in Vegas were never under eighteen. Judy's been around a long time and runs a legal escort service. That means she can't say the girls are for sex, but she doesn't have to. Everyone knows. She steers clear of jailbait, though. Like it was poison. Which it is.'

The thought of that jowly toad even with a girl Alice's age makes Billy's stomach turn. 'When he wanted jailbait he crossed the border.'

'True.'

'I want the fat man's number. Will you give it to me?'

'Are you going after Mr K?'

He is, but he's not going to say so even on a burner phone and believing Nick makes sure his personal phone is whistle clean. He only reiterates his request for Giorgio's number. Nick gives it to him.

'Will he talk to me?'

'If I tell him to. If I say you're going to keep it business. He never would have gone along with this if he didn't need to do something that would force him to change how he's been living. If you want to blame someone, blame me. I didn't need to lose two hundred pounds so the docs would give me a new liver. Like I told you, the money blinded me.'

Billy thinks it's as honest a confession as Nick will ever give anyone. 'Tell him I'm going to keep it business. Joel Allen is water under the bridge.'

'When should I tell him to expect your call?'

'Not tonight, maybe not for awhile. When's the transplant scheduled?'

'It's not, and won't be until December at least. Pigs has got to drink a lot of protein shakes and eat a lot of kale between now and then.'

'All right.' Billy tucks the cell number into his Dalton Smith wallet, behind his Dalton Smith credit cards. 'Take care of yourself, Nick.'

'Wait.'

Billy waits, curious about what else Nick has to say.

'It was never because K didn't want to pay you the million-five. That's pocket change to him. It was because he insisted you be hit once the job was done. Said he wasn't going to make the same mistake he made with Allen. You get that, right?'

'Yes.' And Nick went along with it. He gets that, too.

'Does your Edward Woodley name still work? The account in Barbados?'

'Yes.' Although it's been dormant except for token deposits and withdrawals since 2014 or 2015.

'Check it tomorrow. Thank God you didn't kill Mark Abromowitz. He ain't great and he ain't made, but he's what I got since Pigs went to SA. All I can transfer right now and be safe is three hundred thousand, but I'll put in more when I can. You'll eventually get your million-five.'

For once in your life be honorable, Billy told him when he gave Nick back his life, and damned if the man isn't trying, in the only way he knows how. Money.

'You're not going to say thank you and I don't need you to,' Nick says. 'You're a good workman, Billy. You did the job.'

Billy pushes END CALL without saying goodbye.

8

He cleans himself up with the wipes and baby oil as well as he can, then showers until the brown water running down the drain is mostly clear. But he still gets more smeg on the two bath towels he uses to dry off.

Alice asked him if he'd be able to sleep and he said yes, but for a long time he can't. The time he spent at Promontory Point – probably only an hour, maybe even less, but it seemed like five – keeps running through his mind. Especially going for Edison. The flying splinters. The flushing toilet.

I thought four made guys was pretty serious, Nick said, but Sal the gate guard never got the Mossie off his shoulder, Frank never turned around, and Reggie wasn't carrying, had to go for the boss's hideout gun instead. Only Dana Edison was serious; he took his gun into the crapper with him. And Marge, of course. She was *very* serious, and she had seen through his disguise almost immediately.

Leave a good tip for the housekeeper, he thinks. Leave a twenty.

He rolls over and is on the edge of sleep when something comes to him that he doesn't like and he rolls on his back again, staring up into the darkness. No, he doesn't like it at all. He left Shan's picture of Freddy the Flamingo – aka Dave the Flamingo – taped to the dash of that old truck. He had time to take it but it never even crossed his mind. All he wanted right then was to get the fuck gone.

Forget it, he tells himself. It means nothing.

This may be true, but it doesn't help. Because it is – *was*, he guesses that's the correct tense now – pink like the baby shoe in Fallujah. The one he didn't have when they were ambushed in the Funhouse. He has lost another good luck charm. He can tell himself that's nothing but superstition, no different than folks believing there were ghosts in that old hotel in Sidewinder that burned, but it makes him feel bad. All else aside, that picture was made for him out of love.

Go to sleep, asshole, Billy thinks.

He finally does but wakes up in the dead ditch of the morning, mouth dry, hands clenched. The dream was so vivid that at first he's not sure if he's in a Ramada Inn or his Gerard Tower office. He was working on his story and it must have been early days, because he was still writing in his *dumb self* persona. There came a knock at the door. He answered it, expecting Ken Hoff or Phil Stanhope, more likely Hoff. But it was neither of them. It was Marge, in the big blue dress she was wearing when he approached the Promontory Point service entrance. Only instead of a sombrero she had a Vegas Golden Knights gimme cap jammed down over her hair and instead of a trowel she'd got Sal's Mossberg.

'You forgot the flamingo, you fucking fuck,' she said, and raised the shotgun. The barrel looked as big as the entrance to the Eisenhower Tunnel.

I pulled out of the dream before she could fire, Billy thinks as he walks to the bathroom. While he pees he thinks of Rudy Bell, aka Taco Bell. Bad dreams were common currency in Iraq, especially during the battle for Fallujah, and Taco believed (or said he believed) that if you died in a nightmare, you could actually die in your rack.

'Frightened to death, my man,' Tac said. 'What a way to go, huh?'

But I got out of this one before she could pull the trigger, Billy thinks as he trudges back to bed. She was a piece of work, though. Made Dana Edison with his prissy little manbun look like a street-corner hood.

The room is cold, but he doesn't bother turning on the heater because it will probably rattle – motel wall units *always* rattle. He snuggles under the blankets and goes to sleep almost at once. There are no more dreams.

9

Alice votes for fried egg sandwiches from a drive-thru instead of a sitdown breakfast because she wants to get on the road right away. 'I want to see the mountains again. I really love them, even though I had to gasp for air until I got used to the altitude.'

Billy smiles and says, 'Okay, let's go.'

Shortly after they cross the Colorado line, Billy hears his laptop give a single ding-dong chime for the first time in . . . he can't remember how long. Maybe years. He pulls over at the next turnout, gets it out of the back seat, and opens it. The ding-dong means he's gotten an email from one of his several blind accounts, this one woodyed667@ gmail.com. The message is from Travertine Enterprises. It's an outfit he's never heard of, but he has no doubt who's behind it. He double-clicks and reads.

'What?' Alice asks.

He shows her. Travertine Enterprises has put three hundred thousand dollars in the account of Edward Woodley at the Royal Bank of Barbados. The only notation is 'For services rendered.'

'Did that come from who I think it came from?' Alice asks.

'No doubt,' Billy says. They get rolling again. It's a beautiful day.

10

They get to Bucky's place around five in the afternoon. Billy has called ahead from Rifle with an ETA along with a head-ups about their new ride, and Bucky's standing in the dooryard waiting for them. He's dressed in jeans and a fleece jacket, looking nothing at all like the man who used to live and work in New York. Maybe he's his better self out here, Billy thinks. He knows that Alice is.

She's out of the car almost before Billy can come to a stop. Bucky holds his arms wide and shouts 'Hey, Cookie!' She runs into them, laughing as he enfolds her.

Look at that, Billy thinks. Would you look at that.

CHAPTER 22

1

They stay with Bucky at his mountain retreat long enough to get snowed in (for a day) by an early season blizzard. The ferocity of the storm amazes, delights, and terrifies Alice all at the same time. Yes, she says, she's seen snow in Rhode Island, plenty of it, but never snow like this with drifts higher than her head. When it stops, she and Bucky go out and make snow angels in the backyard. After extended pleading, the hired assassin joins them. Two days later the temperatures are back in the sixties and the snow is melting. The woods are full of birdsong and the sound of meltwater.

Billy never meant to stay so long. It's Alice's doing. She tells him that he needs to finish his story. Her words are one thing. The quiet tone of conviction in which they are spoken is another, and more convincing. It's too late to turn back now, she says, and after some consideration, Billy decides she's right.

There's no electricity in the little log cabin where he wrote about the Funhouse and what happened there, so he lugs in a battery-powered space heater that warms the place up enough so he can write. If he leaves his jacket on, at least. Someone has hung up that picture of the hedge animals again, and Billy could swear that the lions are closer now, their eyes redder. The hedge bull is between them instead of behind them.

It was that way before, Billy insists. It must have been, because pictures don't change.

This is true, in a rational world it *must* be true, but he still doesn't like the picture. He takes it down (again) and turns it face to the wall (again). He opens his story document and scrolls down to where he left off. At first the work is slow and he keeps glancing into the far corner, as if expecting that picture to be magically hanging there again. It's not, and after half an hour or so it's only the words on the screen he's looking at. The door of memory opens and he goes through. For most of October he spends his days on the far side of that door, even trudging up to the cabin in a pair of boots borrowed from Bucky on the day of the big snowstorm.

He writes about the rest of his tour in the desert, and how he decided – almost literally at the last moment – not to re-up. He writes about the culture shock of returning to America, where nobody worried about snipers and IEDs and nobody jerked and put his hands to his head if a car backfired. It was like the war in Iraq didn't exist and the things his friends died for didn't matter. He writes about that first job, assassinating the Jersey guy who liked to beat up women. He writes about how he met Bucky and he writes about all the jobs that followed. He doesn't make himself sound better than he was and writes it all too fast to come out clean, but it mostly does anyway. It comes out like the water running downhill through the woods when the snow melts.

He's vaguely aware that Bucky and Alice have formed a firm bond. He thinks that for Alice it's like finding a fine replacement for the father she lost early. For Bucky it's like she's the daughter he never had at all. Billy doesn't detect the slightest sexual vibe between them, and he's not surprised. He's never seen Bucky with a woman, and while – granted – he never saw Bucky face to face that often, the man rarely talked about women when they were together. Billy thinks Bucky Hanson might be gay, his two marriages notwithstanding. All he knows, all he cares about, is that Alice is happy.

But Alice's happiness isn't his priority during that October. The story is, and the story is now a book. No doubt about it. That no one will ever see it (except maybe for Alice Maxwell) doesn't faze Billy in the slightest. It's the doing that's important, she was right about that.

A week or so before Halloween, on a day of brilliant sunshine and strong upcountry winds, Billy writes about how he and Alice (he has changed her name to Katherine) arrived at Bucky's cabin (name changed to Hal) and how Bucky held out his arms – *Hey, Cookie!* – and she ran into them. It's as good a place to stop as any, he thinks.

He saves his copy to a thumb drive, closes up his laptop, goes to turn off the space heater, and stops. The picture of the hedge animals is back on the wall in that far corner of the cabin, and the hedge lions are closer still. He'd swear to it. That night, over dinner, he asks Bucky if he put it back up. Bucky says he didn't.

Billy looks at Alice, who says, 'I don't even know what you're talking about.'

Billy asks where the picture came from. Bucky shrugs. 'No idea, but I think those hedge animals used to be in front of the old Overlook. The hotel that burned. I'm pretty sure the picture was in the cabin when I bought this place. I don't go up there much when I'm here. I call it the summerhouse, but it always seems cold, even in summer.'

Billy has noticed the same thing, although he chalked it up to the late season. Still, he has done amazing work there, almost a hundred pages. Creepy picture and all. Maybe a chilly story needs a chilly writing room, he thinks. It's as good an explanation as any, since the whole process is a mystery to him, anyway.

Alice has made peach cobbler for dessert. As she brings it to the table, she says, 'Are you finished, Billy?'

He opens his mouth to say he is, then changes his mind. 'Almost. I have a few loose ends to tie up.'

2

The next day is cold, but when Billy gets to the log cabin he doesn't turn on the space heater and he doesn't take the picture down, either. He has decided that Bucky's so-called summerhouse is haunted. He's never believed in such things before, but he does now. It's not the picture, or not just the picture. It's been a haunted year.

He sits down in the room's only chair and thinks. He doesn't want to use Alice in what's ahead – the end of his business – but in this cold room with its strange atmosphere, he sees that he must. He sees something else, as well. She will want to, because Roger Klerke is not only a bad man, he's almost certainly the worst one Billy has ever been hired to take out. The fact that this time he's hired himself is beside the point.

I keep thinking about that horrible man with a child, Alice said. *He deserves to die.*

She didn't want Tripp Donovan dead, and she might not have wanted Klerke dead either if he'd stuck to girls who were seventeen or sixteen, maybe even fifteen. She would have wanted him to pay a price, yes, but not the ultimate one. Only Klerke didn't stick to those. Klerke had wanted *to see what it was like.*

Billy sits with his hands on his knees and growing numb at the fingertips, his breath frosting the air with each exhale. He thinks of a girl not much older than Shanice Ackerman brought to that little house in Tijuana. He thinks of her holding a stuffed animal for comfort, probably a teddy bear instead of a pink flamingo. He thinks of her hearing heavy footsteps coming down the hall. He doesn't want to think about those things, but he does. Maybe he needs to. And maybe this haunted room with its haunted picture on the wall helps him do it.

He takes out his wallet and finds the slip of paper he wrote Giorgio's phone number on. He makes the call knowing the chances of actually reaching the man are small. He may be in the gym of his fat farm prison, or in the pool, or dead of a heart attack. But Giorgio answers on the second ring.

'Hello?'

'Hello, Mr New York Agent. It's Dave Lockridge. Guess what? I finished my book.'

'Billy, Jesus Christ! You might not believe this but I'm glad you're alive.'

Damned if he doesn't sound younger, Billy thinks. And stronger, too.

'I'm also glad I'm alive,' Billy says.

'I didn't want to screw you over that way. You have to believe that. But I—'

'You had to make a choice and you made it,' Billy says. 'Did I like being fucked over by someone I trusted? Do I now? No. But I told Nick it was water under the bridge and I meant it. Only you owe me something and I'm hoping you're man enough to pay up. I need some information.'

There's a brief pause. Then, 'My phone's secure. How about yours?'

'It's okay.'

'I'll trust you on that. We're talking about Klerke, right?'

'Yes. Do you know where he is?'

'He doesn't come to Vegas anymore, so it'll be either Los Angeles or New York. I could find out. He's not hard to keep track of.'

'Do you know who supplies him with girls in LA and NYC?'

'I used to do it with Judy before I retired.' He says it with no discomfort that Billy can detect.

'Judy Blatner? Nick says she doesn't touch jailbait.'

'She doesn't. Nothing under eighteen. And that used to be good enough for Klerke. Then he wanted younger. He'd call. Say he wanted dumplings. That was the code word.'

Dumplings, Billy thinks. Jesus.

'Judy knows guys that are willing to find girls like that. Sometimes I'd deal with Klerke. Sometimes she would do it herself.'

'Does Judy also know guys in Tijuana?'

Giorgio lowers his voice even though his phone is secure. 'You're thinking of the little girl. That didn't have anything to do with Judy, or Nick, or me. That was something the cartel arranged. At Klerke's request.'

'Let me be sure I have it straight. If he's in LA and got the itch for a dumpling, he'd call you or Judy and one of you would put him in touch with someone there. Except what we're really talking about is a pimp.' Billy hunts for the phrase he wants. It goes with dumplings, which isn't surprising. 'A chicken-rancher.'

'Right. And if he's on the east coast at his place in Montauk Point, he'd get the guy from New York. How many dates Klerke's arranged since I left I don't know.'

Dates, Billy thinks. 'He actually gets concierge service?'

'You could call it that. It's what he pays for. Much money changes hands, Billy.'

Now comes the big question. 'Does Judy ever call *him*? Like if she's heard about someone who'd be in his sweet spot?'

'It happens from time to time, sure. More often now that he's reached an age when getting his noodle to stand up is a little more difficult.'

'If you called Judy and said you had a girl he'd like, someone *really* special, would she pass it on?'

There's silence while Giorgio thinks it over. Then he says, 'She would. She'd smell a rat — her nose is what you'd call exquisite — but she'd do it. She hates that guy because of what he did in TJ and if she thought someone was trying to fuck him up, maybe even arrange a hit on him, she'd shout hooray. I feel about the same.'

Although it never stopped you doing biz with him, Billy thinks. Or her. 'Okay. I'm going to call you back.'

'I'll be here. I have no place to go and don't want to. I hated it at first but now I love it. Like alcoholics love sobriety once they get a hold on it, I guess.'

'How much weight have you lost?'

'A hundred and ten pounds,' Giorgio says with perhaps justifiable pride. 'I got another ninety to go.'

'You sound good. Not so wheezy. Maybe if you lose the weight you can skip the operation.'

'Nope. My liver's shot and it's not coming back. They've scheduled the op for two days after *feliz navidad*, so you better finish whatever business you have with me before then. The doc down here is so honest it's brutal. He's saying my odds are sixty-forty against coming through.'

'I'll get back to you.' But I won't bother praying for you, Billy thinks.

'I hope you get that child-molesting perv.'

Who you worked for, Billy thinks again.

He doesn't have to say it because Giorgio says it for him. 'Sure, I carried his water. It was a lot of money, and I wanted to live.'

'Understood.' Billy thinks, But hell will still be waiting for you, Georgie. And if there is such a place, I'll probably meet you there. We'll have a drink. Brimstone on the rocks.

'I always had an idea that stupid act of yours was a shuck.'

Billy says, 'We'll talk soon.'

'Just don't wait too long,' Giorgio says.

3

It's time to fill Alice in on what he has in mind, and Bucky deserves to be a part of the conversation. He tells them at the kitchen table, over coffee. When he finishes, he advises her to think about it. Alice says she doesn't need to, she's in.

Bucky gives Billy a reproachful look that says *you turned her to the dark side after all*, but he doesn't say anything.

'You said you got carded in bars, didn't you?' Billy asks her.

'Yes, but I've only been in a couple. I only turned twenty-one the month before you . . . you know, met me.'

'Never had a fake ID?'

'Wouldn't have worked,' Bucky says. 'I mean, look at her.'

They both look at her. Alice blushes and casts her eyes down.

'How old would you say?' Billy asks Bucky. 'I mean, if you didn't know?'

Bucky considers. 'Eighteen. Nineteen at a stretch. Probably not twenty.'

Billy says to her, 'How young could you *make* yourself look? If you really tried?'

The question interests her enough to forget she's being studied – face and body – by two men. Of course the question interests her. At twenty-one she has undoubtedly considered how she might make herself look older and more sophisticated, but younger? Why would she?

'I could get an elastic binder to make my boobs smaller, I guess. The kind that trans men wear.' The flush returns. 'I know they're not that big anyway, but a binder would make me look, you know, almost flat. Isn't that what Klerke likes? And my hair . . .' She clasps it in one hand. 'I could cut it. Not pixie short, but enough to put it in a little pony-tail. Like a high school girl.'

'Clothes?'

'I don't know. I'd have to think about it. No makeup, or not much. Maybe some pink bubblegummy lipstick . . .'

Billy says, 'Do you think you could get down to fifteen?'

'No way,' Bucky says. 'Seventeen, *maybe*.'

'I might be able to do better than seventeen,' Alice says, getting up. 'Excuse me, I need a mirror.'

When she's gone, Bucky leans across the table and speaks very quietly. 'Don't get her killed.'

'I'm not planning on it.'

'Plans go wrong.'

4

The next day Billy calls Giorgio again from the chilly summerhouse. It has occurred to him that he might not have to use Alice at all. He's a sniper, after all, long-distance delivery his specialty. He keeps his eyes on the picture as they talk, half-expecting the hedge animals to move. They don't.

He begins by asking Giorgio if he could put his sniper skills to work in the matter of Roger Klerke.

'Not a chance. His place on Montauk Point is a forty-acre estate. Makes Nick's place in Nevada look like a tenement.'

Billy is disappointed but not surprised. 'That's where he is now?'

'That's where he is. Calls the place Eos, after some Greek goddess. According to Page Six in the *Post*, he'll stay there until just before Thanksgiving, then whistle up his Gulfstream and head back to LaLa Land for the holidays with his remaining son and heir.'

Lalafallujah, Billy thinks.

'Will he have an entourage with him?'

Giorgio laughs and the laugh turns into a wheeze, so maybe he isn't an *entirely* new man after all. 'You mean like Nick does? No way. Klerke's got a TV in every room, I hear, all on mute and all tuned to different channels. *That's* his entourage.'

'No security?' Billy can't believe it. Klerke is one of the richest men in America.

'Guys on the estate, you mean? Not if he thinks you're dead. And as far as he knows, you had no idea who paid for the Allen job anyway.'

'He'd think I went to Nick's place just to collect my payday.'

'Right. I'm sure he has a security company on call if he needs them, and he's probably got a panic button, but the only full-time guy is his assistant. William Petersen. You know, like the *CSI* guy?'

Billy has heard of the show but never watched it. 'Is Petersen a bodyguard as well as an assistant?'

'Don't know if he's got judo and krav maga skills, stuff like that, but he's young and in shape and you can assume he's good with firearms. Although he might not be actually packing on his hip or in a shoulder rig on the estate.'

Billy files the information away. 'Here's what I need from you. One thing you'll have to send. Do it and we're square.'

'Hold on a sec . . . okay.' All business now. 'I'll do what you want if I can. If I can't, I'll tell you. Give it to me.'

Billy gives it to him. Giorgio listens and asks a couple of questions, but he doesn't raise any problems that Billy hasn't already foreseen.

'It might actually work, assuming you've got a girl that can pass muster. I'll need you to email me some photos. Better send a couple dozen, actually. Mostly face, a few full body but dressed modest. I'll pick the ones where she looks the youngest.' He pauses. 'We're not talking about a real teenager, are we?'

'No,' Billy says. Just *almost* a teenager, one whose only sexual experience was a nightmare muffled (most likely mercifully) by Rohypnol or some similar drug.

'Good. Judy's man in New York is Darren Byrne. Klerke's done business with him before so obviously you can't be him, but you could be his brother. Or cousin.'

'Yes. I could.' Although he supposes he'll need something pimp-appropriate. 'Will Klerke expect her to spend the night?'

'God, no. You park and wait. He does his thing – assuming the Viagra works – and then she's out and back in the car. An hour, two at most.'

Not going to be that long, Billy thinks. Not nearly, and any Viagra he takes will go to waste. 'Okay. We are going to roll east from where we are now—'

'You and Bucky?'

'Me and the girl. When we get placed somewhere close to Montauk—'

'Try Riverhead. Hyatt or Hilton Garden Inn.'

You haven't lost a step, Billy thinks. He almost expects Giorgio to say he'll make them a reservation.

'When we get placed, I'll call you.'

'Okay, but start by sending me some stills of your swing.'

'Swing?'

'The *girl*, Billy. And she's got to be the right kind of girl. Young, yeah, but also wholesome. If she looks trampy, forget it.'

'Understood.' Something else occurs to him. 'Do you know anything about Frank Macintosh? He was alive when I left, but I hit him pretty hard.'

'Doc Rivers got him stabilized but after that there was nothing he could do. He had a brain bleed, and Nick said he might have had a heart attack to go with it. His ma took him to Reno. He's in a long-term facility. Palliative care, they call it.'

'I'm sorry to hear that,' Billy says, and he really is.

'Margie took an apartment nearby. Nick's paying for the whole deal.'

'He's in a coma?'

'It might be better if he was. Nick says Marge told him he sleeps a lot, but when he comes around he talks nothing but gibberish. Has seizures and screams a lot.'

Billy says nothing. He can think of nothing to say.

Giorgio says, and not without admiration, 'You must have hit him *really* hard. Elvis has left the building.'

5

Billy, Bucky, and Alice go to Boulder, where Alice trawls through three different malls, shopping at stores with names like Deb, Forever 21, and Teen Beat. She discusses every choice with Bucky, who will be taking the pictures Giorgio (or Judy Blatner) will send to Klerke. Billy mostly follows them around, garnering suspicious looks from some of the sales staff. Alice buys a lightweight quilted parka, four skirts, two shirts, a blouse, and three dresses. One of the dresses has a boatneck top, but that's as close to sexy as any of the clothes get. Bucky vetoes a pair of low heels in favor of sneakers.

He also vetoes some low-rise jeans she likes, at least for the pictures. 'Buy the jeans for yourself if you want, but he'll want to see you in a dress.'

Once the shopping is done, four hundred dollars' worth, she gets her hair cut at Great Clips. While she's occupied with that, Billy buys shoes, slacks, and a bomber jacket with inside pockets. He shows Bucky a lime green silk shirt and Bucky clutches his head. 'You're not going for the streetcorner pimp-daddy look. Concierge service, remember?'

Billy puts the green shirt back on the rack and selects a gray one instead. Bucky looks it over and nods. 'Collar's a little Rick James for my taste, but never mind.'

'Rick who?'

'Never mind.'

As they walk back toward Great Clips, both of them carrying bags,

Alice comes bouncing out. Her hair is shorter and styled. She's wearing a Colorado Rockies hat with a ponytail threaded through the back. She breaks into a run, the ponytail swishing, and Billy thinks, Holy God, I think this really might work.

'The stylist tried to argue me out of cutting it. She asked me why I wanted to lose such beautiful hair that must have taken me years to grow. But the best part? She asked me if I liked high school so much I wanted to look like I was still there!'

She laughs and raises a hand, palm out. Bucky gives her a high five. Billy does the same, but his enthusiasm is fake. In the excitement of the shopping expedition, Alice has forgotten *why* they're shopping. He thinks Bucky has too, because he's drafting off her happiness. But Billy remembers. He's thinking of that little girl in TJ, clutching a toy and listening to the sound of approaching footsteps.

6

Alice wants to take the pictures as soon as they get back, but Bucky tells her to wait until the next morning, when she's looking her youngest and freshest. He calls it the September morn look.

'Neil Diamond, right?' Alice asks. 'My mom's a big fan.' And to Billy: 'Don't even ask, I called her last night.'

Maybe Bucky is thinking of Neil Diamond, but Billy is thinking of Paul Chabas, and the girl in the house on the outskirts of TJ, and Shanice Ackerman. In his mind the two girls have become a pair.

7

Bucky sets up their little photo shoot the next morning. He wants to use the east-facing window for natural light. The sofa is there, but he says they should move it and put a chair there instead. When Billy asks why, Bucky says it's because sofas say sex, and that's not the look they're going for. Innocent young girl is the look they're going for. Maybe selling herself just this once to help her poor old broke-ass mother.

When Alice comes out in one of her new skirts and tops, Bucky tells her to go back into the bathroom and scrub off most of the makeup. 'You want just a little blush on your cheeks and enough mascara to make your eyelashes look good. Tiny touch of lipstick. Got it?'

'Got it.' Alice is excited, a kid playing dress-up.

When she's gone, Billy asks Bucky how he knows about this stuff. 'Don't get me wrong, I'm glad because I couldn't do half as good a job, just the clothes go a long way toward selling it—'

'No,' Bucky says. 'The clothes are good, but it's mostly the hair. The ponytail.'

'How did you learn that stuff? You didn't ever . . .' Billy trails off. What does he know about Bucky Hanson, really? That he brokered stickup guys, that he's good at getting fugitives out of the country, that he has contacts in the legal profession and maybe even some top echelons of the New York judiciary. If so, Billy doesn't know who any of those guys are. Bucky is discreet. Which is probably one reason why he's still alive.

'Did I ever take pictures of young women dressed up to look like jailbait? No, but it was a thing for awhile in the porno mags like *Penthouse* and *Hustler*. Back in the 80s, when there *were* porno mags. As for taking pictures, I learned at my father's knee.'

'I thought you told me once that your father was a mortician. Somewhere in Pennsylvania.'

'He was, so I also learned a lot about makeup at my daddy's knee. Photography was his sideline – yearbook photos and weddings, mostly. Sometimes I was his assistant. In both jobs.'

'I came to the right place,' Billy says, smiling.

'You did.' But Bucky isn't smiling back. 'Don't you get that young woman hurt, Billy. And if you do, don't come back here because the door will be closed to you.'

Before Billy can answer, Alice comes back. In her white blouse, blue skirt, and knee-socks she looks very young indeed. Bucky seats her in the chair and tilts her head this way and that until the muted morning light is shining on her face to his liking. He's using Billy's phone to take the pix. He says he has a Leica and would love to use it, but that would be a little too pro. Klerke might not register that and be suspicious, but then again he might. TV and movies are a big part of his business, after all.

'Okay, let's get this party started. No big grin, Alice, but a little smile's okay. Remember what we're going for. Sweet and demure.'

Alice tries for sweet and demure, then dissolves in a fit of giggles.

'Okay,' Bucky says, 'that's fine. Get it out of your system, then remember that the man who's going to be looking at these is a fucking pedophile.'

That sobers her up and he goes to work. For all his pre-shoot fussing, the actual photography doesn't take long. He shoots sixteen or eighteen of Ponytail Alice in various outfits (but always, even in the boatneck dress, with the lowtop sneakers). He shoots a dozen more of Barrette Alice and finishes with a dozen of Alice Band Alice. He makes three sets of eight-by-tens on his color printer so they can each look at a stack. Bucky tells Billy and Alice to pick half a dozen they think are the best and says he'll do the same. At one point Alice cries out in a mixture of glee and dismay, 'Jesus Christ, I look about fourteen in this one!'

'Mark it,' Bucky says.

When they're done, they have all agreed on three of the shots. Bucky adds two more and tells Billy to email those five to Giorgio. 'He's pimped for the nasty old lizard before, so he'll probably know whether or not Klerke will bite.'

'Not yet,' Billy says. 'I'll do it once we're on the road and headed to New York.'

'What if Klerke tells Giorgio he's not interested?'

'We'll go anyway and I'll find a way in.'

'*We* will,' Alice says. 'You're not leaving me behind in a motel this time.'

Billy doesn't reply. He thinks it's a decision he'll make when and if the time comes. Then he thinks of what Alice has been through, and what Klerke has done to girls even younger than this one, and realizes it might not be his decision to make.

8

That night he calls Nick for the last time. 'You still owe a million-two.'

'I know and you'll get it. Our friend paid off. As far as he knows, you're dead.'

'Add another two hundred thousand. Call it a bonus for the shit you put me through. And send it to Marge.'

'Frank's mother? Are you serious?'

'Yes. Tell her it's from me. Tell her to put it toward Frank's care. Tell her I did what I had to, but I'm sorry.'

'I don't think your apology will cut much ice. Marge is . . .' He sighs. 'Marge is Marge.'

'You could also tell her that what happened to him ultimately comes back to you, not me, but I don't really expect that.'

There's silence for a few seconds and then Nick asks about the rest of what Billy's owed. Billy tells him exactly how he wants it handled. After some discussion Nick agrees. Does that mean he'll actually do it if Billy isn't around to make sure? Billy has his doubts, because he has no idea how long Nick's gratitude at being spared will last. But he intends to make sure his wishes are carried out, because he has no intention of dying in New York. It's Roger Klerke who's going to do the dying.

'Good luck,' Nick says. 'I mean that.'

'Uh-huh. Just see that Frank is taken care of. And the other thing.'

'Billy, I just want to tell you—'

Billy ends the call. He has no interest in what Nick wants to tell him. The books are balanced. He and Nick are done.

9

Billy is ready to go early the next morning, but Bucky asks him to wait until ten o'clock because he has an errand to run. While he does it, Billy visits the summerhouse one final time. He takes the picture of the hedge animals off the wall and carries it to the end of the path. He looks out over the gorge for a minute or two, across to the place where the reputedly haunted hotel once stood. Alice thought she saw it, but Billy sees only a few charred remnants. Maybe, he thinks, the site is still haunted. Maybe that's why no one's rebuilt on it, although the location looks prime.

He throws the picture over the edge. He peers over the lip of the drop and sees it caught in the top of a pine tree about a hundred feet down. Let it rot there, he thinks, and goes back to the house. Alice has put their little bits of luggage in the Mitsubishi. There's no reason not to drive it east. It's a good vehicle, it can't be tracked, and Reggie won't miss it.

'Where did you go?' Alice asks.

'Just for a walk. Wanted to stretch my legs.'

They are sitting in the rockers on the porch when Bucky comes back. 'I saw a friend and bought you a little going-away present,' he says, and hands Alice a pistol. 'Sig Sauer P320 Subcompact. Ten in the mag plus one in the pipe. Small enough to carry in your purse. It's loaded, so be careful how you grab it if you have to take it out.'

Alice looks at it, fascinated. 'I've never fired a gun before.'

'It's simple enough, just point and shoot. Unless you're standing close, you'll probably miss your target anyway, but you might scare someone off.' He looks at Billy. 'If you have a problem with her carrying, speak up.'

Billy shakes his head.

'One thing, Alice. If you need to use it, *use it*. Promise me.'

Alice promises.

'Okay, now give me a hug.'

She hugs him and starts to cry. Billy thinks that's good, actually. She's feeling her feelings, as they say in the self-help groups.

It's a long, strong hug. Bucky lets loose after thirty seconds or so and turns to Billy. 'Now you.'

Little as he cares for man-hugs, he does it. For years Bucky has just been a business associate, but over the last month or so he's become a friend. He gave them shelter when they needed it, and he's on board with what lies ahead. More important than those things, he's been good to Alice.

Billy gets behind the wheel of the Mitsubishi. Bucky walks around to the passenger side, looking very Colorado in his jeans and flannel shirt. He makes a cranking gesture and Alice powers down the window. Bucky leans in and kisses her on the temple. 'I want to see you again. Make sure I do.'

'I will,' Alice says. She's crying again. 'I sure will.'

'Okay.' Bucky straightens and stands back. 'Now go get that son of a bitch.'

10

Billy stops at the Walmart Supercenter in Longmont, getting as close to the building as possible to improve the WiFi connection. Using his personal laptop, which is VPN-equipped, he sends the pictures of Alice to Giorgio and asks him to post them on to Klerke ASAP.

Tell him the girl's name is Rosalie. She has a window. It opens three days from now and will close four days after that. Price is negotiable but floor is $8,000 for one hour. Tell him Rosalie is 'prime stuff.' Tell him to check with Judy Blatner if he doubts that. If you want, tell him that you will make the arrangements free of charge to compensate for the unavoidable complications on the Allen job. Tell him the delivery rep will be Darren Byrne's cousin, Steven Byrne. Let me know as soon as you hear.

He signs it B.

They stay that night at a Holiday Inn Express in Lincoln, Nebraska. Billy is bringing in their luggage on a courtesy trolley when his phone dings with a text. He observes, with zero nostalgia, that it's from his old literary agent.

'Giorgio?' Alice asks.

'Yes.'

'What does it say?'

Billy hands her his phone.

GRusso: He wants her. November 4, 8 PM 775 Montauk Highway. Text me thumbs up or down.

'Are you sure you want to do this? Your call, Alice.'

She finds 👍 and sends it.

CHAPTER 23

We left Lincoln early and drove east on 1-80. For the first hour or so we didn't talk much. Alice had my lappie open and was reading everything I'd written in the summerhouse. On the outskirts of Council Bluffs a car blipped past us with a clown and a ballerina looking at us from the back seat. The clown waved. I waved back.

'Alice!' I said. 'Do you know what today is?'

'Thursday?' She didn't look up from the screen. It made me think of Derek Ackerman and his friend Danny Fazio back on Evergreen Street, hypnotized by whatever they were looking at on their phones.

'Not just any Thursday. It's Halloween.'

'Okay.' Still not looking up.

'What did you go as? Your favorite, I mean.'

'Mmm . . . once I was Princess Leia.' Still not looking up from what she was reading. 'My sister took me around the neighborhood.'

'In Kingston, right?'

'Right.'

'Get much swag?'

She finally looked up. 'Let me read, Billy, I'm almost done.'

So I let her read and we rolled deeper into Iowa. No big changes there, just miles of flatland. At last she closed the laptop. I asked her if she'd read it all.

'Just to where I came into the story. The part where I threw up and almost choked. That was hard to read about, so I stopped. By the way, you forgot to change my name.'

'I'll make a note.'

'The rest I knew.' She smiles. 'Remember *The Blacklist* on Netflix? And how we watered the plants?'

'Daphne and Walter.'

'Do you think they lived?'

'I'm sure they did.'

'Bullshit. You don't know if they did or not.'

I admitted that was true.

'And neither do I. But we can believe they did if we want to, can't we?'

'Yes,' I said. 'We can.'

'That's the advantage of not knowing.' Alice was staring out the window at miles of cornfields, all brown now and waiting for winter. 'People can choose to believe any old thing they want. I choose to believe that we'll get to Montauk Point, and do what we came to do, and get away with it, and live happily ever after.'

'Okay,' I said, 'I'll choose to believe that, too.'

'After all, you've never been caught yet. All those killings, and you got away with them all.'

'I'm sorry you had to read about that. But you said I should write down everything.'

She shrugged. 'They were bad people. They all had that in common. You didn't shoot any priests or doctors or . . . or crossing guards.'

That made me laugh and Alice smiled a little, but I could tell she was thinking. I let her do it. The miles rolled by.

'I'm going back to the mountains,' she said at last. 'I might even live with Bucky for awhile. What do you think of that?'

'I think he'd like it.'

'Just to get started. Until I can find work and get my own place and start saving up money to go back to school. Because you can start college whenever you want. Sometimes people don't start college until they're in their forties or even their sixties, right?'

'I saw a thing on TV about a man who started when he was seventy-five and got his diploma when he was eighty. My Spidey sense tells me it's not business school you're thinking about.'

'No, regular school. Maybe even the University of Colorado. I could live in Boulder. I liked that town.'

'Any idea what you'd want to study?'

She hesitated, as if something had occurred to her and she'd changed her mind. 'History, I think. Or sociology. Maybe even theater arts.' Then, as if I had objected to the idea: 'Not for acting, I wouldn't want to do that, but the other stuff – sets and lighting and all that. There's so much I'm curious about.'

I said that was good.

'What about you, Billy? What's your happily ever after?'

I didn't have to think about it. 'Since we're dreaming, I'd like to write books.' I tapped the laptop, which she was still holding. 'Until I wrote that I didn't know if I could. Now I do.'

'What about this story? You could fix it up, turn it into fiction . . .'

I shook my head. 'No one but you is ever going to see it, and that's all right. It did its job. It opened the door. And I don't have to give you an alias.'

Alice was quiet for awhile. Then she said, 'This is Iowa, right?'

'Right.'

'Boring.'

I laughed. 'I bet the Iowans don't think so.'

'I bet they do. Especially the kids.'

I couldn't argue with her there.

'Tell me something.'

'I will if I can.'

'Why would a man in his sixties want to be with a girl as young as Rosalie is supposed to be? I don't get that. It seems . . . I don't know . . . grotesque.'

'Insecurity? Or maybe trying to connect with the vitality he's lost? Reaching back to his own youth and trying to connect with it?'

Alice considered these ideas, but only briefly. 'Sounds like bullshit to me.'

It did to me too, actually.

'I mean, think about it. What would Klerke talk about to a sixteen-year-old girl? Politics? World events? His TV stations? And what would she talk about to him? Cheerleading and her Facebook friends?'

'I don't think he's looking for a long-term relationship. The deal was eight thousand for one hour.'

'So it's fucking for the sake of fucking. Taking for the sake of taking. That seems so hollow to me. So empty. And that little girl in Mexico . . .'

She fell silent and watched Iowa roll by. Then she said something, but so low I couldn't make it out.

'What?'

'Monster.' She was still looking out at the miles of dead corn. 'I said monster.'

*

We spent Halloween night in South Bend, Indiana, and the first of November in Lock Haven, Pennsylvania. As we checked in, my phone binged with a text from Giorgio.

GRusso: Petersen, RK's assistant, wants a picture of Darren Byrne's cousin, for identification purposes. Send it to judyb14455@aol.com. She will pass it on at no charge. She'd be happy if RK ran into some bad luck.

Petersen wanting a photo was worrisome but not surprising. He was Klerke's on-site security as well as his assistant, after all.

Alice told me not to worry. She said she would cut and re-style the black wig I'd worn to Promontory Point. ('Sometimes it's good to have a sister who's a hairdresser,' she said.) We went to Walmart. Alice found a pair of aviator-style glasses and some cold cream that she said would give me an Irish pallor. Also a small clip-on gold earring, not too ostentatious, for my left ear. Back in the motel she combed the black wig back from my forehead and told me to prop the aviators on it.

'Like you think you're a movie star,' she said. 'Put on the shirt with the high collar. And remember that as far as Klerke and this guy Petersen know, Billy Summers is dead.'

She took the picture against a neutral background (the brick wall of the Best Western where we were staying) and we examined it together, and closely.

'Is it good enough?' Alice asked. 'I mean, you don't look like you to me, especially with that snarky grin, but I wish we had Bucky to help us.'

'I think it is. As you said, it helps that they think I'm buried in the Pauite Foothills.'

'This is quite a little conspiracy we've got going,' Alice said as we went back inside. 'Bucky, your make-believe literary agent, and now some big shot Vegas madam.'

'Don't forget Nick,' I said.

She stopped halfway down the corridor to our rooms, frowning. 'If any of them called Klerke and told him what's going on, it would probably be a nice payday for them. Not Majarian or Mr Piglielli, and Bucky wouldn't *ever*, but what about the Blatner woman?'

'She won't, either,' I said. 'Basically, they've all had enough of him.'

'You hope.'

'I know,' I said, and hoped I did. In any case I was going in, and it looked more and more like Alice would be going in with me.

★

We stayed in New Jersey on the night of November 2. The following night we checked into the Riverhead Hyatt, fifty miles from Montauk Point. Giorgio had indeed made reservations from his fat farm prison in South America. Because he knew I had no Steven Byrne ID, I was reserved under the Dalton Smith name. And because this place was quite a bit more fancy-shmancy than the motels where we'd previously stayed, Alice had to show her new Elizabeth Anderson ID. Giorgio, maybe thinner but as sharp as ever, had also reserved a double room, prepaid, for Steven Byrne and Rosalie Forester. Klerke wouldn't check, such chores were beneath him, but Petersen might. If the clerk told Petersen that Byrne and Forester hadn't checked in yet, Petersen wouldn't be too concerned. Pimps weren't known for keeping regular schedules.

Before leaving the desk, I asked if there was a package for me. Turned out there was, from Fun & Games Novelties in Las Vegas. A nonexistent company, no doubt. Giorgio had ordered it at my request. I opened it in my room with Alice looking on. Inside was a small unmarked aerosol cannister about the size of a roll-on deodorant tube. No oven spray this time.

'What is it?'

'Carfentanil. In 2002, the Russians pumped a version of this into a theater where forty or fifty Chechen rebels were holding seven hundred people hostage. The idea was to put everyone to sleep and end the siege. It worked, but the gas was too strong. A hundred of the hostages didn't just go to sleep, they died. I doubt if Putin gave a shit. This stuff is supposedly half-strength. It's Klerke we're after. I don't want to kill Petersen if I don't have to.'

'What if it doesn't work?'

'Then I'll do whatever I need to.'

'We,' Alice said.

★

November 4 was a long day. Days of waiting always are. Alice brought out her tank suit and swam in the pool. Later on we took a walk and ate a pickup lunch at a hotdog wagon. Alice said she wanted a nap. I tried to take one and couldn't. Later, while she was re-styling the wig again to match the photo, she admitted she hadn't been able to, either.

'And I didn't sleep much last night. I'll sleep when this is over. Then I'll sleep a *lot*.'

'Fuck it,' I said. 'Stay here. Let me do this.'

Alice cracked a small smile. 'And what would you say to Petersen when you showed up without the eight-thousand-dollar girl?'

'I'll think of something.'

'You might not even get in. If you did, you'd have to kill Petersen. You don't want to do that, and I don't want you to do it. I'm going.'

So that was that.

★

We left at six. Alice had a picture of the estate from Google Earth and directions on how to get there on the GPS. This late in the season the traffic was light. I asked her if she wanted to stop at one of the fast food places on the outskirts of Riverhead and she gave a brittle laugh. 'If I ate anything, I'd throw up all over my nice new dress.'

It was the boatneck, purple with tiny white flowers. She was wearing her new parka but not zipped, so the place where her cleavage began would show. There wasn't much else up front because she was wearing a mid-length binder underneath instead of a bra. Her handbag was on her lap. The Sig was inside. I was wearing my new bomber jacket. The Glock was in one of the inside pockets. The aerosol can was in the other.

'Montauk Highway makes a loop,' she said. I knew that, I'd studied the layout on my laptop that afternoon when I couldn't nap, but I let her talk. She was working on her nerves, trying to sand them down. 'You go past the Lighthouse Museum and take your first left. Eos isn't a seafront estate, he traded that for the view, I guess. I doubt if he water-skis or bodysurfs at his age, anyway. Are you scared?'

'No.' Not for myself, at least.

'Then I'll be scared for both of us. If you don't mind.' She consulted the map on her phone again. 'It looks like number 775 is about a mile in, right after the Montauk Farm Store. That must be handy. For fresh veggies and all. You look good, Billy, Irish as all getout, and can you stop somewhere? I have to pee so bad.'

I stopped at a place called the BreezeWay Diner, about halfway between Riverhead and Montauk. Alice dashed inside and I thought about driving on without her. Everything Bucky had told me not to do with her – to her – I was doing. Soon she would be an accessory to the murder of a rich and famous man, and that would only be if things went right. If they didn't, she might wind up dead. But I stayed. Because I needed her to get in, yes, but also because she had a right to decide.

She came out smiling. 'That is so much better.' And as I pulled back onto the highway: 'I thought you might leave me.'

'Never crossed my mind,' I said. From the look she gave me I thought she knew better.

She straightened in her seat and tugged the hem of her dress to her knees. She looked like a prim and proper high school girl, the kind they don't seem to make anymore. 'Let's do this.'

★

We passed the Lighthouse Museum and the left turn came up less than a hundred yards further on. It was full dark now. Somewhere off to the right was the sound of the ocean. A crescent moon flicked through the trees. Alice leaned over, fussed briefly with my wig, then sat back. We didn't talk.

The numbers on Montauk Highway started at 600, for reasons probably only known to town planners who had long since gone to their final rewards. I was surprised that the houses, although well-kept, were mundane. Most were ranches and Cape Cods that wouldn't have looked out of place on Evergreen Street. There was even a trailer park. A nice one with carriage lamps and gravel lanes, granted, but a trailer park is a trailer park.

The Montauk Farm Store, really just a jumped-up produce stand, was dark and shuttered. There were a few lonely pumpkins in a pyramid by the door and a few more in the back of an old stakebed truck with 4-SALE soaped on one side of the windshield and RUNS GOOD on the other.

Alice pointed at a mailbox beyond the store. 'That's it.'

I slowed. 'Last chance. Are you sure? If you're not we can turn around.'

'I'm sure.' She was sitting ramrod straight, knees together and hands clasped on the strap of her purse. Eyes straight ahead.

I turned onto a piece-of-shit dirt track marked with a sign reading PRIVATE WAY. It became clear almost at once that the dirt track was camouflage to deke curious tourists. Over the first hill it became a tar road wide enough for cars to pass each other comfortably. I crept along using my high beams, thinking that this was my second trip to the estate of a bad man. I hoped this one would be quicker and more efficient.

We rounded a curve. Ahead of us, a slatted wooden gate six or seven feet high blocked the road. There was a talk-box on a concrete pillar, lit by a metal-shaded light. I pulled up to it, rolled down my window, and thumbed the button. 'Hello?'

I thought (Alice and Bucky concurred) that trying for an Irish lilt might be disastrous. And there was no reason why Byrne had to have one, not if he'd lived his whole life in New York.

Meanwhile, the box on the post wasn't talking back to me.

'Hello? This is Steve Byrne. Darren's cousin, yo? I got something for Mr K.'

More silence, giving me – Alice too, from the look of her – reason to think something had gone wrong and we weren't going to get in. Not this way, anyhow.

Then the box crackled and a man said, 'Get out of the car.' Flat and toneless. It could have been a cop's voice. 'You and the young lady both. You'll see an **X** in front of the gate, right in the middle. Stand there and look to your left. Stand close together.'

I looked at Alice and she looked at me, wide-eyed. I shrugged and nodded. We got out and walked to the gate. The **X**, maybe once blue but now faded to gray, was on a concrete square. We crowded together on it and looked left.

'Up. Look up.'

We looked up. It was a camera, of course.

I could hear a faint voice murmur something, then whoever was holding down the intercom button in the house – Petersen, I assumed

– let go and there was only silence. No wind, and too late in the year for crickets.

'What's happening?' Alice asked.

I didn't know, but thought it probable they were listening, so I told her to shut up and wait. Her eyes widened, but then she got it and said, 'Okay, sir' in a meek little voice.

The intercom clicked and the voice said, 'I see a bulge on the left side of your jacket, Mr Byrne. Are you armed?'

That was one hell of a good camera. I could say no and the barrier would no doubt stay closed, no matter how much Klerke wanted the girl. 'Yeah, I'm carrying,' I said. 'For protection only.'

'Take it out and hold it up.'

I took out the Glock and held it up to the camera.

'Put it at the base of the intercom post. You won't need protection here and no one will steal it. You can pick it up on your way out.'

I did as I was told. The aerosol can was much smaller, so there was no bulge on that side of the jacket, and if I could immobilize the man who belonged to the intercom voice, Klerke would be no problem. Or so I hoped.

I started back to the concrete square, but the voice from the intercom stopped me. 'No, Mr Byrne. Stay where you are, please.' There was a pause and then the voice said, 'Actually I want you to take two steps back. Please.'

I took two steps back toward the car.

'Now one more,' the voice said, and I understood. They wanted me off-camera. Klerke wanted to size up the merchandise and decide if he really wanted to buy, or to send us on our way. There was a faint whine from the camera. I looked and saw the lens was now protruding. Zooming the image.

I thought the voice would next ask Alice to show the camera what was in her purse, and the Sig would end up at the base of the intercom post along with the Glock, but that wasn't it.

'Lift your skirt, young lady.'

Petersen's voice, but it would be Klerke looking. Avid eyes in wrinkled sockets.

Staring at the ground instead of at the camera, Alice lifted her skirt to her thighs. The bruises there were long gone. Her legs were smooth. Young. I hated the voice. I hated both of them.

'Higher, please.'

For a moment I didn't think she was going to do it. Then she lifted her skirt to her waist, still not looking up. There was no doubt about her humiliation and I had no doubt Klerke was getting off on it.

'Now look up at the camera.'

She did it.

'Keep holding up your skirt. Mr Klerke would like you to run your tongue around your lips.'

'No,' I said. 'That's enough.'

Alice dropped her skirt and gave me a look that asked what the hell I was doing.

I stepped back into camera range and looked up. 'You seen enough, okay? Anything else is for inside. It's fuckin cold out here.' I thought about throwing in another *yo*, decided not to. 'And I want the money in my hand before she steps through the door. Once she does, the clock is running. You got it?'

There was silence for maybe thirty seconds. I was getting that hinky feeling again. 'Come on,' I said, taking her arm. 'Fuck this shit, we're taillights.'

But then the gate started to roll open on little rubber wheels. The voice from the intercom said, 'It's eight-tenths of a mile, Mr Byrne. I will have your money.'

Alice got in on her side and I got in on mine. She was shaking.

I rolled up the window before telling her, just above a whisper, that I was sorry about that.

'I don't care if they saw my underpants, I just thought they were going to make me open my purse and he'd see the gun on his damn camera.'

'You're a kid,' I said. I looked in the rearview and saw the gate trundling closed behind us. 'I don't think the idea that you were carrying ever crossed his mind.'

'Then I thought he wouldn't let us in at all. I thought that man would say "You're no sixteen-year-old, get out of here and stop wasting our time."'

Now there were old-fashioned lamps lining both sides of the road. Ahead I could see the lights of the house the old man had named Eos, after the rosy-fingered goddess of the dawn.

'You better give me the gun,' I said.

She shook her head. 'I want it. You've still got the spray.'

There was no time to argue about it. The house – the *manor* – was in sight. It was a rambling stone structure on at least two acres of lawn. A rich man's playpen for sure, but with a grace none of the places Nick liked could match. There was a turnaround in front. I pulled up at stone steps leading to a circular entry. Alice reached for the doorhandle.

'Don't. Let me come around and open it for you, like a real gent.'

I went around the hood of the Mitsubishi, opened the door, and took her hand. It was very cold. Her eyes were wide and her lips were pressed together.

I murmured in her ear as I helped her out. 'Walk behind me and stop at the foot of those steps. This is going to happen fast.'

'I'm pretty scared.'

'Don't be afraid to show it. He'll probably like that.'

We walked to the steps. There were four. She stopped at the bottom. The outside light came on and I could see her shadow jump long, hands still clasping her purse. Holding it in front of her as if it could shield her from what was going to happen in the next three hundred seconds or so. The big front door opened, casting an oblong of inside light around me. The man standing there was tall and well-built. With the light behind him I couldn't judge his age or even make out his face, but I could see the holster on his hip. A small holster for a small gun.

'What's she doing down there?' Petersen said. 'Tell her to come up.'

'Money first,' I said. And over my shoulder, 'Stay put, girl.'

Petersen reached into his front pocket – the one on the other side from the holster, which was undoubtedly lined with plastic for a fast, smooth draw should it be needed – and drew out a wad of bills. He handed it to me and said, 'You don't sound like a mick.'

I laughed and started to thumb through the bills. They were all hundreds. 'Man, after forty years in Queens I hope not. Where's the big man?'

'None of your business. Send the girl up, park over there by the garage, and stay in the car.'

'Yeah, sure, but now you made me lose my fuckin count.'

I started again. Behind me, Alice said, 'Billy? I'm getting cold.'

Petersen stiffened slightly. 'Billy? Why does she call you Billy?'

I laughed. 'Ah, man, she does that all the time. It's her boyfriend's name.' I gave him a grin. 'He don't know she's here, get it?'

Petersen said nothing. He didn't look convinced. His hand crept down toward the quick-draw holster.

'This is good, man, pot's right,' I said.

I shoved the money into the pocket of the bomber jacket and brought out the aerosol. Maybe he saw it and maybe he didn't, but he started to draw the little gun anyway. I made a fist with my free hand and brought it down on his, like a kid playing rock breaks scissors. Then I sprayed him. A white cloud of droplets hit him in the face. It was small, but the result was satisfactory. He rocked back and forth twice, then dropped. The gun fell on the stoop and went off with a report like a small firecracker. They are not supposed to do that, so he must have messed with it somehow. I felt the bullet go past my ankle and turned to make sure it hadn't hit Alice.

She came running up the steps looking dismayed. 'Sorry, sorry, that was stupid, I forgot who—'

From inside the house a cracked smoker's voice shouted, 'Bill? *Bill!*'

I almost answered, then remembered that the man lying in the foyer was also a Billy. It's a common enough name.

'What was that?' A loose, phlegmy cough, followed by a throat-clearing sound. 'Where's the girl?'

A door opened halfway down the hall. Klerke came through it. He was dressed in blue silk pajamas. His white hair was combed back in a pompadour that made me think of Frank. He had a cane in one hand. 'Bill, where's the gir—'

He stopped and squinted at us. He looked down and saw his man sprawled on the floor. Then he turned and hobbled for the door he'd come through, hunched over his thumping cane, holding it in both hands, almost pole-vaulting on it. He was faster than I would have expected, given his age and condition. I ran after him, remembering to hold my breath as I went through the foyer, and caught him trying to shut the door. I shoved it against him and he fell over. His cane went flying.

He sat up and stared at me. We were in a living room. The rug he had sprawled on looked expensive. Maybe Turkish, maybe an Aubusson. There were paintings on the walls that looked equally expensive. The furniture was heavy, upholstered in velvet. There was a chrome stand holding a bottle of no doubt expensive Champagne on a bed of ice.

He started to back away from me on his bottom, groping for his cane. His careful comb-job was coming apart, hair falling in clumps around the wrinkled sag-bag of his face. His lower lip, shiny with spit, stuck out in a kind of a pout. I could smell his cologne.

'What did you do to Bill? Did you shoot him? Was that a gunshot?'

He got hold of the cane and brandished it at me as he sat there with his legs splayed. His pajama pants were working down, exposing padded hips and graying pubic hair.

'I want you out of here! Who are you, anyway?'

'I'm the man who killed the man who killed your son,' I said.

His eyes widened and he slashed the cane at me. I grabbed it, yanked it out of his hand, and threw it across the room.

'You had someone set that fire in Cody. Arranged for your camera crew to be the only one at the courthouse when the deal went down. Didn't you?'

He stared at me, upper lip rising and falling. Doing that made him look like an old dog with a bad temper. 'I don't know what you're talking about.'

'I think you do. That diversion wasn't for me, it was way too soon. So why?'

Klerke got on his knees and crawled toward the sofa, giving me a much better view of his ass-crack than I wanted. He pulled ineffectually at the waistband of his pants. I could almost feel sorry for him. Except I didn't. *Mr Klerke would like to see your underwear. Mr Klerke would like you to run your tongue around your lips.*

'Why?' As if I didn't know. 'You need to answer me.'

He grabbed the arm of the sofa and pulled himself up. He was gasping for breath. I could see the flesh-colored button of a hearing aid in one ear. He sat down with a thump and a gasp.

'All right. Allen tried to blackmail me and I wanted to watch him die.'

Of course you did, I thought. And I bet you watched it over and over, both at regular speed and in slow motion.

'You're Summers. Majarian told me you were dead.' And then, with absurd and horrifying outrage: 'I paid that kike millions of dollars! He robbed me!'

'You should have asked for a picture. Why didn't you?'

He didn't reply and I didn't need him to. He had been emperor so long he couldn't conceive of not being obeyed. *Film the execution. Kill the executioner. Lift your skirt and show me your panties. This time I want a really young one.*

'I owe you money. Is that what you're here for?'

'Tell me something else. Tell me how it was, putting out a hit on your own flesh and blood.'

The lip lifted again, showing teeth too perfect for the face they were in. 'He deserved it. He wouldn't *stop*. He was a . . .' Klerke stopped, squinting past me. 'Who's that? Is it the girl I paid for?'

Alice came into the room and stood beside me. She was holding her bag in her left hand. The Sig was in her right. 'You wanted to know what it was like, didn't you?'

'What? I don't know what you're—'

'To rape a child. You wanted to know what it was like.'

'You're crazy! I don't have any idea—'

'It probably hurt. Like this.' Alice shot him. I think she was aiming for his balls, but she hit him in the stomach instead.

Klerke screamed. It was a very loud scream. It banished the harpy who had taken over her head and pulled the trigger. She dropped her purse and put her hand over her mouth.

'*I'm hurt!*' Klerke shrieked. He was holding his stomach. Blood oozed through his fingers and into the lap of his silk pajamas. '*Oh my God I'm HURRRT!*'

Alice turned to me, eyes wide and wet, mouth open. She whispered something I didn't quite hear because the gunshot from the Sig Sauer had been much louder than the one from Petersen's little pistol. It might have been *I didn't know.*

'*I need a doctor, it HURRRRRRTS!*'

The blood was pouring out of him now. He was forcing it out with his screams. I took the gun from Alice's limp hand, put the muzzle to his left temple, and pulled the trigger. He flopped back on the sofa, kicked once, and fell on the floor. His days of raping children and murdering sons and God knew what else were over.

'It wasn't me,' Alice said. 'Billy, it wasn't me who pulled the trigger, I swear it wasn't.'

Only it was. Something inside her had risen up, a stranger, and now she would have to live with its presence because that was her, too. She'd see it the next time she looked in the mirror.

'Come on.' I slipped the Sig in my belt and put the strap of her bag over her shoulder. 'We need to go.'

'I just . . . it was like I was outside myself, and . . .'

'I know. We need to go, Alice.'

'It was so *loud*. Wasn't it loud?'

'Yes, very loud. Come on.'

I led her back down the hall, only noticing now that it was lined with tapestries of knights and ladies fair and, for some fucked-up reason, windmills.

'Is he dead, too?' She was looking at Petersen.

I took a knee beside him but didn't need to feel for his pulse. I could hear his breathing, good and steady. 'He's alive.'

'Will he call the police?'

'Eventually, but we'll be long gone by the time he comes around, and he's going to be fucked up for a long time after he does.'

'Klerke deserved it,' she said as we went down the steps. She swayed, maybe because she'd gotten a little of the gas, maybe because she was in shock, maybe both. I put an arm around her waist. She looked up at me. 'Didn't he?'

'I think so, but I don't really know anymore. What I know is men like him are above justice in most cases. Except the kind we gave him. For the girl in Mexico. And for the murder of his own son.'

'But he was a bad man.'

'Yes,' I said. 'Very bad.'

*

We got in the car and drove the rest of the way around the circle. I wondered if the monitor the two men had been watching had recorded us as well. If it did, it would only show a guy with black hair and a young girl who had lifted her skirt but only once or twice – and briefly – lifted her head. After she got rid of the blonde hair, she'd be next to impossible to identify. I was more concerned about the gate. If we needed a code to open it, we were in trouble. But when we pulled up close, the car broke an invisible beam and the gate trundled open. I stopped beyond it, put the car in park, and opened the door.

'What are you stopping for?'

'My gun. He made me leave it at the bottom of that post. It's got my fingerprints on it.'

'Oh my God, that's right. I'm stupid.'

'Not stupid, woozy. And in shock. It will wear off.'

She turned to me, now looking older than her years instead of younger. 'Will it? Do you promise?'

'It will and I do.'

I got out of the car and started around the hood. I was still in the glare thrown by the headlights, like an actor on a stage, when the woman came out of the trees ten feet from the gate. She was wearing camo pants and a camo jacket instead of a blue dress, it was a pistol instead of a trowel in her hand, she had no business being on this side of the continental United States or anywhere except at her damaged son's bedside, but I knew who it was. There wasn't even a second's doubt. I raised the Sig, but she was faster.

'You fucking fuck,' Marge said, and fired. I fired a second later and her head snapped back. She went down with her sneakers sticking out into the road.

Alice was screaming and running to me. 'Are you hurt? Billy, are you hurt?'

'No. She missed me.' Then I felt the pain start in my side. Not a clean miss after all.

'Who was that?'

'An angry woman named Marge.'

That struck me funny because it sounded like the title of the kind of film smart people go to see in the art cinemas. I laughed and that made my side hurt more.

'Billy?'

'She must have guessed where I was going. Or maybe Nick told her about Klerke, but I don't think so. I think she was just good at keeping her ears peeled while she served lunch and dinner.'

'The woman who was gardening when you drove up to the service gate?'

'Yes. Her.'

'Is she dead?' Alice's hands were at her mouth. 'If she's not, please don't kill her the way you . . . the way . . .'

'I'm not going to kill her if she's still alive.'

I could say that because I knew she wasn't. It was all in the way her head snapped back. I knelt beside her, but only briefly.

'She's gone.' I winced when I stood up. I couldn't help it.

'You said she didn't hit you!'

'In the heat of the moment I didn't think she did. It's just a graze.'

'I want to see!'

I did too, but not right then. 'We have to get out of here before we do anything else. Five gunshots is four too many. Get my Glock from where I put it.'

While Alice did that, I took the gun Marge had used — a Smith & Wesson ACP — and replaced it with the Sig Sauer, after first wiping it clean on my shirt and then curling her dead fingers around it. I wiped the aerosol cannister, put her prints on it, and tucked it into one of her jacket pockets. When I got up the second time, the pain in my side was a little worse. Not terrible, but I could feel the seep of blood staining my high-class pimp's shirt. Worn once and ruined, I thought. What a shame. Maybe I should have stuck with the green one.

I said, 'This is done. Let's get out of here.'

★

We drove back to Riverhead, stopping on the way for Band-Aids, a roll of gauze, tape, hydrogen peroxide, and Betadine ointment. Alice went into the Walgreens while I waited in the car. By the time we got to the hotel, my midsection and left arm had stiffened up considerably. Alice used her key to let us in the side door. In my room, she had to help me off with the bomber jacket. She looked at the hole in it, then at the left side of my shirt. 'Oh my God.'

I told her it looked worse than it probably was. Most of the blood had dried.

She helped me with the shirt and invoked God again, but this time it was a bit muffled because her hand was over her mouth. 'That's not just a *graze*.'

True. The bullet had slashed through me just above the hipbone, parting the skin and the flesh. The wound was maybe half an inch deep. Fresh blood oozed and seeped.

'In the bathroom,' she said. 'If you don't want to leave a lot of blood around—'

'It's almost stopped.'

'Bullshit! Every time you move it starts again. You need to get undressed and then stand in the tub while I dress the wound. Which I've never done before, if you want to know. Although my sister did it to me once when I crashed my bike into the Simeckis' mailbox.'

We went into the bathroom and I sat on the toilet lid while she took off my shoes and socks. I stood up, provoking fresh seepage, and she unbuckled my pants. I wanted to take them off myself but she wouldn't let me. She made me sit on the toilet again, then knelt and pulled them off by the legs.

'Underwear, too. They're soaked through on the left side.'

'Alice—'

'Don't argue. You've seen me naked, right? Think of it as balancing the scales. Get in the tub.'

I stood up, dropped my shorts, and stepped into the tub. She kept a steadying hand on my elbow while I did it. There was blood down my left leg to the knee. I reached for the shower handle and she pushed my hand away. 'Maybe tomorrow. Or the next day. Not tonight.'

She started the tub faucet, wetted a washcloth, and cleaned me up, avoiding the wound. Blood and small clots ran down the drain. 'Dear God, she cut you wide open. Like with a knife.'

'I saw worse in Iraq,' I said, 'and guys were back clearing blocks the next day.'

'Is that really true?'

'Well . . . two days. Maybe three.'

She wrung out the washcloth and tossed it into the plastic-lined waste-basket, then gave me another to wipe the sweat off my face. She took it and tossed it in with the other one. 'Those go with us.' She patted me dry with a hand towel, tossed that into the wastebasket, then helped me out of the tub. It was harder getting out than it had been getting in.

Alice walked with me to the bed, where I sat down – carefully, trying to stay straight from the waist up. She helped me on with my last pair of clean undershorts, then disinfected the wound, which hurt worse than the bullet had when it clipped through me. The Band-Aids were no good. The wound was too long and the edges had spread, creating a wedge-shaped divot in my side. She used the gauze and tape instead. At last she sat back on her heels. Her fingers were stained with my blood.

'Try to lie still tonight,' she said. 'On your back. Don't roll around and break it open and get blood on the sheets. Maybe you ought to lie on a towel.'

'Probably a good idea.'

She went to get one, a bath towel this time. She also brought the plastic bag with the towel and washcloth in it. 'I've got Tylenol in my purse. I'll give you two and leave two for later, okay?'

'Yes. Thank you.'

She looked straight at me. 'No thanks needed. I'd do anything for you, Billy.'

I wanted to tell her not to say that, but I didn't. I said, 'We need to get out of here in the morning. Early. It's a long drive back to Sidewinder, and—'

'Just shy of two thousand miles,' Alice said. 'I googled it.'

'—and I don't know how much of the driving I can do.'

'None would be good, at least to start with. Unless you want to open that wound up again. You need stitches, but I'm not trying *that*.'

'I don't expect you to. I can live with some scarring. A couple of inches farther in and I would have been in real trouble. Marge. Jesus. Fucking Marge. Don't turn down the bedspread, Alice, I'll sleep on top of it.' If I could sleep, that was. The pain wasn't terribly intense now that the sting of the hydrogen peroxide had worn off, but it was steady. 'Just spread the towel.'

She did, then sat where I had been sitting. 'Maybe I should stay. Sleep on the other side.'

I shook my head. 'No. Bring me the Tylenol, then sleep in your own room. You'll need to sleep if you're going to be doing the driving.' I glanced at my watch and saw it was quarter past eleven. 'I'd like to be out of here by eight, at the latest.'

*

We were out by seven. Alice took the wheel as far as the New York metro area, then turned the driving chore over to me, with obvious relief. I got us across New Jersey and into Pennsylvania. At the welcome area just over the state line, we changed places again. The wound in my side was seeping again, and before we stopped for the night – at another off-the-grid motel – we'd have to pick up more gauze. I was going to be okay, but I was going to have one hell of a battle scar to go with my half-missing big toe. And no Purple Heart this time.

That night we stayed at Jim and Melissa's Roadside Cabins, 10% Discount For Cash. The following day I felt better, my side not so stiff and painful, and I was able to do some of the driving. We stopped on the outskirts of Davenport, at a ramshackle motel called the Bide-A-Wee.

I had spent most of that day thinking and deciding what came next. There was money in three separate accounts, one of them accessible only to me as Dalton Smith, an identity that was (by the grace of God) still clean. At least as far as I knew. There would be more in the Woodley account if Nick came through, and I thought he would. His Roger Klerke problem had been solved, after all, and to his great financial benefit.

Before she went into her room, I hugged Alice and kissed her on both cheeks.

She looked at me with dark blue eyes I'd come to love, just as I'd loved Shan Ackerman's dark brown ones. 'What was that for?'

'I just felt like doing it.'

'Okay.' She stood on tiptoes and kissed me on the mouth, firm and long. 'And I felt like doing that.'

I don't know what my expression was, but it made her smile.

'You're not going to sleep with me, I understand that, but *you* need to understand that I'm not your daughter, and my feelings for you aren't in the least bit daughterly.'

She started away. I wasn't going to see her again, but there was one more thing I needed from her. 'Hey Alice?' And when she turned back: 'How are you doing with it? With Klerke?'

She thought it over, running a hand through her hair as she did it. She was back to black. 'I'm getting there,' she said. 'Trying.' I decided that was good enough.

That night I set my phone alarm for one A.M., long after she would be asleep. When I got up, I checked the bandages. No blood and hardly any pain. Pain had been replaced by the deep dry itch of healing. There was no stationery in the Bide-A-Wee, of course, but I had a Staples pad from the Gerard Tower in my suitcase. I tore out a couple of pages and wrote my goodbye letter.

Dear Alice,

By the time you read this, I'll be gone. One of the reasons I wanted to stop here is because of the truck stop, Happy Jack's, half a mile down the road. There I'm sure I can find a long-haul independent who'll let me ride along with him for a hundred dollars. It's got to be west or north, either of those will be okay, just not south or east. I've been there and done that.

I am not deserting you. Believe it.

I rescued you when those three bad and stupid men dumped you on the side of Pearson Street, didn't I? Now I'm rescuing you again. Trying, at least. Bucky said something I haven't forgotten. He told me you'd follow me as long as I let you, and if I let you, I'd ruin you. I know he was right about the following part after what we did at Klerke's estate in Montauk Point. I think he was right about the ruining part, too, but I don't believe it's happened yet. When I asked you how you were doing with Klerke, you said you were trying. I know that you are, and I'm sure that in time you will succeed in putting that behind you. But I hope it won't be too soon. Klerke screamed, didn't he? He screamed that it hurt, and I hope those screams will haunt you long after you've gotten over my going. Maybe he deserved to be hurt after what he did to the girl in Mexico. And his son. And the other girls – them, too. But when you administer pain to someone, not little pain like the healing wound in my side but a killing shot, it leaves a scar. Not on the body but on the mind and spirit. It should, because it's no little thing.

I need to leave you because I too am a bad man. This was knowledge I pushed away from my heart before, mostly with books, but I can't push it away any longer and I will not risk infecting you more than I already have.

Go to Bucky, but don't stay with Bucky. He cares for you, he will be kind to you, but he is also a bad man. He will help you start a new life as Elizabeth Anderson, if that is what you want. There is money in the account of a man named Edward Woodley, and if Nick comes through there will be more. There is also money in the Bank of Bimini, in the name of James Lincoln. Bucky has both passwords and all the account information. He will give you advice on how to manage the flow into your own account and put you in touch with a tax advisor. That part is very important, because money that can't be accounted for is a trapdoor that can open under your feet when you least expect it. Some of the money is for Bucky. The rest is yours, for school and for a start in life as a fine independent woman. Which is what you are, Alice, and what you will be.

Stay in the mountains if you want to. Boulder is nice. So is Greeley

STEPHEN KING

and Fort Collins and Estes Park. Enjoy your life. At some point, perhaps when you are in your forties and I'm in my sixties, you may get a call from me. We can go out for a drink. Make that two drinks! You can toast Daphne and I'll toast Walter.

I have come to love you, Alice. So very much. If you love me as you have said, then bring that love into the world as a real thing by living a fine and useful life.

Yours,
Billy

PS: I'm taking my laptop – it's an old friend – but leaving the thumb drive with my story on it. It's in my room, along with the keys to the SUV. The story ends when we left for Montauk Point, but perhaps you could finish it. Certainly you must be very familiar with my style by now! Do with it as you will, just leave the Dalton Smith name out of it. And yours.

I folded the note around the key to my room, printed her name on it, and pushed it under her door. Goodbye, Alice.

I slung my laptop over my right shoulder, picked up my suitcase in my right hand, and left by the side door. Half a mile down the road I stopped to rest, and to do one other thing. I opened the suitcase and took out the two guns – my Glock and the ACP Marge had shot me with. I unloaded them and threw them as far as I could. The bullets would go into one of the trashcans at the truck stop.

With that taken care of, I started walking toward the lights and the big trucks and the rest of my life. Maybe even toward some kind of atonement, if that's not too much to ask for. Probably it is.

CHAPTER 24

1

It's November 21, 2019, a week from Thanksgiving, but the occupants of the house at the end of Edgewood Mountain Drive aren't in a Thanksgiving frame of mind. It's cold outside − colder than a well-digger's belt-buckle, Bucky says − and snow is on the way. He has lit a fire in the kitchen stove and sits in one of his rocking chairs dragged in from the porch with his sock feet up on the fender. He's got an open laptop, rather scratched and battered, balanced on his thighs. A door opens behind him and footsteps approach. Alice comes into the kitchen and sits at the table. She's pale and at least ten pounds lighter than the first time Bucky saw her. Her cheeks are hollowed out, giving her the look of a half-starved fashion model.

'Finished, or still reading?'

'Finished. Just looking at the end again. That part doesn't make much sense.'

Alice says nothing.

'Because if he left you the thumb drive, the part about him walking down the road and throwing away the guns couldn't be on it.'

Alice says nothing. Since she arrived at Bucky's place, she has said very little, and Bucky hasn't pushed her. What she's done, mostly, is sleep and write on the laptop Bucky now closes and holds up.

'MacBook Pro. Nice gadget, but this one has been around the block a few times.'

'Yes,' Alice says. 'I guess that's true.'

'So in the story Billy took his laptop with him, but here it is. Add the stuff that couldn't be on the thumb drive and it's kind of a science fiction – type story.'

The young woman sitting at the kitchen table says nothing.

'Still, there's no reason it shouldn't hold together. No reason for people who read it to think he didn't just walk away and is living out west somewhere. Or in Australia, he always talked about that. Maybe writing a book. Another one. He always talked about that too, but I never thought it would come to anything.'

He looks at her. Alice looks back. Outside a cold wind is blowing and it looks like snow, but it's warm here in the kitchen. A knot pops in the stove.

At last Bucky says, '*Will* people read it, Alice?'

'I don't know . . . I'd have to change the names . . .'

He shakes his head. 'Klerke's murder was world-wide news. Still . . .' He sees her disappointment and shrugs. 'They'd maybe think it was a *roman à clef*. That's French. I learned it from him. He said it while I was reading this old paperback I picked up at the Strand. *Valley of the Dolls*, it was called.' He shrugs again. 'Just as long as you keep me out of it, I don't care. Call me Trevor Wheatley or something and put me up in Saskatchewan or Manitoba. As for Nick Majarian, that mother-fucker can take care of himself.'

'Is it any good, do you think?'

He puts the laptop – Billy's old standby – on the kitchen table. 'I think so, but I'm no literary critic.'

'Does it sound like him?'

Bucky laughs. 'Sweetheart, I never read anything he wrote, so I can't say for sure, but it sure sounds like his voice. And the voice stays the same all the way through. Put it this way, I can't tell for sure where you took over.'

Smiles have been in short supply since Alice came back, but she gives him one now. 'That's good. I think it's the most important part.'

'Did you make that up about me being a bad man, too?'

She doesn't drop her eyes. 'No. He said it.'

'You wrote what you wished had happened,' Bucky says. 'The hero of the story walks away into the future toting his suitcase. Now tell me what really did happen.'

So she does.

2

They drive back to Riverhead, stopping on the way for Band-Aids, a roll of gauze, tape, hydrogen peroxide, and Betadine ointment. Alice goes into the Walgreens while Billy waits in the car. At the hotel they enter by the side door. Once they're in his room, she helps him off with the bomber jacket. There's a hole in it, and another in his shirt. Not a rip but a hole, and not in the side, as he told her. Farther in.

'Oh my God,' Alice says. Her voice is muffled because her hand is over her mouth. 'That's not a *graze*, that's your *stomach*.'

'I guess it is. Or maybe a little lower?' He sounds bemused.

'In the bathroom,' Alice says. 'If you don't want to leave a lot of blood around.'

But once they're in there and she helps him get his shirt off, she sees there is almost no blood coming from the red-black hole. She's able to cover it with one of the Band-Aids after she's used the hydrogen peroxide and a little Betadine.

She has to help him back to the bed. He's walking slowly and listing to the right. His face is sheened with sweat. 'Marge,' he says. 'Fucking Marge.'

He sits down but gasps when his body bends. Alice asks him how bad it hurts.

'Not too bad.'

'Are you lying?'

'No,' he says. 'Well, a little.'

She touches his stomach to the right of the hole and he gasps again. 'Don't.'

'We have to get you to a hos.' She stops. 'We can't, can we? It's a gunshot wound and they have to report those.'

'You're turning outlaw on me,' he says, and grins. 'You really are.'

Alice shakes her head. 'I just watch too much television.'

'I'll be okay. I saw worse in Iraq and guys were back clearing blocks the next day.'

Alice shakes her head. 'You're bleeding inside. Aren't you? And the bullet's still in there.'

Billy doesn't reply. She stares at the Band-Aid. It looks stupid. Like something you'd put on a scrape.

'Try to lie still tonight. On your back. Do you want Tylenol? I've got some in my purse.'

'If Tylenol's what you've got, I'll take it.'

She gives him two and helps him to sit up so he can take them with water. He coughs, cupping his hand over his mouth. She grabs the hand and looks at it. There's no blood in the palm. Maybe that's good. Maybe it isn't. She doesn't know.

'Thank you.'

'No thanks needed. I'd do anything for you, Billy.'

He presses his lips together. 'We need to get out of here in the morning. Early.'

'Billy, we can't—'

'What we can't do is stay here.'

'I'll call Bucky. He's got connections. One of them might be a doctor in New York who can treat a gunshot wound.'

Billy shakes his head. 'That could happen in a TV show. Not in real life. Bucky's not that kind of fixer. But if we make it back to Sidewinder, to gun country, he'll be able to find somebody.'

'That's almost two thousand miles! I googled it!'

Billy nods. 'You'll have to do some of the driving, maybe even most of it, and we need to make it as fast as we can. If there's a snowstorm, God help us.'

'Two thousand miles!' It feels like a weight on her shoulders.

'There might be a way to speed the plow.'

'Speed the—'

'It's the name of a play. Never mind.' Grimacing, he reaches into his back pocket, brings out his wallet, and hands it to her. 'Find my ATM card. There's a machine on the mezzanine level. My passcode in, 1055. Can you remember that?'

'Yes.'

'The machine will let you take four hundred dollars. Tomorrow morning, before we leave, you can get another four hundred.'

'Why so much?'

'Never mind now. What I'm thinking of may not work anyway, but let's be optimists. Find the card.'

She thumbs through his wallet and finds it. The embossed name is Dalton Curtis Smith. She holds it up, eyebrows raised.

'Go, girl.'

The girl goes. The mezzanine level is deserted. Muzak plays softly. Alice puts in the plastic and punches the code. She half expects the machine to eat the card, maybe even start sounding an alarm, but it pops back out and the money does, too. All twenties, fresh and uncreased. She folds them and puts the wad in her purse. When she comes back to Billy's room, he's lying down.

'How is it?' she asks.

'Not terrible. I was able to go to the bathroom and take a leak. No blood. Maybe the bullet being in there is good. It might be stopping up the bleeding.'

This sounds unlikely to Alice, like her grandmother saying a little cigarette smoke blown into an aching ear would quiet the pain, but she doesn't say so. She roots in her purse instead and comes out with her bottle of Tylenol. 'How about another one of these?'

'God, yes.'

She gets him a glass of water in the bathroom and when she comes back he's sitting up with his hand pressed to his side. He takes the pill and lies down again, wincing.

'I'm going to stay with you. Don't even think about arguing with me.'

He doesn't. 'I'd like to be out of here by six. Seven at the latest. So get some sleep.'

3

'And did you?' Bucky asks. 'Get some sleep?'

'A little. Not much. I doubt if he got any. I didn't know how bad it was, how deep the bullet went in.'

'I'm guessing it perforated his intestines. Maybe his stomach.'

'*Could* you have found him a doctor? If I'd called you?'

Bucky thinks it over. 'No, but I could have reached out to someone who might have been able to reach out to someone else on short notice. Someone of a medical persuasion.'

'Would Billy have known that?'

Bucky shrugs. 'He knows I have a lot of connections in different fields.'

'Then why wouldn't he at least have let me try it?'

'Maybe he didn't want to,' Bucky says. 'Maybe, Alice, he just wanted to get you here and be done.'

4

They leave the hotel at six-thirty. Billy is able to walk to the car unassisted. He says that with a couple more of Alice's Tylenol onboard, the pain is pretty manageable. Alice wants to believe it and can't. He's walking with a limp, hand pressed to his left side. He gets into the passenger seat with the slow, almost glassy care of an old man with arthritic hips. She starts the engine and gets the heater going against the morning chill, then hurries back inside to get another four hundred dollars from the ATM. She snags a trolley for their luggage and trundles it out to the car.

'Let's roll,' he says, trying to buckle his seatbelt. 'Fuck, I can't get this.'

She does it for him, and then they roll.

It's Route 27 to the Long Island Expressway and the LIE to I-95. The traffic gets progressively heavier on the Expressway, and Alice drives sitting bolt upright, hands clutching the wheel at ten and two, nervous about the river of cars passing on both her left and right. She's only had a driver's license for slightly over three years and she's never driven in traffic like this. In her mind she sees half a dozen accidents waiting to happen because of her inexperience. In the worst, they are killed instantly in a four-car pile-up. In the second-worst, they survive but the responding police discover that her companion has a bullet in his gut.

'Take the next exit,' Billy says. 'We'll switch. I'm going to drive us through the metro area, then across New Jersey. Once we're in PA, you can take over. You'll be fine.'

'Can you?'

'Absolutely.' The strained grin she doesn't like appears. His face is damp again, sweat running in little rivulets, and his cheeks are flushed. Can he have a fever-induced infection already? Alice doesn't know, but she knows Tylenol won't stop it if he does. 'If we're lucky, I may even be able to do it in relative comfort.'

Alice changes lanes to line up with the exit. Someone honks and she jumps. Her heart skips in her chest. The traffic is *insane*.

'That was their bad,' Billy says. 'Tailgating son of a bitch. Probably a Yankee fan. There – see that sign? That's what we want.'

The sign shows a hand-waving truck driver jumping back and forth over a sixteen-wheeler outlined in pink neon. Below it, also in pink neon: HAPPY JACK'S TRUCK STOP.

'Saw it on our way out. On a better day, before Marge perforated me.'

'We have almost a full tank of gas, Billy.'

'Gas isn't what we want. Pull around back. And put this in your purse.' From under the seat he takes Marge's Smith & Wesson ACP.

'I don't want it.' This is absolutely true. She never wants to touch another gun in her life.

'I get that but take it anyway. It's not loaded. The chances that you even have to show it are about one in a hundred.'

She takes it, drops it in her purse, and drives around to where she sees dozens of ranked long-haul trucks, most of them grumbling quietly.

'No lot lizards. They must be sleeping in.'

'What are lot lizards? Whores? Truck-stop whores?'

'Yes.'

'Charming.'

'You need to stroll around those trucks, kind of like you were shopping back at those malls where you bought your clothes. Because shopping is what you're doing.'

'Won't they think I'm a lizard?'

This time it's not the grin but the smile she's come to love. He scans her blue jeans, her parka, and most of all her face, which is innocent of makeup. 'Not a chance. I want you to hunt for a truck with the visor turned down. There'll be something green on it, like a piece of paper or celluloid. Or maybe some ribbon on the doorhandle. If the trucker is in the cab, you step up and knock on his window. With me?'

'Yes.'

'If the driver doesn't just wave you off, if he rolls down his window, you say that you're on a long trip, like coast to coast long, and your boyfriend is having back spasms. Tell him you're doing most of the driving and you were hoping to find some pain med stronger than aspirin or Tylenol for him and some stimulants stronger than coffee or Monster Energy for you. Got it?'

Now she understands the two visits to the ATM.

'I'm hoping for OxyContin but Percs or Vikes would be okay. If it's Oxy, tell him you'll pay ten for tens or eighty for eighties.'

'I don't understand.'

'Ten bucks for ten milligram tablets, eighty for eighty milligrams – the greenies. If he tries to jack you up to double that . . .' Billy shifts in his seat and grimaces. 'Tell him to take a hike. Speed for you. Adderall is good, Provigil maybe even better. Got it?'

Alice nods. 'I need to go inside and pee first. I'm pretty nervous.'

Billy nods and closes his eyes. 'Lock up, right? I'm in no shape to fight off a carjacker.'

She pees, picks up some snacks and drinks in the store, then goes out and starts walking around the trucks out back. Someone wolf-whistles after her. She ignores it. She's looking for a turned-down visor with something green on it, or a ribbon blowing from a doorhandle. What she finds, just as she's about to give up, is a rumbling Peterbilt with a green Jesus stuck to the dashboard. She's scared, thinks the man behind the wheel will probably either laugh at her or give her a *you're crazy* look, but Billy is in pain and she'll do anything for him.

She steps up and knocks. The window rolls down. It's a Scandahoovian-looking dude with straw-blond hair and a big old jelly-belly. His eyes are ice blue. He looks at her with no expression. 'If you're looking for help, honey, call Triple-A.'

She tells him about the back spasms and the long drive and says she can pay if it's not too much.

'How do I know you're not a cop?'

The question is so unexpected she laughs, and that's the convincer. They dicker. She ends up parting with five hundred of the eight hundred dollars for ten ten-milligram Oxys, one eighty (what Billy called a greenie), and a dozen orange Adderall tabs. She's pretty sure he jacked her up most righteously, but Alice doesn't care. She runs back to the Mitsubishi with a smile. Part of it is relief. Part of it is a sense of accomplishment: her first drug deal. Maybe she really is turning outlaw.

Billy's dozing with his head back and his chin pointing at the wind-shield. His face has thinned out. Some of the stubble on his cheeks is gray. He opens his eyes when she knocks on the window and leans over to unlock the doors, wincing as he does it. He has to push on the steering wheel to get straight in his seat again and she thinks he won't be able to drive them two miles, let alone across New York and New Jersey in heavy traffic.

'Did you score?' he asks as she slides in behind the wheel.

She opens the handkerchief into which she folded the pills. He looks and says it's good, she did well. It makes her happy.

'Did you have to show the gun?'

She shakes her head.

'Didn't think you would.' He takes the greenie. 'I'll save the rest for later.'

'Won't that knock you out?'

'No. People who use it to get high get sleepy. I'm not using it for that.'

'Will you actually be able to drive? Because I can try—'

'Give me ten minutes, then we'll see.'

It's fifteen. Then he opens the passenger door and says, 'Switch places with me.'

He walks around the car without limping too much and gets behind the wheel without wincing at all. 'Johnny Capps was right, the stuff is magic. Of course that's what makes it so dangerous.'

'You're okay?'

'Good to go,' Billy says. 'For awhile, anyway.'

He swings out of the back lot where the big trucks sleep and merges smoothly onto the LIE, slotting neatly behind a pickup hauling a boat trailer and ahead of a dump truck. Alice thinks she would have hesitated for minutes with exit traffic backing up behind her, honking like crazy, and when she finally pulled out she would have gotten slammed from behind. Soon they're up to sixty-five, Billy moving in and out of slower traffic with no hesitation. She waits for the drug to start messing with his timing. It doesn't happen.

'Get some news on the radio,' he says. 'Try 1010 WINS on the AM.'

She finds WINS. There's a story about a pipeline leak in North Dakota, a plane crash in Texas, and a school shooting in Santa Clara. There's nothing about the murder of a media mogul at his estate on Montauk Point.

'That's good,' Billy says. 'We need all the running room we can get.'

Outlaws for sure, she thinks.

By the time the New York skyline is on the horizon, he's sweating again, but his driving remains firm and confident. They take the Lincoln Tunnel into New Jersey. With Alice calling out directions from her GPS, Billy gets to 1-80. He doesn't make it all the way to the Pennsylvania state line but pulls off at a tiny rest area in Netcong Borough.

'All I can do,' he says. 'Your turn. Take an Adderall now, and probably another two around four o'clock, when you start to fade. Then keep driving as long as you can. Try to make it until ten o'clock. By then we'll have put almost eight hundred miles behind us.'

Alice looks at the orange pill. 'What's it going to do to me?'

Billy smiles. 'You'll be fine. Trust me.'

She swallows the pill. Billy slides slowly from behind the wheel, makes it halfway around the hood of the Mitsubishi, then staggers and has to hold on. Alice gets out in a hurry and steadies him.

'How bad?'

'Not bad,' he says, but her eyes are on him and he says, 'Actually pretty bad. I'm going to get in back and stretch out as much as I can. Give me two of those ten-milligram Oxys. Maybe I can sleep.'

She supports him to the back door as best she can and helps him in. She wants to pull up his shirt and look at the area around the Band-Aid, but he won't let her and she doesn't press him, partly because she knows he wants her to get going and partly because she knows she wouldn't like what she'd see.

The pill is working. At first she thinks it's her imagination, but the way her heartbeat is ramping up isn't imagination, and neither is the way her vision seems to be clarifying. There's grass around the rest area's little brick comfort station and she can see the shadow thrown by each blade. A fluttering potato chip bag looks, there's no other word for it, *delicious*. She discovers that she *wants* to drive now, wants to watch as the Mitsubishi swallows up the miles.

Billy either reads her mind or knows from experience how the Adderall is hitting a girl who's never taken a stimulant stronger than her morning coffee. 'Sixty-five,' he says. 'Seventy if you have to pass a semi. We don't want any flashing blue lights, okay?'

'Okay.'

'Let's roll.'

5

'We rolled, all right,' Alice says. 'My mouth got dry and I finished both my Diet Coke and his Sprite, but I didn't have to pee for the longest time. It was like I left my bladder at Happy Jack's Truck Stop.'

'Speed does that,' Bucky says. 'You probably didn't want to eat, either.'

'I didn't, but knew I had to. I stopped around three o'clock for sandwiches. Billy stayed in back. He was sleeping and I didn't want to wake him.'

Bucky doubts very much if Billy was sleeping, not with internal bleeding and a spreading infection, but he keeps quiet on that score.

'I took two more of the pills and kept driving. We stopped for the night at a no-tell motel – our specialty – outside Gary, Indiana. Billy was awake by then, but he made me check in. I had to help him to the room. He could barely walk. I told him to take more of the OxyContin and he said he had to save them for tomorrow. I got him on the bed and looked at the wound. He didn't want me to, but by then he was too weak to stop me.'

Alice's voice remains steady through all of this, but she wipes her eyes with the sleeve of her sweater again and again.

'Was it turning black?' Bucky asks. 'Necrotic?'

Alice nods. 'Yes, and swollen. I said we had to get him help and he said no. I said I was going to get him a doctor and he couldn't stop me. He said that was true, but if I did, there was a good chance I'd spend thirty or forty years in jail. By then it was on the news. About Klerke. Do you think he was just trying to scare me?'

Bucky shakes his head. 'He was trying to take care of you. If the cops – and the Feebs, they'd be involved – could connect you to what went down at Klerke's place, you'd go away for a very long time. And once the cops put you with Billy at that Hyatt, you'd be connected.'

'You're saying that to make me feel better.'

Bucky gives her an impatient look. 'Of course I am, but it happens to be the truth.' He pauses. 'When did he die, Alice?'

6

Neither of them sleep worth a damn, Billy because he's in pain that must be excruciating, Alice because she's still feeling the remnants of speed-up pills her system has never encountered before. Around four-thirty in the morning, long before first light, he tells her they need to get going. He says she'll have to help him to the car, and he'd like that to happen before the world wakes up.

He takes four of the remaining Oxy tens and uses the bathroom. She goes in after him. He's flushed away the worst of the blood, but there's still some on the rim of the toilet and on the tiles. She wipes it up and takes the plastic trash bag with them: outlaw mentality.

By then the pain pills are working, but it still takes almost ten minutes to get him to the car because he has to rest after every two or three steps. He's leaning heavily on her and gasping like a man who's just finished a marathon. His breath is rank. She's terrified that he'll faint and she'll have to drag him (because she can't carry him), but they make it all right.

Slowly, with a series of little whimpering cries she hates to hear, he manages to crawl into the back seat. But when he's in as well as he can be, with his head pillowed on one arm, he manages a remarkably sunny smile.

'Fucking Marge. If she'd hit just half an inch further to the left, we could have avoided all this mishegas.'

'Fucking Marge,' she agrees.

'Keep it at sixty-five except to pass. Seventy-five once we get to Iowa and Nebraska. We don't want to see any flashing blue lights.'

'No flashing lights, roger that,' she says, and gives him a salute.

He smiles. 'I love you, Alice.'

Alice takes two of the Adderall. She considers and adds a third. Then she gets going.

The traffic south of Chicago is horrible, six or eight lanes in either direction, but with the Adderall on board Alice navigates through it fearlessly. West of the metro area the traffic thins out some and the towns roll by: LaSalle, Princeton, Sheffield, Annawan. Her heart beats in her chest nice and tight. She's locked in, got the hammer down like a trucker in a country song. Every now and then her eyes flick to the rearview and to the prone shape folded into the back seat. And as they leave Davenport behind and enter the wide flat spaces of Iowa, its fields now gray and still, waiting for winter, he begins to talk. It makes no sense; it makes all the sense in the world. He's in the dark, she thinks.

He is in the dark and in pain and looking for the way out. Oh Billy, I am so, so sorry.

There's a lot about Cathy. He tells her not to bake the cookies, to wait until Ma comes home to help her. He tells Cathy someone hurt Bob Raines and he's going to come home mean. He says Corinne stuck up for him, the only one who did. He talks about Shan. There's something about a shooting gallery. He talks about someone named Derek and someone named Danny. He tells these phantoms that he won't take it easy on them just because he's a grownup. Alice thinks he's talking about Monopoly because he says to hurry up and shake the dice and the railroads are a good buy but the utilities aren't. Once he shouts, making her jump and swerve. Don't go in there, Johnny, he says, there's a muj behind the door, throw in a flash-bang first and get him out of there. He talks about Peggy Pye, the girl from the foster home where he stayed after his mother lost custody. He says paint is the only thing holding the goddam house together. He talks about the girl he had a crush on, sometimes calling her Ronnie and sometimes calling her Robin, which Alice knows was her real name. He says something about a Mustang convertible and something about a jukebox ('It would play all night if you hit it in just the right place, Tac, remember?'), he talks about the toe that was partly lost and the baby shoe that was entirely lost and Bucky and Alice and someone named Thérèse Raquin. He returns again and again to his sister and to the policeman who took him away to the House of Everlasting Paint. He talks about thousands of cars with their windshields shining in the sun. He says they were smashed beauty. He is unpacking his life in the back seat of this stolen car and her heart breaks.

Finally he falls silent and at first she thinks he's gone to sleep, but the third or fourth time she looks in the rearview and sees him lying there so still with his knees pulled up she thinks he's dead.

They're in Nebraska now. She pulls off at the exit for Hemingford Home and onto two-lane county blacktop running straight as a string between walls of corn that's finished for another year. The day is almost over. She goes a mile and comes to a dirt road and pulls onto it, driving in far enough to be hidden from the blacktop road. She gets out and opens the back door and is at first relieved to see him looking at her, next terrified by the thought that he's died with his eyes open. Then he blinks.

'Why'd we stop?'

'I needed to stretch my legs. How are you, Billy?'

Stupid question, but what else is there to ask? Do you know who I am or do you think I'm your dead sister? Are you going to be in your right mind for awhile? And by the way, is it too late? Alice thinks she knows the answer to that one.

'Help me sit up.'

'I don't know if that's a good—'

'Help me sit up, Alice.'

So he knows. And he's with her, at least for now. She takes his hands and helps him sit up with his feet on an unnamed dirt road in a town called Hemingford Home. In the mountains of Colorado it will already be almost dark. Here in the flatlands the afternoon has stretched into evening even though it's November. Here the evening redness of the west spills over corn that rustles and sighs in a light breeze. His hands are hot and his face is burning. There are fever blisters on his lips.

'I'm pretty well done.'

'No, Billy. No. You need to hold on. I'll give you two of the Oxys and there are a couple of those speed pills left. I'll drive all night.'

'No you won't.'

'I can do it, Billy. I really can.'

He's shaking his head. She's still holding his hands. She thinks if she let go he'd flop back onto the seat and his shirt would pull up and she'd see his belly, now blackish-gray with red tendrils of infection reaching up to his chest. To his heart.

'Listen to me now. Are you listening?'

'Yes.'

'I rescued you after those men dumped you, all right? Now I'm rescuing you again. Trying to, anyway. Bucky told me you'd follow me as long as I let you, and if I let you I'd ruin you. He was right.'

'You didn't ruin me, you saved me.'

'Hush. You're not ruined yet, that's the important thing. You're okay. I know because when I asked you how you were doing with Klerke, you said you were trying. I knew what you meant, I know that you are, and in time you'll be able to put it behind you. Except in dreams.'

The red light, shining and shining. Painting the corn. It is so silent here and his hands are burning in hers.

'Klerke screamed, didn't he?'

'Yes.'

'He screamed that it hurt.'

'Stop, Billy, it's horrible and we have to get back on the turnpi—'

'Maybe he deserved to be hurt, but when you give pain it leaves a scar. It scars your mind. It scars your *spirit*. And it should, because hurting someone, *killing* someone, is no little thing. Take it from someone who knows.'

Blood is trickling from the corner of his mouth. No, from both corners. She gives up trying to stop him from talking. She knows what this is, it's a dying declaration, and her job is to listen as long as he's able to speak. She says nothing even when he tells her he's a bad man. She doesn't believe it but this is no time to argue.

'Go to Bucky, but don't stay with him. He cares for you and he'll be kind to you, but he's a bad man, too.' He coughs and blood flies from his mouth. 'He'll help you start a new life as Elizabeth Anderson, if that's what you want. There's money, quite a lot of it. Some is in the account of a paper man named Edward Woodley. There's also money in the Bank of Bimini, in the name of James Lincoln. Can you remember that?'

'Yes. Edward Woodley. James Lincoln.'

'Bucky has the passwords and all the account information. He'll tell you how to manage the flow of money into your own bank account so you don't attract attention from the IRS. That's important, because that's how they're most apt to catch you. Unreported income is a trapdoor. Do you . . .'

More coughing. More blood.

'Do you understand?'

'Yes, Billy.'

'Some of the money goes to Bucky. The rest is yours. Enough to go to college and a start in life after that. He'll treat you fair. Okay?'

'Okay. Maybe you should lie back now.'

'I'm going to, but if you try to drive all night you'll be an accident waiting to happen. Check your phone for the next town big enough to have a Walmart. Park where the RVs are. Sleep. You'll be fresh in

the morning and back at Bucky's by late afternoon. Up in the mountains. You like the mountains, right?'

'Yes.'

'Promise me.'

'I promise to stop for the night.'

'All that corn,' he says, looking over her shoulder. 'And the sun. Ever
read Cormac McCarthy?'

'No, Billy.'

'You should. *Blood Meridian.*' He smiles at her. 'Fucking Marge, huh?'

'That's right,' Alice says. 'Fucking Marge.'

'I wrote the password to my laptop on a piece of paper and stuck
it in your purse.'

That said, he lets go of her hands and falls back. She lifts his calves
and manages to get his legs into the car. If it hurts him, he gives no
sign. He's looking at her.

'Where are we?'

'Nebraska, Billy.'

'How did we get here?'

'Never mind. Close your eyes. Rest up.'

He frowns. 'Robin? Is that you?'

'Yes.'

'I love you, Robin.'

'I love you, too, Billy.'

'Let's go down cellar and see if there are any apples left.'

7

Another knot pops in the woodstove. Alice gets up, walks to the refrigerator, and gets a beer. She twists off the cap and drinks half of it.

'That was the last thing he said to me. When I parked with the RVs
at the Kearney Walmart, he was still alive. I know, because I could hear
him breathing. Rasping. When I woke up the next morning at five, he
was dead. Do you want a beer?'

'Yes. Thanks.'

Alice brings him a beer and sits down. She looks tired. '"Let's go
down cellar and see if there are any apples left." Maybe talking to Robin,
or to his friend Gad. Not much of an exit line. Life would be better if

Shakespeare wrote it, that's what I think. Although . . . when you think about *Romeo and Juliet* . . .' She drinks the rest of her beer and some color comes into her cheeks. Bucky thinks she looks a little better.

'I waited until the Walmart opened, then went inside and bought some stuff – blankets, pillows, I think a sleeping bag.'

'Yes,' Bucky says. 'There was a sleeping bag.'

'I covered him up and got back on the highway. Keeping no more than five miles an hour over the speed limit, just like he told me. Once a Colorado State Patrol car came up behind with its flashers going and I thought I was cooked but it went by and on down the road, lickety-split. I got here. And we buried him, along with most of his things. There wasn't much.' She pauses. 'But not too near the summerhouse cabin. He didn't like it. He worked there but he said he never liked it.'

'He told me he thought it was haunted,' Bucky says. 'What comes next for you, darlin?'

'Sleep. I just can't seem to get enough. I thought it would be better when I finished writing his story, but . . .' She shrugs, then stands up. 'I'll figure it out later. You know what Scarlett O'Hara said, don't you?'

Bucky Hanson grins. '"I'll think about it tomorrow, for tomorrow is another day."'

'That's right.' Alice starts toward the bedroom where she has spent most of her time since coming back here, writing and sleeping, then turns back. She's smiling. 'I bet Billy would have hated that line.'

'You could be right.'

Alice sighs. 'I can never publish it, can I? His book. Not even as a *roman à clef*. Not five years from now, not ten. No sense fooling myself.'

'Probably not,' Bucky agrees. 'It'd be like D.B. Cooper writing his autobiography and calling it *Here's How I Did It*.'

'I don't know who that is.'

'No one does, that's the point. Guy hijacked a plane, got a bunch of money, jumped out with a parachute, was never seen again. Kind of like Billy in your version of his story.'

'Do you think he'd be glad that I did it? That I let him live?'

'He'd fucking love it, Alice.'

'I think so, too. If I *could* publish it, you know what I'd call it? *Billy Summers: The Story of a Lost Man*. What do you think?'

'I think it sounds about right.'

8

There's snow in the night, just an inch or two, and it's stopped by the time Alice gets up at seven, the morning sky so clear it's almost transparent. Bucky is still asleep; she can hear him snoring even through the bedroom door. She puts on the coffee, gets wood from the pile beside the house, and builds up the fire in the stove. By then the coffee is hot and she drinks a cup before putting on her coat, boots, and a wooly hat that covers her ears.

She goes into the room set aside for her use, touches Billy's laptop, then picks up the paperback lying beside it and puts it in the back pocket of her jeans. She lets herself out and walks up the path. There are deer tracks in the fresh snow, lots of them, and the weird hand-shaped tracks of a raccoon or two, but the snow in front of the summerhouse is conspicuously unmarked. The deer and coons have steered clear of the place. Alice does, too.

There's an old cottonwood with a split trunk not too far from where the path ends. It's her marker. Alice turns into the woods and starts walking, counting the steps off under her breath. It was two hundred and ten on the day they brought Billy here, but because the going is a trifle slippery this morning she's up to two hundred and forty before she comes to the little clearing. She has to clamber over a fallen lodgepole pine to get into it. In the center of the clearing there's a square of brown earth upon which they have scattered a mixture of pine needles and fallen leaves. Even with the light fall of snow added to the needles and leaves, it's pretty clear it's a grave. Time will take care of that, Bucky has assured her. He says that by next November a random hiker could walk over that patch with no idea of what lay beneath.

'Not that there'll be any. This is my land, and I keep it posted. Maybe when I wasn't here people took advantage, probably used the path to stare across to where the Overlook used to be, but now I'm here, and I plan to stay. Thanks to Billy, I'm retired. Just another old mountain man. There are thousands of them between here and the Western Slope, growing their hair down to their asses and listening to their old Steppenwolf records.'

Now Alice stands at the foot of the grave and says, 'Hey, Billy.' It feels natural to talk to him, natural enough. She wasn't sure it would.

'I finished your story. Gave it a different ending. Bucky says you wouldn't have minded. It's on the same thumb drive you were using when you started in that office building. Once I get to Fort Collins, I'll rent a safe deposit box and put it inside with my Alice Maxwell ID.'

She goes back to the fallen lodgepole pine and sits down on it, first taking the paperback out of her pocket and putting it in her lap. It's good to be here. It's a peaceful place. Before wrapping the body in a tarpaulin, Bucky did something to it. He wouldn't tell her what, but he said there wouldn't be much smell when the hot weather came back, if any. The animals wouldn't disturb him. Bucky said it was the way such things were done in the old days of wagon trains and silver mines.

9

'Fort Collins is where I've decided to go to school. Colorado State University. I've seen the pictures and it's beautiful there. Remember when you asked me what I wanted to study? I said maybe history, maybe sociology, maybe even theater arts. I was too shy to tell you what I really wanted to do, but I bet you can guess. Maybe you even guessed then. I thought about it sometimes when I was in high school because English was always my best class, but finishing your story made it seem possible.'

She stops, because the rest of it is hard to say out loud even when she's alone. It sounds pretentious. Her mother would say she was *getting above herself*. But she needs to say it, she owes him.

'I'd like to write stories of my own.'

She stops again and wipes her eyes with the sleeve of her jacket. It's cold out here. But the stillness is exquisite. This early even the crows are asleep.

'When I was doing it, when I was . . .' She hesitates. Why is the word so hard to say? Why should it be? 'When I was *writing*, I forgot to be sad. I forgot to worry about the future. I forgot where I was. I didn't know that could happen. I could pretend we were in the Bide-A-Wee Motel outside of Davenport, Iowa. Only it wasn't like pretending, even though there's no such place. I could see the fake wood walls and the blue bedspread and the bathroom glass in its plastic bag with writing on it that said SANITIZED FOR YOUR HEALTH. But that wasn't the most important part.'

She wipes her eyes, she wipes her nose, she watches the white clouds of vapor from her exhalations drift away.

'I could pretend that Marge – fucking Marge – only creased you, after all.' She shakes her head as if to clear it. 'Only that's not right. You *were* only creased. You *did* write me that note and put it under my door when I was sleeping. You walked to the truck stop up the road even though the truck stop was back in New York and you went on from there. *Are* going on. Did you know that could happen? Did you know that you could sit in front of a screen or a pad of paper and change the world? It doesn't last, the world always comes back, but before it does, it's awesome. It's everything. Because you can have things the way you want and I want you to still be alive and in the story you are and always will be.'

She stands and goes over to the square of earth she and Bucky dug together. In the real world he's under there. She takes a knee and puts the book on the grave. Maybe the snow will cover it. Maybe the wind will blow it away. It doesn't matter. In her mind it will stay here. The book is *Thérèse Raquin*, by Émile Zola.

'Now I know who you were talking about,' she says.

10

Alice walks up to where the path ends at the knife-cut valley and looks across to the flat ground where the old hotel used to stand – the reputedly haunted hotel, according to Bucky. Once she thought she actually saw it, no doubt a hallucination caused by being unused to the thin air up here. Today she sees nothing.

But I could make it be there, she thinks. I could make it be there just as I was able to make the Bide-A-Wee be there, complete with all the details I didn't put in, like the bagged glass in the bathroom or the stain, sort of like the shape of Texas, on the rug. I could make it be there. I could even fill it with ghosts, if I wanted to.

She stands looking across the gulf of cold air between this side and that, hands in her pockets, thinking she could create worlds. Billy gave her that chance. She is here. She is found.

June 12, 2019–July 3, 2020

ACKNOWLEDGMENTS

Robin Furth and Myke Cole helped me with research, found continuity errors, and made valuable editorial suggestions. My thanks to both of them. It comes with the usual *caveat*: If there's something wrong here, that's on me, not them. I also want to thank Bing West for *No True Glory*, his extraordinary account of the two battles of Fallujah. It was a great help.

Don't miss IF IT BLEEDS, a collection of four uniquely wonderful long stories, including a stand-alone sequel to the No. 1 bestseller *The Outsider*.

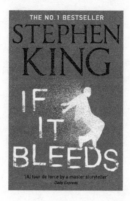

News people have a saying: 'If it bleeds, it leads'.

Following a horrific explosion at a school, Holly Gibney of the Finders Keepers detective agency notices something suspicious about the TV reporter who is first on the scene. In this riveting title story, Holly sets out to discover what he is hiding in her first solo crime case.

Dancing alongside this stand-alone sequel to *The Outsider* are three more irresistible long stories: 'Mr Harrigan's Phone' sees young Craig introduce a curmudgeonly retired businessman to the wonders of the smartphone; 'The Life of Chuck' is a three act life-story – told in reverse order; and 'Rat' sees a struggling author head to a remote cabin in the woods of North Maine, where a deal-making rodent offers him a life-changing pact.

'Exceptionally compelling novellas that reaffirm his mastery of the form' – *Washington Post*

'Suspenseful . . . tender . . . four new stories, all offering vintage King themes with their own particular twist' – *Observer*

HODDER

Described by the *Sunday Express* as 'a masterpiece',
THE INSTITUTE by Stephen King is a stunning novel of
childhood betrayed and hope regained.

Luke Ellis, a super-smart twelve-year-old with an exceptional gift, is
the latest in a long line of kids abducted and taken to a secret
government facility, hidden deep in the forest in Maine.

Here, kids with special talents – telekinesis and telepathy – like
Luke's new friends Kalisha, Nick and Iris, are subjected to a
series of experiments.

There seems to be no hope of escape. Until Luke teams up with an
even younger boy whose powers of telepathy are off the scale.

Meanwhile, far away in a small town in South Carolina, former cop
Tim Jamieson, looking for the quiet life, has taken a job working for
the local sheriff. He doesn't know he's about to take on the biggest
case of his career . . .

'Will keep readers up late at night racing towards a heartbreaking
yet glorious finale . . . a dazzling achievement' – *Daily Express*

'A terrific book – a flat-out pedal-to-the-metal thriller. One of
Stephen King's best' – Linwood Barclay

HODDER

To find out more about Stephen King please visit
www.hodder.co.uk, www.stephenkingbooks.co.uk
and www.facebook.com/stephenkingbooks